Dead
of
Night

J. D. Robb

Mary Blayney

Ruth Ryan Langan

Mary Kay McComas

JOVE BOOKS, NEW YORK

THE BERKLEY PUBLISHING GROUP
Published by the Penguin Group
Penguin Group (USA) Inc.
375 Hudson Street, New York, New York 10014, USA
Penguin Group (Canada), 90 Eglinton Avenue East, Suite 700, Toronto, Ontario M4P 2Y3, Canada
(a division of Pearson Penguin Canada Inc.)
Penguin Books Ltd., 80 Strand, London WC2R 0RL, England
Penguin Group Ireland, 25 St. Stephen's Green, Dublin 2, Ireland (a division of Penguin Books Ltd.)
Penguin Group (Australia), 250 Camberwell Road, Camberwell, Victoria 3124, Australia
(a division of Pearson Australia Group Pty. Ltd.)
Penguin Books India Pvt. Ltd., 11 Community Centre, Panchsheel Park, New Delhi—110 017, India
Penguin Group (NZ), 67 Apollo Drive, Rosedale, North Shore 0632, New Zealand
(a division of Pearson New Zealand Ltd.)
Penguin Books (South Africa) (Pty.) Ltd., 24 Sturdee Avenue, Rosebank, Johannesburg 2196,
South Africa

Penguin Books Ltd., Registered Offices: 80 Strand, London WC2R 0RL, England

DEAD OF NIGHT

A Jove Book / published by arrangement with the authors

PRINTING HISTORY
Jove mass-market edition / November 2007

ISBN: 978-0-515-14367-6

JOVE®
Jove Books are published by The Berkley Publishing Group,
a division of Penguin Group (USA) Inc.,
375 Hudson Street, New York, New York 10014.
JOVE is a registered trademark of Penguin Group (USA) Inc.
The "J" design is a trademark belonging to Penguin Group (USA) Inc.

PRINTED IN THE UNITED STATES OF AMERICA

10 9 8 7 6 5 4 3 2 1

Eternity in Death

J. D. Robb

The Sun's rim dips; the stars rush out,
At one stride comes the dark.
—Coleridge

Whence and what art thou, execrable shape?
—John Milton

Prologue

Death was the end of the party. Worse than death, in Tiara's opinion, was what came before it. Age. The loss of youth, of beauty, of body and *celebrity* was the true horror. Who the hell wanted to screw an old, wrinkled woman? Who cared what some droopy bag of years wore to the hot new club, or what she didn't wear on the beach at the Côte d'Azur?

No-fucking-body, that's who.

So when he told her that death could be the beginning—the real beginning—she was fascinated. She was pumped. It made sense to her that immortality could be bought by those privileged enough to pay the price. All of her life everything she wanted, coveted, demanded had been bought, so eternal life wasn't any different, really, than her pied-à-terre in New York or her villa in France.

Immortality, unlike a penthouse or a pair of earrings, would never get boring.

She was twenty-three, and absolutely at her prime. Everything about her was tight and toned, which she assured herself of by examining her body in the mirror tube in her dressing room. She was perfect, she decided, giving her signature blonde mane a carefully studied, and meticulously practiced, toss.

Now, thanks to him, she would always be perfect.

She stepped out, leaving the double mirrored doors open so that she could watch herself dress. She'd chosen form-fitting, nearly transparent red, with a hem of peacock eyes that shimmered and winked with every movement. Chandelier drops swung at her ears, in the same vibrant tones of sapphire and emerald as the accents on the hem of the short, snug gown. She added her blue diamond pendant, and wide pave cuffs on both wrists.

Her sharply defined lips were dyed to match the dress, and they curved now with smug pride.

Later, she thought, after it was done, she'd change into something fun, something for dancing, for celebrating.

Her only regret was that the awakening had to be done in private rather than at the club. But her lover had assured her all that nasty business about being buried, then having to climb out of some disgusting coffin was just the invention of tacky books and bad vids. The reality was so much more civilized.

One hour after the ritual—which was so frigging *sexy*—she'd wake up in her own bed, eternally young, eternally strong, eternally beautiful.

Her new birthday would be April 18, 2060.

All it would cost was her soul. As if she cared about that.

She strolled out of the dressing room into the bedroom she'd just had redecorated in her new favorite shades of blues and greens. In his bed—canopied to match his mistress's—Tiara's teacup bulldog snored.

She wished she could awaken Biddy as she was about to be awakened. He was the only thing in the world she truly loved almost as much as herself. But she'd given her little sweetie pie the sleeping drug, just as she'd been told. It wouldn't do to have her doggie interrupt the ritual.

Following instructions, she disengaged all security on her private elevator and entrance, then lit the thirteen white candles she'd been told to set around the room she'd chosen for the awakening.

When it was done, she poured the bottle of potion he'd given her into a crystal wineglass. She drank it all, every drop. Nearly time, she thought, as she carefully arranged herself on the bed. He'd slip in quietly, find her. Take her.

Already she felt hot and jittery with need.

He'd make her scream, he'd make her come. And when she was screaming, when she was coming, he would give her that final, ultimate kiss.

Tiara traced her fingers over her throat, already feeling the bite.

She'd die, she thought, running her hands over her breasts and belly in anticipation of him. Wasn't that wild? She'd die, then she'd awaken. And she'd live forever.

One

The room smelled of candle wax and death. In their fat, jewel-toned holders, the candles had pooled into dripping puddles. The body lay in a lake-sized bed canopied with silk, mounded with a multitude of pillows, and stained with blood.

She was young, blonde, with a bright red dress rucked up to her waist. Her eyes, a crystal green, were open and staring.

As she studied the body of Tiara Kent, Lieutenant Eve Dallas wondered if the dead blonde had looked into her killer's eyes as she died.

She'd known him, in any case, almost certainly she'd known him. There was no sign of forced entry, and in fact, the security system had been shut down from the inside, by the victim. There was no sign of struggle. And though Eve was certain they'd find the victim had engaged in sexual intercourse, she didn't believe it would prove to be rape.

She hadn't fought him, Eve thought as she bent over the

body. Even when he'd drained the blood out of her, she hadn't fought him.

"Two puncture wounds, left side of the throat," Eve stated for the record. "The only visible injury." She lifted one of Tiara's hands, examined the perfectly shaped, fussily painted nails. "Bag the hands," she told her partner. "Maybe she scratched him."

"Not as much blood as you'd think there should be." Detective Peabody cleared her throat. "Not nearly enough. You know what they look like, on her neck there? Bite marks. Like, ah, fangs."

Eve spared Peabody a glance. "You think that ugly little dog the maid's got in the kitchen bit her on the neck?"

"No." Peabody angled her head, leaned down with her dark eyes wide and bright. "Come on, Dallas, you *know* what it looks like."

"It looks like a DB. It looks like the vic had a date that went over the top. There's going to be illegals in her system, something that dulled her down or hyped her up enough for her killer to jab something into her throat, or, yeah, sink his teeth into it if he had the incisors filed to points or was wearing an appliance. Then he bled her out, and she lay there and let him."

"I'm just saying it looks like your classic vampire bite."

"We'll put out an APB on Dracula. Meanwhile, let's find out if she was—just possibly—seeing someone with a heartbeat."

"Just saying," Peabody repeated, this time in a mumble.

Eve did another scan of the bedroom before stepping out and into the enormous dressing room area.

Bigger than a lot of apartments, she mused, and outfitted with a security screen, entertainment screen, full round of mirrors. The closet itself was a small department store, ruthlessly organized into categories.

For a moment, Eve stood with her hands on her hips and simply stared. One person, she thought, with enough clothes

to outfit the Upper West Side, and more than enough shoes
to shod every man, woman, and child in that sector. Even
Roarke—and Eve knew her husband's wardrobe was
awesome—didn't rate this high on the clothes-hog scale.

Then she just shook her head and focused on the job at
hand.

Dressed for him, Eve thought. Slutty dress, fuck-me
heels. So where was the jewelry? If a woman was going to
deck herself out for a booty call, down to shoes, wouldn't
she drape on some glitters?

If she had, her killer had helped himself there.

She studied the drawers, the cabinets that ran below the
rungs and carousels and protective domes. All locked, she
noted, all passcoded, which meant valuables housed inside.
There was no sign that she could see of any attempt to
break in.

There were plenty of expensive bits and pieces sitting
around in the penthouse: statuary, paintings, electronics.
She'd seen nothing on her once-over of both levels that
indicated anything had been disturbed.

If he was a thief, he was a lazy one, or a very picky one.

She stood for a moment, evaluating. Eve was a tall
woman, slim in boots and trousers, with a short leather
jacket over a white shirt. Her hair was short and brown,
chopped around a lean face dominated by deep brown
eyes. The eyes, as they studied, were all cop.

She didn't turn at Peabody's low whistle behind her.
"Wow! This is like something out of a vid. I think she had
all the clothes in all the land. And the *shoes*. Oooh, the
shoes."

"A few hundred pair of shoes," Eve commented. "And
she had the requisite two feet. People are screwy. Take
head of building security, see if he's got any knowledge or
documentation of who she's been seeing or entertaining in
the last few weeks. I'll take the maid."

She moved through the apartment, down a level. The

place was full of cops and crime-scene techs, of noise, of equipment. The busy business of murder.

In what she was told was the breakfast room, she found the maid with her red-rimmed eyes, clutching the small, ugly dog. Eve eyed the dog warily, then gestured for the uniforms to step out of the room.

"Ms. Cruz?"

At the mention of her name, the woman burst into fresh sobs. This time Eve and the dog exchanged looks of mild annoyance.

Eve sat so she and the maid were on the same level, then said, firmly, "Stop it."

Obviously used to following orders, the maid instantly snuffled back the sobs. "I'm so upset," she told Eve. "Miss Tiara, poor Miss Tiara."

"Yes, I'm very sorry. You've worked for her for a while?"

"Five years."

"I know this is hard, but I need you to answer some questions now. To help me find who did this to Miss Tiara."

"Yes." The maid pressed a hand to her heart. "Anything. Anything."

"You have keys and passcodes to the apartment?"

"Oh, yes. I come in every day to do for Miss Tiara when she's in residence. And three times a week when she's away."

"Who else has access to the apartment?"

"No one. Well, maybe Miss Daffy. I'm not sure."

"Miss Daffy."

"Miss Tiara's friend, Daffodil Wheats. Her very best friend, except when they're fighting, then Miss Caramel is her best friend."

"Are you putting me on with these names?"

The maid blinked her swollen, bloodshot eyes. "No, ma'am."

"Lieutenant," Eve corrected. "All right, this Daffodil

and Caramel were friends of Miss Kent's. What about men? What men was she seeing?"

"She saw a lot of men. She was so beautiful, so young, and so vibrant that—"

"Intimately, Ms. Cruz," Eve interrupted to stop both the eulogy and the fresh tears. "And most recently."

"Please call me Estella. She enjoyed men. She was young and vibrant, as I said. I don't know them all—some were just a moment, others longer. But in the past week or two, I think there was just one."

"Who would that be?"

"I don't know. I never saw him. But I could tell she was in love again—she laughed more, and danced around the apartment, and . . ." Estella seemed to struggle for a moment with her own code of discretion.

"Everything you tell me may help in the investigation," Eve prompted.

"Yes. Well . . . when you take care of someone, you know when they've had a . . . an intimacy. She had a lover in her bed every night for a week or more."

"But you never saw him."

"Never. I come at eight every morning, and leave at six, unless she needs me to stay longer. He was never here when I was here."

"Was it her habit to turn off her security system from in-house?"

"Never, never." Dry-eyed now, Estella shook her head decisively from side to side. "It was never to be disengaged. I don't understand why she would have done that. I saw it was off when I came in this morning. I thought there must be a glitch in the system, and Miss Tiara would be angry. I called downstairs to report it even before I went up to the bedroom."

"All right. You came in at eight, noted the security was off, reported it, then went upstairs. Is that your usual routine, to come in, go up to her bedroom?"

"Yes, to get Biddy." Estella bent her head to nuzzle the dog. "To take him for his morning walk, then to feed him. Miss Tiara usually sleeps until about eleven."

Estella's brow creased. "Later these last days, since—the new lover. Sometimes she didn't come downstairs until into the afternoon, and she ordered all the windows draped when she did. She said she only wanted the night. It worried me because she looked so pale, and wouldn't eat. But I thought, well, she's in love, that's all."

After a long, long sigh, Estella continued. "Then this morning, Biddy wasn't waiting by the bedroom door. He always waits there for me in the morning. I went in, very quietly. He was coming to the door, but he wasn't walking right."

Eve frowned at the dog. "What do you mean?"

"It was . . . I thought: Biddy looks drunk, and I had to hold back a laugh because he looked so funny. I went in more, and I smelled . . . it was the candles at first. I could smell the candles, so I thought she'd had her lover in the night. But then there was another smell, a hard smell. It was the blood, I think," she said as her eyes welled again. "It must have been the blood and . . . her, I smelled her, and when I looked over at the bed, I saw her there. I saw my poor little girl there."

"Did you touch anything, Estella? Anything in the room?"

"No, no. Yes. Biddy. I grabbed Biddy. I don't know why exactly, I just grabbed little Biddy and I ran out. She was dead—the blood, her face, her eyes, everything. She couldn't be anything but dead. I ran out screaming, and I called security. Mr. Tripps came right up. Right away, and he went upstairs. He was only a minute, then he came down to contact the police."

"Could you tell if anything's missing?"

"I know her things. I didn't notice . . ." Distressed again, she glanced around the room. "I didn't look."

"I'm going to have you look through her jewelry first. You know her jewelry?"

"I do. Every piece. I clean it for Miss Tiara because she doesn't trust—"

"Okay. We'll start there."

She sent Estella to the dressing area with two cops and a recorder. She was scribbling a few notes, adding time lines when Peabody tracked her down.

"Tripps reports that the maid contacted Security at eight-oh-two to report the system was down. She contacted them again at eight-oh-nine, hysterical. He came up personally, went upstairs, verified the death, contacted the police. Times jibe."

"Yeah, they do. What did he say about the system being down?"

"He said—and documented—that Kent told him she would be shutting it down internally near midnight, and would re-engage it when she wanted. He advised against, she told him to mind his own. She did the same every night for the last eight days, though the time of shutdown varied. She'd re-engage before dawn."

Thoughtfully, Eve tapped her fingers on her own notes. "So the boyfriend didn't want to be on the security tapes. Got her to shut it down, came in her private entrance, left the same way. She must've been monumentally stupid."

"Well, she wasn't known for her brains."

Eve slanted Peabody a look. If it was gossip or popular culture, Peabody usually had her finger on the pulse. "What was she known for?"

"Clubbing, shuttle-hopping, shopping, scandals. The usual, I guess, for a fourth-generation—I think it's fourth—megarich kid. She got engaged a lot, broke up a lot—usually publicly and with a lot of passion. Went to premieres, shuttled off to wherever the current hot spot might be. Hobbed and nobbed. Usually something on her in the tabs or one of the gossip or society channels every day."

"Who was she running with these days, and why did I feel I had to interview the maid about her lifestyle when I've got you?"

"Well, she's tight with Daffy Wheats, and Caramel Lipton, recently disengaged to Roman Gramaldi, of Zurich. But she hangs with the sparkles of the young, rich, and looking-for-trouble club."

"Trouble she found," Eve commented, then glanced up when Estella came rushing in.

"Her pendant, her blue diamond pendant, and the cuffs, her peacock earrings. Gone, all gone." Her voice pitched up sharply enough to cut glass. "He robbed my poor little girl, robbed her and killed her."

Eve held up a finger to stop the tirade. "Do you have photo documentation of the missing items?"

"Of course, of course. Insurance—"

"I'll need those. You get me the insurance information of whatever's missing. Go ahead." She waited until Estella hurried out again, smiled grimly. "That was a mistake. Sooner or later some big, fat blue diamond's going to show up. We'll get the details, then inform next of kin. After that, I want to have a chat with Daffy."

Two

As Tiara's mother was living with her fourth husband in Rome, and her father was currently vacationing on the Olympus Resort with his newest fiancée, notification was done via 'link.

Eve left the sweepers to finish processing the scene, and headed out with Peabody to interview Daffodil Wheats.

Another penthouse, Eve thought, another absurdly rich, young blonde. She badged and bullied her way past the doorman, past security, and finally past the housekeeper who might have been a clone of Estella Cruz. It turned out to be her sister.

The apartment was slightly smaller than Tiara's, a bit more tastefully furnished. They waited in a living area done in bold, vibrant colors while Martine Cruz went upstairs to wake her mistress and inform her the police wished to speak with her.

"What's the dish on this one, Peabody?"

"Um, third-generation rich, I think. Not as mega as the vic, but not worried about the grocery bill either. I think the fam made it big in textiles or something back in the day. Anyhow, she's another party girl and gossip channel regular."

"Who'd want to live like that?" Eve wondered.

"They do." Peabody gave a shrug. "You've got as much ready as they do, you can buy some privacy if you want it."

Eve thought back to the acres of mirrors and reflective surfaces at the crime scene. "The type who like to see themselves."

"Yeah, and unless Daffy and the vic were having one of their periodic fallings-out, they were pretty much joined at the hip. Played together, traveled together, and rumor has it shared some of the same men, maybe at the same time. Been tight since they were kids. Vic's father was married to Daffy's mother—or cohabbed, can't remember—for a couple of years."

"Small, incestuous little world."

Eve glanced up. Daffodil Wheats had a short, streaky crop of blonde hair, sleepy blue eyes, and a sulky mouth. She wore a black silk robe that hit her midthigh and gaped open at the breasts so the full white mounds of them played peek-a-boo as she walked down the swirl of silver steps.

"What's the deal?" she said in a blurry voice, then plopped down on the bright red sofa and yawned.

"Daffodil Wheats?" Eve demanded.

"Yeah, yeah. God, it's barely dawn. Martine! I'm desperado for that mocha! I was out 'til four," she explained with a long, feline stretch. "I didn't do anything illegal, so what's what with the badges?"

"You know Tiara Kent?"

"Hell, what's Tee done now?" She slumped, obviously already bored. "Look, I'll bail her, even if she has been a bitch lately. But I have to have my fix first. Mocha, mocha, mocha!" she shouted like an Arena Ball cheer.

"I'm sorry to tell you that Tiara Kent is dead."

The sleepy eyes narrowed a little, then rolled dramatically. "Oh, get off. You tell Princess Bitch that dragging me out of bed to lay it on didn't get a chuckle. Thank God! Thanks, Martine. Life saved." She made kissy noises at the maid as she grabbed the tall white cup of steaming liquid.

"Listen up, *Daffy*." Eve's tone had the blue eyes blinking in surprise. "Your pal was murdered last night, in her bed. So you're going to want to straighten your ass up—and cover your tits, for God's sake—or we're going to take the rest of this downtown."

"That's not funny." Slowly now, Daffy lowered the cup. "That's seriously un." The hand holding the cup shook as Daffy reached out for Martine with the other. "Martine, call Estella. Call her right now and have her put Tiara on the 'link."

"She can't come to the 'link." Peabody spoke now, more gently. "Ms. Kent was killed last night in her apartment."

"My sister," Martine said even as she gripped Daffy's hand.

"Your sister's fine," Peabody told her. "You can go ahead and contact her."

"Miss Daffy."

"Go on," Daffy said stiffly, and the bored young party girl was gone. In her place was a stunned young woman clutching her robe together at her throat with a trembling hand. "Go on, go on. This isn't a joke, this isn't Tee taking a slap at me? She's dead?"

"Yes."

"But . . . I don't see how that can be. She's only twenty-three. You're not supposed to be dead at twenty-three, and we're fighting. We can't be fighting when she's dead. How . . . Killed? Did you say somebody killed Tee?"

Now Eve sat, choosing the glossy white table in front of the sofa so she and Daffy were on a level. "She's been seeing someone recently."

"What? Yeah. But . . ." Daffy looked around blankly. "What?"

Reaching out, Eve took the cup of mocha from Daffy's limp fingers, set it aside. "Do you know the name of the man she's been seeing recently?"

"I . . . She called him her prince. Lots of times she had names for her men. This one was Prince. Dark Prince, sometimes." Daffy pressed her hands to her eyes, then dragged them up over her face, through her hair. "She's only been into him for a week or so. Maybe two. I can't think." She put her hand to her head, rubbed her temple as if she couldn't keep her fingers still. "I can't think."

"Can you describe him?"

"I never met him. I was supposed to, but I didn't. We've been fighting," she repeated as tears spilled down her cheeks.

"Tell me what you know about him."

"Did he hurt her?" Her voice broke on the question as the tears started to gush. "Did he kill Tee?"

"We're going to want to talk to him. Tell me what you know about him."

"She . . . she met him at some underground club. I was supposed to go, but I got hung up, and I forgot. I was supposed to meet her there."

"Where?" Eve prompted.

"Um . . . a cult club, underground, near Times Square, I think. I can't remember. There are so many." When Peabody offered tissues, Daffy sent her a pathetically grateful look. "Thanks. Thanks. She— Tee, she tagged me about eleven when I didn't show, and we got into it because I'd forgotten, and this guy I hooked up with and I decided to zip down to South Beach for the night. I was already down there when she tagged me."

On a long breath, she bent forward to retrieve the cup of mocha, and now sipped slowly. "Okay. Okay." She breathed in and out. "It was my screwup, about the club, so I mea culpa'd the next day. She was all about this guy, this Prince. But she looked out of it, so I knew she'd been using."

Daffy pressed her lips together. "I'm clean, and I've got to stay clean. My father still holds some of the purse strings on me, you know? If I get in any trouble like that again, he said he'd cut me off. He means it, so . . . Shit, you're cops. I'm not going to impress you, so the straight deal is this: Besides the edict from my dad, I've had enough of chems."

"But Tiara hadn't," Eve said.

"Tee's always going to go over the top, it's just her way. Always going to push the limits, then look for the next big thing." As Daffy mopped tears, she managed a wan smile. "But she knows I've got to stay clean. She'd been using, and she'd sworn off six months ago, like a solidarity deal? We took an oath, so I was pissed."

"What was she on?" Eve asked.

"I don't know, but she was strung. We scratched at each other about that, but it was mostly her telling me how I had to go with her to this club, meet this guy and his friends. She said he was complete, the absolute. That they'd banged all night, and it was the best she'd ever had. She nagged me brainless about it until I said I'd go."

Shaking her head, Daffy drank again. "Then later I started thinking how even if I didn't use, she would, and I'd get busted. So I tagged her back and told her I wasn't going, and why didn't we hook up with this guy somewhere else. No go. His club or nowhere."

"His club?"

"Not like he owned it. Or maybe he does. She never said; I never asked. But she got stewed because I wouldn't go, and Carm's in New L.A. until next month, so she couldn't pull her instead of me."

Eve waited while Daffy brooded into the mocha she'd so desperately wanted. "Do you know if anyone else went with her to this club? Any of your other mutual friends?"

"I don't think so. I never heard any buzz about it, not from anyone but Tee. Anyway, we didn't talk for a couple days, then yesterday she came by here, earlier than this even. Like just after sunrise. She looked bottomed. Pale and glassy-eyed. Using again, and she hadn't been using before this run for that whole six months. She was still hyped, talking wild. Going to live forever, that's what she said. Laughing and busting around. She and her prince were going to live forever, and screw me for flipping her off. I tried to get her to stay, but she wouldn't, just told me I'd be sorry, I'd had my chance. Now he was only taking her."

"Taking her where?" Eve asked.

"I don't know. She wasn't making any sense. I'm telling you, she was over. I got pissy right back at her, and we yelled at each other, then she stormed out. And now she's dead."

"That's the last time you saw or spoke with her?"

"Yeah. Did he hurt her? I mean . . . you didn't say how she, she died. Did he hurt her?"

"I can't tell you that yet, I'm sorry."

"She's such a baby about pain." Daffy swiped the back of her hand over her cheek. "I hope he didn't hurt her. I should've gone to the club that night. If I'd gone to the club instead of South Beach, maybe . . . Is it my fault? I should've looked after her better. She got sucked into stuff so easy. Is it my fault?"

"No, it's not your fault."

"She was almost a year older, but I was the one who looked after her—mostly. I could pull her back from the edge when she went too far. But I didn't, you know? I just told her she was being an idiot or whatever. Only Tee would actually believe in vampires."

"Vampires?" Eve repeated as Peabody sucked in her breath.

"Yeah. The prince deal? The Dark Prince. Living forever.

Get it?" Daffy gave a harsh laugh that choked on a sob. "She thought this guy was a frigging vampire, like for real, and he was going to make her one so she'd be immortal. That's what the club was—a wannabe vampire club. Bloodbath! I remember now. It's called Bloodbath. Who the hell wants to go to some club with a name like that?" She swiped at tears again. "Only Tee."

"Didn't I say vampire? I said vampire right off." Peabody gave a smug nod as they exited the building.

"And our vic's going to be deeply disappointed when she just stays dead. Track down this club. I'd love a little chat with the Dark Prince."

"It's not like I believe in the undead or anything." Peabody slid into the passenger seat. "But it wouldn't hurt, once we find this guy, to interview him during the day. In a room with good natural lighting."

"Sure. And requisition some garlic and some wooden stakes while you're at it."

"Really?"

"No." Eve swung out into traffic. "Reach down inside yourself, Peabody, and get a grip on reality, however slippery. Find the club. Right now we're going to visit somebody who knows all about what's dead."

Chief Medical Examiner Morris sent Eve an easy smile as he stood over the naked body of Tiara Kent. He wore a snappy suit the color of good claret with a matching tie thin as straw. His dark hair was intricately braided, and curled into a loop at the nape of his neck.

Eve often thought Morris's sharp fashion sense was wasted on his clientele.

"Running a bit behind today," he told them. "Sent off for tox as you'd flagged that. Shouldn't take long."

She glanced down at the body. Morris hadn't yet made his Y cut. "What can you tell me just from the visual?"

"Lieutenant, this woman is dead."

"Peabody, note that down. We've got a dead woman."

"With excellent breast work," Morris added. "And some very first-class sculpting, belly and butt."

"Jesus, she was twenty-three. Who needs sculpting and new tits at twenty-three?"

Peabody raised her hand, and got a bland look from Eve.

"You're not twenty-three."

"Okay, I've got a couple years on her, but if they're handing out butt sculpting, I'm first in line."

"You have a very nice butt, Detective," Morris assured her, and made Peabody beam.

"Aw, thanks."

"And now, back to our regularly scheduled program?" Eve suggested. "The dead woman on the slab."

"Tiara Kent, party princess. Live fast, die young." Morris tapped his comp screen to magnify the neck wounds. "These are the only injuries or insults to the body. The victim was exsanguinated through these two punctures in the carotid. No visible signs of physical restraint or struggle. Apparently, she lay there and let him suck her dry."

"Suck." Peabody drew a righteous breath through her nose. "See? Vampire bite."

Morris's smile spread to a grin. "Impossible not to have a little play with that, isn't it? The beautiful young blonde, seduced by the Prince of Darkness—or one of his minions—drained of her life's blood while in his thrall. Cue fog and shadows."

"Don't forget the creepy music," Eve added.

"Of course. Mostly, however, I suspect she was drugged to the eyeballs, and was punctured by an appliance during sex."

He lifted his eyebrows as he looked down at Tiara. "Of

course, I could be wrong, and she'll pop up shortly after sundown and terrify the night staff."

"Let's go with number one," Eve decided. "If he actually bit her, appliance or not, there's going to be saliva. Same if he didn't use a cloak for sex. I bet even vampires have DNA."

"I'll send samples to the lab."

"Guy had her convinced he could give her eternity." Eve took one last look at Tiara Kent. "Now she gets a steel box in a cold room."

Three

"Got the club." Peabody studied the readout on her PPC as they drove toward Cop Central. "Daffy had it right about Times Square, it's under Broadway. Got the hours, too. Sunset to sunrise." Peabody tracked her eyes toward Eve's profile. "Vampire hours."

"Owner?"

"Eternity Corporation, no owner or manager listed in this data."

"Dig," Eve suggested.

"Digging. Are we going by the club now?"

"If the guy frequents the place, works in the place, or owns the place, he's not going to be there when the joint's closed. We'll go after dark."

"I knew you were going to say that. Aren't you just a little bit creeped? I mean, at the very least this guy slurps blood."

"Maybe he does, maybe he doesn't." Eve stopped at a light, and watched the throng bull, shuffle, and clip its way along the crosswalk. She saw a pair of transvestites in spangled skin-suits, a tourist approaching three hundred and fifty pounds in his baggy shorts—carrying a variety of cams and vids that had to weigh nearly what he did—a kid in a red cape and skullcap streaking through bodies on an airboard, and a mime.

Whatever weirdos existed, New York made them welcome. A self-proclaimed vampire would fit right in.

"She didn't leave a full pint on the sheets," Eve continued as the light changed. "I don't care how hungry some pseudovampire is, no way he's going to guzzle down more than eight pints of blood in a sitting."

"Right. Right. Well, then what . . ."

"He took it with him."

"I have to say eeuuw."

"Bottled it up, bagged it up. Maybe he sells it, maybe he stores it, maybe he takes a fucking bath in it. But he came prepped for it." She turned into the garage at Central. "So we work that. What's a guy do with several pints of human blood? Let's see if there's a call for it on the black market. And we have the list and description of the jewelry missing from the scene. We've got the club."

She pulled into her slot, climbed out. "We'll see what the sweepers got for us, see if the lab can pull DNA. We'll check like crimes, see if we got anything like this before."

Once inside the elevator, Eve leaned back. The car smelled like cop—coffee and sweat. "Somebody saw her with this guy. She hooked up with him at the club, and somebody saw them together. She goes for thrills, gets drawn in. Starts letting him into her place, fun and games. The way it looks, he could've killed her any time he wanted, robbed her freaking blind. But he waited, and he only took what she either had on or had out.

"He's picky, and he likes the ritual, likes the seduction."

Eve stepped off the car to switch to the glides before the elevator got crowded. "Go ahead and write up what we've got, keep looking for a name to go with the club. I'm going to try to get a session in with Mira, get a better idea of what we'll be dealing with when we take ourselves a Bloodbath."

"I'll bring the rubber ducky."

Eve peeled off in the bullpen, headed for her office. As she expected, her 'link was loaded with calls from the media. A paparazzi darling ends up dead, it's a ratings bonanza, she thought, and ruthlessly forwarded all of the calls to the media liaison.

She tried for Mira first and ran headfirst into Mira's admin—the guardian at the doctor's gate. "Okay, okay. Jesus. Just tell her I'd like five whenever she can spare it. Here, there, in adjoining stalls in the john. Just five."

Eve disconnected, got coffee from her AutoChef. She set up her murder board, wrote up her notes, studied the time line.

Walked right in, that's what he did. She practically showered his path with rose petals. More money than brains.

Did he mark her first, or was it just chance she walked into the club one night? A recognizable face that liked to dance on the wild side. Known more for her exploits than her smarts.

A pathetically easy mark.

But if it had been just for the score, why kill her at all, much less in the chosen method? Because the score was secondary, she decided. The killing was the prize.

Eve glanced toward her tiny window, into the light of a sunny spring day, and calculated the time until sundown.

Thinking of that, she winced, engaged her 'link again. She wasn't just a cop, she reminded herself, but a wife. There were rules in both jobs.

She tried Roarke's private line, intending to leave a voice mail telling him she'd be late, see you when, but he picked up on the first beep. And that face, the heat-in-the-belly sexuality of that face, filled her view screen.

Dark hair framed it. Eyes of wild Irish blue gave her heart just a quick flutter that even after two years of having them look at her, just that way, was a surprise. Those perfectly sculpted lips curved as he said, "Lieutenant," with the wisp of his homeland in the word.

"How come you're not busy buying Australia?"

"I'm just between buying continents at the moment. I believe Asia's up next. And how are you?"

"Okay. I know we had sort of a thing on for tonight—"

"Dinner, I believe it was, followed by naked poker."

"That was strip poker, as I recall."

"You'd be naked soon enough. But I'm thinking that competition's been postponed. You have Tiara Kent, I take it."

"Heard about her already?"

"Multimillionaire bad girl murdered in her luxury penthouse?" His eyebrows lifted. "Word travels. How did she die?"

"Vampire bite."

"That again?" he said and made her laugh.

"She was into some kind of vampire cult crap, and it came back to, well, bite her. I've got to check out this club where she likely met her killer. It doesn't open until sunset, so I'm going to run late."

"Almost as interesting as naked poker. I'll meet you at Central by six. Darling Eve," he continued before she could speak, "you can't expect me to pass up the opportunity to accompany my wife into the den of the undead."

She considered a moment. He'd be useful; he always was. And another pair of eyes, another set of reflexes would come in handy underground.

"Don't be late."

"I'll leave in plenty of time. Should I pick up some garlic and crosses on the way?"

"I think Peabody's on that. Later," she said, and clicked off.

While she was at her desk, she contacted the lab to give them a not-so-gentle push, then began to research vampire lore. She broke off when Peabody poked her head in.

"Did you know there are dozens of websites on vampirism, and any number of them have instructions on how to drink from a victim?"

Peabody cocked her head. "This surprises you because?"

"I know I say people suck, but I didn't mean it literally. And it's not just kids in their I'm-so-bored twenties into this."

"I've got a couple of names we might want to look at, but meanwhile, Tiara Kent's mother just came in. I had one of the uniforms take her to the lounge."

"Okay, I'll take her, you keep digging." Eve pushed back from her desk. "Roarke's going to tag along tonight."

"Yeah?" Relief showed on Peabody's face before she controlled it. "It doesn't hurt to have more of us when we head down."

"He's an observer," Eve reminded her. "I'm waiting for a callback from Mira. That comes through, tag me."

Eve made Iris Francine the minute she stepped into the lounge with its lines of vending machines and little tables, and chairs designed to numb the ass after a five-minute sit-down.

Her daughter had favored her, taking the blonde hair, the green eyes, the delicate bone structure from her mother.

Iris sat with her hand clutched by a man Eve imagined was husband number four, Georgio Francine. Younger than his wife by a few years, Eve judged, and dark and sultry where she was light and elegant.

But they sat like a unit—she recognized that. Like two parts of a whole.

"Ms. Francine, I'm Lieutenant Dallas."

Iris's eyes looked exhausted as they lifted to Eve's, a

combination Eve also recognized as grief, guilt, and simple fatigue.

"You're the one in charge of . . . in charge of what happened to Tiara."

"That's right." Eve pulled up a chair. "I'm very sorry for your loss."

"Thank you. Will I be able to see her?"

"I'll arrange that for you."

"Can you tell me how she . . . what happened to her?" Iris's breath hitched, and she took two slow ones to smooth it out. "They won't tell me anything really. It's worse not knowing."

"She was killed last night, in her apartment. We believe she knew her killer, and let him in herself. Some pieces of her jewelry are missing."

"Was she raped?"

They would always ask, Eve knew. For a daughter, they would always ask, and with their eyes pleading for the answer to be no. "She'd had sexual relations, but we don't believe there was rape."

"An accident?" There was another plea in Iris's voice now, as if death wouldn't be as horrible somehow if it were accidental. "Something that got out of hand?"

"No, I'm sorry. We don't believe it was an accident. What do you know about your daughter's activities recently, her companions? The men in her life?"

"Next to nothing." Iris closed her eyes. "We didn't communicate much, or often. I wasn't a good mother."

"*Cara.*"

"I wasn't." She shook her head at her husband's quiet protest. "I was only twenty when she was born, and I wasn't a good mother. I wasn't a good anything." The words were bitter with regret. "It was all parties and fun and where can we go next. When Tiara's father had an affair, I had one to pay him back. And on and on, until we loathed each other and used her as a weapon."

She turned her shimmering eyes to her husband as he lifted their joined hands, pressed his lips to her fingers. "Long ago," he said softly. "That was long ago."

"She never forgave me. Why should she? When we divorced, Tee's father and I, I married again like that." Iris snapped her fingers. "Just to show him he didn't matter. I paid for that mistake six months later, but I didn't learn. When I finally grew up, it was too late. She preferred her father, who'd let her do whatever she liked, with whomever she liked."

"You made mistakes," Georgio told her. "You tried to fix them."

"Not hard enough, not soon enough. We have an eight-year-old daughter," she told Eve. "I'm a good mother to her. But I lost Tiara long ago. Now I can never get her back. The last time we spoke, more than a month ago, we argued. I can never get that back either."

"What did you argue about?"

"Her lifestyle, primarily. I hated that she was wasting herself the way I did. She was pushing, pushing the boundaries more all the time. Her father's engaged again, and this one's younger than Tee. It enraged her, had her obsessing about getting older, losing her looks. Can you imagine, worried about such things at twenty-three?"

"No." Eve thought of the mirrors again, the clothes, the body work Tiara had done. Obviously, this was a young woman who obsessed about anything that had to do with herself. "Did she have any particular interest in the occult?"

"The occult? I can't say. She went through a period several years ago where she paid psychics great gobs of money. She dabbled in Wicca when she was a teenager— so many girls do—but she said there were too many rules. She was always looking for the easy way, for some magic potion to make everything perfect. Will you find who killed her?"

"I'll find him."

Even as Eve made arrangements to have the Francines transported to the morgue, she saw Mira come in. After an acknowledging nod, Mira wandered to a vending machine.

She'd cut her hair again, Eve noted, so it was short and springy at the nape of her neck, and she'd done something to that soft sable color so that little wisps of it around her face were a paler tone. She sat, trim and pretty in her bluebonnet-colored suit, with two tubes of Diet Pepsi.

"Iris Francine," Mira stated when Eve came over. "I recognized her. Her face was everywhere a generation ago. I always thought her daughter was hell-bent on outdoing her mother's youthful exploits. It seems she succeeded in the hardest possible way."

"Yeah, dying will get you considerable face time, for a while."

"Quite a while, I'll wager in this case. Vampirism. I had a meeting one level up," Mira explained, "and thought to catch you in your office. Peabody gave me the basics. Murder by vampire proponents is very rare. For the most part, it's the danger, the thrill, the eroticism that draws people—primarily young people. There is a condition—"

"Renfield Syndrome. I've been reading up. What I'm getting from the people who knew the vic was a predilection to walk the edge, a desperation for fame, attention, a serious need to be and stay young and beautiful. She'd already had bodywork. And you have to add in sheer stupidity. I get her. She's not unusual, she just had more money than most so she could indulge her every idiocy."

Eve paused as she broke the seal on the Pepsi tube. "It's him. The method of killing was very specific, planned out, and there was no attempt to disguise it. He took jewelry, but that was more of the moment than motive. He went there to do exactly what he did, in exactly the way he did it."

"The compulsion may be his," Mira considered. "A craving for the taste of blood, one that escalated to the need to drain his victim. Have you gotten the autopsy results as yet?"

"No."

"I wonder if they'll find she drank blood as well. If so, you may be dealing with a killer who believes he's a vampire, and who sought to turn her into one by taking her blood and sharing his own with her."

"And if at first you don't succeed?"

"Yes." Mira's eyes, a softer blue than her suit, met Eve's. "He may very well try again. The rush, the power—particularly when coupled with sex and drugs—would be a strong pull. And she made it so easy for him, even profitable."

"How could he resist?"

"And why should he?" Mira concurred. "He was able to enter her highly secured building undetected. More power, and again cementing the illusion of a supernatural being. She gave herself to him, through sex, through blood, through death. Held in thrall—whether by his will or chemicals—another element. He removed her blood from the scene. A souvenir perhaps, a trophy, or yet another element of his power. His need for blood, and his ability to take it. You believe she was drugged?"

"I haven't had that confirmed, but yeah. Her closest pal states she'd been using, and heavily, the last week or so."

"If he drank any of her blood, he'd have shared the drug." Seeing Eve had already considered that, Mira nodded. "More power, or the illusion of it. From what you know, they'd only met a week or two earlier. It wasn't eternal love, which is one way of romanticizing vampirism."

"I don't get that." Interrupting, Eve gestured with her drink. "The romantic part."

Mira's lips curved. "Because you're a pragmatic soul. But for some, for many, the idea of eternity, that seeking a mate throughout it, coupled with the living by night, the lack of human boundaries is extremely romantic."

"Takes all kinds."

"It does. However, the way he left the body wasn't romantic, or even respectful. It was careless, cold. Whether or not he believes he could sire a vampire through her, she was no more than a vessel to him, a means to an end.

"He'll be young," Mira continued. "No more than forty. Most likely attractive in appearance and in good health. Who would want eternal life if they were homely and physically disadvantaged?"

"This vic wouldn't have gone for anyone who wasn't pretty anyway. Too vain. Her place was loaded with mirrors."

"Hmm. I wonder how she resigned herself to the lore that she'd have no reflection as a vampire."

"Could be she only bought what she wanted to buy."

"Perhaps. He'll be precise, erudite, clever. Sensual. He may be bisexual, or believe himself to be as in lore, vampires will bed and bite either sex. He will, at least for the moment, feel invulnerable. And that will make him very dangerous."

Eve drank some of her soft drink, smiled. "Knowing I'm mortal makes me very dangerous."

Four

Eve grabbed the tox report the second it came through. Then she stared at the results. She engaged her interoffice 'link, said only, "Peabody," then went back to studying the lab's findings.

"Yo," Peabody said a moment later at Eve's office doorway.

"Tox report. Take a look." Eve passed her a printout while she continued to read her computer screen.

"Holy crap. It's not what she took," Peabody decided, "it's more what didn't she take."

"Hallucinogens, date-rape drugs, sexual enhancers, paralytic, human blood, tranq, all mixed in wine. Hell of a cocktail."

"I've never seen anything like this." Peabody glanced over the printout. "You?"

"Not with so many variables and with this potency. It's new to me, but let's run it by Illegals and see if it's new to them. According to the results, and the time line, she downed this herself, before she disengaged the alarm, or just after. Maybe she knew what was in it, maybe she didn't. But she drank it down, on her own."

"Hard to say, seeing she's dead, but she pretty much wins the stupid prize."

"All-time champ." Eve paused as her machine signalled another incoming. "And we may have a runner-up. We've got DNA." She scanned the data quickly. "Semen, saliva, and the blood she ingested. All the same donor."

"Pretty damn careless of him," Peabody commented.

"Yeah." Eve frowned at the screen. "It is, isn't it?"

"Another conclusion is he just didn't care—being a vampire." Peabody shrugged as Eve glanced back at her. "He doesn't care if we match his DNA because he'll just, I don't know, turn into a bat and fly off, or poof into smoke. Whatever."

"Right. A whole new scope on going into the wind."

"I'm not saying it's what I think, but maybe what he thinks."

"We'll be sure to ask him when we find him. Meanwhile, go ahead and run the cocktail by Illegals. I'll do a standard search for the DNA match. Maybe he's in the system."

But she didn't think so. He wasn't careless, Eve thought. He was fucking arrogant. It didn't surprise her when her search turned up negative.

"Lieutenant."

She glanced over, experienced that quick heart punch when her eyes met Roarke's. He was dressed in the dark suit he'd put on in their bedroom that morning, one of the countless he owned tailored to fit his long, rangy frame.

"Right on time," she said.

"We aim to please." He stepped in, eased a hip onto the corner of her desk. "How goes the vampire hunting?"

"I don't think we'll have to call in Van Helsing." When he lifted his brows and grinned, she shrugged. "I do my research. Plus I've sat through some of those old vids you like so much."

"And so armed, we'll venture into the den of the children of the night. Never a dull moment," he added and flicked his fingers at the choppy ends of her hair. "Your case is all over the media."

"Yeah. Bound to be."

"I noticed the primary hasn't given a statement."

"I'm not going to play the game on this one, or give this asshole the satisfaction. She drugged her own brains out prior—mix of Zeus, Erotica, Whore, Rabbit, Stunner, Bliss, Boost, along with a few other goodies, including her killer's blood."

"There's an ugly recipe."

"And my money says he provided the brew, pushed on her vanity and stupid buttons, got his rocks off, then drained her like a faulty motor."

"For what purpose?" Roarke wondered.

"Best I can tell, he wound her up because he could. And he killed her because he could. He'll want to do it again, real soon."

"Foolish of him, don't you think, to have chosen such a high-profile victim?"

She'd considered that, and had to appreciate being married to a man who could think like a cop. "Yeah, smarter, safer to bite a vagrant off the street. But this was more fun, more exciting. Why snack on street whores or sidewalk sleepers, the nobodies, when you can gorge yourself on the prime? Plus, it was profitable. A street level LC isn't going to be sporting blue diamonds. He's stoked, believe it, watching all the media coverage."

"Unless he's spent the day napping in his coffin."

"Ha, ha." She pushed up, instinctively brushed a hand over the weapon at her side. "Almost sundown. Let's go clubbing."

Peabody was lying in wait, along with her cohab, E-Division Detective McNab. He wasn't just a fashion plate, but an entire place setting, and was decked out in pants of neon blue that appeared to be made up almost entirely of pockets. He'd matched it with a bright green jacket with streaks of yellow jagged across it and some sort of skinny tank that melded all the colors of the spectrum in a kind of eye-searing cloudburst.

"I thought we could use another pair of eyes," Peabody began even as Eve's eyes narrowed. "You know, strength in numbers."

"I did a rotation in Illegals when I was still in uniform." McNab grinned out of his pretty, narrow face. "And when I worked Vice, we ran into all kinds of freaky shit."

"You don't want to miss a chance to cruise a vampire club."

He smile turned winsome. "Who would?"

She could use him, Eve thought, but she gave him the hard-eye first, just for form. "This isn't a damn double date."

"No, sir." So he waited until Eve turned her back to walk to the elevator before hooking pinkies with Peabody.

"Illegals hasn't worked the combo," Peabody began once they'd shoehorned into the elevator. "They don't even have Bloodbath on their list of watch points. But they have worked a combination of Erotica, Bliss, Rabbit, with traces of blood—usually animal blood—in cases of vampire fetishism. They call it Vamp, and the use generally skews young. They haven't had any homicides as a result of."

"Our guy upped the stakes, considerably. Have to wonder why the club hasn't made their list."

"It's new," Peabody told her. "Way underground. Hadn't hit their radar until I contacted them regarding our investigation."

"Underground clubs pop up faster than weeds," McNab put in. "Live or die on word of mouth. Since it's more than urban legend that people tend to go down and not come back up, they don't get heavy tourist traffic."

"Tiara Kent found out about it somewhere." Eve strode off the elevator and into the garage.

"Crowd she runs with." Peabody jerked a shoulder. "New place with a jagged edge? It would be right up her alley."

"And in less than two weeks from the first time she goes down, she's guzzling a new, exciting illegals cocktail, and dies from a neck wound." Eve slid behind the wheel of her vehicle. "That's fast work, smooth work when you consider the security in her building never made him." She glanced over at Roarke. "How much would a few pints of human blood net on the black market?"

"A few hundred."

"What about famous human blood?"

"Ah." He nodded as she drove out of the garage. "Yes, that might drive up the price to the right buyer. Are you thinking she was specifically targeted?"

"It's an angle. She's known, and she's known to take risks, to slut around, to live wild. Her best friend hadn't heard of the club before Kent clued her in. So maybe the idea or an invitation got passed straight onto the vic. In any case, she hooked up with her killer there, so someone saw them together. Someone knows him."

"You know," McNab speculated, "if you factor out the blood-sucking, soulless demon angle, this should be a slam dunk."

"Good thing none of us believe in blood-sucking, soulless demons." But Peabody's hand crept over and found McNab's.

Eve caught the gesture in the rearview, just as she caught the way the fingers of Peabody's free hand snuck between the buttons of her shirt to close over something.

"Peabody, are you wearing a cross?"

"What? Me?" The hand dropped like a stone into her

lap. Her cheeks went pink as she cleared her throat. "It just happened that I know Mariella in Records, who just happened to have one, and I happened to borrow it. Just for backup."

"I see. And would you also be carrying a pointy stick?"

"Not unless you mean McNab."

McNab smiled easily as Eve stopped at a light, turned around in her seat. "Repeat after me: Vampires do not exist."

"Vampires do not exist," Peabody recited.

With a nod, Eve turned back, then narrowed her eyes at Roarke. "What's that look on your face?"

"Speculation. Most legends, after all, have some basis in fact. From Vlad the Impaler to Dracula of lore. It's interesting, don't you think?"

"It's interesting that I'm in this vehicle with a trio of lamebrains."

"Lamebrained to some," Roarke replied equably, "open-minded to others."

"Huh. Maybe we should stop off at a market on the way, pick up a few pounds of garlic, just to ease those open minds."

"Really?" Peabody said from the back, then hunched her shoulders as Eve sent her a stony stare in the rearview mirror. "That means no," Peabody muttered to McNab.

"I translated already."

Eve had to settle for a second-level street slot five blocks from the underground entrance. The sun had set, and the balmy April day had gone to chill with a wind that had risen up to kick through the urban canyons.

They moved through the packs of pedestrians—heading home, heading to dinner, heading to entertainment. At the mouth of the underground entrance, Eve paused.

"Stick together through the tunnels," she ordered. "We can work in pairs once we get to the club, but even then, let's keep visual contact at all times."

She didn't believe in the demons of lore, but she knew the human variety existed. And many of them lived, played, or worked in the bowels of the city.

They moved down, out of the noise, out of the wind, into the dank dimness of the tunnels. The clubs and haunts and dives that existed there catered to a clientele that would make most convicted felons sprint in the opposite direction.

Offerings underground included sex clubs that specialized in S&M, in torture dealt out for a fee by human, droid, or machine, or any miserable combination thereof. In the bars, the drinks were next to lethal and a man's life was worth less than the price of a shot. The violent and the mad might wander there, sliding off into the shadows to do what could only be done in the dark, where blood and death bloomed like fetid mushrooms.

She could hear weeping, raw and wild, echoing down one of the tunnels, and laughter that was somehow worse. She saw one of the lost addicts, pale as a ghost, huddled on the filthy floor, panting, pushing a syringe against his arm, giving himself a fix of what would eventually kill him.

She turned away from it, passed a sex club where the lights were hard and red and reminded her of the room in Dallas where she'd killed her father.

It was cold underground, as it had been cold in that room. The kind of cold that sank its teeth into the bone like an animal.

She heard something scuttling to the left, and saw the gleam of eyes. She stared into them until they blinked, and they vanished.

"I should've given you my clutch piece," she said under her breath to Roarke.

"Not to worry. I have my own."

She spared him a glance. He looked, she realized, every bit as deadly as anything that roamed the tunnels. "Try not to use it."

They turned down an angle beyond a vid parlor where someone screamed in a hideous combination of pain and delight.

She smelled piss and vomit as they descended the next level. When a man with bulging muscles stepped out of the dark, turned the knife he held into the slant of light so it gleamed, Eve simply drew her weapon.

"Wanna bet who wins?" she asked him, and he melted away again.

From there, she followed the strong vibration of bass, the scent of heavy perfume, and the ocean surf roar of voices.

The lights here were red as well, with some smoke blue, fog gray shimmered in. Mists curled and crawled over the floor. The doorway was an arch, to represent the mouth of a cave. Over the arch the word BLOODBATH throbbed in bloody red.

Two bouncers, one black, one white, both built like tanker jets, flanked the arch, then stepped together to form a wall of oiled muscle.

"Invitation or passcode," they said in unison.

"This is both." Eve pulled out her badge, and got twin smirks.

"That doesn't mean jack down here," the one on the left told her. "Private club."

Before she could speak again, Roarke simply pulled out several bills. "I believe this is the passcode."

After the money passed, the bouncers separated to make an opening. As they walked through, Eve shot Roarke an annoyed look. "I don't have to bribe my way in."

"No, but you were going to hurt them, and that's a lot messier. In any case, it was worth the fee as you take me to the most interesting places."

The club was three open levels, dark and smoky, with the pentagram bar as the center. A stage jutted out on the second level where a band played the kind of music that bashed into the chest like hurled stones. Fog crept over it like writhing snakes. Patrons sat at the bar, at metal tables, lurked in corners or danced on platforms. Nearly all wore black, and nearly all were well under thirty.

There were some privacy booths and some were already occupied with couples or small groups smoking what was likely illegal substances inside the domes, or groping each other. Eve's gaze tracked up to note there were private rooms on the third level. The club had a live sex license, and no doubt all manner of acts transpired behind the doors.

She approached the bar where a man or woman worked at every point of the pentagram. Eve chose a woman with straight black hair parted in the center to frame a pale, pale face. Her lips were heavy and full and dyed deep, dark red.

"What can I get you?" the woman asked.

"Whoever's in charge." Eve set her badge on the slick black metal of the bar.

"There a problem?"

"There will be if you don't get me whoever runs this place."

"Sure." The bartender drew a headset out of her pocket. "Dorian? Allesseria. I've got a cop at station three asking for the manager. Sure thing."

She put the headset away again. "He'll be right down. Said I should offer you a drink, on the house."

"No, thanks. Have you seen this woman in here, Allesseria?" Eve drew out Tiara's ID photo.

She saw recognition immediately, then the quick wariness. And then the lie. "Can't say I have. We get slammed in here by midnight. Hard to pick out faces in the crowd, and with this lighting."

"Right. You got anything on tap here but beer and brew?"

Once again, Eve saw the lie. "I don't know what you mean. I just run the stick at this station. That's it, that's all. I got customers."

"She's not only a poor liar," Roarke observed. "She's a frightened one."

"Yeah, she is." Eve scanned the crowd again. She saw a man barely old enough to make legal limit actually wearing a cape, and a woman, nearly a decade older, all but bursting out of a long, tight black dress, who was wrapping herself around him like a snake on one of the dance platforms.

Another woman in sharp red sat alone in a privacy booth and looked mildly bored. When a man wearing mostly tattoos glided up to the bar, ordered, Allesseria poured something into a tall glass that bubbled and smoked. He downed it where he stood, throat rippling, then set the glass down with a snarling grin that flashed pointed incisors.

Eve literally felt Peabody shudder beside her. "Jesus, this place is creepy."

"It's a bunch of show and theater."

Then Eve saw him coming down the corkscrew of steps from the top level. He was dressed in black, as would be expected. His hair, black as well, rained past his shoulders, a sharp contrast to the white skin of his face. And that face had a hard and sensual beauty that compelled the eye.

He moved gracefully, a lithe black cat. As he reached the second level, a blonde rushed toward him, gripped his hand. There was a pathetic desperation about her as she leaned into him. He simply trailed his fingers down her cheek, shook his head. Then he bent to capture her mouth in a deep kiss as his hands slid under her short skirt to rub naked, exposed flesh. She clung to him afterward so that he had to set her aside, which he did by lifting her a foot off the ground in a show of careless strength.

Eve could see her mouth move, knew the woman called to him, though the music and voices drowned out the sound.

He crossed the main level, and his eyes locked with Eve's. She felt the jolt—she could admit it. His eyes were like ink, deep and dark and hooded. As he walked to her, his lips curved in a smile that was both knowing and confident.

And in the smile she saw something that didn't cause that quick, physical jolt, but a deep and churning physical dread.

"Good evening," he said in a voice that carried a trace of some Eastern European accent. "I'm Dorian Vadim, and this is my place."

Though her throat had gone dry, Eve gave him an acknowledging nod. "Lieutenant Dallas." She drew out her badge yet again. "Detectives Peabody and McNab. And . . ."

"No introduction necessary." There was another quality to him now, what seemed to be a prickly combination of admiration and envy. "I'm aware of Roarke, and of you, Lieutenant. Welcome to Bloodbath."

Five

She knew what she saw when she looked at him. She saw in those pitch-dark eyes her greatest single fear: She saw her father.

There was no physical resemblance between the man before her and the one who had tormented and abused her for the first eight years of her life. It went, she understood, deeper than physical. Its surface was a calculated charm thinly coated over an indifferent cruelty.

Under it all was utter disregard for anything approaching the human code.

The monster that had lived in her father looked at her now out of Dorian Vadim's eyes.

And he smiled almost as if he knew it. "It's an honor to have you here. What can I get you to drink?"

"We're not drinking," Eve told him, though she would have paid any price but pride for a sip of water to cool the burning in her throat. "This isn't a social call."

"No, of course not. Well then, what can I do for you?"

Eve slid the photo of Tiara across the bar. Dorian lifted it, glanced at it briefly. "Tiara Kent. I heard she was killed this morning. Tragic." He tossed it down again without another glance. "So young, so lovely."

"She's been in here."

"Yes." He affirmed without an instant's hesitation. "A week or two ago. Twice, I believe. I greeted her myself when I was told she'd come in. Good for business."

"How did she get the invitation?" Eve demanded.

"One may have been sent to her. A selection of the young, high-profile clubbers is sent invitations periodically. We've only been open a few weeks. But as you can see . . ." He turned, gestured to the crowd that screamed over the blasting music. "Business is good."

"She came alone."

"I believe she did, now that you mention it." He turned back, angling just a little closer to Eve, until the hairs on the back of her neck prickled. "As I recall, she was to meet a friend, or friends. I don't believe she did. I'd hoped she'd come back, with some of her crowd. They spend lavishly, and can make a club such as this."

"Underground clubs aren't made that way."

"Things change." He picked up the drink Allesseria had set on the bar, watching Eve over the rim as he sipped. "As do times."

"And how much time did you spend with Kent?"

"Quite a bit on her initial visit. I gave her a tour of the place, bought her a few drinks." He sipped again, slowly. "Danced with her."

Her father had smelled of candy from the mints he chewed to cover the liquor. Dorian smelled of musk, yet she scented the hard sweetness of candy and whiskey. "Went home with her?"

He smiled, and when he set down his glass his knuckles lightly brushed Eve's hand. "If you want to know if I fucked her, you've only to ask. I didn't, though it was tempting. But bad for business. Wouldn't you agree?" he said to Roarke. "Sex with clients is a tricky business."

"It would depend on the client, and the business." Roarke's voice was a silky purr, a tone Eve knew was dangerous. "Other things are bad for business as well."

As if acknowledging some unspoken warning, Dorian angled his head in a slight nod, shifted his body away from Eve's.

"Did you tell her you were a vampire?" Eve demanded. "That you could turn her?"

Dorian slid on a stool and laughed. "Yes, to the first. It's part of the atmosphere, as you can clearly see. The core clientele come here for the thrill, the eroticism of the cult, the thrill of possibility. Certainly part of the draw is the fear and the allure of the undead, along with the dark promise of eternal youth and power."

"So you sell it, but you don't buy it."

"We'll just say I very much enjoy my work."

"Tiara Kent was exsanguinated, through a two-pronged wound through the carotid artery."

He lifted one arched black brow. "Really? Fascinating. Do you believe in vampires, Lieutenant Dallas? In those who prey on the human, and thirst for their blood?"

"I believe in the susceptible, in the foolish, and in those who exploit them. She was drugged first." Eve took a careless glance around and hated, *hated* that her chest felt tight. "I wonder how many illegals I'd net if I ordered a sweep of this place?"

"I couldn't say. We both know such things aren't as . . . regulated underground." He stared deeply into her eyes. "Just as we both know that's not what you're here for."

"One leads to another. Her killer left his DNA behind."

"Ah, well. We can, at least, settle that one particular element." Watching her still, he rolled up his sleeve. "Allesseria, I'll need a syringe with a vial. Unopened."

"You keep needles behind the bar?" Eve snapped out.

"Part of the show. We serve several drinks that contain a dram or two of pig's blood, and it's added with a syringe for flourish." He took the needle from the bartender. "Should you do the honors," he asked Eve, "or I?"

"A swab of your spit would be easier."

"But not nearly as interesting." He pumped his fist until a vein rose, then slid the needle neatly—expertly, Eve thought—into it. Depressed the plunger. "Allesseria, you'll witness I'm providing the lieutenant with my blood voluntarily."

When the bartender didn't speak, Dorian turned his head toward her slowly, stared.

"Yes. Yes, I will."

"That should be enough." He flashed a hard smile at Eve, then removed the needle, capped off the vial. "Thank you, Allesseria." Flipping the syringe agilely, he held it out, plunger first. "Dispose of that properly," he ordered, then handed the vial to Eve. "You'll mark and seal that in our presence?"

As she did, Dorian swiped his fingertip over the drop of blood on the tiny puncture in his flesh, then laid it on his tongue. "Is there anything else?"

"Did you see Miss Kent with anyone in particular, see her leaving with anyone?"

"I can't say I did. I believe she danced with any number of people. Feel free to ask any of the staff, and I'll be happy to ask myself."

"You do that. We'll need an address, Mr. Vadim."

"Dorian, please. I'm known as Dorian. I can be reached here. I'm living upstairs at the moment. Let me give you a card." He waved his fingers, flicked them, and a glossy black card appeared between the index and middle finger. As he passed it to Eve, his fingers brushed down her palm, lingered for just an instant too long. Then he smiled. "I tend to sleep days."

"I bet. One more thing. Can you verify your where-abouts from midnight to three this morning?"

"I would have been here. As I said, I'm most often here."

"Anybody vouch for that?"

His lips quirked again, in a kind of smug amusement that put her back up. "I imagine so. You might ask any of the staff or the regulars. Allesseria?" He turned his black gaze from Eve's face to the bartender. "You were on last night. Didn't we speak some time after midnight?"

"I was on until two." Allesseria kept her eyes locked on Dorian's. "You were, ah, working the floor before I left, came by the bar for a spring water just before I clocked out. At two."

"There you are. Lieutenant, it's been a pleasure." He took her hand, held it firmly. "But I really need to get back to work. Roarke. I hope you'll both come back, for the entertainment."

Through the fog that shimmered and curled, he glided off again, easing his way through the crowd. Eve shifted her body, stared hard at the bartender. "You want to tell me why you lied for him?"

"I don't know what you're talking about." Busily now, Allesseria wiped the bar.

"You don't see a woman whose face is all over the screen and mags, and she comes in at least twice, hangs with your boss. You don't make her." Some of the anger she felt for herself snapped out in her voice. "But you remember Do-rian got a spring water at two in the morning."

"That's right."

"I need your full name."

"You're going to cost me my job if you don't back off."

"Full name," Eve repeated.

"Allesseria Carter. If you have any more questions, I'm calling a lawyer."

"That'll do it for now. You *remember* anything, get in touch." Eve laid one of her cards on the bar before she stepped away. "If that wasn't Kent's Prince of frigging Darkness pigs are currently dive-bombing Fifth Avenue."

"Blood will tell," Roarke said quietly.

"Bet your fine ass."

Once they were out on the street, Peabody's sigh was long and heartfelt. "Man. Creepshow—even if the Lord of the Undead is intensely sexy."

"Looked like another freak to me," McNab muttered.

"You're a guy who likes women. If you were a woman who liked men, we'd still be rolling your tongue back into your mouth. He completely smoked, right, Dallas?"

Women had found her father attractive, Eve thought. No matter what he'd done to them.

"I'm sure Tiara Kent thought the same even as he was draining the life out of her. I'm going to call a black-and-white for you. I want you to take the blood sample directly to the lab, wait while it's logged in."

"Got it." Peabody took the sample, stowed it in her bag.

"I'll run our host, and the bartender. This isn't his first time around the block—and she was lying about seeing him this morning. Lab comes through quickly enough, we'll be giving Vadim a very unpleasant wake-up call."

They separated, and as she walked Eve gave Roarke a quick hip bump. Now that she was on the street, away from Vadim, away from those pulsing lights, she felt herself again. "You're quiet."

"Contemplating. He was scoping you, you know. Subtle but quite deliberate." When she started to jam her hands into her pockets, Roarke took one, brought it casually to his lips. "He wanted to see your reaction—and mine."

"Must be disappointed we didn't give him one. Or much of one on your part."

"More puzzled, I'd think."

"Okay, why didn't you slap him back?"

"It was tempting, but more satisfying to let him wonder. In any case, he's not your type."

She snorted. "Nah. I don't go for the tall, dark, gorgeous types who exude sexuality like breath."

"You don't go for sociopaths."

She glanced up at him. He'd seen it, too, she realized. He'd seen at least that much, too. "You got that right."

"Besides, I'm taller."

Now she laughed, and because really, what did it hurt, she turned as she climbed the platform to the car, feigned judging his height as she laid her hands on his shoulders. She pressed her lips to his, warm, ripe, real, then eased back. "Yeah, I'd say you're exactly tall enough to fit my requirements. You drive, ace. I want to start the runs on the way home."

She used her PPC, and though it was limited to a mini-screen, Dorian Vadim's ID photo still had punch. His hair had been shorter when it was taken, but it still brushed past his shoulders. It listed his age at thirty-eight, his birthplace as Budapest, where according to his data, he still had a mother.

It also listed a very impressive sheet.

"Grifting's a specialty of our suave Mister V," Eve related. "Lotsa pops there, starting with a juvie record that was never sealed. Bounced around Europe and came to the States, it seems, in his early twenties. Arrests for smuggling—no convictions on that. Illegals, some pops, some questioned and released. Worked as an entertainer—mesmerist and magician. Hmmm. A lot of dropped charges, heavy on the female vics. Was questioned about the disappearance of two women he reputedly bilked. Not enough evidence to arrest, and no DNA in his records.

"Slithered through the system like a snake," she muttered. "No violence on record, but wits recant or poof with regularity." She frowned over at Roarke. "You buy into that mesmo stuff?"

"Hypnotism is a proven art, you know Mira uses it in therapy."

"Yeah, but mostly I think it's bull." Still she remembered the odd sensation she'd felt when Dorian had stared into her eyes. Her problem, she told herself. Her personal demons.

"Anyway, the man's bad news. And he's got a pattern of victimizing women, wealthy ones particularly."

She did a quick run on the bartender and found no criminal on Allesseria. "Bartender's clean. Divorced, with a kid just turning three." Eve pursed her lips as Roarke drove through the open gates toward home. "I get her in the box, even alone at her own place, I can break her. She's lying about seeing Dorian. I could snap her statement in five minutes without him around. He scares her."

"He's a killer."

"Yeah, no question."

"I mean she knows it, or believes it. You're capable of snapping her statement, and he's equally capable of snapping her neck—and with a great deal less passion."

"Wouldn't disagree. I just wonder why you'd say that after one conversation with him."

"I would have said it after one look at him. His eyes. He's a vampire."

Her mouth dropped open as he stopped the car. She hadn't managed to get words working with her thoughts until she'd pushed out of the car, rounded the hood to meet him. "You said what?"

"I mean it literally. His type sucks the life out of people, and does it for momentary pleasure, just as effectively as any fictional vampire. And he's just, darling Eve, as soulless."

Like her father, Eve thought. Yes, Roarke had seen it, too. He'd seen all of it. There was nothing strange or frightening about recognizing a monster.

It only meant she understood her quarry.

Eve stepped in, pulled off her jacket. She gestured toward Summerset, Roarke's majordomo, who—as he inevitably did—stood waiting in the foyer in his funereal black suit. "I always figured vampires looked like that. Pale, bony, dour, and dead." She tossed the jacket on the newel and started up the stairs.

"Will you be having dinner in the dining room like normal human beings this evening?" Summerset asked.

"Got work, and nobody who looks like you should toss around words like 'normal'."

"We'll get something upstairs," Roarke said placidly.

He strolled with Eve into her office, then immediately whipped around and boxed her against the wall. "I think I'll start with an appetizer," he said, then crushed his lips to hers.

Her blood went to instant sizzle. She could all but feel her brains leaking out of her ears as his mouth ravaged hers with a kind of feral impatience that thrilled. Even as she gripped his hips, he was doing torturous things to her body with those quick and clever hands.

She gulped in air, and simply gave herself to the wild and wanton moment. And to him.

She would always give. He knew no matter how much he wanted, she would always be there to give, or take, to meet those endless, urgent needs with her own. Her mouth was a fever on his. A moan poured from her as he tugged her shirt apart, then found that warm, trembling flesh with his lips, his teeth.

The taste of her incited a fresh and mammoth wave of hunger.

Her hands yanked at the hook of his trousers as his yanked at hers. And she pressed erotically against him, core to core.

Her eyes were dark when he looked into them and, for one brilliant moment, went blind when he plunged inside her.

She matched him, beat for frantic beat, riding and racing the violent pleasure as he dragged her arms over her head, as he pinned them there. As he battered them both over the last turbulent crest.

Her breath whistled in and out; he rested his cheek on her hair as he caught his own. And in sweet opposition to the force of their mating, he brushed his lips at her temple, soft as gossamer wings.

"I believe I was a bit more than mildly annoyed by having some poster boy for Dracula hit on my wife in front of my face."

"Worked for me." Grateful for the wall behind her, Eve leaned back, managed to focus on Roarke's eyes. "Feel better?"

"Considerably, thanks."

"Anytime. You know what, I feel like a big, fat hunk of red meat. How about you?"

He smiled, touched his lips to hers. "I could eat."

Six

She had an enormous hamburger while she backtracked through Dorian Vadim's criminal record. She burned up the 'link as she ate, as Dorian hadn't just slithered through the system, but had wound his way around the country and in and out of Europe while he did so. She spoke to detectives and investigators in Chicago, Boston, Miami, New L.A., East Washington, and several European cities.

She took copious notes, requested files, and made promises to keep other cops in other cities in the loop.

At some point during the process, Roarke wandered out. She'd set up another murder board, typed up her notes, and was talking to the head of security at Tiara Kent's building when Roarke wandered back in again.

She held up a finger.

"Go back as far as you can. If you see this guy on any of your discs, at any point, I want to know. Yeah, day or night. Thanks."

She disconnected. "Gist from the cops I've talked to across the frigging globe is Vadim is a smart grifter with the conscience and agility of a snake, an ego as big as . . . how big is Idaho?"

"There are bigger," Roarke considered, "but I'd say that's big enough."

"Okay, we'll go with Idaho, and an appetite for rich females and illegal substances. I'm damned if he'll slip through my fingers. Going to wrap him up quick, going to wrap him up tight," she told Roarke. "If we get him on any of the building's security discs, it's one more—ha, ha—nail in his coffin."

"Then you might be interested in what I ferreted out, regarding his financials."

Her expression went from intent to annoyed. "I don't have authorization to ferret in his financials, as yet."

"Which is why I used the unregistered. I don't like him," Roarke said very clearly before Eve could complain.

"Yeah, loud and clear on that. But I don't need his financial data at this point, and I can't use anything you found by illegal means, so—"

"So don't use it. And if you're not as curious as I was, I'll keep the information to myself."

He walked over, opened a wall panel, and got out the brandy. She lasted until he'd poured himself a snifter.

"Damn it. What did you find?"

"He's not officially listed as the owner of the club, but he owns it—such as it is. He's built several fronts, and is registered as its manager."

"Shady," she commented, "but not strictly illegal."

"He's also sunk quite a bit into the club—more, in my opinion, than makes good business sense on an underground establishment. I'd say Idaho might be lacking in square miles, after all. His overhead's considerably more than his take, particularly considering his payroll."

"You hacked into his books for Bloodbath?"

"It wasn't any trouble." He swirled, then sipped brandy. "Not much of a challenge. He's losing money on it, every week. Yet his personal finances don't reflect that. Instead there's a nice steady build. Nothing that would wave flags, which tells me he's very likely tucked away other accounts. I only scraped off a few layers on this run."

"What's his other income?" Eve wondered, and Roarke smiled.

"That's a question."

"Illegals are likely one chute. Bilking, blackmail, extortion. Once a grifter . . . He could've been milking Kent, but if it was just about money, why kill the really rich cow before she runs dry? It's not just about money," she said before Roarke could. "That's a shiny side benefit."

"Agreed. And I'm going to wager very shiny. I can take a hard look at Kent's finances, but I suspect she was the type who flung money about like confetti on New Year's Eve."

"Yeah, she had hundreds of shoes."

"I don't see the correlation, however," he continued as she rolled her eyes. "With enough time, I could find his hidey-holes, and jibe any unusual income with the same outlay from Kent's."

"Given enough time," Eve repeated. "Hours or days?"

"From the subjects in question, it could take a few days."

"Crap. Poking there won't hurt. But that's not what's going to get him."

"Again, we agree." He strolled over, sat on her desk. He liked it there, where he could look down into those whiskey-toned eyes. Those cop's eyes. "It may be weight, but it won't be your hammer. And as for the club, he's certainly got a second set of books on that, one that includes any exorbitant, and likely illegal membership fees, illegals transactions, and the like. Which I'll find for you, in time, as well."

"You're really handy to have around." She tapped his knee with her finger. "And not just for the sex."

"Darling, how sweet. I'll say the same of you." He bent down to kiss her lightly—another reason he liked sitting in just that spot. "On Vadim, if he were smarter, he'd be keeping his income and outlay closer on his official records. But he's not as smart as he thinks he is."

"But you're smarter than even he thinks he is." She paused, thought that through. "If you get me."

"Aren't we full of compliments tonight? I'll have to bang you against the wall more often."

She laughed, then picked up her coffee. She drank it even though it had gone cold. "I'll have the DNA match in the morning, maybe get lucky and get a blip of him on Kent's building's security. I'm going to corner the bartender and break down her corroboration of his bullshit alibi. I'll have him in a cage by noon. Then we can take his finances and his records apart, piece by piece. You can add weight to my hammer."

Roarke angled his head. "Except? I can hear an 'except' in your voice."

"Except it's too easy. Roarke. It's all too goddamn easy on his end. He gave up his blood without a blink, and with a smile."

"I particularly dislike his smile," Roarke commented.

"Yeah? With you on that. He has to know he left DNA at Kent's that can hang him, but he didn't demand I get a warrant. And the fact is, it might have taken me some fast talking to get one for it. He may not be as smart as he thinks, but he's not stupid either. He's not worried, and that worries me."

"So, he has an ace in the hole somewhere. You'll just have to trump it. Now, tell me, what else is it that worries you?"

"I don't know what you mean."

"You went somewhere else in your head once or twice when we were in the club. And you've been there again a time or two since. Where did you go that worries you?"

"I've got a lot to push through, think through," she began.

"Eve." It was all he said. All he needed to say.

"I saw my father. I stood there in that ugly place, and he came toward me. Toward me," she repeated. "Not us, not the group of us, but me."

"Yes. Yes, he did."

"Like a dream, in a way. The fog, the lights, the noise. I knew it was for effect, for show, but . . . I got a hook in me, I guess, and then I looked in his eyes. You said sociopath. You said killer. And yeah, I saw that. But I saw more than that. When I looked into him I saw whatever monster it was that lived in my father. I saw it staring out at me. And it . . . it sickens me. It scares me."

Roarke reached down, took her hand. "Knowing monsters exist, as you and I do, Eve, may not always make for easy sleep, or even an easy heart. But it arms us against them."

"It was like he knew." She tightened her grip on his hand. There was no one else she could have told such things to. There had been a time when there'd been no one at all she could have told such things to. "I know it was my imagination, my own . . . demons, I guess you could say, but when he stared back into me, it was like he knew. Like he could see what was small and scared inside of me."

"You're wrong on that. What he saw was a woman who won't stand down."

"I hope so, because for a couple seconds I wanted to run. Just rabbit the hell out of there." She let out a shaky breath. "There are all kinds of vampires, you said that, too. Isn't that what my father was? Trying to suck the life out of me, trying to make me into something less than human? I put a knife into him instead of a stake. Maybe that's why he keeps coming back in my head."

"It's you who made you." He leaned down now, framed her face with his hands. "And what you are your father would never have understood. Neither would Vadim. No matter how he looks, he'll never really see you."

"He thinks he does."

"His mistake. Eve, do you want to talk to Mira about this?"

"No." She considered it another moment, then shook her head and repeated, "No, not now anyway. Dumping on you levels it out a little. Taking him down, all the way down—that'll take care of the rest."

For a moment she studied their joined hands, then shifted her gaze up to his. "I didn't want to tell you I'd been scared, much less why. I guess that was stupid."

"It was."

She scowled. "Aren't you supposed to say something like 'No, it wasn't. Blah, blah, support, stroke, let me get you some chocolate'?"

"You haven't read the marriage handbook, footnotes. It's another *woman* who does that sort of thing. I believe I'm allowed to be more blunt, then ask if you'd like a quick shag."

"Shag yourself," she said and made him laugh. "But thanks anyway."

"Offer's always on the table."

"Yeah, yeah, and the floor, in the closet, or on the front stairs. Time to work, ace, not to play."

She pushed up to study and circle her murder board, and he knew she was soothed and settled.

"Prior bad acts, and plenty of them. Mysterious income. Contact with the vic, and the profile fits him like a tailor-made suit. Bullshit alibi. He's running a game in that club, skinning rich idiots with his vampire fantasy, maybe blackmailing them, selling illegals. But that's only part of the picture. He's got something," she said in a mutter now. "He's got something, and he's feeling fucking smug about it."

"Heads up, Lieutenant," Roarke warned.

She glanced his way, caught the candy bar he tossed across the room. She grinned, tore the wrapper, and biting in, continued to study her board.

When Allesseria finished her shift, she was careful not to rush, careful to do everything just as she did every night. She closed down her tabs, keyed in her codes, passed her station off to her replacement.

She stretched her back as she walked, casually, to the employee-only area where she stowed her bag and her jacket every shift. Even there, behind closed doors, she kept her expression neutral and her movements routine. Everyone knew there were cameras in every section of the club, the boss had made that clear.

You never knew who was watching.

Her yawn wasn't entirely feigned. It had been a long shift, and a busy one as the crowds that patronized Bloodbath liked to stay thoroughly lubed. As she always did, she transferred her tips to her bag, zipped them into its inside pocket. After fitting the bag's strap across her body, she put her jacket over it.

She hung the illuminated cards, given to all employees, around her neck so that one glowed between her breasts, the other between her shoulder blades.

With the gleaming gold pentagram with its boldly red double B's in the center like a shield front and back, nobody would bother her on the way out of the club, on the nasty route through the tunnels. It was something else Dorian had made clear from the get-go, and he'd made an example of a souped-up chemi-head who'd tried a move on one of the waitresses the first week the club opened.

Rumor was the guy had ended up in pieces, and there hadn't been enough blood left to so much as stain the ground.

It was probably bullshit. Probably. But it was enough to keep the path clear for anyone coming or going from Bloodbath who wore the sign.

Still, she checked her pocket, as she always did, for her ministunner and panic button.

An ounce of prevention was worth a lot of peace of mind.

She headed out, and as was usual at shift changes, she left the club with a group of other employees. Safety in numbers. There wasn't much chatter, there rarely was, so she could huddle inside her own thoughts as they wound through the stink and the shadows, through the pounding music and wailing screams.

She'd thought she could handle it, the money was too good to pass up. With salary and tips, if she was frugal, she could move out of the city, plunk down a down payment on a nice little house.

A yard for her kid, a day job.

It seemed like the perfect plan, and she knew how to take care of herself. But it was too much, she had to face that now. The club, the tunnels, the boss himself. It was all too much, and she was going to have to go back to working street level, pulling doubles just to put a few extra aside every week. The house in Queens, the yard, the dog, would all just have to wait a few more years.

She'd walked out of Bloodbath for the last time.

She'd send in written notice, that's what she'd do, Allesseria decided as she finally came out to the sidewalk. She'd use her son as an excuse. Dorian knew she had joint custody, but she could use the night work as too strenuous, too difficult.

Nothing he could do about it, she assured herself as she pulled off the glowing cards and stuffed them in her pocket. Nothing, that she could think of, that he'd want to do. At the salary he offered, he'd replace her in one crook of the finger.

Let somebody else mix pig's blood—God, she *hoped* it was just pig's blood—in gin to make Bloody Martinis, or handle dry ice to make a Graveyard. She was done.

The cops had been the last straw. She couldn't take any more.

He'd made her lie for him, so there was a reason he needed the lie.

As Allesseria went underground again, this time to catch the subway home, she admitted she'd lied before he'd asked. Something had warned her she'd be better off playing dumb.

Never seen that face before.

Tiara Kent, who'd knocked back a half-dozen Bloodies on her first visit to the club—and had spent a hell of a lot of time up in Dorian's private office.

Okay, she hadn't seen them leave together, but in fact, she hadn't seen either of them leave when Tiara had come to the club. Which meant they might have slipped out through Dorian's office.

And Allesseria hadn't seen Dorian from sometime before midnight last shift. He hadn't come down to work the floor as she'd told the cop he had. He hadn't worked the floor, not once that she'd noticed, after Tiara Kent had gone up those stairs with him.

And she always noticed him because of the way her skin started to crawl.

He could've killed Tiara Kent. He could've done it.

With her arms protectively crossed over her torso, Allesseria sat on the train, struggling with what she should do, could do. A dozen times she told herself just walking away was enough. It wasn't her responsibility, and she'd be smarter to just mind her own business. Quitting was enough. More than enough.

But when she got off at her stop, she thought of her son, how she tried to teach him to do the right thing, to stand up for what he knew was right. To be a good man one day.

So she pulled out the card the cop had left on the bar and her pocket 'link as she walked the dark street home.

Nerves prickled at the base of her spine, crawled up to the back of her throat. Even though she told herself it was foolish, she shot anxious glances over her shoulder. Nothing to worry about now, *nothing*. She was blocks from the club, and back on street level. As far as Dorian knew she'd backed him up, 100 percent.

She was nearly home. She was safe.

Still, she stayed in the streetlights where she could as she recited Eve's office code. When she reached voice mail, she took a long breath.

"Lieutenant Dallas, this is Allesseria Carter, the bartender at Bloodbath."

She paused, looking over her shoulder again as those nerves dug in like claws. Had she heard something? Footsteps, a rustle in the breeze?

But she saw nothing but light and shadow, the black, blank windows in the buildings.

Still, she increased her pace, felt her knees tremble as she hurried. "I need to talk to you, um, talk to you about Tiara Kent. If you could contact me as soon—"

He came out of nowhere, charging in like some dark and brutal wind. Shock had her sucking in air as she whirled around, as she stumbled back. She managed one choked-off scream as his hand closed over her throat, squeezing out even that single panicked gulp. The black eyes stared into hers when her 'link went flying. As if she weighed nothing at all, he lifted her off the ground.

"You," he said in a quiet, almost pleasant tone, "made a very tragic mistake."

She kicked, her legs dancing and dangling like a hanging man's when he dragged her out of the circle of light from the street lamp. Red dots exploded in front of her eyes while her lungs screamed for air and her hand fumbled wildly for her panic button.

Her feet thudded on broken steps, and tears spurted out of her eyes. They bulged in horror when he smiled and she saw, impossibly, the flash of fangs.

In the dark, those gleaming points sank into her neck.

The minute she was dressed in the morning, Eve snagged a second cup of coffee. "I'm going to check my home office machine, see if I got anything from the lab overnight."

"Being a bit obsessive, aren't you?" Roarke asked from where he sat, scanning the morning financials on the bedroom screen. "It's barely seven."

"You have your obsessions." She nodded toward the maze of numbers. "I have mine."

"Check it from your pocket 'link then. Have something to eat while you're about it."

"How am I supposed to check my office messages with my pocket 'link?"

Roarke only sighed, rose. He walked to her and held out a hand. "They're all connected, my technology-challenged darling, hence the term *'link*."

"Yeah, yeah, but then you have to remember all these codes and sequences, and it's just easier to . . ."

He punched a command while she frowned at him. "Relay any new incomings on home unit Dallas," he ordered.

Acknowledged . . . There are no incomings since last operator use on home unit Dallas . . .

"Huh. Okay, not as complicated as I thought. Can I check my unit at Central?"

He only smiled. "Relay any new incomings on office unit Dallas, Cop Central."

Acknowledged . . . There is one new incoming transmission on voice mail . . .

"Damn it." She grabbed the 'link out of Roarke's hand. "I told them to contact me here as soon as they had—"

Lieutenant Dallas, this is Allesseria Carter, the bartender at Bloodbath.

"Conscience got to her," Eve decided, watching the face on screen. "Walking home, it looks like. Looks spooked."

I need to talk to you, um, talk to you about Tiara Kent. If you could contact me as soon—

There was a sound—a rush of wind? Eve saw a black-gloved hand, the blur of it whip in and close over Allesseria's throat.

"Fuck! Goddamn it." Eve's own hand clamped on Roarke's arm as the screen image blurred, the 'link struck the sidewalk, and the display went black.

"Play it back again," she ordered Roarke as she yanked out her communicator. "Dispatch, Dallas, Lieutenant Eve. I need a unit, closest possible unit at . . ." She flipped quickly through her memory to the address she'd pulled out of Allesseria's data, then snapped it out. Repeated it. "Possible victim of assault is Carter, Allesseria. Female, Caucasian, thirty-four, black hair, medium build. I'm on my way."

"I'll go with you," Roarke told her. "I'm closer than Peabody. You can contact her on the way. You know you won't find her in her apartment," he added as they rushed downstairs.

"Maybe she got away. Maybe he just wanted to scare her. Goddamn it, I picked her out for him. I set her up."

"You did nothing of the kind." He snatched up her jacket from the newel, tossed it to her as he snagged his own. "He chose her, the minute he asked her to lie for him, he chose her. I'll drive."

He'd get there faster, Eve knew, and it freed her to contact Peabody, then take the report from Dispatch. There was no response at Allesseria's apartment.

"Get inside," Eve snapped. "The victim's life is in immediate jeopardy. I have probable cause. Get the fuck inside."

She thumped her fist against her leg as she waited, waited, as Roarke maneuvered her police-issue through streams and clogs of morning traffic.

Dispatch, Dallas, Lieutenant Eve. Officers report the apartment is currently unoccupied. There is no sign of break-in or foul play.

No, Eve thought, there wouldn't be. He didn't take her there. "Start an immediate search in a five-block radius. Repeating description. Subject is female, Caucasian, age thirty-four, black and brown, last seen wearing black pants, black shirt, red jacket."

Eve ended the transmission, stared out the windshield. "I know it," she said, though Roarke had said nothing. "I know it. He didn't leave her alive."

Seven

Eve scanned sidewalks, the buildings as they approached Allesseria's apartment. It was a tough, low end of the lower-middle-class neighborhood. Most self-respecting muggers would hunt for scores a few blocks away in any direction.

Pickings would be slim here, and the population willing to fight for what they carried in their pockets. Street level LCs would troll for johns elsewhere, too. All in all, the handful of blocks were safe simply because they were poor enough not to warrant much trouble.

But Allesseria Carter hadn't been safe.

Eve's gaze zeroed in on a subway exit. "Pull over, park wherever you can. She'd take the subway, wouldn't she? Cheap and quick. If she did, this would've been her route home."

She slammed out of the car the minute Roarke stopped, then pulled out her 'link to replay the message. Looked for landmarks. "It's dark, and it's mostly her face, but . . ." She held up her own 'link as if relaying a message, then looked over her left shoulder. "See here, could be that building in the background."

She kept walking, studying the screen, the street. "Here, he took her right about here. Somebody would've picked up her 'link by now, or he did, but it was right about here he attacked."

She scanned again, focused on a narrow building sagging between a Thai market and a boarded-up storefront. It was plastered with graffiti, and what looked like an old, torn CONDEMNED sign.

Eve took out her communicator, requested backup at the location. Then drawing her weapon, she started toward the door. "You carrying anything besides half the wealth of the world in your pocket?"

"Burglary tools, though this won't require them."

She nodded, reached down, and took her clutch piece out of its ankle holster. "You're deputized, ace." She sucked in a breath, kicked in the door.

She went in low and to the right while he took high and left in a routine they'd danced before. Sunlight dribbled through the broken windows, striking off shards of glass, filth, vermin droppings.

And blood.

Eve could smell it—not just the blood, but the death. That heavy human stench.

Roarke took out a penlight, shone it on the trail of smeared red.

He'd left her splayed on the floor, arms and legs spread out so her body formed a gruesome human X. Most of her clothes had been torn off, leaving only ragged remnants of black clinging to skin mottled with bruises.

Her blood spread out in a pool from the puncture wounds in her throat. Her eyes hadn't lost their horror with death, but stared at the ceiling in a fixed expression of abject terror.

"Didn't take her blood with him this time," Eve said

quietly. "Didn't come prepared for that. But he made sure to hurt her plenty before he bled her out. Got off on her pain, got off on the power. See how he spread her out? Motherfucker."

Roarke touched a hand to Eve's shoulder. "I'll get your field kit."

She worked the scene; it's what she did. What she had to do. She could follow the trail of blood, of smeared footprints, and see Allesseria being dragged inside.

Kicking, Eve thought, her work shoes thudding hard against the broken concrete steps. Hard enough to cut through the cheap canvas before he'd hauled her inside.

He'd punctured her throat immediately, only steps inside the door. There was spatter against the dirty wall where she'd gushed. Where she'd collapsed. Dragged her unconscious from there, she noted. Gave himself a little more room to work. To beat her with his fists, to rape her. All while the blood ran out of her.

But he'd taken some, too. Ingested it, bottled it. She'd find out.

"Time of death oh-three-thirty," she said for the record. "Took her about an hour to die." She sat back on her haunches. "A block and a half from home."

She looked over at Roarke. He stood, his hands in the pockets of his jacket. The morning air fluttered in the broken windows, stirred his dark hair. And lifted the smell of ugly death all around them.

"He could've taken her in the club, anywhere in the underground. She might never have been found, and we'd never prove a thing if she'd been murdered down there."

"He wanted you to find her," Roarke agreed. "He's making a statement."

"Yeah, oh, yeah, because he didn't have to do this. Even if she recants, he'd find ten others to back his alibi. Ten others he'd bribe or intimidate. He didn't have to kill her, and certainly not like this."

"He enjoyed it." Roarke shifted his gaze, met Eve's eyes. "Just as you said. Payback was secondary to the killing."

"And he wanted it to be me who found her," Eve added. "Because of that click last night, that mutual recognition. But he's too cocky for his own good. There'll be DNA again, and he'll have picked up some of this dirt. Shoes, clothes. He'll have transferred some of this dirt, this blood, and the sweepers will find it."

"He attacked her while she was on the 'link—to you, Eve." Reaching out, Roarke took her hand, lifted her to her feet. "That's another statement."

"Yeah, and I'm hearing him. Just like he's going to hear me, really soon." She looked over as Peabody came in.

"Nothing on the canvass so far," Peabody reported. "I got in touch with the ex-husband. He lives a few blocks from here. He's on his way."

"We'll take him outside. He doesn't need to see this." Nobody needed to see what cops had to see. "Body can be bagged and tagged. There's nothing else she can tell us here. Let's see what she says to Morris."

She went out, grateful for the sunlight, and for the smell that was New York rather than death. She started to reach for her 'link to nag the lab yet again, when she spotted a six-and-a-half-foot black man with a body like a linebacker sprinting across the street against the light.

He wore short dreads, sweatpants, and a T-shirt, and an expression of fear in his topaz eyes. When he tried—and was well on his way to succeeding—shoving past the uniforms at the crime-scene barricade, she called out, went over.

"Rick Sabo?"

"Yes. Yes. My wife—my ex-wife. A detective called and said . . ."

"Let him through. I'm Lieutenant Dallas, Mr. Sabo. I'm sorry about your ex-wife."

"But are you absolutely sure it's her? She had a panic button, a ministunner. She knew how to handle herself. Maybe—"

"She's been identified, I'm sorry. When did you—"

She broke off when he just crouched down, dropped his head in his hands as a man would if pierced by a sudden and unspeakable pain. "Oh, God, oh, God. *Alless*. I can't . . . I told her to quit that goddamn job. I told her."

"Why did you tell her to quit her job?"

He looked up, but since he didn't straighten, Eve hunkered down with him. "She worked in this cult club— vampire shit—which is bad enough. But it was underground, off Times Square. It wasn't safe, it's not safe down there, and she *knew* it."

"Then why'd she work there?"

"Made three times what she made on street level. Sometimes four with tips. No doubles. She wanted to buy a house, a little house, maybe in Queens. We've got a boy." His eyes watered up. "We got Sam, and she wanted a place out of the city. We share custody of Sam. But, Jesus, I told her it wasn't worth it. I went down to check it out right after she took the job. Goddamn pit in a goddamn sewer. Alless."

There was love here, Eve thought. Maybe not enough to make a marriage work, but there was love. "Did she talk about her work, the people she worked with? For?"

"No, not to me. Not after we went a round about it. Haven't fought like that since we split. Don't know that we fought like that before we split. I was scared, if you want to know the truth. Scared for her, and I handled it wrong."

His hands dangled between his knees now, and he stared at them as if they were foreign objects. "Flat out told her she was *going* to quit, and I know that's just the way to make her dig into something. If I'd handled it better, she might've . . ."

He looked up, looked past Eve. There were people gathered on the other side of the barricades, as people always did.

What happened? they'd ask, and as word trickled down, they'd think how awful, how terrible, even as they continued to gawk, to linger, to hope to catch a glimpse of the dead body before they had to head off to work.

Because it wasn't them, it wasn't theirs the city had swallowed up. So they could gawk and linger and congratulate themselves that it wasn't them or theirs—and the next time it might be.

Sabo didn't see them, Eve knew that, too. Because for him, it was the next time.

"Mr. Sabo, did you meet any of her coworkers or her employer while you were in the club, or after?"

"What? No. No." He scrubbed his hands hard over his face. "Didn't want to. I only stayed about twenty minutes. Illegals passing around like party favors. People coming out of the private rooms licking blood off their lips, or it looked like it. She wanted a damn house in Queens."

"Mr. Sabo, I have to ask. It's routine. Can you verify your whereabouts between two and four A.M. this morning?"

"In bed, at home. I got Sam. I can't leave Sam alone at night." He rubbed at his eyes now before his hands dangled uselessly again. "I have building security. In and out. You can check. Whatever you have to do so you don't waste time, so you find who hurt Alless. Was she raped?"

Before Eve could respond, he shook his head. "No. No. Don't tell me. I don't think I want to know either way. Walk from the subway, after two in the morning, alone. Because of that damn job. Now what am I going to tell our boy? How am I going to tell our Sam his mama's gone?"

"I can have a grief counselor contact you, one who works with children."

"Yes. Please. Yes." His throat worked on a swallow. "I'll need help. Alless and I, well, we couldn't stay married, but we were a team when it came to Sam. I'll need help. I have to get back to my kid. I left him with the neighbor. I have to get back to Sam. Can you let me know when . . . when I need to do whatever I need to do?"

"We'll contact you, Mr. Sabo." Eve watched him walk away. "Peabody?"

"I'll take care of the grief counselor. Poor guy."

"Murder kills more than the victim," Eve said quietly. "We need to wrap up here, get into Central. Feeney may be able to clean up some of her last transmission from my unit. We get even a glimmer of this bastard . . ."

"I could help with that." Roarke stepped up beside her.

"You've got your own work."

"I do, but I'd be interested in, let's say, hammering one of those nails."

"If Feeney—" She broke off as her 'link signalled. "Hold on a minute." She moved aside, answered.

Roarke noted the instant change in her body language—the stiffening, the aggressive stance. When she turned back, he saw it mirrored in the temper that heated her eyes.

"DNA doesn't match Vadim's."

"But—"

"No but about it," Eve cut Peabody off. "There's a fuck-ing screwup somewhere. You want in," she said to Roarke, "you're in. You can round up Feeney at Central, do what-ever the two of you can do with the transmission. Peabody, with me. We're going to the lab. Contact Morris." She moved quickly as she snapped out the order. "I want him to personally take the DNA samples from this vic, have them hand-delivered to the lab. That's red-flagged."

"Got it."

Eve glanced back at the building one last time. "No way, no goddamn way he slithers out of this."

Peabody had to all but leap into the car to keep up. "Maybe he didn't kill her."

"Screw that."

"What I mean is, maybe he had her killed. Set it up."

Peabody jerked her safety harness tight as it looked like they were in for a hell of a ride.

"No. He wouldn't deny himself the pleasure of the kill." Monsters didn't want to watch, to be *told*. They wanted to do. They wanted the smell of the blood. "He did them both. Kent because it's what he set out to do, Carter because he was smart enough to know she wasn't going to hold up his alibi, and it slaps at me. He picked her, put her on the spot, then he took her out. The lab screwed up, or I did. I did if he switched the vials."

"We were right there. He drew his own blood right in front of us."

"Hand's quicker than the eye," Eve muttered. "He worked as a magician, he's worked the grift all of his life. He offered the blood sample without a blink because he knew he could swing it so it wouldn't match."

And she'd been distracted, she couldn't deny it. Tight chest, dry throat, pumping heart. Her own fears had dulled her senses.

"Either way," Peabody commented, "without the match, with Allesseria vouching for him and being unable to recant, we've got nothing on him."

"That's what he's counting on. I played into it, and that pisses me off. Dark club, all that movement and noise. Guy draws his own blood at a bar. Not something you see every day." Looking into his eyes, she remembered. Caught in them for a few seconds too long, shuddering inside at what she'd seen there, and she's conned. "Son of a bitch."

She strode into the lab, only to be cut off by the chief, Dick Berenski.

His egg-shaped head was cocked aggressively as he jabbed one of his long, thin fingers at her. "Don't think about coming into my shop and saying we fucked up. I ran those samples twice myself. Personal. You want to argue with science, you go somewhere else. I can't make a match when there's no match."

He was called Dickhead for a reason, and it had everything to do with his personality. Eve throttled back. "I think he switched them on me. It's his DNA on the vic, but it's not his in the vial you have. I've got an idea how he pulled it off, but the question right now is: If it's not his blood in the vial, whose is it?"

It was obvious Berenski had been expecting a battle. Now, caught off guard, he was more accommodating than he normally would be without a substantial bribe. "Well, if we got the DNA in the system, I can find it for you."

"I did a standard search, crapped out."

"Global?"

"Yeah, do I look like this is my first day on the job? But I didn't run deceased."

"Blood from a corpse? How's that going to end up in some mope's veins?"

"Not in his veins, in a damn vial he palmed off on me. Can you do a global search, deceased donor?"

"Sure."

"How fast?"

He wiggled his spidery fingers. "Watch and learn."

He went back to his station, the long white counter with comps and screens and command centers. Sliding back and forth on his stool, he began to work—verbal orders, manual keys.

While he ran the searches, Eve drew out her 'link and tried Feeney.

Her old partner and the captain of EDD popped on her screen. He had a Danish in one hand, and a mouth full of the hefty bite missing from it. "Yo."

"Roarke's on his way in. Put him to work. I've got a 'link trans, voice mail, from a vic while she was being attacked. Lost the trans almost as soon. It's dark, it's jumpy, but if you can clean it up, I might burn this bastard quick."

"Take a look." He swallowed. "This your vampire?"

"Come on."

"Hey, before your time I took down this asshole who was grave robbing, then sewing body parts together. Thought he could make himself a Frankenstein. Weird shit happens. He take another one?"

"Yeah, early this morning."

Contemplatively, Feeney took another bite of Danish. "McNab said he pulled out a syringe and gave you blood right on the spot."

"Yeah. There was a screwup there. Looks like mine. I'll fill you in later. Anything you can do on the trans, Feeney, I'd appreciate."

"Your man gets here, we'll do some magic. Meanwhile, you go up against this guy, wouldn't hurt to take a cross along." He lifted his eyebrows when she just stared at him. "Kid, weird shit happens because people are fucking crazy."

"I'll keep that in mind."

She clicked off just as Berenski made a sound of victory. "Got your blood. And I'm forced to say, 'Damn good call, Dallas'."

"I'm forced to say, 'Damn fast work'."

"I'm the best. Pensky, Gregor." He tapped the ID picture on his screen.

Square face, Eve noted. Small eyes, pinched mouth. The data put him at two-ten and six-one, with a long sheet of violent crimes.

It also listed him as dead for nearly a year.

"How'd he get to be a corpse?" Eve demanded.

"Son of a bitch." Berenski pursed his thin lips. "Been running DNA on a DB." He called for the data.

"Body found in the woods in freaking Bulgaria, where it was believed he headed after escaping from a work program on his latest visit to their version of the State Pen." Eve shook her head. "Work program for a guy with this kind of sheet. Bludgeoned, partially dismembered, and how about this, exsanguinated. Peabody, let's get the full

ME's report on this. I'm betting among his other injuries, there were a couple of puncture wounds in his throat."

"This vampire shit's creepy."

Eve glanced at Berenski. "It would be, if vampires existed. What happened to science?"

He jutted out what he called a chin. "You got science, you got the para side of it. I'd be sharpening stakes if I were you, Dallas."

"Yeah, that's on my list."

"Really?" Peabody asked when they got back into the car.

"Really what?"

"The stake-sharpening detail."

"Peabody, you're making my eye twitch."

"I know it's out there, but you have to consider all the information. Blood from a corpse. Vampires are corpses, essentially. No trace of Vadim on the first vic, scientifically at this point in time."

"Because he switched the fucking vials."

"Okay, okay." Peabody held up both hands, palms out. "But if you bought into the vampire lore, he could've sired this Pensky guy, then—"

"Then his body wouldn't have been real available for the Bulgarian ME."

Peabody considered. "There's that. But do we know, for absolute *sure*, that it stayed available?"

Give up, Eve told herself. Logical debates can't be made out of illogical theorems. "You be sure to check on that. While you do, I'll just stick with the more pedestrian theory that Vadim hooked up with Pensky, killed the shit out of him, and stored the blood he drained out for later use. It's smart, but it would've been a hell of a lot smarter to get blood from some unknown. We're also going to see if we can pin Vadim's whereabouts for the time of this Gregor's murder. What do you bet he was in Bulgaria?"

"He'd've been in Bulgaria if he vamped him, too," Peabody said under her breath. "Guy's got devil eyes."

"On the last part we heartily agree." She pulled into the garage at Central. "And we're going to give him a shot right between them. All data on Gregor Pensky's autopsy, Vadim's whereabouts at the time in question—and last night. Another DNA sample from that slippery son of a bitch."

Mentally kicking herself one more time on that score, Eve slammed the door of her police-issue. "This one spit—and it's going to be taken by a certified criminalist. Going to wrap him up before the day ends. He's not going to bite anyone else."

"Dallas?" Peabody scrambled inside the elevator. "Do you figure he's fatally bitten someone before? Bulgaria's a long way from Times Square. And there are places farther away. Places where bodies might never be found." Even if, Peabody thought, they stayed buried.

"I don't think he took a year off between Pensky and Kent." Eve scowled at the elevator doors. "So yeah, I think there'll be others."

"So do I. And listen, whether or not you—I mean we—believe in vampires, who's to say he doesn't? I know how he played it at Bloodbath. Like it was a show, a con—but a legal one this time. Maybe it isn't."

"Mira's initial profile allowed for him deluding himself into believing himself immortal, but his sheet screams con. We get him in the box," Eve decided, "we'll see how he plays it."

"I'm thinking if he does believe it, he's feeling pretty full of himself right now. Sucking out two vics in two nights."

"As of now, he's going on a no-hemoglobin diet."

Inside Central, Eve turned toward the Homicide bullpen. Stopped. Swags of garlic hung from the door frame like some odd holiday decoration. She caught the snickers from up and down the corridor, decided to ignore them, just as she ignored the surreptitious glances shot her way when she walked inside.

She arrowed in on Baxter, strolled to his desk. "How much did it run you?"

"It's fake." He grinned at her. "I'd have sprung for real, even though it's steep, but it's hard to come by enough to make a real impact so we got the fake stuff, too. You gotta admit, it's funny."

"Yeah, inside I'm cracking up. I'm going back down to reinterview Count Dracula. Get your boy, you're backup."

"Underground." His grin vanished into a look of pure disgust. "I just bought these shoes."

"Now I'm crying on the inside." She pushed him aside with a satisfied grin, and commandeered Baxter's computer.

Moments later, her suspicions were confirmed. Two puncture wounds had pierced Gregor Pensky's carotid artery and had been attributed to an animal bite. She had news for Bulgaria, and the standing medical examiner. But for now, she contacted her own.

"What've you got?" she demanded of Morris.

"Saliva and semen, and I had my top man walk them to the lab. Exsanguination was COD. She was beaten pre- and postmortem, he used his fists on her, and wore gloves. Her larynx was partially crushed by manual strangulation. Tox just came back. Traces of the same cocktail inside Kent, administered through the neck wounds."

"He transferred the drug through the bite?"

"Yes. She didn't consume any blood, or alcohol."

"This one wasn't a party. Thanks, Morris." She sat back for a moment, organizing thoughts and strategy.

"Peabody," she said as she got to her feet. "Baxter, Trueheart. Let's move." She strode to the doorway, flicked a bulb of garlic with her finger. "You can take some of this along if that does it for you. Me?" She tapped her sidearm. "I'll stick with this."

Eight

Baxter might like to joke, and bitch about damage to his slick wardrobe, but he was a solid cop. His uniformed aide, Trueheart, hadn't shaken off all the green, but he was dependable as sunrise.

There wasn't a cop on the job—or not a sane one—who would be thrilled to traverse underground, day or night. But there weren't any who would back her up more reliably.

She took point, left Baxter to take the rear. Below the streets, time vanished. In the world, the day was sunny and heading toward warm. Here, it was as dark and dank as midnight in a winter graveyard. Still, at this hour most of those who inhabited the tunnels were huddled away in their holes and burrows.

Some of the clubs and arcades ran 24/7, and the harsh music still pumped, the ugly lights still glared. Those who came or stayed to do business were more interested in the pain or gain than confronting four armed cops.

A few threats and insults were hurled. One brave soul

invited *the girls* to have a taste of the appendage he was proud enough of to whip out and dangle in their direction.

Eve paused long enough to glance down. "Only thing down here interested in a taste of that is the rats, but they generally like bigger meals."

This comment caused hilarity among the flasher's companions.

"Sir," Peabody said, with feeling, "I really don't think you should tease the animals."

"The rats can handle it."

Eve turned down the next tunnel as the insulted flasher shouted inventive suggestions about what Eve might do with his pride and joy.

"Gotta give him points for originality," Baxter commented.

"And optimism," Trueheart added, and made his partner hoot with laughter.

Despite herself, Eve tossed a grin over her shoulder. His young, handsome face might have been pale and just a little clammy, but Trueheart was game.

The shouts echoed away as they reached Bloodbath. It was locked down tight.

She used the number Dorian had given her. With the video blocked, he answered in a slurred and sleepy voice.

"Dallas, official police business. Open up."

"Of course. One moment."

It took a bit longer than one, but the locks clicked, the security lights blinked to green. And the barred doors slid slowly open.

Eve saw the extra minutes had given Dorian time to set the stage.

Inside the lights were a dim and smoky blue with pulsing red undertones. The screen behind the stage flickered on, filled with images in black and white of women being attacked or willingly baring their necks for fangs. The blood that ran down flesh was black as pitch.

Dressed in black, his shirt open to the waist, Dorian stood above the screen on one of the open balconies. He seemed to float there on a thin river of fog, as if he could, at any moment, simply lift his arms and rise into the air. His face was ghost pale, his eyes and hair black as ink.

"I see you brought company." His voice flowed, echoed. "Please . . ." He gestured toward the steps. "Come up."

"That's a spider to the fly invite," Baxter murmured, glanced at Eve. "You go first."

She hated that her heart stuttered, that her blood ran cold under her skin. Though her stomach clenched in protest, she crossed the club floor where more fog was beginning to curl and snake, and her bootsteps echoed on the iron steps as she climbed.

Smiling, slowly smiling, Dorian stepped back. And vanished in the mist.

She drew her weapon. An instant later she had to fight not to jolt as he seemed to materialize directly in front of her. His eyes were so dark she couldn't tell pupil from iris. In them, if she let herself look, were all the horrors of her childhood.

"Nice trick," she said casually. "And a good way to get stunned."

"I trust your reflexes. My home." He gestured again, then led the way through an open door.

Black and red and silver. He'd played up the gothic touches, Eve noted, but didn't lack for plush. Iron chandeliers held white candles, wall niches showcased statuary of demons or nudes in pornographic poses.

There were curved black divans and black high-backed chairs studded with metal, and a single life-sized painting of a woman in a diaphanous white gown, bent limply over the arm of a black-caped man. Her eyes were wide with terror, her mouth open in a scream, as he bent toward her neck with fangs exposed.

"My humble home," Dorian said. "I hope you approve."

"A little too theatrical for my taste." She turned and looked him directly in the eyes. Eyes that triggered memories and fears she couldn't completely bury. "I'm going to need another sample, Dorian. I'll need you to come in for this one."

"Really? I'd think I gave you more than enough blood . . . for police purposes. A drink for you or your companions?"

"No."

"Excuse me while I get one. I'm not used to being up so early in the day." He moved to a bar, opened the minifridge behind it. He took out a squat black bottle, poured red and thick liquid into a silver cup.

"We'll arrange your transport, have you back for your morning nap."

"I'd like to oblige you, but it's just not possible." He gestured an apology with one hand. "I'm under no legal obligation, after all."

"We'll discuss that at Central."

"I don't think so." Carrying his cup, he walked to a desk. "I have here a document that lists me—quite legally—as unable to tolerate sunlight. Religious reasons." He passed the document to her. "As to the sample, I'm afraid you'll need a warrant this time. I did cooperate."

He sat on the sofa, arranged himself in a lazy sprawl. "If this is about Tiara Kent, I have witnesses putting me here in the club at the time she was killed. You spoke with one yourself just last night."

Studying the paper, Eve answered without looking up. "Your alibi was killed early this morning."

"Really?" He sipped negligently. "That's a great pity. She was an excellent bartender."

"Where were you between two and four A.M. this morning?"

"Here, of course. I have a business to run and patrons to entertain."

Now her eyes flashed to his. Let him see, she told herself. Let him see that I *know*. That I won't back down. "And witnesses to intimidate?"

"As you like." He shrugged a shoulder, and there was a laugh on his face now, a gleeful amusement smeared with viciousness. "I find religious prejudice tedious, but understandably . . . human. Those outside the cult often fear it, or smirk at it. For myself, I enjoy it and find it profitable. And there are other, more intimate benefits."

He rose again, moved across the room, opened a door. "Kendra, would you come out for a moment?"

She was covered in a robe so thin it might've been air, and it showed a generously curved body. Her hair was tumbled, her eyes blurry with sleep, and—Eve was certain—chemicals.

She recognized the blonde that had approached and pawed over Dorian the night before. She moved to him now, wrapped her arms around his neck, rubbed her body suggestively to his. "Come back to bed."

"Soon. This is Lieutenant Dallas, and her associates. Kendra Lake, a friend of mine. Kendra, the lieutenant would like to know where I was this morning, between two and four."

She turned her head, aimed eyes with pupils big enough to swim in toward Eve. "Dorian was with me, in bed, having sex. Lots of sex. We'd be having sex now if you'd go away. Unless you want to stay and watch."

"What are you on, Kendra?" Eve asked.

"I don't need to be on anything but Dorian." She rose on her toes, whispered something in Dorian's ear. He laughed, a low rumble, then shook his head.

"That's rude. Why don't you go back in, wait for me. I won't be long."

"Kendra," Eve said as the blonde started back toward the bedroom. "Did he promise you'd live forever?"

Kendra looked over her shoulder, smiled. Then shut the bedroom door behind her.

"Was there something else, Lieutenant?" Dorian asked. "I hate to keep a beautiful woman waiting."

"This might hold up." She set the document down. "Or it may not. Either way, we're not done. You shouldn't have used Gregor Pensky's DNA, because I'm going to link you to him." She stepped closer, ignoring the tickle at the back of her throat as those dark eyes pierced hers. "We'll talk again real soon, Dorian."

He grabbed her hand, brought it to his lips. She told herself she hadn't yanked it away to prove a point. But she wasn't entirely sure.

"I'll look forward to it."

Watching him, she dipped a finger in his cup, sucked the liquid off her finger. "Tasty," she said as his eyes blurred with what she recognized as excitement.

She walked out, down the stairs. With an effort she kept her expression cool as he once again materialized in front of her, in the mists that now clouded the club.

"I always escort my guests to the door. Safe travels, Lieutenant. Until we meet again."

"How'd he do that?" Even as her eyes tracked the tunnels, Peabody stuttered out the question. "How'd he do that?"

"Elevator, false doors. Smoke and fucking mirrors." It irritated Eve that he'd nearly made her jump, disturbed her so that her skin crawled as if he'd run his fingers over it.

She had to remind herself she'd bearded him in his own den, and she hadn't cracked. Her pulse wasn't steady, but she hadn't cracked.

"Damn good trick though," Baxter commented from the rear. "Did you get a load of the blonde? I might try a little blood sucking if you score that kind of action."

"She's an idiot, and a lucky one," Eve tossed back. "He needs to keep her alive, unless he's bone stupid."

"She was using. You were right on that one, Lieutenant." Trueheart's voice was just a little breathy. "I saw plenty of zoners and chemi-heads when I did sidewalk sleeper detail. She was zoned to the eyeballs."

"Okay, so he likes his women toked, and plays magic tricks. Not so scary," Peabody decided. "And the stuff he was drinking? Syrup, right? Just red syrup."

"No." Eve avoided a smear of some unidentifiable substance on the tunnel floor and aimed for the dim light ahead. "That was blood."

"Oh." Peabody gripped the cross at her neck. "Well."

On the street, Eve snapped out orders as she moved to her vehicle. "Baxter, I want you and Trueheart to find me a connection, any connection between Vadim and Pensky. Use EDD, if necessary, and see if you can pin Vadim in the area Pensky was killed. I'll get you the data I have. Peabody, push harder on the jewelry from the first vic. Turning the glitters liquid may be too hard to resist. We need to run this Kendra moron. My money says she's got a deep well. His pattern is to bilk rich women. However he's escalated, whatever the game, that's his base."

She shoved her way into traffic. "I'm going to the PA. I need a damn warrant, and I want to shatter his religious shield into a lot of tiny pieces."

But an hour later, Eve stood, stunned and furious, in APA Cher Reo's office.

"You've got to be kidding me."

"I'm giving it to you straight." Reo was smart, savvy, and ambitious, a small blonde dynamo. And she tossed up her hands. "I'm not saying we couldn't have the order overturned, I'm saying it's a tricky business, and one that would take time and a lot of taxpayer dollars. The boss won't move on it, not with what you have. Bring us evidence, even a real glimmer of probable cause on the homicides, and we'll start the war. And war is the word. The courts don't like to mess with religious objections and predilections, even when they're obvious bullshit."

"This guy bled two women to death."

"Maybe he did. You say he did, I'm going to agree with you. But I can't give you a warrant for his residence, his place of business, on what you've got. I can't break down his objection to daylight hours with what you've got. Worse, the DNA you took—the vial with your initials on it, doesn't match."

"He switched them."

"How?"

"I don't know how." She kicked Reo's desk.

"Hey!"

"Reo, this guy's just getting started. He's pumped. He's using God knows what to keep pumped, and the killing's got him flying on his own importance. He's got a club full of opportunities every damn night. Like a damn all-you-can-eat buffet."

"Bring me something. I'll go to the wall for you, you know that. Bring me something I can use. Until you do, I'll do some research on precedents for breaking through a religious objection. If you can wiggle something that rings on the use or possession of illegals, I'll get you a warrant to search and seize on those grounds. It's the best I can do, Dallas."

"Okay. Okay." Eve raked her hands through her hair. "I'll get something." She thought of Allesseria's ex. Illegals passed around like party favors, he'd said. Add three cops and another civilian who had been in the club and they'd all swear they'd witnessed illegals bought, sold, and consumed. "Yeah, I can get something for an illegals raid."

"Make it work. And you know," Reo cast a glance at her office window, "I think I'm going to be damn sure I'm home and behind a locked door before sunset."

Nine

Eve hunted up Feeney and Roarke in a lab in EDD. She could see them both standing, hands in pockets, as they studied a screen—in the same way she'd noted men often studied motors or other gadgets.

Physically, they couldn't have been less alike with Feeney nearly a head shorter even with the explosion of the mixed ginger and silver bush of his hair. Feeney habitually slouched, just as he was habitually rumpled and wrinkled. Roarke may have ditched his suit jacket and rolled up the sleeves of his crisp white shirt, but the contrast remained very broad.

Inside, she knew they often ran on the same path, particularly when it came to e-work. Geeks born of the same motherboard, she thought.

It was a relief to see them, and not so hard to admit. A relief to see these two men—so essential to the life she'd made—after coming from her confrontation with Dorian, and the demons he woke in her.

She stepped in. "Did you clean up the transmission?"

Feeney turned to her, droopy eyes, mournful expression. Roarke shifted, eyes of an almost savage blue. There was a click here, too, but a good solid one, one that made her smile.

Roarke angled his head. "Lieutenant?"

"Nothing." But she thought: *Who needs crosses and holy water to fight demons when you have two men like this?* Dorian would never have understood that bright and brilliant human link. Her father had never understood it.

"So." She crossed to them, and because it amused her, slid her hands into her pockets to mirror their stances. "What's the word?"

"Good news," Feeney began. "We got her clean. Bad news, there's not much of him."

"I don't need much."

"Going to need more than what we've got. Computer, run enhanced transmission."

Acknowledged . . .

Eve watched Allesseria's face. It was crystal clear now, as was the night around her, as was her voice. A streetlight beamed over her. The movement—rather than the jerky bounce of her quick walk—had been smoothed out, slowed down.

There was a sound, a *whoosh* of air, a ripple of fabric on the breeze. Eve watched the gloved hand snake in, between the 'link and the victim's face. There was an upward jerk, an instant of pain and terror in Allesseria's eyes. Then the image flipped as the phone tumbled: sky, street, sidewalk. Black.

"Crap" was Eve's comment, and her hands fisted in her pockets now. "Anything when you magnify and slow it down?"

"We can enhance so you can count the stitches in the seams of the glove," Feeney told her. "Can use the scale program to get you the size of it. We can give you the attacker's probable height calculated from the size, the angles. But we can't put on screen what's not there. Got some snatches of audio though, for what it's worth."

He set the comp again, made the adjustments, then played it back.

What she heard first was silence.

"We backed out her voice, her footsteps," Roarke explained, "the ambient city noises. Now . . ."

She caught it. Feet on pavement, the faintest rustle, then the rush she identified as a run followed by a jump or leap. There was a breath, expelled in a kind of laugh as the hand shot out and clamped Allesseria's throat. And as the images rolled and tumbled on screen, a single low word. *You.*

"Not enough for a voiceprint," Feeney pointed out. "Never hold up in court even if we could match it on one syllable."

"He doesn't have to know that." Eve narrowed her eyes at the screen. "Maybe what we've got is just enough to shake him, to make him think we have more."

Feeney grinned at Roarke, tapped a finger to his temple. "She's got something cooking up there."

"Yeah, I do. This time, we con the con."

Roarke stepped into Eve's office, closed the door. "I don't like it."

She continued across the cramped little room to her AutoChef, programmed coffee. "It's a good plan. It'll work." She took the two mugs of hot black out, passed him one. "And I didn't figure you'd like it. That's one of the drawbacks of having you inside an investigation."

"There are other ways to run him to ground, Eve."

"This is the quickest. There's no putting standard surveillance on him," she began. "There are dozens of ways in and out of those tunnels. I can't know what kind of escape hatch he might have in that club, up in his apartment. He decides he's bored here, or there's too much heat, he'd be in the wind before we got close."

"Find a way to shut down the club. Illegals raid will put him out of business."

"Sure, we could do that, we *will* do that. And if that's all we do, he'll be smoke. There are fronts to the business," she pointed out. "You said so yourself. And it'd take time we don't have to cut through them and dig down to him. By then he's gone."

He set the coffee down on her desk. "All right, even agreeing that all that's true, or very likely, it doesn't justify you going in alone. You're setting it up this way because the DNA crashed on you, and you're blaming yourself."

"That's not true." Or not entirely, she amended silently. "Sure, it pisses me off he pulled that over on me, but I'm not doing this to even the score." Or not entirely.

Logic, she decided, was the best way to lay it out. Not as satisfying as a fight, she thought, but quicker. "Okay, look. I go in there with troops or other badges, he's not going to talk, even if he sticks around long enough for me to corner him. He doesn't have to stick around at this point. I can't even pry him aboveground and get him in the box for interview. It has to be on his turf, and it has to be between him and me."

"Why—on the last point?"

"Why didn't you like him, from the get?"

She could see irritation cross Roarke's face before he picked up the coffee again. "Because he scoped my wife."

"Yeah. He'd like to take a bite, not only because I'm the cop looking at him, but because I'm married to you. Be a big ego kick for him to score off you. And if he thinks he has a shot at that, he'll take it, and I'll be ready."

"Eve—"

"Roarke. He'll kill again and soon. Maybe tonight. He has a taste for it now. You saw that, and so did I, the first time we met him. I'm telling you I saw more of it today. I see what he is."

This was the core, he knew, whatever she said. Whatever the other truths, this was the heart of it for her. "He's not your father."

"No, but there's a breed, and they're both of it. The smoke, the blood, the insinuation: Is he or isn't he an undead, bloodsucking fiend? That may tingle the spine, rouse superstitions, even tease the logical to entertain the illogical. But it's what's under it, Roarke. It's, well, shit, it's the beast that lives there that has to be stopped."

"The one you have to face," he corrected. "How many times?"

"As many as it takes. I want to walk away from it. Hell, I get within five feet of him, I want to run from it. And because I do, I can't."

"No." He traced his thumb down the shallow dent in her chin. "You can't." That, he knew, was what he had to face—again and again. Loving her left him no choice. "But this rush—"

"He's flying on the moment. Whatever drugs he's on, they're not as potent as the kill. As the blood. If I don't try this, and he gets another, how do I live with that?"

He searched her face, then lifted a hand to her cheek. "Being you, you don't. You can't. But I still don't have to like it."

"Understood. And . . ." She took his hand, squeezed it briefly. "Appreciated. Let's just count on me doing my job, and the rest of you doing yours. We'll shut him down, nail down that lid, before he knows what the hell's going on."

"He best not get so much as a nibble of you. That's my job." He leaned down, caught her bottom lip between his teeth. After one quick nip, he sank in, drawing her close, taking them both deep.

Her initial amusement slid away into the dreamy until she could float away on the taste of him, glide off on the promise. When she sighed, eased back, her lips curved up.

"Good job," she told him.

"I do my best."

"Maybe later you can put in some overtime."

"Being dedicated to my work, I'll be available."

"But for right now, let's go get the team together for a full briefing. I don't want any screwups."

"Lieutenant." He caught her hand before she reached the door, and tugged her back around. Out of his pocket he drew a silver cross on a silver chain, and dangled it in front of her.

"Knew I forgot something." But when he draped it over her head, she goggled. "What? You're serious?"

"Indulge me." He planted another kiss on her lips, this one brief and firm. "I'm a superstitious man with a logical mind that can entertain the illogical."

Staring at him, she shook her head. "You're full of surprises, pal. Just full of them."

She used a conference room for the briefing. On screen was a diagram of Bloodbath, and a second of the apartment—or the area of the apartment Eve had seen. Both were sketched from memory, with input from the others on the team who'd been inside the club.

As was often the case with underground establishments, no recorded blueprints or work orders could be located.

"There will be alternate exits," Eve continued. "It's likely at least some of the staff are aware of them, and will use them. Detaining and arresting waitresses and naked dancers aren't priorities."

"Speak for yourself," Baxter shot out, "on the naked dancers angle."

"Moving civilians out," Eve said, ignoring him, "without inciting a riot is a primary goal. Anyone wants to make collars for illegals, that's a personal decision and can be determined at the time. A couple dozen busts will add weight to the op, and hang on Vadim as manager. Anything and everything we get on him is a plus, but not at the expense of the primary target."

She scanned faces. "Nobody moves in, nobody tips the scales until I give the go. My communicator will be open for said go. Nothing, I repeat, nothing, is to be recorded from that source. I'm not having this slime skate on a technicality."

She paused, ordered the computer to show the diagram of the club only. "Our warrant covers only this area. No personnel are to move outside the club area in search or pursuit without probable cause. All weapons low stun."

Once more, she switched the screen image. Now Dorian Vadim's face filled it. "This is primary target. Unless specifically ordered or cleared, he is not to be detained or apprehended. If I can't pull this off, we have no cause for arrest. Suit up," she ordered. "Vests all around. Report to squad leaders for transportation to target."

She laid a hand on her sidearm. "Let's go kick ass."

As she bent to check her clutch piece, Baxter tapped her shoulder.

"What?"

"Got something for you." He held it out as she straightened.

"You're a laugh a minute, Baxter."

"Yeah, you gotta admit." He gave the wooden stake an agile toss.

Because she was amused despite herself, she caught the stake in one hand, then stuck it in her belt. "Thanks."

He blinked, then roared with laughter. "Eve Dallas, Vampire Slayer. One for the books."

Ten

She went in alone, the way it had to be, as a cop, as a woman fighting her own demons.

She walked the now-familiar path down from the world to the underground, through the fetid tunnels with misery skulking in dirty shadows.

She'd come out of the shadows, Eve thought. So she knew what hid there, what bred there. What thrived there.

Light killed shadows, and it created them. But what loved the dark would always scuttle back from the light. Her badge had given her the light, Eve knew. Then Roarke had simply, irreversibly, blasted that light straight through her.

Nothing could pull her back again, unless she allowed it. Not the nightmares, not the memories, not whatever smear the man who'd made her had left in her blood.

What she did now, for the job, for two women, for herself, was only another way to cast the light.

She moved toward the ugly pulse of red and blue, the bone-rattling thrum of violent music.

The same bouncers flanked the arched door, and this time they sneered.

"Alone this time?"

Still moving, she kicked the one on the left solidly in the groin, smashed her elbow up and out into the bridge of the second's nose.

"Yeah," she said as she strode through the path they made as they stumbled back. "Just little old me."

She walked through the jostling crowd, through the sting of smoke, the crawl of fog. Someone made the mistake of making a playful grab for her and got a boot down hard on his instep for his trouble. And she never broke stride.

She reached the steps, started up their tight curve.

She felt him first, like the dance of sharpened nails along the skin. Then he was there, standing at the top of the stairs, mists swirling dramatically around him.

"Lieutenant Dallas, you're becoming a regular. No escort tonight?"

"I don't need an escort." She stopped on the step below him, knowing it gave him the superior ground. "But I'd like some privacy."

"Of course. Come with me." He held out a hand.

She placed hers in it, fought off a jitter of revulsion as his fingers twined with hers. He led her back, away from the crowd, then keyed in a code on his private door. "Enter Dorian," he said for the voice command, and the locks gave.

Inside candles were lit, dozens of them. Light and shadow, Eve thought again. On the wall screen various sections of the club were displayed, the sound muted, so people danced, groped, screamed, stalked, in absolute silence.

"Some view." Casually, she stepped away from him and stepped over as if to study the action on screen.

"My way of being surrounded and alone at the same time." His hand brushed lightly over her shoulder as he walked behind her and over to his bar. "You'd understand that."

"You talk as if you know me. You look at me as though you do. But you don't."

"Oh, I think I do. I saw the understanding of violence, of power, and the taste for it in you. We have that in common. Wine?"

"No. Are you alone here, Dorian?"

"I am." Despite her answer, he poured two glasses. "Though I planned to entertain a woman later." This time his gaze traveled over her, boldly intimate. "How interesting it should be you. Tell me, Eve, is this a professional or a personal call?"

She let herself stare at him, into those eyes. "I don't know. I guess we'll find out. I know you killed those women."

He smiled slowly. "Do you? How?"

"I feel it. I see it when I look at you. Tell me how you did it."

"Why should I? Why would I? Lieutenant."

As if impatient, she shook her head. "I don't have a warrant. You know that. I haven't given you your rights. I can't use anything you tell me. You know that, too. I just need to know what you are. Why I feel the way I do around you. I don't believe in . . ."

There was no mistaking the *hunger* on his face as he walked toward her. "In what?"

She could hear her father's voice whispering in her mind. *There are things in the dark, little girl. Terrible things in the dark.*

"In the sort of thing you're selling out there." She gestured toward the screen. "Turn that off, will you? It feels crowded in here."

"You don't like to watch?" he said, silkily. "Or be watched?"

"Depends," she answered with what she hoped sounded like false bravado.

"Screen off," he ordered, and smiled again. "Better?"

"Yeah. It's better with it off."

"That's the signal." Feeney nodded to Roarke. "All units, move in. Move in. She's playing him," he said to Roarke. "She'll walk him right into it."

"Or he's playing her." With Eve's voice in his ear, Roarke rushed into the dark.

Into the terrible things.

"Hold it." There was the slightest hesitation in her order as she slapped a hand against Dorian's chest and shoved. "I have obligations. I have loyalties."

"None of which fill your needs."

"You don't know my needs."

"Give me five minutes to do as I like with you, and you'll know differently. You came to me." He trailed his fingers over her cheek. "You came to me alone. You want to know what I can give you."

She shook her head, stepped away. "I came because I need to understand. I can't settle, I can't focus. I feel like something's trying to crawl out of my skin."

"I can help you with that."

She glanced over her shoulder at him. "Yeah, I bet you could. But I'm not like Tiara Kent. I'm not looking for cheap thrills. And I'm not like Allesseria Carter. I don't need your goodwill. I'm not afraid of you."

"Aren't you? Aren't you afraid of what I could make you?"

She looked at the portrait. "Like that?" Her voice was just a little breathless. "I'm not that gullible."

He lifted one of the wineglasses, drank deeply. "There's more in the world that slips in and out of what's deemed reality."

"Such as?"

He drank again, and his eyes went even darker. "Such as powers, and hungers beyond the human. I'll take you there. I can show you a glimpse without causing you harm. You should drink. Relax. Nothing will happen to you here. It's not my way."

"No, you go to them. Kent practically spread rose petals on a path to her bed for you."

"Hypothetically, invitations are required."

"In an occupied building," Eve agreed. "Not in an abandoned one. Like the one where you dragged Allesseria, where you killed her."

"Does it excite you to think so, to look at me and see her death?"

"Maybe it does."

"You seek death." He laid his fingertips under hers, lifted her hand. "Surround yourself with it. Isn't that what I sensed, what I saw, in you that first moment our eyes met? It connects us, this . . . fondness for death in a way the man you give yourself to can never understand. He can't reach that dark bloom inside you. I can."

She let her fingers curl to his for an instant, then eased back again. "I don't know what connects us, but I felt something when I heard your voice come in on Allesseria's 'link message to me. It was a mistake to say anything, Dorian, a mistake not to make certain the 'link was down and the transmission broken before you spoke to her. We'll have your voiceprint match by morning."

He lowered the glass he'd lifted to his lips. "That's not possible."

"Would I be here now otherwise? Risking all this so I could see you tonight? This goes down tomorrow, and my part in it's over. I need answers for me. Why would I tell you we have evidence building that could take you down, give you time to poof? I have to know. For me."

"I have an alibi," he insisted.

"Kendra Lake? Another spoiled rich girl running on hormones, vanity, and chemicals. She won't help you. She'll crack, we both know it. She's on the juice, she's your lover. It won't hold."

"You're lying." He gulped down the rest of the liquid in the glass, heaved the glass aside. "You're lying. You bitch."

Okay, Eve thought, time to change directions.

Outside the apartment it was hell. Screams and shouts echoed through the mist some clever soul had boosted up when the small army of cops had burst in, announcing a raid.

Roarke flung one attacker aside, dodged the swipe of a knife from another. Preferring fists to stunner, he used them viciously. Despite the cacophony, he heard Eve's voice clearly in his head.

"She's losing him," he yelled to Feeney. Whirling, Roarke sprinted for the stairs through streams of stunner fire.

"Caught me," Eve said. "I'm lying about any pretense I find you attractive or compelling on a personal level. About the rest, that's a wrap. You not only ran your mouth where it could be heard on Allesseria's 'link, EDD's working on cleaning and enhancing a few seconds on screen during the trans. You moved partially into view.

"Added to that," she continued, "we're about to link you to one Pensky, Gregor. Shouldn't have used a former known associate as a fall guy. Even a dead fall guy, Dorian. Little slips, they'll kill you every time."

She glanced idly around the room. "I bet you saved some of Tiara Kent's blood for a souvenir. I get that warrant in the morning, I'm going to find it, and the jewelry you took off her dead or dying body. You scum. That'll put you down for three counts of murder. Anything else you want to add to the menu?"

"Do you think you can threaten me?" His eyes were black pools. "Play with me?"

"If you're trying for thrall, you're missing. I'll have you locked on Allesseria in a matter of hours. The rest will tumble right into the pile. You're done. I just wanted the satisfaction of telling you personally before— Don't," she warned. She laid her hand on her stunner when she saw the move in his eyes. "Unless you want to add assaulting an officer to the mix. In which case, I can haul you out of here. Sun's down, Dorian."

"Yes, it is." He smiled, and to Eve's absolute shock, showed fangs.

He leaped, almost seemed to fly at her. She drew her weapon, pivoted, but she wasn't quick enough. Nothing could have been. She got off two shots as he hurled her across the room. He took both hits, and just kept coming. She felt it in every bone as she hit the stone wall, and though the stunner spurted out of her hand on impact, she managed to roll, then kick up hard with both feet. The force knocked him back far enough to give her room to flip up.

She braced for the next attack, but instead he hissed like a snake, cringed back. She flicked her gaze down, saw he was staring at the cross that had come out from under her shirt.

"You've got to be kidding me." He snarled as he circled her. "You actually believe your own hype."

Whatever he'd drunk had juiced him up good, she determined. So good, she'd never be able to take him in hand-to-hand. She held up the cross as she tried to gauge the distance to her stunner, and her chances of reaching it.

"I'll drink you dry." His tongue ran over his long incisors.

"Almost dry. And make you drink me. I'll change you into what I am."

"What? A babbling lunatic? Why didn't Tiara change?"

"She wasn't strong enough. I drank too much of her. But she died in bliss under me. As you will. But you're strong, strong enough to be reborn. I knew it when I saw you. Knew you'd be the first who'd walk as I walk."

"Uh-huh. You have the right to remain silent."

He sprang, leaping like a great cat. She blocked the first blow, though she felt the force of it sing down her arm, explode into her shoulder. But the second sent her sprawling. She thudded hard against one of his metal tables, and tasted her own blood in her mouth as she rolled painfully onto her back.

He was standing over her now, fangs gleaming, eyes mad. "I give you the gift, the ultimate kiss."

Eve swiped the blood off her mouth. "Bite me."

Grinning, he fell on her.

Outside the door, Feeney pulled out his master and a bag of electronic tricks to bypass the locks.

"I've got it." Blood seeped through the ragged tear in Roarke's jacket where a knife point had slipped through. He flipped out a recorder, closed his eyes to focus first on the tones of the beeps.

Quickly, he played his fingers over the keypad in the same order, then held the recorder to the voice command.

"Enter Dorian," the recorder replayed.

"Hey, Dallas said nothing was to be recorded."

Roarke spared one glance over at Feeney's wide grin. "I'm a poor team player."

They pushed in the door, Roarke going low as he knew Feeney preferred high.

She was flat on her back, blood soaking her shirt. Even

as Roarke rushed toward her, she pushed herself up on her elbows. "I'm okay. I'm okay. Call the MTs before that asshole bleeds to death."

Roarke barely spared a glance at the man lying on the floor with a wooden stake in his belly. His own stomach muscles were knotted in slippery fists. "How much of this is yours?"

She looked down at her shirt in some disgust. "Hardly any. Missed the heart. Bastard was on top of me. Gut wounds are messy. Feeney?"

"Contacting the MTs," he told her. "Situation below is nearly contained. Hell of a show. But looks like you're the headliner here. Jesus, what a freaking mess."

"I can't believe I'm going to have to thank Baxter for being a smart-ass. Lost my weapon. He'd've done some damage before you got through if I hadn't had the pointy stick."

She started to stand, and with Roarke's help made it to her feet. Once there, she swayed and she staggered. "Just a little shaken up. Hit my head on various hard objects. No, no, don't carry me."

He simply scooped her into his arms. "You're doomed to have me disobey." Then he pressed his lips to the side of her throat where he saw the faint wounds. "Got a taste of you, did he?"

She heard the rage, and tried to tamp it down. "Told him to bite me. It's the first time anyone's ever taken that suggestion literally. Except you." She turned Roarke's face with her hand so that he looked at her rather than Dorian. "Put me down, will you, pal? This seriously undermines my authority."

"Hey, hey!" Crouched over Dorian, Feeney stopped even his half-hearted attempt to stanch the blood flow. "Is this guy sporting fangs?"

"He must've had them filed down that way," Eve said.

"Then had them capped. Easy on, easy off. We'll sort it out."

Peabody ran in. There was a darkening bruise on her cheekbone and a nasty scrape along her jaw. "Unit's heading out to escort the MTs in. Holy crap!" she added when she saw Dorian. "You staked him. You actually staked him."

"It was handy. Let's get those medics in here. I don't want this guy skipping out on multiple murder charges by dying on me. I want to know the minute he's able to talk. I think we're going to get an interesting confession."

"It's supposed to be the heart," she heard Peabody mutter. "It's really supposed to be the heart."

Eve blew out a long breath. "Keep it up, Peabody, and I may have Mira shrink your head after she's done with this second-rate Dracula. I want some damn air. I'm going up to the real world."

Once she had, she took the bottle of water Roarke passed her and drank like a camel. She lifted her chin at the blood on his sleeve. "Is that bad?"

"It damn well is. I liked this jacket. Here, take a blocker. If you don't have the mother of all headaches yet, it's only due to adrenaline. Take the blocker, and I won't haul your stubborn ass into a health center for an exam."

She popped the blocker without a quibble. Then since it was there, she sat on the edge of the floor through the open door of the police van.

"He believed it," she said after a moment. "He actually believed he was a vampire. Drugs probably pushed the act into his reality. Mira nailed the profile from the get. It was the pretending to be the Prince of Darkness that was the pretense, for him."

"More likely he was just pushing the con as far as it would take him—and gambling to use it to plead insanity."

"No. You didn't see his face when he looked at this."

She held up the cross. "And thanks, by the way. It bought me a few minutes when it counted."

Roarke sat beside her, rubbed a hand over her thigh. "Illogical superstition. Sometimes it works."

"Apparently. He's got himself some kind of super-Zeus recipe, is my guess. Not just the whacked brain it causes, or the temporary strength. Speed, too. The bastard was fast. Magician training, grift experience, drugs. I wonder when it turned on him, stopped being a way to case marks."

Gently, Roarke traced a fingertip over her neck wounds. "There are all kinds of vampires, aren't there? Darling Eve."

"Yeah." Very briefly, since all of the cops running around were too busy to notice, she leaned her head against Roarke's shoulder. "Under it, he wasn't really like my father. Not the way I thought. My father wasn't crazy. Dorian, he's bug-shit."

"Evil doesn't have to be sane."

"No, you're right about that." And she'd faced it—and she'd beaten it. One more time. "Well, the bad news is he's going to end up in a facility for violent mental defectives, not a concrete cage. But you take what you can get."

Roarke's hand rested on her knee. She laid hers over it, squeezed. "And right now, I'll take a hot shower and a fresh shirt. I've got to go in and clean myself up, and clean this up, too."

"I'll drive."

"You should go home," she told him, but her hand stayed over his. "Get some sleep. It's going to take hours to close this up."

"I have this image I can't shake." He got up, drew her to her feet. "Of the sun rising, all red and gold smears over the sky. And you and I walking toward home in that lovely soft light. So taking what I can get, I'll take sunrise with you."

"Sunrise it is."

She kept her hand in his as she pulled out her communicator to contact Feeney, Peabody, the team leaders to check on the status below.

With her hand linked with Roarke's, the demons that plagued her were silent. And would stay silent, she thought, through the night. And well past sunrise.

Amy and the Earl's Amazing Adventure

Mary Blayney

For Mikey and Dawn
For Steve and Laura
And 2006, the year of the diamond

One

"What do you do when you're just days from leaving a place that calls to your soul?" the girl asked.

The tour guide nodded encouragement and was delighted when she continued.

"I can't imagine leaving England. The thought of Topeka makes me shudder and not just because spring is slow in coming this year."

What had prompted Amy Stevens to ask him that question? He was a tour guide, a docent, in a small house, on a quiet street in Mayfair. She could not possibly be confusing him with an Embassy official. God bless her. He knew no more than her name, and that from her passport. And what did it say about modern London that picture identification was necessary for a house tour?

Even without her name he had *known* that she was a crucial element in the puzzle he had been trying to solve for so long. He had thought he would lose her and wished with desperation that she would ask a question, any question. Praise the Lord, she had asked him the *perfect* question, had given him the opening he needed.

"Why can't you stay?"

"I have to go to a wedding in June. I want to be there and I have to be there. Jim says I can come back here but—"

"Who's Jim?" the docent interrupted. A boyfriend could complicate the whole situation.

"A friend. We've both spent the year here in grad school. See, he's the one getting married back home *and* his fiancée is one of my best friends. Once I'm home there's my family and my other pals. They won't want me to leave. Not one of them would understand. They think Topeka is perfect."

"For them it may be." Not for her though. Wasn't she the first person who had listened to the story of the magic coin? She had even asked him if it was true, had not brushed the magic away as a fanciful tale. With complete confidence he took the dented coin from the display case and handed it to her. "Take this with you as a memento and believe that anything is possible."

"You can't give that away," she said, putting her hands behind her back.

"I can give it to anyone I choose." The docent shrugged. That was the truth even if the next would be a lie. "I can get another one easily."

In her heart, Amy Stevens wanted that coin, a fairy-tale memento of this fabulous year. So in the end she let the docent talk her into keeping it, knowing she would buy a chain and wear it around her neck forever.

She hurried through Mayfair to Earl's Place, the pub just off Piccadilly that she and Jim had claimed as their own. Along with a hundred other soccer fans. The pub was crowded and she could not get Jim's attention. She could wait. He wouldn't be interested in anything until the match was over anyway.

Amy sank onto a stool at the bar, took out the coin, and stared at it. The docent's story graced it with magic. In his tale this coin had changed the lives of the three people who had wished on it. All for the better.

What were the chances that it really could grant a wish? Zero.

Who would it hurt to pretend?

No one.

Placing the coin on the bar in front of her, she tried out a few wishes, then picked up the coin and held it tight. She whispered, "I wish there was a way for me to stay here."

The coin felt warm and she frowned at it. The whole place was filled with people, the room overheated, the crowd cheering their favorite team.

The bartender worked his way to her spot at the end of the bar. Not the usual guy. An extra hired to help handle the crowd? He wore the Earl's uniform of jeans and button-down shirt with sleeves turned up. His white shirt was spotless despite his busy routine. What kind of magic was that? she wondered. She followed his progress down the bar, mesmerized by the rhythm with which he took orders, handed out drinks, and made change.

He was nice enough looking and then he smiled. It changed his pleasant face to fabulous. It was a smile that made her want more from him than his practiced chatter.

"What'll you have?"

His accent was different, not at all suited to a pub. His voice belonged at Eton or Oxford. Or somewhere with Prince William.

She pointed to the wine bottle he held, for some stupid reason not wanting to open her mouth and betray the fact she was an American. She forgot about the magic coin and it fell from her hand, rolled along the bar toward him, and onto the floor.

She gasped and leaned over the bar trying to spot it.

"Under the cooler," he said. "Is it important to you?"

"Oh, yes. It's very special."

"Right then." He squatted down, reaching under the cooler. He looked up at her with a grimace. "Time to do some cleaning down here." He stretched a little farther and with a triumphant, "Have it," stood up, glanced at the coin. He seemed taken aback by it, but handed it back to her with a smile.

"Thanks," she said, "thanks a lot."

He nodded, held up the wine bottle and when she said, "Please," poured her a glass.

She dug in to her jeans pocket for some money, but he waved off payment.

"Give me a good look at the coin, would you? That's all the pay I want."

She was about to hand it back to him when the room erupted into shouts and cheers. The match was over and any number of thirsty sports fiends surged toward the bar.

"If you like, I can wait until the crowd's gone."

He leaned across the bar, resting on his arms, his smile as warm as an embrace. "Great, that's exactly what I wished you'd say. There's a table in the back corner. It's a little quieter there."

Amy nodded. She'd hoped for more from him than chatter. And it looked like she was going to get it. She wound her way through the crowd and sat down at the table the bartender had pointed out.

Jim came over to her a minute later. "Did you see that last goal, Amy? World Cup here we come!"

"Jim, you've been saying that for years," she answered, trying to match his enthusiasm.

"Yeah, but the matches begin in June. Admit it," he challenged in that patronizing way he had, "you don't even know what two teams were playing."

"Nope. No idea. You can call it football, or soccer the way we do at home, and it still has no appeal to me. I'd rather play tennis or volleyball than watch someone else work out."

Jim nodded. Yeah, Amy thought, he'd heard that a hundred times before. Fair trade. She had to listen to soccer stats ad nauseum.

"I'm off with the rest of the guys to the pub with the free food. Are you with us?"

"No, thanks. I'm waiting to talk to someone."

"Oh?" Jim looked over his shoulder. "I saw you chatting up the bartender." He wiggled his eyebrows. "Remember, we're leaving soon and somehow I don't think Topeka would appeal to him."

"I want to hear what he has to say about a coin I found, that's all."

"Sure," Jim said, smiling as though he were part of a romantic scheme. "It's your choice. I'm outta here. I've got my phone. Text me if you need help escaping." He headed for the door along with most everyone else in the place. The noise level dropped considerably.

She raised a hand in farewell, then gave all her attention to the coin warming her hand. Well, not all of it. Half her mind was on the bartender. Could he be the owner? Was he Earl? Hopefully not. Or, she thought with a spurt of excitement, was he the Earl of Someplace? And the chances of that were a million to one.

So why did he want to see the coin? It was old, maybe even valuable. Or maybe not. It looked like it was minted from some worthless metal. Did that make a difference?

"What I want to know is where you bought that coin."

The bartender stood beside her, a mug of something hot in his hand, watching the disappearing Jim as he spoke. The noise might have left with him, the testosterone had not. The bartender's once-friendly expression was now more suspicious than curious. Not any less handsome, though, even if his looks—the full Kiefer Sutherland lips and the blond hair that fell onto his forehead—were less appealing than they had been an hour ago when he had been smiling.

"Someone gave it to me." When he looked less than convinced, she nodded. "I know, I thought it was weird, too. But he insisted. Do you know that nineteenth-century house museum on Norfolk Street? I'm a sucker for anything about the Regency."

He shook his head as though the words had no meaning. She tried again.

"Near Hyde Park. It has a bright blue door. I spent a few hours there today. The docent on duty gave me the coin."

"Gave it to you?" He put his mug on the table and leaned toward her, which raised the intimidation factor considerably. "He just handed you a coin like that?"

Amy pushed her chair back and stood up. "I don't know if arrogance comes with the Prince William accent or the fact that you own this place." She picked up the coin and kept her gaze steady.

His amazing dark blue eyes softened as she watched.

"Sorry." He backed off. "It's been a long day."

As apologies went it was bare bones. So if this wasn't an imaginative pick-up line, then what was it? Was he really that interested in the coin? "I've been coming here for the better part of a year," Amy said. "I don't ever recall seeing you before."

"I'm a temp. My regular job is teaching."

"So you're *not* the owner?"

"No, this bit's my brother's investment." He made a gesture that included everything around them: the chairs they were sitting in, the pub, maybe even the building. "Now, sit down and tell me about the coin." He nodded toward her chair as he sat down opposite it.

She stayed right where she was. So, he was not Prince Charming. And he didn't give a flying fig what her name was, much less what she was doing for the rest of her life.

He just wanted to know about the coin. Oh well. For all of two seconds she considered telling him the story the tour guide had told her, about its magic, but knew he would scoff at her. Instead she went with ignorance.

"I don't know much about it. Do you?"

"It has some moghul writing on one side," he said slowly, as though the words were being tugged out of him. "Underneath that there's an X and the word 'cash' next to the X. The other side has a crest."

He was a teacher now. Very reserved, a little superior.

"Yes," she said, finally taking her seat, curious and excited in spite of his detachment. "You saw all that when you picked it up off the floor?"

His gesture could have meant either yes or no.

"So what kind of language is moghul?" she asked, folding her other hand over the fist that held the coin. She would pull the information out of him even if it was one question at a time.

"The moghuls conquered India in the sixteenth century and were the power there until the British took over."

"You make that sound a lot easier than it was. They hardly went *knock, knock* on the palace door and announced 'We're here now.' I may not be British but I know better than that."

"Aha, you've read history," he said. "I'll quiz you on that later. It's the coin I'm interested in right now." He was relaxing a little. The tension was still there, though, in the way he held his body, the way he watched her so intently. Too bad that look wasn't for her. He reached across the table and tapped one finger gently on the back of her hand.

"Please? May I see the coin?" He looked down at her hand even as he asked.

She heard what he said, but what her mind (and body) focused on was the point of contact, finger to wrist, and the flood of awareness that slammed through her, a purely physical flash from his fingertip to every pulse point. In an instant she was restless and wanting. *Wow,* she thought, straightening in her chair. *And I don't even like him. Does he feel this?*

Apparently not, as his gaze was still fixed on her hand. *It's about the coin, stupid.* She put it down and pushed it in front of her, far enough so that he had a clear view of it. He shook his head. His smile was the kind you would see on a boy with his newest, finest toy.

"I know a lot about this coin," he said, not looking up. "It was minted in 1808."

"You're right!" she said after she had turned the coin over so she could check the date.

"It was commissioned by the East India Company." He leaned closer to it. "That's their crest above the date. All the coins were packed in wax and then in barrels and put on a ship bound for India. It sank in a squall that pushed the ship onto the Goodwin Sands beyond the Straits of Dover. The whole lot of them were lost until 1985, when the ship was found and some of the coins were recovered. This is one of them. And this particular one has a dent in it."

"Does the dent diminish its value?" She reached over and fit her nail into the little indentation.

"No, it's what makes it important. To me at least."

"It's important?" Amy picked up the coin, examining it with new respect. "How do you know this? I never heard of it before."

"I've been studying it for a long time," he said, "and trying to find one for almost as long."

"Wow. And I walk in with one. Isn't that odd?" *Magic?* She pushed that thought aside. "If it's so rare and valuable, why would the docent give it to me?"

"It does seem odd," he said after a long minute.

"Yes, it does." She was speaking aloud, mostly to herself. Then that mistrust in his voice registered. She realized, with some surprise, what he was implying. "Do you think I stole it?"

Two

The bartender held up his hands as if that would protect him from her verbal assault.

"You don't even know my name or anything else about me and you believe I'm a thief?" She sat back in her chair. "That's insulting. My name is Amy Stevens. I'm from Topeka, Kansas. I've been studying here for a year and I'm scheduled to head home next week. Until about a minute ago I was really, really sorry to be leaving. As a matter of fact, until a minute ago I didn't have a bad thing to say about my experience here." Folding her arms, she gave him as haughty a look as she could muster. "And you are?"

"Simon West," he said, lowering his hands. He started tapping a rhythm on the table's edge.

"I told you that the docent gave me the coin," she repeated. "I did not steal it."

"All right, but this has to be more than a coincidence." He stopped tapping.

"What is?"

"That you're here with a coin I've wanted for years."

"Do you think I came here to sell it to you? You really are too much." Amy reached out to pick up her coin and leave.

He leaned over and took her hand. "I do not think you took it or came here to sell it to me. That would be much too simple."

"Now you're talking in riddles." Her words came out in a whisper, her response to his touch once again overriding her annoyance with him.

Oh hell's bells, how could this be one-sided?

You are a fool, Simon West. Yes, she was adorable with her wayward auburn hair and lively eyes. Were they green or brown? No matter. She was up to something. "Sorry, Amy. I *am* talking in riddles."

The coin, here and now, was too big a coincidence to be anything but a con. Or magic—which was absurd. He'd play along with her game because he wanted that coin, not because he was taken in by her. She'd probably spent the year studying acting.

"So you believe me? That I didn't steal the coin?"

Her accent was delightful. The Queen's English as a second language. He loved the way Yanks tried to speak the mother tongue. It charmed him the way a French accent charmed others. *Pop a top on it, you idiot. Think with your head.*

"I want you to tell me that you believe me," she insisted.

"She is telling the truth, sir. She did not steal it nor come here to sell it to you. I can promise you that."

With a start Simon turned to find a man dressed in an old-fashioned naval uniform standing beside the table.

"May I ask who you are?" Simon asked, then, seeing Amy's pleased surprise, he raised his hand for silence. "You're the docent from the museum."

"Yes." Amy and the newcomer spoke in unison.

Of course he is. Simon waited, wondering what was next.

"You doubt me, sir?" The older man drew himself up to his full height. "Indeed I am a docent. Wentworth Arbuckle is my name. I work at the house with the blue door three blocks north."

"Right, maybe you are." Simon tried to figure out this new spin. No one knew of his studies. There was no money in the coin or his research. He'd kept it a tight secret largely because he disliked being called a fool. "Tell me why you would give away a coin like that. I'm sure your employer would not approve."

"What do you know of that coin?" the docent asked, apparently unconcerned about the suggestion of theft.

Simon looked from the docent to Amy, who was watching for his answer with an expression that all but shouted, "Don't make us wait!" What the hell. They must know the answer already. Why else would they be here?

"I've seen the coin in a portrait," he said, addressing the docent directly.

That one sentence brought a complete shift of energy.

"A portrait? Where is this painting?" Arbuckle asked, his bearing changing from calm to excited in an instant.

"In my office." Simon spoke slowly, feeling the plot deepen.

"And you have the actual coin, miss!" the docent exclaimed, slapping his hands together as though they were on the verge of discovering something incredible. "Please, I beg of you, sir. May I see the painting?"

Simon took a minute to think it through. "Why not?" It would be easy enough to pretend to be won over by the man's enthusiasm. "I'll trade one look at the painting for another look at that coin."

"Sure," Amy said without a moment's hesitation, as though she was as innocent as she was pretty.

He looked away from the vivid face. "Let me tell the

staff." Without waiting for an answer he went over to the man at the door.

Amy would have called the guy Simon was talking to a bouncer, even though she had never seen him do anything but call a cab for someone too drunk to make it home on his own. West talked to him for all of a minute. Whatever he said had the man looking at them with suspicion and nodding his understanding.

He's backup, Amy decided as she pocketed the coin. In case we're bad guys. She looked at the tour guide to see if he was offended. Not at all. He was smiling, ready to burst with anticipation.

Simon West then had a quick word with the other bartender and gestured to them. He then opened the door to the back office and led the way.

She was not impressed with the space, a cramped office filled with business junk. And no sign of a portrait. Confused, Amy decided she would let Mr. Arbuckle go ahead of her.

West turned as he put his hand on a doorknob at the other end of the room. "It's not here. The portrait with the coin in it is in my study upstairs."

"Is there anyone else home? Your wife, maybe?" Amy asked. Being from Topeka did not mean she was naïve—a little slow at self-protection maybe, but not naïve.

"No wife," West said. "Just a sec. I'll see if any of the staff is about." He disappeared through the door and she heard him shout, "Tandy? Roger? Is anyone home?"

"I'm polishing the brass in the front hall," a female voice bellowed back. "Roger's in the upstairs loo fixing the leak. You need something you come up here."

With a nod, Simon held the door again for Amy and the docent. He directed them down a wide hall that ended in what reminded Amy of servants' stairs, the kind that typically ended with a green baize door. The door opened onto a stunning foyer.

Amy took in the black-and-white tiled floor, the great clock, and a woman—Tandy she assumed—cleaning a doorknob. The air was filled with the odd, combined scent of polish and the sweetness of Asiatic lilies, coming from the flowers near the door. Wow, Amy thought, it was so elegant. Not your usual bachelor flat.

"I'm taking Miss Stevens and this gentleman to see the portrait."

"All right," Tandy said. "Call me if you want some tea."

With a nod to Tandy, Simon led them up the stairs.

Amy waved at the maid, who nodded back with a friendly smile, even as she followed Simon and the docent up the rise of gleaming wood steps. The staircase formed a U at end of the hall opposite the front door. A long landing connected the two stairways and Amy walked very slowly, examining the paintings that lined the wall.

She stopped in front of one. "Is this a Rembrandt?" she asked, raising her head to find Simon watching her.

"A Rembrandt? We dearly wish, but no, my fine art observer, it's a fake. Of Rembrandt's school, of his time and *not* by him."

"I'm no expert, but surely it's a very good fake," Amy said, standing back and considering it carefully.

"Yes, it fooled a lot of people until the thirties, when Berenson and his cronies doubted its attribution. Now there are dozens of *almost* Old Masters around."

Even a fake Rembrandt from the 1600s must be worth money, she thought, or at least more than she would ever spend on a painting. Too bad it wasn't the real thing.

With a nod of sympathy she followed Simon the rest of the way up the stairs, wondering who he was. "So this place is half magnificent townhouse and half football pub?"

"Yes." Simon's single word was abrupt. "My brother was sure it was the solution to all financial ills."

By his tone Amy assumed it was not. She could hear her mother's voice in that part of her memory reserved for life lessons—"It's impolite to ask about money"—and quelled the overwhelming urge to quiz him for details.

The U-shape of the staircase had her all turned around and when they reached the final landing she looked out the huge arched window to get her bearings. The building was placed crosswise at the end of a cul-de-sac. The twilight edging to dark made it impossible to see more than that it was a quiet neighborhood, very quiet. How could she have come to Earl's Place for a year and not known that Earl's was half of a house with a split personality? Amazing.

No less amazing than the room Simon ushered them into. It had more arched windows on two walls and she could imagine it in the daytime, filled with light.

It was more like a library than a study, lined with shelves that were filled with books. There was a desk and a table, the wood surfaces barely visible under endless stacks of books, papers, and files. A state-of-the-art computer showed the room for the anachronism it was.

Even with all that to look at, it was the painting that dominated the space. "That portrait's from the Regency," Amy said with real pleasure.

"Right," Simon agreed. "George III gone crazy and his son named Regent. That and Napoleon's ego made the early 1800s pretty interesting."

Amy moved closer to the portrait. "The Regency is my favorite period in English history. I've read Jane Austen, seen exhibits, visited museums, and read at least a hundred historical novels." She loved it, and not because the men were as compelling as the one in this painting. He resembled Simon West so much that she wondered if he had posed for it and this was his idea of a practical joke.

Not possible. Why would he do that? Besides, he said he had never seen the actual coin before today. This painting had to be the real thing.

The man in the painting posed with casual elegance, seated at the side of a desk, not behind it. On the desktop were a toy train, a miniature of a woman, and the coin. It was the smallest item, but somehow it caught and held one's attention. Was it because it was so carefully rendered, right down to the dent?

"It has a dent," Amy said. "Like mine. That is seriously weird."

"Now you see why I was so amazed when you showed up with it?" Simon turned to find the docent and include him in the conversation. He was standing in the shadows near the fireplace, seeming more ghostlike than real, but he nodded at Simon.

"Who is this, Simon? Some relative, for sure," Amy asked.

"A many times great-grandfather, the third Earl of Weston."

She could feel the flush of embarrassment creep up her cheeks. And she had teased him about his "Prince William accent." "And when did you inherit the title?" She tried to sound casual and not completely out of place.

"My brother's the earl, not me."

So much for her fantasy. Bartender or not, Simon West was related to an earl, not to mention his six feet of blond good looks with an accent that was as seductive as a glass of champagne. He was probably dating a supermodel.

"So you're the second son? Like Prince Harry? You have a title, too, don't you? Not prince, ummm . . ." She paused a second, trying to recall. "Lord Simon, isn't it?"

"No, my brother has the use of that title as well. I'm simply Mr. West." A little bow accompanied Simon's exaggerated accent.

Simon watched as she made a conscious effort not to be impressed with his rank. Good for her. American through and through. That didn't mean she wasn't a grifter of some kind. He still could not see how they were going to make money from him, short of picking up a bit of silver and walking out with it.

Not that there was any silver to pinch.

"The earl in the portrait looks so much like you, Simon. Doesn't it feel odd to know he's been dead for two hundred years?"

"My brother and I are twins," he began. So far they hadn't asked a single question that wasn't easily available. Except for the request to see the portrait. He looked around for Wentworth Arbuckle again and did not see him. Damn, was that it? She would chat him up and the old man would see what he could steal. He was just about to be shot of both of them when the docent stood up from the wing chair facing the fireplace and nodded to him.

"You're a twin?" she asked.

"Right," he said. "Having someone look like me is the norm. Besides, I bet you've seen pictures of your great-grandmother or some distant relative and everyone comments on how much you look like her. Not that much difference."

"There's a big difference between a family photo and a huge portrait you see every day." Amy laughed at the comparison. "So you are the son and brother of an earl, you teach, occasionally tend bar, and spend the rest of your time in here. What are you studying?" She picked up a book and looked at the title. "*The East India Company*?"

Now she was prying. Using those guileless eyes to find out what he was doing. Why? It meant nothing to anyone but his family.

"Oh, I know," she said, acting as though she had this moment realized something. "Are you trying to figure out what the connection is between the earl and the coin?"

"Why do you care? What possible interest could this be to you?"

She stepped back as though he had thrown a punch she had to dodge. "I'm sorry. Am I being too personal? It's just that it hardly seems an accident that I should be here with the coin that is in the painting. Doesn't it seem odd to you?"

"Yes."

"Well, see, there is something we agree on. And now here's something else. If you want me to leave, I will."

"I want to see the coin," he said, holding out his hand. "Then you can go."

"But of course, Mr. West." She said his name exactly the way Tandy did when she was annoyed with him, the little edge to her voice that made "mister" an insult. She took the coin out of her pocket, handed it to him, and turned her back to him and her coin.

Arbuckle came up to them. Simon hadn't heard him move from the fireplace to his side, had not heard the floor creak the way it always did.

"I was afraid you'd left," Amy said, her relief evident. She and the docent studied the painting, ignoring Simon.

The coin felt warm, and glinted the way it did in the painting. Simon turned it over and over with one hand. It seemed an anticlimactic end to a years-long search. He put the coin in the center of the nearest empty table, wondering if she *would* sell it to him. He was about to ask, when the docent spoke up.

"Here is what I wish to know," the docent said, talking to Amy, but loud enough for him to hear. "The coins were not recovered until 1985. I ask you"—he turned to Simon, his eyes as intense as his voice—"how was it returned to the Regency? I know much of its history in that period, but have been searching for the answer to that question for longer than you can imagine."

Amy thought the answer to that question was obvious. She said it anyway. "Isn't it possible that a few of the coins made their way onto the streets?"

"No." This time it was Simon and the docent who answered together.

"All the coins were sealed and shipped from the mint," the docent said, unwittingly corroborating the story that Simon had told her an hour ago.

"Yes." Simon nodded. "And though graft and corruption are almost as old as man, no one has ever intimated that some were stolen." He looked at the painting for a long moment and then at the docent. "The more unanswerable question, sir, is how a coin minted in 1808 could be in a portrait painted in 1805?"

Three

Wow, he was right. How had the coin come to be in the painting if it was not created until 1808? That was weird.

Now they all stared at the painting as if Simon's ancestor would explain. The coin glinted as though trying to communicate its secret. The earl regarded them with an earnestness that made her wonder what he knew that they did not.

"I know how it was done, Mr. West," the tour guide said. "If I could take you to the place where it happened, would you be willing to go?"

Amy nodded as if Simon needed a prompt.

"Sure," Simon answered too quickly. "And while we're at it, can you tell me what the third earl did with the Guardi painting the family used to own?"

"A what painting?" Amy asked.

"The artist's name is Guardi. He painted in the second half of the eighteenth century. The second earl bought it in Venice when he was on his Grand Tour. It was what one did in those days. Bought a painting by Guardi or Canaletto. They sell for millions of pounds now."

"And the third earl lost it?" Jeez, that was a true disaster. She thought about it for all of three seconds. "Maybe he sold it," she said, turning to him. "Even without today's death taxes I bet the estate was expensive to maintain. It was the same then, wasn't it? The estate eats up every pound and is still starving to death."

"That's the easy explanation, but there's no record of it. The only notation is in the house steward's book. April 10, 1805. Family lore has it that the third earl gave the Guardi to his mistress as a farewell gift."

"What, she already had enough jewelry?"

"No, the earl had recently bought a spectacular race-horse and hired a Spanish trainer, so he was a little low on funds. *That* we have a record of. The only thing we know is that it was discovered missing on April 10, 1805." He shook his head and stopped talking. "Sorry. The missing Guardi fascinates me almost as much as the coin."

Did he think he had said too much? Exactly what could she do with that information? Or was he still convinced that they were trying to get something from him?

"Mr. West, if you would like to wish on the coin perhaps you can find out what happened to the work by Guardi." The docent spoke for the first time in a while.

"Wish on the coin? Is that before or after you answer my first question?" Simon West sounded as though he was reaching his limit.

"I can answer your questions about the coin," the docent said, nodding. "If the answer to your question about the painting is to be known then the coin will respond."

Simon made a sound of annoyance.

"That surprises you?" the docent asked.

"Surprise is not the word I would use. Coins do not talk."

"No, but they can respond. Feel warm, turn brighter. Just the way the one in the painting looks brighter than the rest of the items around it."

They all turned back to the portrait and Simon nodded. "I've noticed that before. It's a trick of the light or the way the artist painted it." He raised his hands as if he wanted to ward off its influence. "This is nonsense. I have to close up the pub."

"Please, sir," the docent urged. "Why not sit on the sofa and try. I promise you will lose no time at all."

The docent looked desperate. He might not be playing with a full deck, Amy thought, but this was important to him.

"Oh, come on," Amy said. "Loosen up and give it a try. Wish for us to be gone." She winked at the docent who gave her a faint smile in return. He really didn't look well. "Simon." She waited until she had his complete attention. "Please. Who can it hurt?" She moved close enough to whisper. "It will cost you no more than a few moments and it will please a very tired old man."

How could anyone resist those earnest eyes? She made him feel like an uncaring fool, instead of the practical realist he was. Right. He would wish. He would wish for them to be gone. With a nod, he sat on the sofa.

"Very good and thank you, Mr. West."

Arbuckle's words were conventional but his profound relief was evident. Why was this so important to him?

"If you will pick up the coin it will be my pleasure to aid you in the process. Miss, you may wish as well."

"I wished already." Amy shrugged. "I figured it couldn't hurt. I can't say that I believed it would mean anything."

"Then you had best wish again. Believing in the magic is what makes it happen. You can wish as many times as you want. The coin decides which wish is the truest."

"Oh, I like that." Simon's words meant one thing, his tone another. "An inanimate object knows what's best for me."

"Yes, Mr. West, it does."

The docent had the critical air of a father disappointed in his son. Simon felt properly chastened and wondered exactly who was in charge here. Or what. He looked at the coin.

Amy sat on the small settee near the fireplace. Simon sat next to her. Arbuckle pulled a chair from the desk and sat across the small table from them. He picked up the coin, seemed to make a wish of his own, and then handed it to Amy. Simon watched her take it. She wrapped her fingers around it and held it tight. "Can I make a different wish than the one I made before?"

"Yes, my dear. As a matter of fact, I think you should."

She closed her eyes and held the coin close to her heart. Simon's own heart skipped a little. He wished he had half her faith and a solid dose of her trust. With a nod she opened her eyes and then closed them again and added a soft, "Please." He smiled, wondering if the coin had any maternal instincts.

Her worried expression was eclipsed by surprise and she opened her palm. The coin glowed gold and she laughed. "Does that mean I made the right wish?"

Simon wasn't taken in. A sleight of hand would explain it.

The docent could not resist her enthusiasm. He took the coin from her. It immediately dulled. He offered it to Simon, who let him place it in his palm. He left his hand open so they could watch it as he made his "wish."

"You do know this is pointless, don't you?"

"Simon, Simon, take a chance," Amy said. "What will it hurt to try, to believe, just for one minute, that your dreams can come true?"

If that dream included her he might be willing to give it a try. He thought about wishing for that but decided it was too venal. He considered wishing for an end to this absurdity and then remembered the Guardi. He had always wanted to know what happened to it. That would be something worth wishing for. As for believing, if Amy Stevens was not part of this silliness then she had enough faith for both of them. He wished he had half of her conviction. Or was it confidence? He cried out, "Ouch!" and dropped the coin on the carpet.

All three of them watched it glowing white hot, though it did not singe the rug. Arbuckle continued to stare at it even as he spoke. "Impressive wishes, both of them." As it dulled, he moved to pick up the coin and set it again on the small coffee table nearby.

"So what's next?" Simon asked. "How long will it take for my wish to come true?" He looked from the girl to the old man. "You don't know, do you?" He shook his head at the docent's regretful nod.

"Do you know if they will come true?" Amy asked.

"Oh yes, they certainly will. If you believe in the possibility and are willing to do what wish fulfillment entails."

"Is it anything illegal?"

Amy asked the question as though an illegal element was a deal breaker. If she was not as honest as the sun, then she should do well on stage.

"Nothing illegal is necessary, miss," the docent said. "Mr. West, I offered to help you find out how the coin appeared in the painting in 1805."

"You said you would take me to the place it happened."

"I can send you there, but not take you."

"All right, can Amy go, too?" he asked the docent, and watched for her reaction.

They both spoke at the same time. Amy's "Oh, please" in chorus with the docent's "Yes."

"It was part of my wish. That I get to go with Simon."

"Then it's not surprising that it is granted. The coin did bring the two of you together."

"Was that magic?" Amy wondered aloud.

"Fate or chance?" Simon added.

"It is one, both, or all three, Mr. West, Miss Amy. You see, there are certain things that are *meant* to be. It is the choices made by man that dictate *when* they will happen."

"That sounds like predestination to me," Amy said with a disapproving frown.

"Not at all. There are an infinite number of ways that an end can be reached. What is predetermined about that?" He did not wait for a rebuttal. "You, miss, are not the first person to whom I told the story of the coin and the wishes it granted. You are, however, the first to listen with your heart.

"You, Mr. West, know the story of the coin as well as I do. Your head is so filled with the details that you have yet to make sense of them. From the moment I saw you at that table I knew it was the two of you who were the key to my puzzle. I thought Miss Amy's role was to bring us together, Mr. West. I am wrong. The coin brought the two of you together to complete the work I have started."

Arbuckle so firmly believed in the coin that it was contagious, Simon thought. Amy was nodding, absorbing every word, and God help him, it almost made sense to him, too.

Simon offered Amy a hand and began to stand up when the docent spoke. "Oh, please stay seated. You will be more comfortable traveling from there. I am sending you to the year 1805, with the coin." He picked it up from the table and handed it to Amy. "You will give the coin to the earl and then return to the present."

Time travel? Had he said time travel? He made it sound as easy as hailing a cab on a sunny day.

"You mean man can control travel through time?" Amy said sounding, for once, as skeptical as he felt.

"If you believe it, you can. Time travel is certainly within the coin's power, though perhaps not man's."

"Oh, for God's sake. This is ridiculous."

"Wait a minute and listen, Simon, it might be possible," Amy said.

"We just have to believe in the magic coin. Right. *Back to the Future* is one of my favorite movies." Simon aimed his exasperation at the docent. "Did you have anything to do with that?" He stood up and walked away from them just in case this insanity was contagious.

"Listen to me, Simon." Amy came between the two. "According to Einstein's general theory of relativity, there is nothing in the laws of physics to prevent time travel."

"Is that what you've been studying here? Physics?"

"Good grief, no. I barely made it through required science in college. I'm not sure where I heard that. Maybe I read it."

"Did your college courses include Einstein's general theories?" He could tell she was considering a lie by the vaguely guilty look on her face. Then she shrugged and her expression cleared.

"Okay, I hate to admit this, but I just remembered where I heard it. To be completely honest, I was quoting a TV character on the show *Stargate Atlantis*." She waited.

He was about to say something scathing when he realized that at least she was being honest. Who but the scrupulously honest would admit that their scientific data came from a TV show?

"I know it stretches credulity, Mr. West." The docent's words fell into the silence.

"Yes, it does." Simon crossed his arms. "Answer this: If time travel is within the coin's power, then why haven't you taken it back?"

"Don't you think I've tried?" Arbuckle said. "A hundred times at least and in a dozen different places."

It was hard not to believe him. He spoke so earnestly.

"But now I see. The presence of the coin in this room and in the portrait is the key. You take the coin back to your ancestral home, Westmoreland in 1805."

"Westmoreland? I've heard of Westmoreland," Amy said. "That's where it all started?"

Simon could only shake his head. What an elaborate scheme. To what end? He still had no idea.

"Mr. Arbuckle," Amy began gently, "how are you so sure that Simon is the one to take the coin and that 1805 is where its magic begins? What happens after that?"

"There is no need to worry about that. His only responsibility is to make certain the coin is given to the earl."

"If we leave the coin there, then how do we return?"

Her question was so right on that Simon thought she was as much a dupe of this crazed man as he was. "We can come back because the coin guarantees a round trip once our chore is done," he said. "I'm making that up, but I bet I'm right, aren't I?"

The docent shook his head. "I am not at all sure, Mr. West. Our goal is to be sure the coin is in the time it was meant to be. Man, fate, and fortune will enable the rest."

"That's leaving way too much to chance," Amy said. "Your faith in the coin must be very strong."

It was leaving so much to chance that Simon decided to call his bluff. "Let's sit down and do it, shall we, Arbuckle? Do we close our eyes?"

When the docent nodded, Amy reached over and swiped the coin off the table and pushed it into the pocket of her jeans. She sat down and reached for Simon's hand. If it meant as a distraction, it had worked. Her palm was soft, her fingers long and fine. That sweet hand in his aroused more than protective feelings.

"Very well, Mr. West. Thank you both. You are right. It is best to go in the dead of night when there are fewer people to see your arrival." He waited a beat and Simon nodded. "I am sorry, Miss," the docent said to Amy. "You cannot hold hands or sit too close. You will be in the same place and time although not together."

Simon moved a few inches to the left.

"All you must do is close your eyes and visualize where you would like to go."

"Westmoreland, the year the portrait was painted. With Amy nearby," Simon said. Fatigue overcame him before he could question how he had been drugged. He let his head fall back on the sofa. In a second he was sound asleep.

Four

"No, my lady, your new companion has not arrived yet."

The voice woke Amy from a deep sleep, one filled with dreams, not all of them sweet. Echoes of delight, regret, pleasure, and loss faded, leaving her exhausted and anxious. She forced her eyes open. Surely the real world would be easier to deal with.

She shut her eyes as quickly. The sofa, Simon, the docent, and the office were gone. Good God, where was she? Where was Simon?

"I am sorry, Lady Anne." The same woman spoke again. "I know Mrs. Braintree is sending someone as quickly as possible. It has rained so much the last few days. No doubt, carriages are later than usual."

Carriages? Amy's anxiety blossomed into excitement. She ignored the fear.

"You are making excuses, Martha," a young female voice answered. "This is not the last century. It is 1805 and the roads are in much better repair."

1805? Either she *had* time traveled or she was in a very

elaborate reality stunt. The docent hadn't seemed like the reality show type, and wouldn't she have had to sign some kind of consent form? Besides, the *Regency House Party* reality show had been a bomb. It wasn't likely anyone would try that again.

Amy opened one eye and then the other. She was in some sort of small room, on a narrow bed tucked under a window. The sky was the bright gray of dawn or bad weather. The room was filled with three large chests and a trunk that was open. There were hooks on the wall, but they were all empty. Is that how Regency people stored their clothes? She knew they did not have hangers then. And she thought she knew so much. If the first thing she saw confused her, this time-travel visit would be full of pitfalls.

"The earl came home last night, my lady."

"Weston is here? Not in London?"

"He is to sit to have the last bits done on his portrait."

Weston? Portrait? Wow.

Her doubts vanished.

Amy Stevens—from Topeka, Kansas—was in a nineteenth-century room, in a nineteenth-century house with two nineteenth-century people talking in the other room. Where was Simon? Had he come home with the earl?

Amy's first impulse was to leap from the bed, make her presence known, then find Simon as quickly as she could. And be sent to the nearest insane asylum.

Keep still, look around, figure it out. It took four repetitions before she was able to do more than lie still. How long before someone found her here? Wherever here was. She forced her eyes open. Keeping them closed was like an ostrich burying its head in the sand.

"Not only do I have to deal with Mrs. Braintree's idea of a companion, but now Weston will nag me endlessly about sitting for a portrait."

The well-bred voice sounded acerbic rather than petulant.

"Where *is* my new companion? The bed in the dressing room was made up for her. Was she not supposed to arrive yesterday?"

"Yes, my lady, but the roads, you know. From the rain, you understand. It could be—"

"Weston is home," the other woman interrupted. "He found the roads passable."

Amy sat bolt upright in her bed. She'd bet this was a dressing room. Was *she* supposed to be the lady's companion they were talking about?

Amy decided to get up and tiptoe to the door.

As she pushed back the thin blanket, she drew a deep breath and sneezed. Then sneezed again. Her dreams had been as filled with the scent of lilacs as the air was now. Too sweet and too much of it.

A girl popped through the door, vital, animated. Not at all constrained by the sober dress and apron she was wearing.

Hell's bells, she thought. Nothing like jumping right into the story with no idea of anything other than that she was confused. And scared. Not paralyzed by it. Not yet. But it wasn't far off.

"Thank heaven, you *have* arrived, miss. Mrs. Braintree promised you would be here by this morning. When I went to bed and there was no sign of you I had my doubts."

Amy nodded.

"You must have arrived so very late. The night porter should have told Mr. Stepp instead of sending you off to bed. Sorry, but could you please dress quickly. Lady Anne is working herself into a state. She has been so anxious about your arrival."

Amy nodded again, trying to take in the names at least. Stepp must be the butler. Lady Anne, the woman she would be working for.

"Come on now. Up, if you please, miss. Let me help you with your stays and dress."

Amy got up, her chemise a mass of wrinkles. At least it was a chemise and not the jeans and T-shirt she had been wearing in the twenty-first century. "My name is Amy Stevens. I beg your pardon, who are you?" And wasn't that an odd thing to be asking somebody who was helping you put on the Regency version of underwear?

"Martha. My name is Martha Stepp. How could I not tell you? I do beg pardon, Miss Stevens."

"You are related to the Mr. Stepp you mentioned?"

"Yes, miss, my father," the maid said as she laced the stays. It was not as uncomfortable as she had expected. Of course, Martha was not lacing it tightly. Was that because tiny waists did not matter in the empire-style gowns that were so fashionable now? As Martha finished the lacing, it occurred to Amy that the coin had been in the pocket of her jeans. Where was it now?

"My mother is Mrs. Stepp, the housekeeper."

Pay attention, Amy, she commanded herself. You can worry about the coin if they don't kick you out. Would her accent give her away completely? She'd done her best to sound English. Even after a year she sounded anything but.

"The Earl and the Countess Weston have had Stepps in their service for more than a hundred years."

"That's impressive. It's not very often you hear of such loyalty. That never happens where I'm from."

"Well, of course not. Your work lasts only a Season or two. Once the young miss is engaged, you have to move on to the next one who needs what you can give."

And what exactly was that? Amy wondered. Before she could ask, the maid spoke again.

"I beg your pardon, miss. Do you come from Scotland? Or Wales? Your accent is," she paused, and Amy waited for her adjective, "a bit different."

How could she explain it? She closed her eyes and wished for inspiration. "I spent my childhood in the Orkneys and have been working in the Midlands for the last five years." Wow, her imagination must be working overtime.

"Oh, the Orkneys."

Martha made it sound like it was the North Pole. Amy was pretty sure the Orkneys were in Scotland.

"You must miss your family terribly."

"No, I'm an orphan."

"Oh." Clearly Martha Stepp could not decide if that was more fortune or misfortune.

"I'm looking forward to meeting Lady Anne," Amy said. Definitely better to steer the conversation away from her background.

"She's a lovely young woman," Martha said, then leaned closer to whisper, "though she has been given to megrims lately, ever since her governess left and her brother took so long contacting Mrs. Braintree for a companion."

Amy had read that word "megrim" dozens of times and always wondered exactly what it meant. Now she would find out. The recollection of those romances gave her a boost of confidence. Clearly they were expecting someone who would help the young lady of the house prepare for her first Season. From her reading she had a good idea what a companion did. Though she had always associated them with older women. Plucking a storyline from one of the books, she forged ahead. "My most recent client in Leicestershire decided to marry her childhood sweetheart, so she had no need of me for the Season. When Mrs. Braintree called I was only too happy to find another position so quickly even if it meant a move to Sussex."

"Indeed, Miss Stevens. It worked out like magic."

Yes, it certainly had. What would she do when the real companion arrived? Like Scarlett O'Hara she decided to worry about that tomorrow.

"If Mrs. Braintree went all the way to York to call on you that certainly is a sign of how highly she regards you."

As she watched Martha rummage through the small bag at the foot of the bed, Amy made a mental note. *No phones in the Regency. "Call" means something entirely different in 1805.*

Martha pulled out a lovely lilac dress, sadly wrinkled, and then an even prettier dress, this one a pale green, its wrinkles not quite so noticeable. And no magic coin. Maybe it was in the bottom of the bag.

"You must have been exhausted not to have shaken out your clothes. If you wear the lilac, I will iron the green for you to wear at dinner."

"Thank you." She bit her lip to keep from asking a dozen questions.

"No need to thank me, Miss Stevens. I am not the housekeeper yet, though I hope to be someday. Let me introduce you to Lady Anne and then I will see what is keeping the chocolate." She scooped up the wrinkled dress as she spoke.

"My hair!" Amy exclaimed, raising her hand to what she knew was bed head at its worst.

"The knot at your neck has held quite nicely. I will help you with it later."

Another bit of magic, Amy thought, mightily relieved. She followed the maid into the bedroom. Where was the coin? Where was Simon? She must have looked as nervous as she felt. The maid patted her arm and added, "Not to worry, miss. Lady Anne is nervous, too. She won't even notice what sort of accent you have."

The girl awaiting them was small, not much bigger than a preteen. Fine-boned with wispy blonde hair that was cut short and framed her face. Her dress was white, too white for her very fair skin. It made her look pale and sickly. Her nervousness, or at the very least shyness, was betrayed by her hands. She was twisting them in an anxious rhythm that Lady Macbeth would have admired.

Amy had to push panic to a deep, dark corner as she

realized that they did not shake hands in the Regency era. She would have to curtsey. Where was the Regency version of Miss Manners?

She decided against a deep, royal curtsey. One thing she had learned this year is that royal was different from aristocrat. She went with a medium curtsey, like she'd seen on the Austen videos, more than a bob but not much more than that.

The next twenty minutes were no more awkward than they would have been between any two strangers. If one was barely interested and the other was trying to make a good impression. If Lady Anne was being "quite lovely" Amy did not want to see her when she was bitchy.

It took only a few questions from Amy and the rather limiting "yes" and "no" responses from Lady Anne before the girl/woman raised her head with an imperious frown. "Where are you from?"

Martha gave a long explanation of the Orkneys, her lack of family, and ended with a reminder that Mrs. Braintree had considered it a rare stroke of good fortune that Miss Stevens was available.

"Thank you, Martha," Lady Anne said in freezing tones. "Do your job and go find our chocolate."

Martha took no offense at her mistress's rudeness and excused herself. Amy felt abandoned by her only ally.

"Martha is new to her work as a lady's maid and I have little hope that she is teachable. Too spoiled by her parents."

Having dealt what sounded like a death blow to Martha's aspirations, Lady Anne took a step away from Amy. "You have no connections and no money?"

What a snot. Remembering Simon's arrogance she wondered if maybe all the Wests were like that when you first met them. Swallowing her pride, Amy bobbed a half-curtsey just because it seemed the humble thing to do. "I am sure my background is a disappointment, my lady. May I remind you that no one will ever see me? I am like Madame d'Aulnoy's fairy godmother who wants only to help." Amy never knew she was so good at sucking up. What was Simon putting up with?

"A very young fairy godmother. I do hope you have brought a magic wand." Lady Anne smiled a little.

If I had one I'd turn you into a flower seller. With that thought it struck Amy that Lady Anne was trying to make her feel incompetent. She'd had enough psych classes to know that Lady A's aloofness was rooted in fears of her own inadequacy. "I have no need of a wand, my lady, as you are far from a hopeless case."

While her ladyship tried to figure out if that was a compliment or an insult, Amy pushed on. "May I ask what you are most looking forward to this Season?" She mentally ran through a list of possibilities, completely missing the one that made Lady Anne's eyes shine.

"Oh, the music, of course," she said without a moment's hesitation. "I assumed Mrs. Braintree had told you of my specific interests and needs."

"Yes, she did," Amy said. Had she ever read any novels with heroines who loved music? None came to mind. "It is only that I wanted to know how to make time for the other aspects of the Season. Of those items you will need to have in order to appear to your best advantage."

"Oh, you mean clothes, stockings, bonnets. All of that." She waved a dismissive hand. "You can handle that. I am much more concerned about what kind of pianoforte is at the town house and whether Weston has secured a box at the opera and managed to make my wishes known regarding musicales."

They talked, or rather, she let Lady Anne talk. When it came to music the woman had plenty to say. Amy considered it a crash course and wished she could take notes.

Martha came back with the chocolate and handed a cup to Lady Anne and one to her.

"Miss Stevens," Lady Anne said, before Amy had a

chance to take one sip of her chocolate. "Would you find the earl and ask him if he was able to secure the items from the list I gave him?" She looked at Martha.

"I do believe he is in the conservatory," the maid said.

"Good. Since you are going there, please find the music sheets I left on the music stand and bring them back here."

"Yes, my lady." Amy rose.

"Oh, finish your chocolate first." An impatient sound allowed Amy to sit down again. "I am not that selfish."

How interesting, Amy thought. She always thought self-awareness a facet of modern life.

"Tell me why you enjoy the Season so much."

Amy felt like she had been given the cue for her soliloquy to begin. She crossed her fingers, hoping she would not commit some revealing faux pas. How she wished she could remember more of what she had read. *I am so out of my element here.*

She took a sip of the chocolate and almost swooned at the fabulous taste. It was so much better than the add-milk variety she drank at home. And the caffeine didn't hurt either. It was like a boost of confidence. *Here goes,* she thought.

Five

"The Season is all about new adventures, new acquaintances, new sights, my lady. And new clothes." She added the last in a conspiratorial whisper.

"I suppose so. Not that there is anything truly *new*. It has been the same for years. The dress styles have changed and not much else."

Lady Anne sipped some more of her chocolate, patted her lips daintily with a serviette while Amy wondered if she would be looking for new employment before she even had a chance to look for the coin.

"Tell me why you so enjoy being a 'fairy godmother,' as you call it."

"Because, Lady Anne, the lesson I teach is very simple and does not require a magic wand at all." Good save, Amy thought.

Lady Anne leaned forward and Amy took another sip of the chocolate. It was as good as the first one. *Yum.* Now what is the lesson? She hoped the pause seemed dramatic rather than desperate. Fear was too damn distracting so she pushed it aside. The success of this was in her control. No one would ever guess who she really was or where she was from.

And that was her answer. It was all about control.

"The Season and its success are entirely in your control, my lady. If there is one thing that I want to convince you of, it is that."

"In my control." Anne sat back with a puff of disappointment. "Nonsense. I live in my brother's house, meet the people who are our social equals. Men will court me after my brother gives them permission and we will stay as long as Parliament is in session or the weather permits. None of that is in my control."

Lady Anne's answer only made Amy more certain she was right. It was exactly like her year abroad. "No matter what the constraints, you can make choices and enjoy the Season on your terms. Yes, there are some invitations that you must accept—I am sure your brother will insist and, for a fact, so will I—but you can balance them with all the music you want. You will find like-minded friends and what now seems so overwhelming a spectacle will be the most fun you have ever had."

"You make it almost sound bearable." Her admission was grudging, but her frown lines eased even when she added, "I hate crowds."

Aha, thought Amy. *Those psych courses pay off once again.* Here was the heart of it. The woman was an introvert and just thinking about the size and scope of the Season was exhausting.

"It will be more than bearable, I promise you." Amy hoped that was enough about Lady Anne's expectations. Translating twenty-first-century self-help talk into Regency English was hard work.

It's in your control, Amy, she reminded herself. "Lady Anne, you said before that there is still so much to do. Does your brother have a firm date for leaving Westmoreland?"

"Not really. We will go when Parliament demands more of his attention than his horses do. Until then, we are close enough to town that he can go back and forth in a day if he chooses."

"Very well. For now we will look at the fashion books, decide what must be ordered here and what can wait for town, and practice your music so that you will be ready for all the invitations for you to sing."

Lady Anne shook her head, still not convinced.

Martha had been bustling about the room, tidying and listening to every word that was said. Her smile and gesture must be the Regency version of two thumbs-up. It looked like she had done something right.

Amy stood up, deciding it was best to leave and call this a victory. Although she had a feeling this was a mere skirmish in her battle to convince Lady A to make the most of the next few months.

"If you will excuse me, Lady Anne, I will refresh myself and then go to find the earl, collect your music. Where shall I meet you?"

"The small music room."

With a curtsey, Amy went into the dressing room and grabbed the bag that was still on the floor. She emptied it out on the bed, but all she could find were the sorts of things a Regency lady might need when traveling. Not a coin in sight. As a matter of fact, no money at all. That could be inconvenient. Surely Simon had the coin. What was the point of their time travel if the coin had not come with them? It was not lost. That simply was not an option. Mr. Arbuckle had been very specific about *giving* the coin to the earl.

Amy fussed with her hair and her skirts and made her way through Lady Anne's bedroom one more time. Her ladyship ignored Amy's passage as she was once again berating Martha. This time for not cleaning the hair from her brush. Martha appeared to be attending though not particularly upset by the reprimand.

Poor thing, Amy thought. *She is going to have her cheerfulness crushed if this keeps up.* And then Amy realized that she had no idea where the conservatory was. Or what floor they were on. Or how big the house was.

There was a man standing by the stairs, wearing what looked like a costume in satin. Pants that stopped at the knee and a wig. Surely that was old-fashioned in 1805. Aha, she thought, a footman in livery.

She went up to him, thought about bobbing a curtsey but stopped herself. As her ladyship's companion, she was senior to him and no such courtesy was necessary. What book had that tidbit come from?

"Would you please direct me to the conservatory?"

He bowed and announced he would take her there. It must have taken them three minutes of walking twisting and turning hallways and at least two flights of stairs, one up and one down. Amy tried to memorize the route and gave up when she realized there were footmen stationed everywhere, surely to serve the same purpose as her current guide.

She was out of breath when she reached the conservatory, not only because of the distance covered. Amy Stevens was about to meet the third Earl of Weston.

The footman knocked on the door and when a voice called "Enter," he opened it for Amy. She stepped into the room.

The conservatory was lovely. What she would call a greenhouse, but in the giant proportions that matched the scale of Westmoreland. There were several trees, palms and some fruit trees—orange or lemon she thought—and orchids blooming near a small pool. She saw no sign of the music sheets Lady Anne wanted her to collect. Following the sound of the water, she turned a corner and stopped with a gasp. There, seated beside a desk, was a man who could only be the Earl of Weston. Or Simon West.

Though the furniture and pose were familiar to her from

the earl's portrait, they were so totally out of place in this garden of green and light that Amy thought she was hallucinating.

With one more step it made complete sense. An artist was busily at work. The portrait. She was looking at the man who had painted the portrait of the earl. I'm still sane, she thought, with real relief.

She looked back toward the desk. If this was not Simon, how would he explain that he looked so much like the earl himself?

Amy curtseyed again, more deeply this time. "I beg your pardon, my lord."

The earl turned his head when he heard her voice. His eyes betrayed interest though the rest of his expression remained impassive.

"My lord, do not move!" the artist insisted.

"I will take a break now. Come back in an hour."

"No, remain seated. The light will be gone in an hour."

The earl stood up. "Then we will resume tomorrow." He left the conservatory without looking at her. Amy followed him anyway, after grabbing the sheet music she noticed on the stand near the entrance.

"Excuse me," she said, annoyed that she sounded so intimidated.

"We will not stand here talking in the hall where every footman can hear us. I do not even know your name," the earl said, giving her no more than a glance.

"I am Miss Stevens, my lord. Lady Anne's new companion." She was talking to his back and he stopped to confront her.

"I assumed so. You will not do at all. You are too young, too pretty, and too free with your words. We will talk in the library, Miss Stevens."

She followed him in silence, around and up and down again, terrified that she had lost her position, so full of worry that she paid no attention to the route they were taking until they reached a door that another footman promptly swung open. It was not the library. It was a bedroom. Obvious, as the bed was the biggest one she had ever seen. It was unmade, adding an intimacy that made her Regency self uncomfortable.

"I beg your pardon, miss." The earl took a step back with an arrogance that belied the apology. "This is not the library."

That was stating the obvious. How could he get lost in his own house?

"I have a book I want you to take to Lady Anne," he said, picking one up from the table near the bed. "The footman will take you to the library and I will join you in a moment."

"Do you require assistance, my lord?" A man had come through a door at the far end of the room.

"No, Miss Stevens has been asked to retrieve this book."

What? Lady A had not asked for a book. That had been his idea.

The valet came toward them, took the book from the earl, and handed it to her. "I am Fancett, my lord's valet."

Ooooh, power struggle, Amy thought. One of those issues that persisted over time, from the Bible through Jane Austen to *Days of Our Lives*: Which one of us is more important?

There was no doubt in her mind any more than there was in Fancett's—the earl's valet certainly outranked his sister's companion. In length of service if nothing else.

"Fancett, did you know that Miss Stevens is related by birth to Lord Allbryce Stevens? Surely you remember him."

How did he know that? He hadn't even known her name. She bit her lip to keep from asking.

For his part, the valet wilted just a little. Her pedigree outranked his and that outranked length of service. What a silly game.

"Leave us, Fancett."

A woman in any century would be uncomfortable in a bedroom alone with a man she did not know. She edged toward the door. "Thank you, my lord," Amy said, curtseying. "I will take this to Lady Anne and come to you in the library."

"In a moment." His imperious tone stopped her in her tracks. Amazing how a voice of command could conquer self-interest. Before she could move away, he came to her, leaned down as though he was going to kiss her neck.

How did she recognize him? Without even looking at him she knew it was Simon. The energy he radiated? The smell of him? The feel of his breath on her neck? Relief flooded her, with a sexual charge not far behind.

Even as she recognized him, he whispered, "Amy, it's me, Simon West. Is everything all right?"

She turned her head. He was so close that half a step would mean she could kiss him. "No, everything is not all right. I don't have the coin. Do you?"

He shook his head.

She could hear Fancett rummaging about and could only imagine what they looked like. She pushed Simon away with a cautionary "We both have a role to play."

She clapped her hands together in what she hoped would sound like a slap and spoke loud enough to be heard by listeners. "I do not want my reputation ruined, my lord. You can fire me or we can speak of what you wish in the library as you first suggested."

Amy flounced out of the room, shooting daggers at the footman, who remained impassive. "Show me the way to Lady Anne's wing." It felt good to be the one giving orders. Who did the footman give orders to?

Lady Anne's room was empty and she walked through to toss the book on her cot. No way was a tome on farming in Sussex truly intended for the earl's sister. She gave the music to Martha, explaining that she was to meet with the earl in the library.

Martha agreed cheerfully, dropping the music on the table near the fireplace. Her "It's about time he took an interest in her ladyship's Season" didn't indicate that a private appointment with the earl was asking for trouble.

As she followed the footman to the library, some of the hallways looked familiar. The painting and statuary at least. Before he opened the door, the footman turned to her. "I will be out here, Miss."

"Thank you," Amy said, touched by his gallantry though not sure exactly how he could help if this situation were real. Fascinating, she thought. Westmoreland was its own small kingdom and the earl its ruler, having won the right by nothing more than the fate of his birth. How times had changed.

The footman opened the door and closed it gently after her. Simon turned from his consideration of a group of paintings. "I'm sorry, Amy."

"Why in the world did you take me to your bedroom?" She wasn't quite ready to forgive him though she could feel his genuine regret eroding her anger.

"I didn't do it on purpose," he said. "In 2006 that room is the library, or one of them. Then, after I realized my mistake, I thought that if we were pretending to have a liaison it would give us an excuse to be together."

"Simon, the earl doesn't need a reason to see a servant. All you have to do is command her presence."

"Yes, yes. That's true." He ran a hand through his hair. "How could this happen? How could we have actually traveled through time?"

"I have no idea. You're the one who said, 'Let's do it,' before we knew all the details."

"Right. Admit it: You thought it was all a bit dodgy, too."

She had to give him that. "If we were skeptical, then how did it happen? Didn't the docent say we had to believe?"

"He believed enough for both of us."

Simon said it with such certainty that Amy didn't argue.

"So we're here, without the coin, and with no idea how to travel back."

"Thank God we have each other."

She couldn't think of any other time in her life that a man had sunk his pride enough to admit that a situation was beyond his control.

Amy practically ran into the arms he held out for her. They stayed in the embrace a long time, as if one or the other of them would disappear. It was such a comfort that she thought she might stay in his arms forever. And then, suddenly, it was more than comfort. She could feel his heart, his breath, her body awakening to the feel of him.

She leaned back and stepped out of his arms. "What happened? What are you doing pretending to be the earl?"

"Believe me, it wasn't my idea." He let her go. "I woke up in a carriage as the coachman was opening the door. I was alone, dressed in period clothes, and he said, 'My lord, we are at Westmoreland.'"

"So if they think you're the earl, what do we do when the real earl arrives?"

Six

Simon shook his head slightly. "The whole thing is a mess. Who do they think you are?"

She explained about being Lady Anne's companion. He nodded.

"At least you know the era. I started shaving myself this morning. It almost gave Fancett a heart attack and then I let him tie my cravat. Apparently, the earl always 'works his own linen.' I told him that I had hurt my fist in a boxing match." He paused and exercised his hand as though it were hurting him. "They did have boxing then, didn't they?"

"Yes, and it would be exactly the sort of thing the earl would try. Good guess."

"What do I do when the real earl arrives?"

"I think he must have been with you last night, Simon. It's true that Regency folks didn't travel at night, but the moon was near full and this time of year it's almost as bright as daylight. With outriders, it would have been safe enough."

"I tell you, Amy, I was alone in the coach."

"It's like you switched places." As she said it, she saw his expression switch from uncertainty to shock just as the same thought had occurred to her.

"Is it possible," she said, "that the real earl is waking up in the London town house? Do you think that could be it? That he is there with the real lady's companion?"

Simon was quiet for longer than she wanted him to be. *Think faster.* She bit her lip to keep from saying it. Finally, he nodded.

"It could be the explanation. Doesn't it make sense that matter would have to displace other matter? That only so much can exist in the same time and place?"

"Is that from *Star Trek*?" Narrowing her eyes, she tried to read his.

"No, I made it up."

"I'm not sure if that makes me feel better or not." Amy considered his idea for a second. "But it does make sense."

"Thank you," he said gravely, as though he had just won the Nobel Prize for physics.

"What do you think the two of them are doing in the twenty-first century?" It could be disastrous. And she was not going to say that word out loud. No need to send a hint of it into the cosmos.

"Hopefully, Arbuckle will keep them from doing anything disastrous."

Amy hid her dismay at his choice of words and watched as he raked a hand through his hair again, pushing a blond wave off his face. *Why, he's as confounded as I am. He just hides it better.* "At first, I thought maybe this was some kind of reality show."

"No. We are at Westmoreland in 1805," he added in case she had any doubts. With an arm around her shoulders he turned so they faced the paintings. "Look at this. The Guardi painting. Right where it's supposed to be."

"Wow." Amy moved closer to the painting and stared at

it for a minute. "I totally believe we are here, but my heart is still hammering and my head whirling. How must those poor people feel? The ones who took our place? They had no idea they would be time traveling. At least we were warned."

"Amy, listen. We have to concentrate on what is happening here. What is happening in my study is beyond our control."

The idea of "control" brought back her conversation with Lady Anne. What made sense then seemed like drivel now. Her eyes filled. She turned away, pretending to examine the paintings, hoping he would not see her tears. "I am so glad that I'm not facing it alone."

Simon put his hands on her shoulders and it was like a cue for tears to start. She did her best not to sniff, but even without a sound he knew and turned her so they were facing each other.

"Why the tears, Amy? Where's your sense of adventure?"

"We're so far from home." Amy leaned into him. "No one knows where we are. We can't give the coin to the earl. He's not here and we seem to have lost it. Simon, how will we get back?"

"Hey, come on, you're the one who told me to 'believe.' I think that applies all the way. I have no idea how or when we'll get back. What I do know is that we have a job to do. And we don't know how much time we have to do it."

"It feels like a *Mission Impossible*. And while you are every bit as fabulous as Tom Cruise, I am not cut out for this kind of adventure."

"Why not? If I'm Tom Cruise then it's obvious you are the remarkable and talented Amy Stevens from Topeka, Kansas."

He kissed her on the forehead. She shook her head, pretending that she believed him, and in about ten seconds she actually began to.

All right, she thought, this is strange and no one will ever believe it. But we have each other. It will be as much fun as we make it. She straightened, stepping away from Simon.

"You know, you've done a complete turnaround. I had you pegged as a first-class cynic, a younger, hip Professor Higgins."

"Fair enough. I thought you were on the dodgy side of honest. That you and Mr. Wentworth Arbuckle had some scheme to cheat me of something. God knew what it could be. Then I was sorting through wishes and half wished I had as much faith as you did. The coin didn't give me a chance to pick. That was it.

"But let me tell you—even without the coin's magic, it's hard *not* to believe in time travel when I see Westmoreland looking the same, but not. Or when I have linen wrapped around my neck. It makes a tie seem civilized."

"Is it that bad? The stays are not nearly as uncomfortable as I thought they would be."

"What are stays?"

"The Regency version of a corset."

He smiled and she could imagine what he was visualizing. Corset and stockings with some kind of sexy garters. Which, in fact, was what she was wearing. No way was she telling him that.

"Amy, how did you learn all this?"

"In the romance novels I read. Don't make a face," she said before her words could even register. "Most of them are written by intelligent, educated women who value research. God bless writers like Mary Balogh and Sophia Nash."

"I'll send them a personal letter of thanks once we're home. Come to that, from now on I am not going to be so cavalier about alien sightings either."

"I'm not sure if it's the kiss on my forehead or your confidence, but I'm feeling much better."

"Right-o—let's see what this will do." With his hands framing her face, he kissed her lips.

If his shoulder had been comfort, his mouth was persuasion. His lips held her as surely as his hands. She welcomed it and opened to him, the sweetness of the kiss exploding into a tumult of delight that echoed through her body, tempting, taunting, teasing her until she needed him as surely as she needed breath. The feel of starched linen, the smell of spice, the clean, cool taste of him—she wanted all of it.

Her breath of disappointment as they drew apart had him pressing his forehead to hers. "Wow."

"Right-o," she said back. They stood still, conversation more than either of them could manage for a minute. Her arousal matched his. Wisdom dictated that they step away from each other, that they try for some measure of decorum.

Imprudence won out and she raised her face to his once again.

He showered kisses on her eyes, her cheeks, her lips as she whispered, "The first time you touched me. It was nothing more than a tap on my hand. That touch was as intimate an invasion as a kiss."

"It was the look of you that cornered me. All this wonderful hair, your incredible eyes, the way life radiates from you. And then there was your accent."

"See, you are Professor Higgins." As they traced back the attraction, they moved apart. Amy felt her hair escaping from the tight knot at her nape, and did her best to twist it back into shape.

The sight of her with her hands raised to fix her hair was so arousing that Simon turned away and walked to the window. What was it about that pose that made him ache? *Concentrate on something else.* There wasn't much activity outside. Spring sunlight spilled through the trees along the drive. The trees stood as they had for hundreds of years and still did in his time. Later he would take Amy for a walk, show her his favorite spots, spend an hour at the folly.

"After that kiss, Simon, anything is possible." She was near the Guardi painting, but her eyes were on him. "Amy and the earl are going to have an amazing adventure."

Is a kiss all it would take to make her smile again? Now that was a welcome prescription.

"How do we find the coin, Simon?"

She wasn't smiling now.

"I think we have to let the coin find us. It could be anywhere. It could have been left behind."

"All right. Hard as it is not to tear apart my room and the coach and your bedroom, I can see your point."

She bit her lip and he knew she was holding back. With a long breath, she let it go. Turning away from him, she gave her full attention to the painting.

Would they be able to travel back if they did not do what they had been sent to do?

"So this is the Guardi. The real thing." She leaned very close to it, examining it as though she could read something in each brushstroke.

"It is," he said, taking her lead. "Painted around 1780 and brought from Italy two years later. One of his classic scenes of the Grand Canal in Venice."

"You will note that it is still here. Not given away, stolen or otherwise lost. Not yet anyway."

"That in itself is intriguing, isn't it? It means that someone noticed it was gone almost as soon as it disappeared."

"Of course they would."

"No, Amy. Think about it. It's one of a dozen paintings in this room. That big one over the fireplace is the focal point. It could be missing for days, even weeks before someone noticed it was gone. You know how that is."

"Okay. That's happened to me a few times. I guess it's possible. So what do we do now, my lord earl?"

"Watch and wait, I guess."

"And you're sure the last time anyone saw it was in this room?"

"That's what Stepp's records indicate."

"You started to talk about that in your study. So the house steward kept a written record?"

"Right."

"And you still have it?" At his nod she went on, "Wow. That is so cool. Can I see it when we get back?"

"Sweetheart," he said with a teasing edge in his tone, "when we're back in our time you can sleep with it if you want."

She grinned at the thought, or was it because she was thinking of sleeping with him rather than the household record? He smiled back. One could only hope.

"So," she said, moving away from him. "Stepp would make notations in the book?"

"Yes, it covered all manner of household incidents. If a glass was broken, or if dry rot was found. The item listed before the painting is about the dismissal of a servant after an 'accident.' There is a notation that the painting is missing on April 10, 1805, and the next item is a discussion of spring plantings in the kitchen garden and some changes to be made."

"You have a darn good memory."

"I've looked at that page a hundred times."

"The fact that there is no additional information would argue for the earl intervening. In this little kingdom, the earl is head of state and no one questions him."

"Right."

"So that means the painting will disappear within the next few days. How do we solve a mystery that hasn't happened yet?"

"Spend a lot of time in this room while we figure out who we should give the coin to?"

"Simon," she said as though his suggestion was one a five-year-old would make, "you're joking, aren't you?"

"What do you think we should do? Start a full-scale investigation before it even goes missing?"

"No, it's only that if we're hanging around here no one will come to take it away."

"Right." Simon covered his face with his hands. "I feel a headache starting."

"You don't mean to prevent the disappearance, do you?"

There was a small commotion outside, and Simon walked to the window.

"I mean, you want to know what happened to it?"

"Right. Right," he said as a man rode into the yard leading a horse. Simon closed his eyes as he thought about Amy's question. "So, we go about our daily routine, whatever that is, and check on the painting every few hours."

"I'm not sure that will make it any easier to figure out who took it."

"Of course it will." He turned his back on the horse and rider to watch her look at the painting. He loved the little tendrils of hair that escaped her attempt to control it. They tickled her neck at the exact spot he next wanted to kiss.

He was quiet too long and she looked over her shoulder. There was that smile again. He could read her mind as surely as she could read his. He stayed right where he was. For now.

"It will be easier to find out who took it," he said. "For one thing, the household will be talking about it when it does disappear. There will be rumors even if Stepp says the earl took it. And you, as Lady Anne's companion, will be in the perfect spot to hear it all, above, and below stairs."

"So our plan is to be on the lookout for the coin and to watch out for any gossip about the missing painting?"

"Right." There was a knock at the door before Simon could say anything else.

It was Fancett. He did not so much as look at Amy. "My lord, Stepp asked me to tell you that your new horse has arrived. It's being settled in the stable and everyone is awaiting your arrival."

The valet stepped out and as he turned he did glance at Amy. His expression was so impassive that Simon was sure he knew exactly what the man was thinking. There might be ten feet between the earl and Miss Stevens, but hormones were singing in the air. Ah well, the man was his valet and was surely used to less than discreet aristocratic behavior. Hopefully, he was snob enough not to share the gossip below stairs.

"Does part of his job description include being a condescending jerk?" Amy walked over to the looking glass near the door. He saw her wince at her reflection and begin fiddling with the pins that held her hair. He could not look away. When their eyes met in the mirror, he saw her smile.

"You are a minx, you know that."

She faced him and blew him a kiss. "I suppose we shall see each other at dinner, will we not?" Without waiting for an answer, she opened the door, paused, and then closed it again.

"One more thing, my lord. Who is Lord Allbryce Stevens?"

"Stevens? A bloke I met at University. His family lives in the Orkneys and I'm pretty sure the title dates back beyond time."

"That is so weird, Simon. I told Lady Anne and her maid that I'm from the Orkneys and I don't even know where they are."

"Off the north coast of Scotland. So not likely Lord Bryce will turn up here."

"It's weird, Simon," Amy insisted.

"Weird does not make it magic."

"You know," she said, putting her hands on her hips, "I would think that after time traveling to 1805 the idea of magic in the cosmos would be a little more believable."

He put his arm through hers and tugged her through the door. They left the room laughing, the sound echoing up the stairway.

Seven

Even with the door to the small music room closed, Amy could hear the pianoforte. Passion was the word that came to mind and she found it hard to believe that the aristocratic snob she had met upstairs was capable of such feeling.

Indeed she was. Lost in the music, she did not seem aware that Amy had entered the music room. A moment later, Amy heard someone else enter the room and turned to see Simon, who came to stand beside her.

When Lady Anne finished the piece, she raised her head to the ceiling with her eyes closed. The power of the music swam in the air around them and she seemed to draw in what energy she had lost with one deep breath.

She stood up, twirled around, and curtseyed to their applause.

"That was wonderful, Anne."

"Thank you, Weston," she said with a sincere smile.

One of the footmen came in to tell the earl, again, that his newest horse had arrived and the groom was awaiting him at the stable.

"Tell him he will have to wait a little longer." As he spoke, Simon gave his attention to Lady Anne, missing the look of complete surprise on the footman's usually impassive face.

"Did you not hear him, brother?" Anne asked. "Your new horse is here."

"Yes, yes," Simon answered irritably. "The horse will still be there in twenty minutes. For now I should like to hear you play something else."

"Weston, are you feeling quite well? The last time I played you were restless after five minutes."

"That was before Miss Stevens told me how important music is to you. You have only to play that piece and all London will be at your feet."

"Oh nonsense. How do you know? You are deaf as a post when it comes to anything musical."

He was? There were so many pitfalls when you were trying to be someone else.

"You have been at the brandy already, haven't you?"

Talk about a woman who could not accept a compliment. Amy decided that Simon needed rescuing and abandoned her attempt to try to blend in to the wall, as any good paid companion should.

"I am sure Lady Anne appreciates your praise." Amy turned to her patron and knew at once that she had made a mistake.

"I do not need lessons in conduct from you, Miss Stevens," she said stiffly. "You are not my governess."

"That was rude, too, Anne," her brother added.

"Indeed," she said, the lady of consequence triumphing over the artist. She curtseyed to her brother, as formally as if they had just met. "Thank you for the extravagant compliment, Weston. I shall treasure it always." She sat down again at the pianoforte. "Now if you will leave me, I am going to continue my practice."

With a bow and a curtsey, they left the room.

"I'd best go to the stable to see the blasted new horse the earl has spent too much money on."

Amy turned to face him. "Footmen have ears," she whispered. "Play your role." And then added in a louder voice, "May I walk part of the way with you? Lady Anne asked me to see if the roses were ready to be cut."

As they made their way to the front door, the sound of the pianoforte reached them again. This time it was Beethoven. Angry, almost vicious music left no doubt of Lady Anne's mood. Well, Amy thought, at least the footman would be entertained.

"No doubt about it, that was my first big mistake," Amy said. "I am not her governess."

"Not to worry. You don't have to face a job eval. That kind of reaction to criticism is a family trait. You're all but asking for a bloody nose if you tell my brother Will that he's driving badly or drinking too much. I, of course, am exempt from all the West failings."

"Of course, my lord." She was sure he was joking. Pretty sure. "I wonder how her governess handled it. A shame she's gone."

"You will find a way back into her good graces. Now toss those worries away and run off to the garden to check the roses, which, by the way, are nowhere near blooming. I think you must have misspoken and meant tulips."

"Indeed I did." She watched as he walked off and then turned abruptly for the garden. *Please, let no one see me looking at him as though he were a god.*

"Fine figure of a man, is he not?"

An old, old woman was tottering down the pathway, coming from the garden. A maid followed her, a basket filled with the tulips that Amy was supposedly on her way to inspect.

"I beg your pardon." Amy curtseyed, sure that no matter her station, a woman this old deserved the courtesy.

"My nephew," she said, nodding toward the now distant

figure. "The earl is my nephew. His father was the second earl's brother. The second Earl of Weston was my husband."

The genealogy was hardly confusing; still, it took Amy a second to reason out who this woman was: the Dowager Countess of Weston. How many more of the earl's relatives called Westmoreland home?

Amy curtseyed again. "How do you do, my lady."

"We had no children and so William inherited."

How disappointing for them. What did one say to a woman who had failed at her only responsibility? Providing an heir. No matter how the modern world saw it, the Regency placed the blame squarely on the woman. "I am Amy Stevens, Lady Anne's companion for the Season."

The countess's pleasant smile became a grimace and Amy's own smile stiffened. Yet another supercilious aristocrat. She was beginning to have some sympathy for the French, if not their awful method of ridding themselves of the *aristos*.

"Amy Stevens? What happened to Miss Kemp? I specifically asked Mrs. Braintree to send her."

"She will come as soon as she can. Miss Kemp was detained." *More likely being held hostage in the twenty-first century. Please, Lady Weston, please leave it at that,* Amy prayed.

"Are you related to the Stevens family? The ones who live in those horrible islands north of Scotland?"

"The Orkneys? Yes, my lady, I am."

"This must seem like Paradise to you then. Does the sun ever shine there?"

"It is lovely here, and I have not been in the Orkneys since I was a child. When my parents died I went to live with my godmother in Yorkshire. It was through her that I came to Mrs. Braintree's attention." Maybe she should try her hand at a novel when this was over. Her imagination was in high gear. She was certainly better off than the earl and Miss Kemp.

"I should like to hear about that." The dowager countess shook her cane at the maid next to her. "Angston, take those flowers to the cutting room. They will wilt if they are not in water soon. You may begin to arrange them. Miss Stevens will give me her arm and I will come to see how you are doing. Then we must dress for dinner."

It was hardly the third degree, but by the time Amy went up to dress for dinner she was exhausted. She lay down on the cot, only for a moment, thinking over the questions fired at her and the answers she returned. The first few were easy: How old was she? Twenty-four. How had she met Mrs. Braintree? Through the headmistress at the York-shire Academy for Young Ladies. Surely there was one. The other questions were more difficult. Who seemed likely to make a match this Season? Were there any ducal heirs or perhaps a marquis? Yes, always. And the best way to meet them was through the mothers and grandmothers who were the dowager countess's friends.

Quickly, before the dowager could get another question in, Amy had shot one back. "Who did you think we should call on?" It was the perfect question. Soon Amy had a list that would be useful.

Her biggest misstep came when Amy dared suggest that someone with a taste for music might be most suitable.

"Making the right match is not about who likes to hear music in the evening, it is about increasing position and power. You know that as well as anyone, Miss Stevens."

Amy fell asleep wondering how she was supposed to know that. Because she had no position or power except what was given her by her employer? How could servants stand that kind of dictatorship?

She dreamed of a world where love and lust were fueled by power, where a man could claim you with only money as a measure of his worth as a husband. Loyalty, honesty, generosity meant nothing. Where sex between married strangers was little more than mating to ensure the same game would be played by the next generation. It was a nightmare.

"Miss, miss, you must wake up."

Amy surfaced from the heavy, too-short nap.

"It's Martha, miss. I have your dress and am sorry I have taken so long. I promise you will not be late."

• The maid hurried her through her toilette and then led her down to the dining room.

Simon was waiting, as were the rest of the dinner guests. He did not look at her as she came in. A well-dressed man had his complete attention. Amy guessed that the woman beside him must be his wife.

Stepp announced dinner the moment she arrived. It saved her the effort of trying to figure out whether she should simply sit unobtrusively or join the conversation as an equal. More than one person had made it clear she was not.

The group that sat for dinner was eclectic. The earl, the dowager countess, and Lady Anne were to be expected. Besides herself, there were five others, all unknown to her though it was easy enough to figure them out. There was the portrait artist who wore his badge of honor—a smear of paint on the collar of his cravat. Then there was a hearty man, dressed in a flamboyant style. He was introduced as a cousin who acted as the estate librarian. Judging by his appearance, he seemed an unlikely bibliophile.

There was one more relative, the first earl's brother, a very old man, who held the title of chaplain.

The estate steward and his wife made up the last of the group. They were a delightful couple who seemed on comfortable terms with the family. Mr. Smithson was the gentleman Simon had been talking to when she came into the room. He had the Weston smile, which left little doubt in Amy's mind that he was some relation to the family.

By the time the ladies left the gentlemen to their port, it was clear that despite the egalitarian nature of the meal, everyone knew whether they belonged above or below the salt. She followed the ladies into the large music room and found a corner where she could observe.

This world did not seem to welcome strangers with neither money nor rank. She had known that from her novels, but living it was decidedly frustrating.

Was the British aristocracy still like that? Or had the tax structure and industrialism been the great equalizers? As fascinated as she was by Simon West, she could not imagine living in a world where your value hinged on something less than ability.

Conversation was desultory while the ladies sipped tea. The dowager countess prosed on about the virtuous Miss Kemp, while Lady Anne played some light, vapid tunes, even as she absorbed every word her aunt was saying.

It was Mrs. Smithson who came to sit beside Amy. "As you can tell from our dinner companions, the earl is very kind to his relations and his staff. He will not turn you off without finding another post for you."

Which translated to "he might be a dictator but he is a benevolent one." "Do you think that is what will happen? Is the dowager countess deliberately undermining my influence with Lady Anne?"

"Yes," she answered bluntly. "For all her charm, the dowager countess is willful and still wants things run her way. The earl has made it clear that the estate is his. Lady Anne is in a tug-of-war between them."

Amy did not know whether to be worried or not. Hopefully her stay would be short enough that she would not become a point of contention between the countess and her supposed nephew.

The gentlemen joined them for tea, the earl the last one to come into the room. He ignored her and for a moment Amy worried that it was the real earl and not Simon. She tried to catch his eye and when she did he winked at her. It made her smile and she pursed her lips when she saw the librarian looking from one to the other of them.

The arrival of the men was a signal of sorts. Lady Anne stopped playing and the whole evening sped up. Fresh tea arrived instantly and in less than thirty minutes it was gone and the good-nights were said.

It was not yet bedtime. What did people do? She decided that with the moon still full she would take a few moments to walk outside. Her brief almost-visit to the garden had been all she had seen of the estate grounds.

With a word to Martha Stepp and her assurance that Lady Anne would be playing in the small music room, Amy grabbed a shawl and found her way to the side door that opened onto a patio and down to a path that would ensure she would not get lost.

A moment later, she heard someone behind her. Her dress was the color of the leaves so she stepped into the trees and watched to see who it was. Simon came along, not in a hurry, but moving as though he was looking for her.

"Simon," she whispered, "I'm over here."

He turned sharply.

She stepped away from the tree and curtseyed. "Is it not a perfectly gorgeous evening?" She drew a deep breath of the sweet spring air. "It feels like twenty-first-century Ireland on a good day."

He laughed, drawing a deep breath himself. "Clean, and sweet, with only a hint of damp. You're right."

She went to him and they fell into step together.

"And quiet," she continued. "So blessedly quiet. Without that constant hum of electricity, not to mention leaf blowers, and traffic. I think the quiet is my favorite part." She stopped and spoke to his back. "How did you know where I was?" she asked, only slightly distracted by his broad shoulders and the way his Regency-era jacket emphasized his fine body.

"I asked and one of the footmen told me he had seen you leave," he said, facing her.

"Can anyone keep any secrets here?" They looked back toward the house where they would still be visible from the upper-floor windows. They resumed walking.

"So far we've done pretty well."

"Think about it, Simon. Westmoreland is huge, but one is rarely alone. Footmen and the rest of the gang of servants outnumber the residents. Both the servants and your family must feel as though they are always playing before an audience. And after a while it becomes second nature. How often do the people here let their true selves show? This experience has completely ruined my fantasy of Regency life."

"Which was?" he prompted.

"A world where the ladies shopped and drank tea and had nothing more to worry about than what novel to read next." She twisted a flower from a stem and twirled it as they walked. "Now I know that in between tea parties they worried about producing an heir, whether they would catch pox from their faithless husbands, if their children would survive infancy . . ."

"Except for the particulars, it's the same in our time." Simon took the flower from her and tucked it in her hair. "You have one face for the world and keep your worries to yourself."

"Like you did when you thought I was a con artist."

"Right. Both of us have a lot to learn about each other, don't you think? Secrets to share, if you will. Which only goes to prove that details may change, but man remains the same."

They came to a fork in the path and Simon nodded to the left. "This way, it's a bit of a walk but worth it." The turning put an end to their conversation. Amy marveled at the way he listened to her, treated her ideas as though they had merit.

Moonlight lit the way, the treed path giving way to a clear hillside. Now she could see their destination.

"It looks like the Jefferson Memorial!"

"I guess it does," he said. "It's called a 'folly.' "

"Oh! I've read about them. I've always wanted to see one."

She ran a little ahead of him. He slowed and watched as she stopped in front of it. In her green dress she stood out against the moon-bright white of the folly, the slight breeze pressing her clothes against her. With her hands clasped together she looked like a windswept supplicant before the temple of a god.

He wanted her. He wanted all of her. Her mind, always questioning, always interested. Her heart, so open and generous, and her body, so soft, so welcoming. He had always made light of his parents' story—now he understood how it could happen.

When he was beside her, he waited a moment, watching her watch the play of light on the façade. Finally, she looked his way, and he decided to tell her exactly what was on his mind.

Eight

"Did you know that my father proposed to my mother on the night they met?"

"Really?"

He could tell by her smile that she thought that was romantic.

"What did she say?"

"That's not the point," he said, hoping he didn't sound too much like a teacher correcting a student. "The thing is that he knew the minute he met her that she was the one."

"Which means she said no to him."

"True, but now that he's gone she tells us that she wasted two whole months that they could have been together."

Amy was quiet for about a second. But not silent. Her eyes told him as surely as words that she understood the feeling. She spoke with a laugh. "Wow, that's off the chart on the romantic scale. And you might be right about it not taking more than a touch to know you've found the one. You have to admit, though, these are not the usual boy-meets-girl circumstances."

He walked up the steps, into the folly's one room. He could hear Amy following him. When he faced her, she was looking out over the vista, down to the river. "You're right about that. This is not the usual. As a matter of fact, I can't recall anything as strange. Except that time I drove by this outdoor photo shoot. It was the middle of winter and a Victoria's Secret model in a teddy jumped into my car and told me to turn the heat up."

"Awful pun." Amy let go of the vista and gave him her full attention as she grimaced, then laughed out loud.

He loved that laugh, so he went on. "I proposed to her right away, like my dad had. Didn't work. So I learned my lesson and am waiting until we know each other for at least a few hours."

"You can't be serious."

"Oh yes, I am. After that first kiss, is there any doubt left?"

"Just a little," she said, wrapping her arms around his neck.

He'd always thought that love would blind him to all but the beloved. He had never understood that it would be all-consuming in a completely different way. With her body pressed against his, her mouth teasing him with kisses along his neck, all he could think of was Amy Stevens. No other woman came to mind, no other love tickled his memory. Amy was his touchstone and his world.

She pressed her lips to his and his thoughts were flooded with a storm of sensations. There was nothing but the feel of her, the taste, the scent, the gift. It swirled though his brain, his body, his heart.

Holding her back in his arms, her breasts pressed against him, he could barely hear her over the thunder of his need. He lowered his head and kissed the sweet, smooth skin where the bodice of her dress barely covered her breasts. Her moan was all the encouragement he needed.

He pushed the dress down and edged the chemise aside.

Her welcome was a sound of pure delight that enchanted him, made him want to give endlessly. They shared the pleasure of learning the other's secrets, undressing each other; their own heat was warmth enough even on this cool evening.

It was magic and madness until need eclipsed feeling.

"There's no bed here, Amy."

"We'll find one next time. Please don't stop," she begged.

He smiled as he used his jacket to protect her from the cold stone wall at her back, promised more with a kiss and filled her with passion as fully as his heart filled her with love.

The night wrapped them with its quiet. Simon matched his breathing to hers, felt the beat of her heart, the warmth of her around him, and knew a moment of perfection. No words were needed, as a lifetime of possibilities opened before him.

"I noticed you the minute you came through the pub door. When you ignored the football game and sat down I thought I knew it was more than looks. Amy, that was even before I saw the coin."

"Your smile, Simon. It was your smile that made me think that I wanted more from you than a few words."

They shared kisses with their confessions, but Simon could feel the air cooling and knew that they had to find their clothes and walk back to the house.

Dressing in unfamiliar clothes in the dark was a process as absurd as it was arousing. By the time Amy had her stays tied and had helped Simon into his close-fitting jacket, they were both cursing and laughing and swearing that valets and maids earned every pound of their pay.

As they walked back to the house, Simon suggested a plan. "At least it is fully dark. Less chance of discovery. You go in through the large music room. Can you find your way from there?"

She nodded.

"I'll go on down to the barn and check on the status of my new horse. He really is a beautiful animal," he said as he turned her to face him. He smoothed her hair and drew the shawl around her. "Much too high strung for my tastes. Good to know that the third earl died in his sixties from a lung inflammation and not as the result of a riding accident. I'll see if I can surprise any of the grooms gambling."

He kissed her, a quick touch on her lips, the kind any longtime couple would share. It was anything but casual for her, reviving every fine memory of the last hour. She could feel him watching her to the door, where she turned to wave him on.

It could not be much later than nine o'clock, not what one usually thought of as the dead of night, but the house seemed so still and quiet it might as well be midnight. As she made her way past the library, she saw the light under the door and wondered who was still up or if the light was left on until the earl retired.

The stairs were a gray marble and easy to see. She skipped up them quick and quiet. The sound of the pianoforte drifted from the small music room and Amy knew that Lady Anne was still practicing. Was the endless practice her way of finding privacy? Where did she escape to in her music?

One more long hallway and she was at the door to Lady Anne's suite of rooms. She might not be Lady Anne's maid, but she thought it would be best if she remained dressed and available until she came up for bed. There was a full mirror in the corner of her sitting room and Amy used it to make sure she did not look as though she had just come from a romantic tryst.

No amount of hair brushing or shaking of her skirts could erase the softness from her eyes or the fullness of her lips, and if she did not stop smiling, she would be called a simpleton.

She found a chair in Lady Anne's sitting room, near the single lit candle, leaned back, closed her eyes, and yawned, part glorious fatigue and part the exhaustion that came with dealing with the oddest day of her life.

I wish we could find that coin. Simon could give it to Martha to give to the earl and they could find a way home. She picked up the book that was at hand. It was a work of art in itself. Lovely leather binding in dark blue, lovely gilt edging on the pages. Before she could do more than admire the workmanship, the sound of arguing came from the bedroom. Amy recognized Martha Stepp's voice. The other was definitely not Lady Anne.

"I found it. I found it on the floor in the conservatory and it's mine. It's no proper coin anyway."

"It may well be yours, Florrie, but we must ask the earl first. Give it to me."

"You are not the housekeeper. I doan have to."

"Florrie! Give it to me, this minute."

"I wish you would get what you deserve, Martha Stepp!"

As Amy made sense of the conversation she was out of her seat and at the door as quickly as possible, still too late to prevent the wish. The moment before she pushed through the bedroom door, the other door opened and Lady Anne came into the sitting room.

"And on whom, may I ask, are you eavesdropping?"

"No one, Lady Anne. They were arguing and I wanted to see if I could help them."

The bedroom door opened and Florrie raced out of the room, her apron raised to cover her face. Even with that protection, the sound of gulping tears was unmistakable.

"What is this, Martha?" Lady Anne asked at her most demanding.

Martha was red-faced. "I'm so sorry, my lady. Miss Stevens. This is not the place for such a thing. I do beg your pardon."

"For what, Martha?" Amy asked. "Florrie ran out of the room in tears. Surely that was not your fault."

"She found a coin today and insisted it was hers. I told her that she had to first show it to Mr. Stepp and the earl to be sure it was not of some importance to them or one of the guests."

"Where is this coin?"

Martha came toward her, but as she handed it over she bumped the small side table. The music sheets that Martha had left there earlier in the day fluttered off and into the fire. It did not take Lady Anne's cry of distress to make Martha reach into the flames to rescue them. Amy was one step behind, but could do nothing when Martha dropped the flaming music sheets. They fell on the chair nearest the table. Lady Anne's nightrobe was there and it and the chair began to flame.

Amy grabbed the flower vase from a table nearest the window and poured the contents, both tulips and water, on the fire, stopping it before it had a chance to spread. The final insult was the splash of water that soaked the hem of Lady Anne's elegant evening dress.

"That is the last straw, Martha Stepp. You are dismissed. Clean this mess up and pack your things."

Martha looked stricken. Her face went white. "Yes, my lady" was all she said.

"But Lady Anne, it was an accident." It was too unfair to blame Martha, Amy thought.

Anne would have nothing to do with her either. "You might as well pack your things and leave tomorrow, too, Miss Stevens. I will wait for Miss Kemp. The last thing I want is a companion who listens at doors or one who does not know who pays her wages."

The coin lay on the floor, twinkling as it always did. Amy was beginning to wonder if it was a *cursed* coin and not a magic one. For surely what Martha deserved in Florrie's mind was not fair at all. Despite the fact that she was still learning to be a lady's maid, Martha's loyalty and good nature were unteachable assets.

Following the maid's lead, Amy curtseyed. "As you wish, my lady. Please, though, the coin is mine."

"It is?"

"Yes, it was a gift from my father." Oh right, she forgot, her father was dead. "He gave it to me before he died. It must have fallen out of my bag this morning."

Martha picked up the coin and made to hand it to her. Lady Anne put her hand out. "I will take it and give it to the earl in the morning. He can decide whose it is."

Yes! Amy bit her lip to keep from saying it out loud. She could handle being fired if she thought the coin was finally going to wind up in the right hands.

"You can gather your things in the morning, Miss Stevens. Go and have Stepp find someplace else for you to sleep."

Martha was near tears and left the room without another word. Amy made her way down the front stairs more frustrated than worried. Poor Martha Stepp. With her hopes of being housekeeper so thoroughly crushed, what would she do? How could Florrie have made such a stupid wish? And above all, why had the coin granted a wish that was so wrong, would bring so much pain?

What she needed to do now was find Simon. He was the earl. He could rehire Martha. And she could tell him that they could return home. She would go to his bedroom if she had to. Brave Fancett's superciliousness. It didn't matter to her what he thought. Or it shouldn't.

She stopped at the massive front door, with its smaller inset door, and asked the still bright-eyed porter if the earl had returned from the stables.

"No, miss," he said, touching his forelock. "I won't be off duty until he goes up to bed. Then I can lock the door, check all the other locks, report to Mr. Stepp, and go to me own bed. Let the night porter start his rounds."

"Thank you." She made her way to the stairs, stopping at the first landing, just out of sight. She leaned against the pillar, then sank down onto the stair, all the elation draining from her. It was positively selfish to be so happy when almost everyone in this house was miserable.

Waiting was torture. Oh, she wished he would hurry. She was having a staring contest with a statue when she heard the small door swing open. She peeked around the column and saw Simon step through.

He and the porter exchanged a few words that had Simon searching the stairs. With a final good-night, he hurried up the steps two at a time, stopping short when he saw her.

She jumped up. "Simon—!"

He pressed a finger against her lips and took her hand. "Let's go to the library."

When they reached the top of the stairs, Simon checked to make sure that the hall was empty. With a sign from him that all was clear, they tiptoed into the room and she burst out laughing. "I feel like I'm a teenager looking for a place to make out. Not that I ever did that."

He swooped her into his arms and kissed her like a pirate claiming a prize. When he let her go, they were breathless. "You are a liar or a natural-born kisser."

Amy pressed her hand to her chest and opened her mouth, hoping she had enough breath to talk. "Simon, listen, I found the coin!"

He handed her the small glass of brandy he had just poured and, as he quickly filled another, proposed a toast. "Here's to Amy Stevens!" he sang out. "What a woman."

I wish that were true. She put the glass on the table. "Simon, we have to find a way to leave. We've already had too big an influence on your family's history." She gave him a brief account of what had happened upstairs.

He shook his head.

"Don't you see—?"

"You're the one who doesn't see, dear heart. Time travel

is not some chance event. We're supposed to be here as surely as the dowager countess, the artist, everyone who is originally a part of this time and place. We're as real as they are. What is happening now is exactly as it should be."

"How do you know that?"

"Arbuckle told us. He said that there are certain things that are meant to be. Man decides how and when they will happen. We are meant to be. The proof of that is you and me. Do you have any doubt that we were destined to be together?"

"No, but I do think there might have been an easier way to do it. And if that's true, then Martha will get what she truly deserves."

"We've done our job and now we go back so the earl can claim the coin." He sat down and patted the seat next to him. "Sit here and visualize where you want to be."

His lack of concern about Martha was like a knife. How could he not be worried about someone who had been wronged! Would it be possible to love someone, build a relationship with him, if his values were so different? Were they moving too fast?

"Both of us have to do this, Amy." He spoke gently as if he thought her hurt look was pain at the thought of leaving.

"You think it will be that easy?" she asked as she sat close to him, but not touching.

"I think so. I am fairly certain that this settee is the one that is in my study, recovered and rebuilt once or twice."

She looked at the slightly worn cushions. "Okay, though I do feel bad if some ancestor of your friend Allbryce Stevens comes to visit. My name is mud in 1805."

"He can disown you, say you were a connection the family does not recognize because of your poor work performance or your loose morals or whatever."

Is that the way it worked in his social circle? Were servants like the Stepps the only people in whom one found loyalty?

"Then there is poor Mrs. Braintree, who came to call on me in Yorkshire."

"I feel confident that Miss Kemp will completely restore her into the family's good graces."

Amy looked around the room, trying to take in all the details. She had not even been here long enough to write down any of her impressions. Not even twenty-four hours. She should have written down the names of all the paintings. Oh, the painting! How could they have forgotten? "Simon! We won't find out what happened to the Guardi!"

Nine

"I thought of that," he said, nodding. "Obviously it wasn't the right wish." He squeezed her hand. "My other wish, the one I hope the coin will grant, is much more important." He let her go without further explanation. "It's time to go home. We have a life to live there."

The study in London in her time was easy to visualize. She let the room fill her thoughts, the stack of books, the one on the East India Company, the portrait of the third earl, the sleek computer. The huge windows. The smell of old books and history, the constant buzz of London life just outside the window. Would the docent be waiting? It would be so good to be home again.

Nothing happened.

She opened her eyes, terrified that Simon had gone and she had been left behind. No, he was sitting beside her, his hands on his knees, as real as the cushions on which they were sitting.

"What did we do wrong?" she asked.

"I don't know."

"It felt wrong. I was so tired when we traveled before I couldn't keep my eyes open."

"Right. Same here."

"What did we forget?" She wasn't afraid. Not with Simon beside her. "Do we need the coin?"

"No, the docent was quite clear about that. The docent's wish was to find how the coin reached the Regency. We've done that. It makes no sense for us to bring it back to the present."

They sat next to each other, now holding hands. It wouldn't be the worst thing in the world if they had to stay here. Yes, it would. She could not stand living in the same house as these small-minded, status-conscious people.

"Could it be . . ." Simon's words came out slowly, as though he was still piecing the thought together. ". . . Could it be that just as we switched places with people so as not to distort the relationship of mass and space and time, things must also switch places?"

"I guess it could be," she said, after thinking about it for a second.

"What? *Stargate Atlantis* never covered that?"

"No," she said, more touched than embarrassed that he remembered that silly explanation. "But your theory makes sense. Our clothes didn't come with us."

"The coin did."

"All right," Amy said, "so what matters is that the coin is here and we have to take something back with us so we do not cause space and time to come crashing down."

"Now there's a nonscientific explanation that totally works for me."

"So all we have to do is pick something to take back with us. No one would miss a comb or a brush."

"Right, and we could donate it to the Regency museum."

"Or, Simon, you could sell it and use the money to keep Westmoreland in good repair. You know, the eating pence and pounds thing?" She looked at the painting and the idea hit her so hard that she jumped up from the settee and gasped. "The painting, Simon! We are the ones who took the painting."

"What?"

"Yes, don't you see? We exchanged the coin for the painting. Your family can sell it if you want and have all the money you will ever need to keep Westmoreland in repair and in the family."

"It's too much like stealing."

He was tempted, she could tell, even as he shook his head.

"It is not. Besides, we have to take it. It was meant to be. Don't you understand? It's exactly as you said before. We are as much a part of this time and place as the earl and his aunt and Lady Anne and all the rest."

Simon nodded and then shook his head. "How will I explain that I found a Guardi painting?"

"You've been researching all year, for heaven's sake. Tell them that the earl brought it to town and put it in a safe place and then forgot about it. It's possible, isn't it? It wasn't worth millions of pounds then."

"Still, it's a stretch."

"We can make it work. It's been owned by your family for more than two hundred years. Lost and now found. Its provenance is not in question. Its validity can be sworn to. They can test forever and all they will be able to prove is that it's a Guardi painting."

"You might be right. If we leave it here there is a good chance that the useless fifth earl will sell it. He sold everything else that wasn't entailed." He reached up and took the painting off the wall.

"It will look perfect in your study," she said, "in that space to the right of the door." She could see it quite clearly in her mind's eye. "You'll see it every time you leave the room."

She heard his "Yes, I can see it there, too," but was so overcome with fatigue that she sank onto the nearest chair and fell asleep before she could reply.

There was no mistaking the sounds of London at night. A distant siren, the sound of a trash pickup woke him and the scent of hot tea roused him as surely as a cock crow in the country. It was not daylight yet, even if the city was awake. He could feel Amy beside him. Her eyes were closed, her body restless with a time traveler's dreams. Bits of his dreams persisted, an aching sense of loss, a euphoric victory, despair so deep that death would be easier, the relief of love trumping all. There were no details, only the sensations. Was this his life? Could he be that blessed?

Light from his desk lamp gave the room shape and shadow. He watched as Amy opened her eyes, a long tear moving down her cheek. He kissed it. "We're home, Amy," he whispered and felt the anxiety drop from her. She turned her head and kissed him, still sleepy-eyed. It was more sweetness than desire, more warmth than fire, more love than passion. The perfect welcome home.

The kiss energized them both and they sat up as one. Simon saw the Guardi on the floor, lying face up, looking exactly as it had in the library at Westmoreland.

"Are we alone? Where's Mr. Arbuckle?" Amy asked.

Simon stood up and went to turn up the desk lamp, though he was sure they were the only ones in the room.

"The portrait, Simon. Look."

"What? It looks the same to me." He walked closer to it and tried to see any changes. The coin glimmered— golden—the model train sat nearby, the earl still looked intent. "What do you see that I'm missing?"

"No, no, you're right. Nothing has changed."

He heard the relief in her voice and understood, even as she explained.

"I was so afraid that we had messed with history," she confessed.

He had to admit he was relieved as well. Not that he hadn't believed it when he told her they were meant to be in 1805 as surely as Lady Anne and Fancett were. To his way of thinking, a bit of uncertainty was man's greatest strength, not a weakness.

"Did you make tea for me? How sweet." Amy stood up, stretched, and oh, did the glimpse of her skin distract him. She made her way to the tea table.

"Sorry, not my doing. The smell of it was so familiar that it didn't occur to me to think of it as odd."

Amy raised the pot to the painting. "Thank you, my lord."

"More likely, 'Thank you, Miss Kemp,'" Simon corrected. "I might have only been the earl for twenty hours or so but I can tell you brewing tea would never occur to him."

She poured for both of them and only hesitated a moment before taking a sip. "Tastes normal."

"Right, but if there is a magic elixir in it, don't you think that the sorcerer would be clever enough to have it be tasteless?"

"I saw that episode of *Angel*, too, though I find it hard to believe it's a show you'd be into."

"No, it's not, but a friend of mind had a part. The kind of role where you die before the third commercial."

She sipped the tea. "This is so weird, Simon. We've been to 1805 and back and now we're talking about a television show. Do we just go back to our normal lives?"

"I bet there are records at Westmoreland that have never been studied. I imagine the Stepps have some as well."

He went over and picked up the diary of the nineteenth-century Mr. Stepp. "You do realize that the entry about the 'accident' and the dismissal of the servant was a reference to his daughter, Martha, and the fire." He held out the notebook.

"Wow. Of course," Amy said, taking it from him and holding it against her heart as if it were worth her life to protect. "Where do you think the docent went, Simon? I wish there was a way we could find out."

She went to hand the old notebook back to him when a piece of paper fell from it. Amy picked it up and handed it to Simon with a pained expression on her face. "Did a page fall out?"

"No, this is a letter. One I've never seen before." He scanned it and then smiled. "Amy, listen to this:"

Dear Mr. West and Miss Stevens,

Thank you for your efforts on my behalf. I have been trying to return the magic coin ever since I was given charge of it and failed to see it safely to India. Now I see that returning it to the nineteenth century was not a task meant for me.

I was at the helm when the coins were lost. It is why I was here until now. How could I allow a burst of temper from Mother Nature and my incompetence ruin lives that might have been changed for the better by this special coin?

I knew all the wishes this magic coin had granted, but never knew how the coin was returned to the past. Now I do. Thank you for believing. Now my wish has been granted as well.

With eternal gratitude,
Wentworth C. Arbuckle

They were both silent a long time.

"Do you think he time traveled?" Amy asked.

"Or was he a ghost?"

"That could be. He always did have that fey quality. Like he would disappear until he was needed." Silence settled between them again. Simon was sure that Amy's thoughts were on the docent. His most definitely were not.

"Oh, Simon, I know you don't care that much, but I want to know what happened to Martha. And what did the earl and Miss Kemp do while they were here?"

"What makes you think I don't care?" he asked, as surprised as he was offended.

"You were so casual about the mess we left behind."

"To be honest, at the time I was more worried about us returning to the right place and time." Simon pointed to the painting. "I expect that the earl figured out that investing in trains was a sound financial move. And that miniature. I'll bet money that it's Miss Kemp. As for Martha Stepp, I do care. But it wasn't our job to make her wish come true. Now that we are safe, we can spend the rest of our lives finding out the answers." He put down his cup and took her hand. "Darling girl, listen to me." He took her other hand in his. "*We* is the important word in that sentence. I hope you don't want to go back to your old life any more than I do. Who can I talk to about ghosts and time travel? No one else will believe it." That sounded way too practical. *Don't bugger this, Simon, old boy.* "Amy, I love you. I want you to be part of my life. I want to marry you."

She didn't give it more than two seconds' thought. "No, Simon, I'm so sorry. It wouldn't work. Our lives are too different. Our stay in the Regency proved that to me. You're Simon West of Westmoreland and I'm Amy Stevens from Topeka, Kansas. You go to Ascot and I go to Disney World."

"I've never been to Ascot."

"Then Wimbledon or—"

That was so nonsensical he cut her off. "Amy, I teach kids in one of the worst parts of London, in a school founded to give them a chance. The bartenders at Earl's Place earn more than I do. The only time I've ever seen either prince is on the telly. Our lives are more alike than you think."

She took a step back from him. Skepticism did not become her.

"Right," he conceded. "Don't marry me tomorrow. Hang around a bit, meet my mum. See what my life is like."

The tears in her eyes gave him hope. "I have to leave next week. There's a wedding I can't miss. I'm the maid of honor."

"Then invite me to the wedding. I've always wanted to see the fruited plain. Does Kansas have any amber waves of grain? My school leave ends in three months. What do you say?"

She laughed. "I think you're insane. You thought I was a complete liar when we met and now you want me to marry you. It's too soon. We haven't known each other two days."

"Amy darling, we've been together for two hundred years." And if that did not convince her, his kiss did.

Timeless

Ruth Ryan Langan

To all those old souls who search for truth and love.
And for Tom, my heart and soul.

One

*

"What you are seeing now is the most recent addition to MacLennan Fortress, completed in 1832, though renovations continue even today." The tour guide led the cluster of tourists across highly polished wood floors that gave not a hint of the thousands of visitors that had walked this space since the castle had been opened to the public as a five-star hotel and restaurant. In the upper gallery they strode past portraits of the early lairds of the fierce MacLennan clan.

Laurel Douglas trailed the others, taking time to study the proud, handsome faces of the men, warriors all. Despite the gradual change of clothing, from simple plaid to ornate kilt, and the hundreds of years that separated them, from the earliest laird in the fifteenth century to contemporary times, all bore a striking resemblance to one another. Whether fierce, proud, or simply amused, there was a haughty bearing and a defiant glint in the eyes that said each was aware of his position, and completely, utterly comfortable with himself.

Laurel still couldn't believe she was here in the Scottish Highlands. It had been a dream for so long, since her grandmother had lulled her to sleep with tales of noble warriors and beautiful maidens. Though her grandmother had left her native Scotland as a child, her love of the land of her birth had never faded. She'd filled her only granddaughter's head with visions of fog-shrouded lochs where monsters swam deep beneath the murky waters, and castle ruins guarded ancient secrets.

Just days ago, after a year in the planning, it had looked as though Laurel's dream trip would be canceled. After working her way up the corporate ladder in New York City's commercial real estate, a field dominated by men, she'd been persuaded to take her first real vacation in years. She had planned to go with her best friend, Chloe Kerr, who had handled all their reservations, from the airline tickets to the rental car to the hotel.

Then came Chloe's frantic midnight call to relate a family emergency.

"Laurel, it's my mother. She's been rushed to the hospital. They say it's her heart. They're talking about a bypass, if the stent won't work. I'm really sorry, but I have to be here."

"Of course you do." Laurel paused, twirling a strand of hair around her finger as she always did when she was thinking. "I'll call and see if the airline will allow us to reschedule."

"But you've already blocked this time off work."

Laurel was thinking the same thing, but declined to mention it. She glanced at her appointment calendar. So many clients had been rescheduled to accommodate this longed-for vacation. None of them would be pleased if asked to change yet again. "Look, Chloe, things like this happen. You know my motto: There's no such thing as an accident. It's all part of some grand plan in the universe. There's nothing to be done about it. We'll go another time."

"You know better than that, Laurel. It took me years to talk you into this. I can't even imagine how long it will take to get you to agree again. You didn't even go on our senior trip."

"My grandmother was sick."

"And after all those years of study at the university, you blew off graduation to go to work."

"I didn't have anybody there to cheer for me anyway." Laurel sighed. "We've been through all this before, Chloe. What's the big deal?"

"This trip is the big deal. You planned your entire year around these next two weeks. I can't stand knowing that you're going to miss this, too." There was a pause. "You could go alone." Her friend's voice wavered. "I know it won't be as much fun traveling solo, but at least you'll get to see and do all the things we've planned."

"It won't be any fun without you."

"I'd feel the same way. But I'll feel even worse if you stay home because of me. We've talked of nothing else for so long now. Please, Laurel. At least give it some thought."

After hanging up, Laurel brooded. The money she would have to forfeit on the airline and hotel fees didn't matter, but the hassle of time on her hands with no clients to deal with did matter. She'd go mad with nothing to do and time on her hands. Why not go ahead as planned? She'd be just fine traveling to Scotland alone. It wasn't what she'd hoped for, but then, she mused, how much in life actually went according to plan? Besides, wasn't she really good at being alone? She'd had plenty of experience.

She'd lost her parents when she was six, and had been raised by her grandmother. At eighteen she'd vowed on her grandmother's grave that she would make her proud. To that end, after earning her business degree, she'd spent the past ten years working her way up the corporate ladder. There'd been no time for such things as romance, courtship, marriage. Oh, there'd been the occasional interlude with a coworker, or a friend of a friend, and she would wonder if this would be the one to change her life forever. But in time, as if by mutual consent, they would drift apart and move on. Laurel never looked back. And certainly never grieved the loss of something she'd never even had. She was very good at living her life on her own terms.

If, at times, she felt a twinge of regret at the things she'd had to sacrifice for success, she was able to nudge it aside. She made a very good living while enjoying a satisfying career. She had a circle of friends she could count on, and an enthusiasm for life that was the envy of all who knew her. That was enough to fill her life.

Her thoughts were interrupted by one of their tour group, a retired bank president from St. Louis. "What about a tour of the castle ruins and the ancient tower?"

Laurel nodded in agreement. That was what she wanted, more than anything. It was her fondest wish to walk through the ancient ruins. To get a sense of those who had lived and died here. After a lifetime of reading about them, she wanted a closer look.

Their leader shook his head. "Because of its age and fragile condition, we no longer allow tours of the original bones of the old castle and the tunnels beneath. It was built in the fifteenth century by the laird of the MacLennan clan, Conal MacLennan, who was called Con the Mighty by both his friends and his enemies. Though we don't permit an actual tour of his early home, if you'll follow me along this hallway, I'll take you up to the adjoining tower. It offers an excellent view of the ruins below, and the Highlands spread out around it. In the tower room we offer a detailed map of the ancient castle as it once looked. For as far as the eye can see, this land once belonged to the Clan MacLennan, some of Scotland's finest and fiercest Highland warriors."

While the others moved ahead, Laurel stopped to study

the portrait of Conal MacLennan. Now there was a warrior. His arms and torso were bare, revealing a body corded with muscles. He wore nothing more than a length of plaid, belted at the waist by a leather scabbard. In his hand was a jewel-encrusted sword. His forehead was broad; his features so perfect they could have been chiseled from stone. His eyes stared into hers with such intensity, she couldn't look away. She marveled at the ancient artist who had captured his likeness so perfectly.

She trailed the others to a circular staircase. Up ahead she could hear the voice of their guide.

"If you'll look to your left, you'll see through that window the crumbling ruins of the original tower. It's said that Con's beloved wife fell or was pushed from that tower during a siege. Her body was never found, and the great laird of the MacLennan clan vowed to move heaven and earth to find her."

Laurel heard a woman ask the question they all wanted answered. "Did he succeed?"

The tour guide's voice drifted back. "Rumor has it that he roams the Highlands still."

Laurel shivered before her attention was caught by an ancient tapestry that hung along the staircase. It must have been nearly ten feet high, and at least as wide. Their guide had said that all the tapestries in the castle had been made by the women who once lived here.

Since needlework had been one of the skills her grandmother had passed along to her, Laurel found herself tracing her finger over the delicate scrolls and circles and marveling at the patience of the women who had created such a work of art by hand.

She could imagine them sitting around the fireplace at night, heads bent, working needle and thread through the wool, forming the intricate patterns while their men sharpened the blades of their broadswords and dirks, and spoke in low tones of war.

What must life have been like in those primitive times, with the threat of invasion always hanging over them? Did the women weep when their men went off to battle? Or were they stoic, holding back their tears until they were alone in their beds?

Laurel thought of her grandmother, fueling a child's imagination with bedtime tales that were both thrilling and romantic.

As Laurel started to turn away, a drop of moisture landed on the toe of her white beaded sandal. She noted with disgust that a dark stain had begun to spread in an ever-widening circle. She looked up, but could see nothing leaking from above. Bending, she touched a finger to the warm, sticky spot, and was stunned when she realized what it was.

Blood!

Where had it come from?

Curious, she took hold of the edge of the tapestry and moved it aside. It had been cleverly hung to hide a niche in the wall. At first Laurel thought the figure in the recessed area was a statue, until she had a quick impression of her own shock and surprise mirrored in his eyes.

Not a statue. A man. But this was no ordinary man. He was dressed in the manner of an ancient Highlander. His arms and legs were bare, with nothing but a length of plaid to cover his torso. But what caused her even more fear than the sight of this stranger was the sight of the very large, very deadly jeweled sword he was holding in a menacing manner.

She gasped and shrank back. Before she could flee, his hand snaked out, catching her roughly by the shoulder.

"No! I . . ."

Her cry broke off as she was caught by strong arms and yanked off her feet. She saw, to her dismay, the flutter of the tapestry as it slid closed behind her, engulfing her in darkness.

Without a word the man lifted her as easily as if she weighed nothing at all. Though she bit and kicked and fought him with all her might, she was no match for his almost superhuman strength. He tossed her over his shoulder and began racing along a darkened passageway.

Her cries and shouts of alarm bounced off the cavernous walls in an echoing chorus.

Laurel's heart was pounding in time to his every footfall. As her eyes adjusted to the gloom, she realized that they were heading deep into the dungeons beneath the original castle ruins.

From the history she'd read, she knew that this was where the clans would gather during a siege. There were tunnels leading to various rooms that were large enough to shelter livestock, store grain, and permit entire families to live in safety within the castle enclosure while their men fought back intruders.

As they rounded a corner, the man came to an abrupt halt and in one fluid movement set her on her feet before shoving her roughly behind him. As Laurel took in a breath and prepared to flee, she heard the clash of steel upon steel, and looked up to see her captor facing a band of warriors.

There were nearly a dozen of them, their faces streaked with mud, their voices screaming words that were unintelligible to Laurel. But this much she understood: They were determined to kill both her captor and her.

Some of these men wore only animal skins to cover their nakedness. They lifted knives and swords menacingly as they surrounded their prey.

Laurel's captor never even hesitated as he plowed through the circle of warriors, his sword cutting a swath of death and destruction through all in his path. Despite the fear that gripped her, Laurel couldn't help admiring his courage in the face of such overwhelming odds. One after another, the attackers fell to his blade.

Just as it seemed safe, she watched in horror as two more attackers crept up from the shadows. "Behind you."

At her shout, he turned and drove his blade through the chest of the one nearest him.

Seeing that the other was about to thrust his blade into her captor's back, Laurel looked around for something, anything to use. Without even thinking, she yanked her cell phone from her pocket and tossed it as hard as she could. It caught the warrior on the side of his temple. Startled, he turned on her, ready to defend himself. It was all the distraction necessary for her captor to overpower the man. With an arm around his neck, he pulled a small, deadly knife from his waist and slit the attacker's throat.

At the sound of hurried footsteps coming toward them, he again thrust her behind him before turning to await the next attack.

A warrior garbed in the same plaid as her abductor came to an abrupt halt. "Ye've come back, m'laird."

"I have. To find barbarians in my own household." The voice rang with righteous anger.

"They caught us by surprise, m'laird. Without your leadership, we feared all would be lost, but we managed to fight them off. This was the last of them. I'd feared they'd already made good their escape."

"They would have, had I not been here to change their plans. See to them."

Without another word, Laurel's captor closed a hand over her wrist and hauled her through the carnage. They moved quickly along a darkened hallway and up a flight of stairs. At last he slowed his pace and stepped through a doorway into a suite of rooms that, though primitive, seemed surprisingly comfortable. The floors were covered with rushes. A cozy fire was burning in a massive stone fireplace. Around it were gathered chairs and settees strewn with animal hides.

The stranger drew Laurel inside before securing the door. When he turned, he surprised her once again by dragging her roughly into the circle of his arms.

"At last." His words, raw and passionate, were whispered against her temple. "I thought I'd lost you, love." His lips nuzzled her cheek, her jaw. "Oh, my bonny, bonny Laurel. I've been searching for you everywhere. The fear of what might have happened to you nearly caused my poor heart to stop."

Without waiting for her reply, he lowered his head and kissed her long and slow and deep, like a man starved for the taste of her.

Laurel tried to push away, but she was no match for him. He seemed completely unaware of her resistance. Instead, caught up in the moment, his hands moved over her body while his fevered kisses smothered her protests until they died in her throat.

She was assaulted by such a rush of conflicting feelings, she couldn't sort them out. Shock. Outrage. Fear. And somewhere deep in the recesses of her mind, the realization that she'd never in her life been kissed like this. Possessively, as though this man owned her, body and soul, and had the right to expect such passion in return. He touched her, held her, like one who already knew her intimately. His kiss spoke of desperation, and then, in the blink of an eye, of reverence, as though he held in his arms some rare and perfect creature that must be treated as the greatest of treasures.

Maybe it was a reaction to what she'd just gone through. Perhaps she was in a state of shock. Whatever the reason, though she tried to deny it, her body responded in a purely sexual way.

"I was lost without you, love. My heart was so shattered . . ." He ran hot, wet kisses down her throat, pausing to nibble the sensitive hollow between her neck and shoulder until her flesh nearly sizzled. Already a spark of heat skimmed her spine, adding to her jumble of emotions. How could she think, when this man's kisses were doing such things to her?

But think she must. "Wait. Stop."

At her words he lifted his head, but kept his hands at her shoulders, as though afraid to let her go for even a moment.

"How . . ." She had to struggle to find her voice. "How do you know my name?"

He regarded her with a humorous lift of the brow before gathering her close. His strong fingers began gently massaging her scalp. "Was it a blow to your head, my love? I've heard of such things during battle. Has it left you dazed?"

Again she pushed away, dragging air into her lungs. The press of his fingers through the tangles of her hair was far too intimate a caress. "Who are you?"

"Now I know you tease me." His eyes crinkled. "I'm the lad you've loved since you were no more than a wee lass. And you're my own true love, Laurel. The one I've cherished all my life. When I couldn't find you after the siege, I was beside myself. Some said they'd seen you falling from the tower, but your body was never found. I'm afraid I went a little mad with worry. I searched the length and breadth of the forest, refusing to tend to my duties, or even to return to my fortress until I'd found you. But you're home now." He dragged her against him and kissed her full on the mouth. "Home to stay." Against her lips he whispered, "Now come to bed, love. For I've been searching for you for such a long time, I've built up a powerful need."

"But I . . . Wait." She'd never felt so dazed, so disoriented, so thoroughly confused in her entire life.

How could this be happening? It was like a dream. All disjointed. Out of sync. But she was wide awake, and this was all too real. Those attackers had intended to kill her, and had ended up giving their lives. She'd seen the carnage with her own eyes. Had heard their death cries with her own ears. The brutality of that bloody scene was an image that would remain in her mind forever.

And this man, this stranger from another era, was also real. A warrior who seemed to have no fear of his enemy's weapons. A warrior who was calling her by name, behaving as though he'd known her for a lifetime, and was preparing to take her to his bed.

She had to put the brakes on this now, before it went any further. "We need to talk."

"Aye, love." With no effort at all he lifted her in his arms and carried her across the room to the chaise, softened with animal skins and set before a roaring fire.

As he lowered her to the plush hides, he lay beside her and drew her into the circle of his arms.

With his mouth warm on hers he muttered, "We'll talk. I give you my word on it. As soon as I've had time to offer you a proper welcome home, my bonny, bonny wife."

Two

Wife? He actually believed she was his wife?

Couldn't he see that she was a stranger? Didn't he question the difference in their clothes? In her strange American accent?

Yet he seemed to know her as intimately as she knew herself. He was prepared to make her welcome. And what a welcome. He pressed soft kisses to her temple, her brow, her cheek. And all the while his hands moved over her, at first soothing, then gradually exciting, until they were both aroused.

She had to put a stop to this before they crossed a line.

"You've made a terrible mistake. I'm not . . ." She struggled to make her brain work in sync with her mouth. "I mean, I am Laurel, but I'm not your Laurel."

He merely grinned. "You've been mine since long before our families agreed to our betrothal, love. You were mine the minute I set eyes on you at market day all those years ago. You, with that dark tumble of curls around the face of an angel. I carried the look of you in my heart until the day

I was old enough to speak to your father and mine, and arrange our future together. Now kiss me before I go mad with wanting you."

His mouth moved over hers with a hunger that had the blood pounding in her temples.

"What about . . . ?" Sucking air into her starving lungs, Laurel leaned up on one elbow, determined to distract him. She may not have the muscles to fight him, but there was nothing wrong with her brain. Thinking quickly, she stared pointedly at his shoulder. "What about your wound?"

He touched a hand to it, and stared without emotion when his fingers came away bloody. " 'Tis nothing, love."

"Nothing?" A lesser man would have been staggered by the pain of it. "It looks serious to me."

"A barbarian's sword. 'Twill be the last he'll ever lift against a Highlander." He made a sound of disgust. "I've been so blinded by the loss of you, I grew careless. But now that you've been returned to me, I'll make it up to my people. I'll concentrate on the safety of my clan, and should the invaders return, we'll be ready for them."

"What do they want?"

He looked at her as though she were daft. "What they've always wanted. Our flocks. Our crops. Our women."

"Why don't they have their own?"

"Bloody barbarians would rather pillage and steal from us than do the work involved to prosper."

"Why do you wait for them to attack? Why not send your warriors out to find them before they wreak their havoc?"

Again that arched look before he smiled. "I promised my people peace and prosperity. It is not our way to take from others. But we will die before we will give in to the barbarians. It is my sworn duty to protect my people, my flocks, and my land from invaders. You and they would think little of their laird if I did not. And I would rather die than have you think ill of me, my beloved. Now that I know you're safe, I'll see them all routed from these shores." He rubbed idly at his shoulder, giving Laurel the opportunity she'd been waiting for.

"You're losing too much blood. Let me tend that wound." She eased herself from the settee and glanced around the room. Spying a basin and pitcher, she motioned him to follow her.

With a sigh of resignation he crossed the room and plunged his arms into the basin while she poured water over the wound. "Woman, have you no heart? You know what I want."

"And I want . . ." *To wake from this nightmare,* she thought. She bit back the words she'd been about to hurl and cautioned herself to speak with care. ". . . I want you strong and healthy."

He gave her a mysterious smile that had her heart tripping over itself. "I'd be happy to show you both my strength and my health, if you'd but cooperate, wife."

"One thing at a time." She picked up a linen square and dried his arm, then looked around for something with which to disinfect the wound.

As if reading her mind, Con filled two goblets with ale. After handing one to her, he splashed some of his on his wound, gave a quick indrawn breath at the sharp pain, then drained his goblet.

He tore a length of linen into strips and bent close. "Here you are, my love." His mouth brushed her cheek, causing the most amazing sensations to ripple along her spine. "You've always had such a light touch when tending to my needs."

She took the linen strips from his hand. Oh, what she wouldn't give for some antiseptic ointment and an antibiotic, not to mention a doctor to stitch this deep, bloody gash. This whole scene was so primitive. But since it was all she had, she would do what she could to stem the bleeding, and pray the wound healed without infection.

While she carefully wrapped a strip of linen around his shoulder and tied the ends, she couldn't help but notice the perfect symmetry of his body. Despite the many battle scars that marred his flesh, his was the most beautiful body she'd ever seen. All hard, tight muscle and sinew, without the bulk of a bodybuilder. This was a lean, fit warrior, who would put the men in her New York office to shame, even though many of them spent hours each week with their personal trainers in a gym, sweating on their treadmills and exercise bikes to stay in shape.

She gathered her courage. "You are Con the Mighty? Conal MacLennan?"

"I see your memory is returning. A good sign. You had me concerned. Do you remember your name now?"

"I've never forgotten." She couldn't help grinning. "Laurel."

"Aye. My beloved Laurel, of the Clan Douglas. What happened to you, love? Were you pushed from the tower as I'd feared?"

"I . . . don't know." She turned away to avoid those piercing eyes. How could she possibly make this man understand that she didn't belong here? That she was caught up in some sort of mad dream, even though wide awake? "None of this makes any sense."

At once his hands were at her shoulders, drawing her back against him. He circled his arms around her, his big hands resting just beneath the fullness of her breasts, causing a strange tingling deep inside her. She'd never known someone so powerful to be so gentle, so caring.

His words, spoken against her ear, vibrated with tenderness and passion. "You're not to worry yourself about it, my love. The memories will come to you in time. These things often happen after a blow to the head."

"But you don't understand. I'm not . . ." She turned to him, intent upon explaining. But when she saw the look in his eyes, her mind seemed to go blank. No man had ever looked at her with such fierce, abiding love. Even if she didn't deserve it, even if she wasn't the one he really loved, she was helpless against such a tidal wave of feeling.

What must it be like to be completely, utterly loved? Hadn't she always wondered? It would be so easy to pretend, for a little while, that she was the woman he really wanted. Yet she knew in her heart that it wouldn't be fair to accept, for even one moment, the love this man meant for another. But, oh, how she wished it were so.

She took a deep breath. "There's something you should know."

"Aye, love?" He drew her close, his mouth pressed to a tangle of hair at her temple.

She could feel his breath, warm on her cheek. And his strong, steady heartbeat keeping time with hers. "I come from another time. Another place."

"That would explain your strange garb." He looked her up and down. "The barbarians took you with them and forced their clothes and customs on you."

"The clothes are mine. I wore a business suit on the plane. And when we got here, I thought I'd just exchange the skirt for comfortable slacks while we took a tour of the castle."

He smiled at her as if she'd just babbled in a foreign language. "How did you escape your captors?"

She sucked in a breath, determined to make him understand. "I didn't need to escape. I was never . . ."

"Nay." He touched a finger to her lips to silence her. "It matters not how you did it. It is enough that you are back where you belong. Here in my arms. Safe in my fortress. But know this. If they harmed you in any way, my love, I'll make them pay in ways they will regret even after they lie in their graves."

She shook her head, more determined than ever. "It isn't like that, Conal."

"Conal." He gave her a wicked smile that had her heart

actually fluttering. "Besides my mother, you are the only woman who dares to call me that." He put a hand beneath her chin, forcing her to look at him. "You know what it always does to me. But then, that was your plan, love, was it not?"

"Con . . ." It was too late. His mouth claimed hers in a blazing kiss. As he lingered over her lips, tasting, devouring, she could actually feel the floor beneath her feet begin to dip and sway, until she was forced to wrap her arms around his waist or risk falling.

"There's the Laurel I know and love." He kissed the tip of her nose before lifting his head and taking hold of her hand. "You've tended my wound. We've quenched our thirst. Now, love, there is a hunger, deep and abiding, that must be fed."

As he started toward the settee there was a quick rap on the door.

Con looked up in annoyance. "Enter."

A young warrior with red hair, his handsome face clean-shaven, paused in the doorway, looking from Con to Laurel. For a moment he seemed so startled at the sight of her, dressed in her man-tailored slacks and white shirt, he couldn't seem to find his voice. For the longest time he merely stared in stunned silence.

Finally he managed to say, "I see ye've found her."

"Aye. Just beyond the wall of the keep. She'd managed to flee her captors and was making her way home. What is it, Duncan?"

When the man continued to stare at Laurel in silence, the warrior standing behind him pushed him aside. "Ye must come, m'laird. Our warriors caught one of the barbarians."

"That's grand. Bind him, lad. I'll see to him later. There are . . ." Con turned to Laurel with a burning look. ". . . things here I must see to before I deal with him."

The warrior gave a quick shake of his head. "Ye'd best

come now, m'laird. The intruder has made wild claims that his leader knew before the attack how to breach our defenses."

Con's eyes narrowed to dangerous slits. "Is he saying there's a traitor in our midst?"

The warrior nodded. "'Twould seem so, m'laird. But you know these barbarians are sworn to never speak the truth."

Duncan suddenly composed himself enough to say, "Leave me alone with him and I'll get the truth out of him before I slit his throat."

"Nay. I want him alive." With a hiss of anger, Con released Laurel's hand. "I'm sorry, my love. I have no choice but to deal with this immediately."

Laurel felt a sense of elation. She'd won a reprieve. But even as the thought rushed through her mind, she wondered at the chill she felt when he released her.

Con lifted a hand to her cheek and gave her a look so loving, so tender, she could feel herself blushing. "I'll send Brinna to tend to you until I return."

"Brinna?"

"The lass from the village." He took hold of her hands. "'Twill all come back to you in time." He seemed torn between duty and desire. "I waited so long to find you. I hate to leave you for even a little while." He surprised her by pressing a kiss to each of her palms before closing her fingers over the spot. "Until I return, hold this as a token of my love."

He turned and strode from the room.

Laurel stood perfectly still, wondering at the way her heart behaved in response to the simple touch of this man. She ought to be terrified by this entire situation. Instead, almost from the beginning, this strange, primitive warrior had been able to put her at ease.

What patience he showed for the woman he believed to be his wife. What passion. What a deep, abiding love.

Still, she had no time for romantic notions. The capture of one of the intruders had given her a chance to escape. She dare not squander this opportunity. She would use the moment to slip away before the girl from the village arrived.

There had to be a way to get back to her own world.

She opened the door, peering around anxiously before stepping from the room.

Though she'd been too shocked to pay much attention which direction they'd taken through the darkened passageways, she was fairly certain she could find her way back. Like anyone who lived and worked in New York City, she had a keen sense of direction.

A short time later, after becoming lost in a maze of darkened passageways, and retracing her steps many times, she spied a doorway up ahead. Though it wasn't the niche behind the tapestry, she was hopeful that it would lead to freedom. Shoving the heavy wooden door open she stepped outside and stared around in confusion.

There were no ruins. No tumbled stones. Instead, the once ancient fortress and tower now rose up like a gleaming beacon in the fading light of evening. The newer additions to the castle, which housed the five-star hotel and restaurant, were nowhere to be seen. They had completely disappeared, like ghostly wisps of fog over the loch.

She became aware of something else. An eerie silence seemed to have settled over the land. Except for the call of an occasional bird, and the hum and buzz of insects, there was no sound. No planes overhead. No cars or trucks. No curving ribbon of driveway leading to the fortress. No people milling about. No lights, except for a flickering candle at several of the tower windows, and far off, in the distance, the fairy lights of what appeared to be a village.

Civilization as she knew it had disappeared. Now there was only this towering fortress. And around it, a wild and primitive Highland wilderness.

Time hadn't stopped; it had been reversed. Laurel could see nothing familiar or comforting. Though she looked the same, and felt the same, she had fallen into some sort of time warp, with no apparent way out.

She stared around to convince herself that she wasn't dreaming. She could feel the breeze on her face. Could smell the dank, rich tang of freshly turned earth, and the wonderful fragrance of baking bread wafting from the castle. And she could still taste Con, strong and dark and mysterious, on her lips.

If this wasn't a dream, if this was truly happening, it wasn't some mere accident. Laurel was far too pragmatic for that. Hadn't she always believed that everything that happened in life had a rhyme and reason?

How did she happen to come to this particular castle, only to learn that she shared the same name as the laird's wife?

It had to be Fate.

But why?

Was there a mystery to be solved? A life to be saved?

Would her actions here alter the course of history? Or at least the course of the MacLennans' history?

Deep in thought, recognizing that she had nowhere else to go, she turned and let herself back into the castle. This time she managed to find her way back to the suite of rooms with no trouble.

She stepped inside and began to pace.

She wasn't dreaming. This was actually happening to her. But why? What was her purpose in all this? And how could she best fulfill this strange new role that had been thrust upon her?

For now, she decided, until she could find a way back to her own world, her own time, she would watch and listen and hope to learn what she was meant to do here.

She no longer feared for her life. Despite this primitive existence, she felt safe here in Con's castle.

Con the Mighty.

Though she may be safe from the intruders, there was something else, equally dangerous. Her own foolish heart. For as handsome and intriguing as Conal MacLennan may be, he was wed to another. Trying to avoid giving in to his obvious charm may prove to be the greatest challenge of all.

Three

"My lady." Laurel's musings were interrupted when the door to her chambers was opened and a young woman hurried inside carrying an armload of clothing.

"Brinna?"

"Aye, my lady." Because her hands were occupied, the young woman nudged the door closed with her hip before laying the clothes carefully across the chaise.

When she turned, it was obvious that she was out of breath from her efforts. She was taller than Laurel by a head, with flaming hair and icy blue eyes.

She gave her mistress a brittle smile. "I didn't believe it when the laird sent word that you'd been found."

"And why is that?"

"You've been gone so long, we were certain you were dead at the hands of the barbarians." She made it sound like an indictment, as though Laurel had somehow chosen to be kidnapped and that her return had merely created more work.

Remembering her manners, the servant gave a slight bow. "Welcome home, my lady." Her words, spoken quickly, were anything but welcoming.

"Thank you." Laurel glanced at the array of garments. "Are these for me?"

"Aye, my lady." The girl was openly staring at Laurel's strange clothing. "'Tis true then? You were indeed captured by the invaders. Did they treat you badly?"

Laurel looked away. "I'd rather not speak of it."

"Of course. Forgive my boldness. I'm sure you'll want nothing left to remind you of your captors." The young woman indicated a soft, white wool gown. "You will feel better when you are dressed in your own clothing."

While she helped Laurel out of her slacks and shirt she made disapproving sounds about the strange bra and bikini panties underneath.

"Barbarians." She spat the word. "Why did they bind you so?"

Laurel bit back a smile and managed to shrug. "I suppose it's their custom."

"If you'd like, my lady, I'll gladly toss these in the fire."

Laurel caught her hand. "I'd rather keep them."

"Aye. To stoke your hatred of the ones who treated you so shamefully, I'd wager." The girl tossed the blood-stained clothing to the floor with a look of disdain before helping Laurel into fresh undergarments. A soft, delicate chemise that tied in front with ribbons. Wool hose. And finally a gown of unbleached wool, with a low, rounded neckline and long narrow sleeves that fell in little points over the backs of her hands.

When she was dressed, Brinna led her to a stool. "If you'll sit here, I will dress your hair."

Because there was no mirror, Laurel had no idea how her hair looked, or what the lass would do to it. Not that it mattered. What she needed was information. Something that would tell her how she'd come to be here, and how to get back home. But this girl seemed so sullen, so distant, she wondered where to begin.

"Are there any other fortresses in this area, Brinna?"

"None, my lady. For as far as the eye can see, the land belongs to none but the MacLennan Clan."

Laurel pushed aside the little twinge of regret. She'd hoped to find yet another castle in the area that might offer a way home. A room, perhaps, that would resemble the tower stairs where she'd slipped into this other dimension.

"How long have you served the laird in his castle, Brinna?"

The girl's hands paused in their work. "You've known me all my life, my lady."

"Of course. But I can't seem to recall . . ."

"Oh, aye." The girl clapped a hand to her mouth. "The laird warned that you suffered some lapses in memory."

"Perhaps you can help me remember, Brinna. Tell me about your . . . our village."

"Ours is a prosperous village. In my grandfather's day, our people roamed the Highlands to avoid the invaders, refusing to settle in one place. The laird persuaded us to build our huts here, for the soil is rich and the crags and hills make us impervious to attack. Under the laird's protection our crops grow lush, and our herds of sheep grow fat. But now the barbarians have once again found us, and there is talk among the villagers of leaving this place and seeking a haven elsewhere."

"Where would they go?"

Brinna shook her head. "I know not where."

"Don't they trust their laird to protect them?"

The girl's voice held a trace of anger. "When you disappeared, the very heart seemed to go out of our laird. He could think of nothing except finding you. Because of it, he could no longer look out for the welfare of his people. When he left on his quest to find you, he charged his half brother with the care of the castle and our village and even of your son until he returned."

Laurel's head swiveled. "I have a . . . ?" She paused to consider her words more carefully. "My son? Is he here in the castle?"

"Aye, my lady. In the chambers of the laird's half brother, Fergus, and his wife, the lady Dulcie."

"When will I see him?"

"My lady Dulcie insists that the lad bathe before he comes to you."

Laurel started to rise. "He doesn't need to be clean. I want to see him now."

"Soon." None too gently, Brinna eased her back to the stool. "Donovan rode with his uncle and the warriors during the attack, and they spent many days in the forest. The lad returned looking more like a barbarian than a Highlander."

"He rode with the warriors? How old is Donovan?"

Brinna's hands went still. "Why, he is ten and two, my lady."

Twelve. She'd expected a two- or three-year-old.

Laurel sensed the girl's disapproval over the fact that she couldn't even recall her own son. To cover her unease, she began firing questions at Brinna. "Do Fergus and Dulcie have children?"

"Alas, they have not been blessed with wee ones of their own. But they lavish much love on your son."

"Is Fergus as capable a warrior as the laird?"

Brinna's voice rang with pride. "No warrior compares to the laird. Not even the laird's man-at-arms, Duncan, though they are old and dear friends." The girl paused. "Not that any of us blame my lord Fergus for his lack of battle skills. He wasn't privileged to learn to be a warrior from his father as was the laird. Nor could he be faulted that the barbarians chose this time to attack us. They couldn't have known that our laird was away, searching for his wife. But because of the laird's distraction, the invaders managed to inflict much pain and death before they were driven off. The entire village is rejoicing at the knowledge that our laird has returned, for it was surely his presence that caused the last of the invaders to flee."

Her words had Laurel's mind working overtime. The warrior with Duncan had told Con that there may be a traitor in their midst. That could mean that it had been no coincidence that the attack had come when the laird was distracted.

Could it be that the plot went deeper than that? Had someone deliberately pushed the laird's wife from the tower and spirited away the body, hoping that Con the Mighty would be so distraught that his people would be easily overcome without his leadership? If the love of the laird for his lady had been common knowledge, there were many who could have predicted his reaction to such a loss.

Or had she been watching too many cop shows on TV recently? The clever detectives always uncovered hidden agendas among the petty crooks and thieves who preyed on the good and the helpless. But, Laurel reasoned, evil was evil, whether in the fifteenth century or the twenty-first. And most crimes were committed for simple reasons. Greed. Passion. Jealousy.

Was someone jealous of Con? Of his position as laird, perhaps? Had someone lusted after his wife? Not likely, since they'd used her disappearance to distract him. But then, she could have been cooperating with his rival. Still, Laurel couldn't help but believe that a man who loved as deeply as Con the Mighty would be deeply loved in return. She found it hard to believe that the Laurel he adored so completely would betray him.

If not his wife, then someone close to him. Someone he trusted, who could cooperate with the barbarians without fear of being discovered.

What did Con have that someone else might want? From what little she'd seen, he shared his wealth with all the clan. This fortress was open to all the villagers. In times of siege, this was their home. They shared their crops and herds.

If not possessions, perhaps power? Did someone else hope to be laird? Since a Highland laird was chosen by the will of the people, that would require turning his people against him.

Some might see his search for his wife as abandonment of the people who depended on him. Would that be cause enough for them to turn against him?

Laurel decided to pursue this angle, and see where it led.

"Are there places in your village that I frequently visit?"

The girl thought a moment. "The stalls on market days. You especially enjoy the bits of ribbon and lace."

"Market days. Conal mentioned it as the place we met as children. It sounds like a pleasant place to be."

"It is, my lady. The entire village turns out, even the warriors and lads."

"So Conal and Donovan go with me?"

"Aye. They wouldn't think of missing. And though you disapprove, the laird and young Donovan always manage to find an extra coin to buy some sweets."

Laurel began to relax. Except for the time difference, it would seem that people were the same here as they were in the twenty-first century. Working, playing, fretting over their loved ones' health while they enjoyed a special treat.

"Where else do I frequently visit?"

"The huts of the villagers whenever a wee one is born. The women all remark on your lovely handwork. Your bonnets and coats and blankets are highly prized by the village women."

"I sew?"

Brinna regarded her thoughtfully. "Aye, my lady. You sew a very fine seam."

Laurel thought about the tapestry. Was there some significance there? Hadn't she been admiring the handiwork of the women who'd made it when she'd discovered Con hiding behind it? Could his Laurel have been one of the women who'd helped to create that tapestry?

Brinna set aside the comb. "I have dressed your hair so often, my lady, and always I am pleased at the way it curves just so around your face."

Laurel went very still. It was yet another thing she shared with Con's wife. Neither Con nor Brinna could tell that they had an imposter in their midst.

Or was she?

What did she really know about reincarnation? The theory had long fascinated her. The thought of returning, to live one's life again, and being given the opportunity to right some of the wrongs, was something she'd often played with in her mind. But it had always been mere fantasy. She'd never given serious thought to it.

Hadn't she always felt a particular kinship with ancient Scotland, especially the Highlands and this castle? But her love for this place had developed because of her grandmother's bedtime stories. They had simply fueled a little girl's imagination.

Or had there been more to it than that?

After a lifetime of Highland lore, she could no longer tell which came first—her love of all things Scottish or the intriguing tales her grandmother wove that whetted her appetite for more.

Could she actually be the missing wife of Con the Mighty? Had she once lived in this long-ago era?

How else to explain the disappearance of the modern sections of the castle, and the reemergence of the ancient keep? She certainly wasn't imagining the fact that life as she'd known it had been swept away in the blink of an eye.

She lifted her hands to rub her temples, where the beginning of a headache throbbed. There were too many theories, too many possibilities, whirling through her mind. And all of them troubling.

This mind of hers, always able to see all sides to an argument, always willing to look at all the possibilities of a thorny issue, had helped her climb to the very top of the corporate chain. But there were times when it was a curse instead of a blessing.

"I see you are suffering one of your spells."

"Spells?" Laurel's head came up sharply.

"Those sudden pains in your head. You've suffered them since you were a lass. That is why many in the village fear you as a witch."

"They do?"

She turned to see a look in the girl's eyes that had her puzzled. It wasn't so much fear as wariness.

Again she pressed her hands to her temples. "You know I'm no witch, Brinna."

"Here." Brinna took Laurel's hands and lowered them to her lap, before pressing her own fingers to Laurel's temples and massaging gently.

Laurel leaned back and gave a sigh of pure pleasure. "Oh, that feels heavenly."

"'Tis what I've always done to soothe you, my lady."

With her eyes closed, Laurel tried to clear her mind. But the thought of all her similarities with the laird's wife continued to taunt her.

Was it possible that she had once been Laurel of the Clan Douglas, who lived in the fifteenth century, as wife to Con the Mighty, Laird of the MacLennan Clan?

Had something happened to cause her to somehow become mired in a kind of limbo, lost between centuries?

If so, what had brought her back now? Was there some critical event about to happen that required her participation?

Would she be given the chance to do something good? Something noble?

Maybe it wasn't about her at all, but rather this laird. Would she be the one to urge Con to travel a path he wouldn't otherwise consider? A path that might forever change his life and reverse the course of history?

Or . . . a nagging little thought tormented her . . . was she simply losing her mind?

Four

Laurel and Brinna looked up at the sound of a quick rap on the door.

It was thrown open and a lad came rushing in, looking much the way a puppy would, all happy and wriggling with excitement. Quick as a flash, he crossed the room and flung himself into Laurel's arms.

"Mother! I couldn't believe it when I heard the news. Father and I have been so worried. What happened? Where have you been? We've been looking . . ."

"Donovan." A woman stood framed in the doorway, watching with a look of disapproval. Though she didn't raise her voice, her tone was pure ice. "I told you not to ask too many questions. Remember what the laird said. Your mother suffered a blow to the head that has left her frail."

"Sorry." The boy quickly straightened.

Before he could pull away, Laurel caught his hands and held him to her. "Nonsense. I'm not at all frail. Just forgetful. Now, let me look at you."

He was the image of his father. Tall and straight as a

young sapling, with dark hair curling softly around his shoulders. He shared his father's eyes as well. Dark and piercing, with a hint of teasing humor in their depths. The length of plaid he wore belted at the waist revealed thin arms and legs, with just the beginnings of muscles. Any mother, Laurel thought, would be proud of such a fine, handsome son.

"Oh, you look so good."

Her words brought back his smile, warming her heart as nothing else could.

She turned her attention to the woman in the doorway. She was young, plump as a ripe peach, with pale hair that fell in corkscrew curls to below her waist. Her eyes looked a little too wide, a little too wary, as though they were beholding a ghostly specter. She wore a pale woolen gown loosely belted, with a dagger tucked into the sash at her waist. Had all the women of the keep adopted this fashion since the invasion? Or did she fancy herself a female warrior? Except for the dirk, she looked too pale, too utterly feminine to do battle.

"You would be Dulcie."

The woman stepped closer, lips pursed in disapproval. "You remember?"

Laurel gave a quick shake of her head. "Not really. But Brinna has told me that you and Fergus have been caring for Donovan, and for that I'm so very grateful."

The woman dismissed her gratitude with a wave of her hand. "Why wouldn't we care for him? We are, after all, family. We could not love Donovan any more if he were our own son."

Laurel squeezed the lad's hand. "I can see why."

Dulcie studied Laurel with a critical eye. "How is it that you managed to escape the barbarians, when so many others perished at their cruel hands?"

"I wish I knew." Laurel pressed her fingertips to her temple, where a shadow of the headache lingered.

Seeing it, Dulcie took a step back. "I can see that you are not yet recovered. We will leave you."

As she started to turn away, Laurel placed a hand on the boy's arm. "Stay awhile, Donovan. I want to hear all about . . ." She hesitated, then amended, ". . . all the things you've been doing while I was gone."

Dulcie's voice was sharp. "You need your rest. The laird will be furious if he learns that the lad stayed overlong and made you weary."

Laurel's voice was equally insistent, though she fought to keep any sign of impatience from her tone. The last thing she wanted was a catfight between herself and this woman who might prove to be a valuable ally. "I assure you, nothing will soothe me as much as a visit with my son." She emphasized the last words, leaving no doubt that she had no intention of letting the lad go.

"You will remember not to tire your mother." Dulcie shot him a warning look before taking her leave.

Brinna made ready to stay, until Laurel suggested that she and her son wished to be alone.

The young servant hesitated in the doorway. "Shall I bring you and Donovan refreshments, my lady?"

"Thank you. That would be grand."

As the girl hurried away, Laurel turned to Donovan. "At last. Now that there are no distractions, we can speak freely. I want to hear all about you. Tell me everything." At his quizzical look, she amended, "Tell me everything you've done since I've been away."

The lad settled down at her feet, his eyes grave. "Father and I were so worried when we couldn't find you. I begged to be allowed to join him in the search, but he ordered me to stay with my uncle."

"He was only looking out for your safety, Donovan. It was hard enough losing a wife. Think of a father's pain if his son should disappear, as well."

"Aye. That's what Father told me. But I hated having to

be here, knowing you were lost somewhere in the forest, and at the hands of those wicked barbarians. All I wanted was to be with you. To comfort you. To protect you. If I'd been there, I'd have fought them as Father taught me, until there were none left to harm you."

Laurel felt her heart melt at his vehemence. What woman could ask for more than such devoted love?

"Don't dwell on it. I'm home now." She touched a hand to his head. "Where were you when the barbarians invaded?"

He looked up, eyes bright with excitement. "I was asleep in the chambers of my uncle. I awoke to hear the cry of alarm that they were storming the fortress. At first I thought I was surely dreaming. No barbarians would dare enter the fortress of Con the Mighty. But then the voices grew louder, and it was impossible to ignore the battle cries."

He lowered his voice. "Had it not been for the many villagers who had taken refuge here at the keep while Father was away searching for you, all would have been lost. Somehow the invaders had slipped past the guards and were already fanning out along the many passageways. A village woman, awakened through the night by the cry of her babe, was the first to spy a barbarian, and sounded the alarm. 'Twas taken up by other women and children, and then by their men. The ensuing battle was fierce and bloody. When we rousted them, Uncle Fergus permitted me to ride with him on the chase through the forest, hoping to capture some of the invaders alive."

"Would your father have approved you being exposed to such danger?"

The boy laughed. "You and Father are far too protective. As Uncle Fergus was quick to point out, I'm more man than boy now. If I'm ever to learn the ways of a warrior, I must leave the safety of the fortress and ride with the men into battle."

Laurel could see the pride burning in his gaze, and felt a sudden flash of worry. Despite the dangers, he was absolutely fearless. Leave it to the young to feel so invincible. He didn't see the danger of facing the swords of the invaders. He saw only the adventure, the pride in having taken part in securing his father's fortress.

A few years from now, when he'd had his fill of bloody battles, his words would no doubt come back to haunt him.

Even though he wasn't hers, she couldn't help but worry about what the future held for this lad, and for all the lads of the village, who would have a lifetime of wars ahead of them. Scotland's history was a bloody one. Barbarians from across the sea. The British just beyond their borders. And even their own. Clan against clan. But how could she possibly warn him, when all of those threats had not yet come to be? There was no way she could explain her knowledge of the future to this innocent lad. And so, though it cost her to keep silent, she decided to change the subject.

"Do you get on well with your uncle and aunt?"

The lad nodded. "Well enough. Except when my aunt speaks against my father."

Laurel's interest was instantly piqued. "Why would she do such a thing?"

"It isn't only my aunt. She claims that many in the village feel that Father was not doing his duty to his people by deserting them in their hour of peril. But as I pointed out, Father had no way of knowing when or if the barbarians would attack. He knew only that his life would be meaningless without you, Mother."

Laurel huffed out a breath. "That should have been obvious to them. To anyone who dared criticize Conal for what he did."

Seeing her sudden flash of temper, the boy chuckled. "I should have known what your reaction would be. You have always been Father's fiercest defender."

She blushed. "Have I?"

"Aye. The love you share is spoken of with great interest by all. It makes me proud to hear the way the villagers speak of you and Father, and the love that burns between you."

She met his look. "You know that you are equally loved."

His smile was quick and radiant. "Aye, Mother. For you and Father have made it abundantly clear."

"What do you know of the relationship between Fergus and the laird? Brinna told me that Fergus wasn't trained in the art of battle by his father."

"'Tis true. Father and my uncle shared the same father, but had different mothers."

"How did Fergus come to live here?"

"When word of his mother's death reached Father, he asked his half brother to share the shelter of his fortress."

"How old was Fergus when he joined the laird's household?"

"Ten and three. My uncle often reminds me that he was the sole protector of his mother until she died. By the time he was brought to live in the laird's fortress he needed no one to come to his aid. But he is grateful that Father is willing to share his home and his clan, for his life alone with his mother was a lonely time for him."

Laurel's mind was working overtime. It seemed the classic sibling rivalry scenario. The successful brother, doted on by both mother and father. The outcast, craving the love of a father, and now, though sharing the brother's largesse, still smarting from those years of neglect. "Do you sense that Fergus resents the years he was forced to care for his mother, without benefit of a father?"

"I know not. He rarely speaks of those days."

They both looked up at a sharp rap on the door.

It was opened to reveal a warrior poised in the doorway.

At once Donovan was on his feet. "Uncle."

Intrigued, Laurel studied the man who was staring at her with such open curiosity.

At the sight of her, his jaw had dropped. "I'd not have believed had I not seen with my own eyes."

Fergus looked nothing like his half brother. Where Con was tall and dark, Fergus seemed pale by comparison, with fair hair that fell to his shoulders, and eyes the color of a cloudy sky. He wasn't nearly as tall as Con, but he was broad in the trunk and shoulders, and his arms rippled with finely honed muscles.

Laurel could imagine those strong arms wielding a dirk or broadsword with deadly accuracy.

"Fergus. Will you join us?" She held out her hand, but he remained in the doorway, his face registering no pleasure at the sight of her. If anything, he seemed to be regarding her with open suspicion.

"My lady." He gave a slight bow. "The laird said you are not yet recovered from your ordeal."

"I'm fine, as you can see."

"It is customary for the barbarians to render their captives unable to escape, either by breaking their legs, or otherwise inflicting enough pain that they have no choice but to remain."

"Then I consider myself indeed fortunate to be here."

Abruptly he composed himself and turned to the lad beside her. "Your father summons you to join him in the stables."

The boy's face came alive with delight. "Does this mean we will resume our search for the barbarians?"

"I know no more than you. I was in the village when a rider ordered me to return to the fortress. Come, lad. It wouldn't do to keep the laird waiting."

Donovan paused to brush a kiss over Laurel's cheek. "Forgive me, Mother. I must go."

"Of course you must." She closed his hand between both of hers. "I so enjoyed our visit, Donovan. Promise me you'll return."

"Aye. Though I know not when. I am at the bidding of my father." He shot her a radiant smile before following his uncle from the room.

As the door closed behind him, Laurel leaned her head back and closed her eyes, deep in thought.

Of the people she'd met thus far, there were only two she felt she could trust completely. Con and Donovan. Father and son. Both had been desperate to find their long-lost Laurel. And both were elated at her return.

It was impossible to fake that kind of love. The man and boy were deeply devoted to the lady Laurel.

The same couldn't be said for the others. Brinna, Dulcie, and Fergus all seemed not only astounded by her sudden reappearance, but also somewhat dismayed by it. Which only suggested to her that one or all of them may have had a hand in the disappearance of the laird's wife.

Still, she could be wrong. They could be simply too overcome to express their true emotions. Which would mean there could be others who had been involved in the lady Laurel's disappearance.

Until she could learn more about these people who surrounded Conal and Donovan, she intended to trust no one but herself. She would watch and listen. And learn all she could about the secrets they kept hidden in their hearts.

She was more and more convinced that this thing that had propelled her back in time was no mere accident. She was here for a reason. Perhaps she was sent here to help Con the Mighty determine the identity of the traitor in their midst. Or maybe she was meant to use her knowledge of the future to educate his people in some area in which they were lacking.

Whatever the reason, she had no doubt it would be revealed to her in time.

For now, she must be cautious. She must be attentive to all that was said. And to all that was left unsaid, as well.

She struggled to ignore the tiny thread of uneasiness that curled along her spine.

Someone had gone to great pains to get rid of the laird's wife. The first Laurel may be already lying dead somewhere in a shallow gràve. If that were the case, for as long as she continued to pretend to be that woman, her life was equally in danger.

She had no doubt that those who'd been willing to kill once wouldn't hesitate to kill again, given the opportunity.

And so she would watch and listen, and do all she could to protect herself until this dream, this nightmare, this . . . crazy twist in time was resolved.

Five

"My lady." Brinna glanced around in puzzlement. "Is the lad gone, then?"

"I'm afraid so. He was summoned to join his father in the stables."

The serving girl set down the tray she'd retrieved from the refectory. "Cook baked Donovan's favorite scones."

"I'm sure he'll happily devour them as soon as he returns."

Brinna straightened. "Cook sends word that she and the servants are planning a lovely banquet this eventide to welcome you home, my lady."

"Thank them for me, and tell them I look forward to it."

The girl understood that she was being dismissed. "Aye, my lady. Will you rest now?"

Laurel nodded and pretended to stifle a yawn. But as soon as she was alone, she moved around the suite of rooms, hoping to learn anything she could about the woman who had recently occupied them.

Atop a small cabinet she found needles and a skein of yarn. In a drawer were a series of brushes and pots containing various plant and tree dyes. It would appear that the laird's wife had also been an artist. Laurel thought about the tapestry, and the lovely drawings set amid the embroidery, depicting everyday life in the castle. She was convinced that some of the work on that tapestry had been done by Laurel's hand.

Intrigued, she opened a wardrobe and studied an array of gowns, both day- and nightwear, as well as a shawl, a bonnet, and several lengths of ribbon that would have been useful as colorful sashes. Holding each gown to her, Laurel realized that she and the laird's wife had been the same size. That should hardly surprise her, since everyone who had seen her so far had mistaken her for the missing woman. Still, now that she was touching Laurel's clothes she was once more reminded of the fact that this was not some harmless game. While she was here, feeling safe and pampered, the laird's wife was being held somewhere against her will. Or worse, dead—her abductors smug in the knowledge that their victim would never be able to reveal their villainy.

Except that she was back, and walking among them.

Whether they believed in ghosts, or bought into her story of an injury-induced lapse of memory, sooner or later, they would feel compelled to dispose of her, in order to protect their involvement in this wicked scheme.

While Conal and Donovan were rejoicing in her safe return, they might be tempted to relax their guard. She could afford no such luxury. She would have to remain alert to every danger. Not the least of which, she thought with a sigh, was the laird's determination to take her to his bed. If it weren't for Laurel's damnable sense of right and wrong, that much, at least, could have been satisfying indeed. But the thought of lying with a man while his wife was in grave peril was repugnant to her. And since she couldn't make him believe that she was not his beloved Laurel, this promised to be the most dangerous threat of all.

She looked up when the door was thrust open and the man she'd just been thinking about stepped into the room.

His eyes were narrowed in thought, his mouth a grim, tight line of concentration.

"What is it, Conal? What did you learn from the prisoner?"

"Not nearly enough. With my sword at his throat, he admitted that he'd known in advance how to slip past the guards, and which passageways would take him to the chambers of the villagers, so that they could be silenced before sounding the alarm. But he denied knowing the name of the one who'd given such information, claiming that only his leader had that knowledge." Con tossed aside his sword and dirk and filled a goblet with ale, drinking deeply.

"Do you believe him?"

He shrugged. "When a man is about to die, he has no reason to speak falsehoods."

"Where is the prisoner now?" She held her breath, wondering if the blood on Con's sword belonged to the unfortunate prisoner.

"I left him with Fergus and Duncan. Fergus is convinced that he can make the barbarian give up his secrets."

Laurel felt an involuntary shudder at the thought of what the prisoner would be forced to suffer. "And if he's telling the truth and truly doesn't know the name of the traitor?"

Another shrug of those powerful shoulders. "Then he will welcome his death."

Laurel had a sudden fear. "What about Donovan? Dear heaven, you didn't leave him there to witness such brutality?"

Con managed a smile. "Always the fierce she-bear when it comes to our son. Have no fear, my love. I sent Donovan to the village to fetch the apothecary."

"For your wound?" Without thinking, she touched a hand to the clean linen that bound his shoulder.

He closed a hand over hers. "Nay, love. For yours."

"Mine?" She tried to draw away, but he held her fast. "I have no need of any medicine."

"I want the apothecary to see to the blow to your head. Brinna told me that you could not even recall our son."

"It was . . ." Laurel's mind raced. "It was a momentary lapse. Nothing more. I'm a little confused. But I certainly don't need anyone examining my head."

"Then you'll submit to it for my sake." He gathered her close and pressed his mouth to a tangle of hair at her temple. "I cannot bear the thought that you've been harmed by those barbarians, my love."

She tried to ignore the sizzle of heat that curled along her spine, but it was impossible. Though she had no right to his affection, she was being drawn ever closer to the heat of his passion. Sooner or later she was bound to become incinerated.

What a way to die.

She felt the bubble of laughter rising up to her throat as she wrapped her arms around his waist and decided to stop fighting it and just give herself up to the pleasure. Pushing aside the nagging little guilt that tugged at the edge of her conscience, she lifted her face for his kiss.

"Did I call you a she-bear?" He brushed her lips with his. "I should have said vixen."

She was about to make a teasing reply when she felt his quick intake of breath a moment before he crushed her to him and kissed her with such intensity, she had no choice but to give herself up to it.

And then she was lost.

Lost in a haze of sensations unlike anything she'd ever before experienced. How could one man's lips bring so much pleasure? At once sensual and worshipful. As though she were the most alluring goddess ever created. Whispering over her face, her neck, her throat. Promising a banquet of delights. And his hands. Those big, warrior's hands that could wield a sword with such power now moved over her as softly, as gently, as though she were fragile glass. His fingers sought out each line and curve of her body with the absolute certainty that every part of her belonged to him.

They were so lost in each other it took them a moment to realize that the door to their chambers had opened.

Two heads came up sharply. Two chests rose and fell as they struggled for each ragged breath.

Duncan stood in the doorway, looking completely un-apologetic about having violated the laird and his lady's intimacy.

"M'laird." He gave a quick bow of his head, though his gaze remained on Laurel. "Yer presence is requested in the great hall."

"Nay, my friend. Tell Cook that Laurel and I will sup alone in our chambers. I've yet to welcome my wife prop-erly." Con kept his arms around Laurel, holding her when she attempted to draw away.

Seeing that he was being dismissed, the handsome young warrior cleared his throat. "The staff and villagers have planned a banquet to celebrate the lady's return."

Though Con said not a word, Laurel could hear the growl of frustration in his words. "Is there no way to stop this?"

Duncan gave a shake of his head. "The hall is already filled with villagers, ready to feast. 'Twould be an insult to send them home now."

"Aye." Reluctantly, Con released Laurel and gave a wry smile. "Come, my love." He caught her hand and led her out the door and along yet another hallway. As they walked, he leaned close to whisper, "I dare not curse the Fates that are keeping us apart, since those same Fates brought you safely home, wife. Besides, sooner or later, the others will need their beds. And when they do, I'll show you all the love I've been storing up just for you."

Laurel found herself shivering, and wondered whether it was caused by fear or anticipation.

When they reached the great hall, they were joined by a beaming Donovan, who emulated his father and offered his arm to his mother.

"The apothecary is here, Father."

"For now, he'll join in the celebration, and see to his work another time."

Con's words had Laurel relaxing. She'd been given a reprieve.

As she stepped through the doorway of the great hall, Laurel realized with a start that she hadn't been at all prepared for the pageantry of the occasion. A bonfire of burning logs blazed on a hearth at either end of the room, casting a fiery glow over all. The room was filled to overflowing with men and women seated at long tables, while serving wenches scurried about filling goblets. There were shouts and bursts of raucous laughter that erupted around the hall. But when Laurel was spotted standing between her husband and son, the voices became a roar like thunder that threatened to shake the very timbers soaring high above.

"Welcome, m'lady."

"Here she is now. Welcome home, Lady Laurel."

"To our lady."

Goblets were lifted. Men raised their swords in a salute, while many of the women wiped away tears of joy as she moved slowly through the crowd.

Against her ear, Con whispered, "See how they love you?"

Laurel ignored the rush of heat as his breath fluttered the hair at her temple. "From the sound of them, I'd say the ale has been flowing freely for some time."

He chuckled. "And why not? They've fretted and suffered right along with their laird. Now is the time to celebrate our good fortune."

A little girl rushed forward and thrust a bouquet of wildflowers into Laurel's hands. Touched, she knelt and drew the child close while pressing a kiss to her cheek.

When she straightened, she saw the girl's parents openly weeping.

What had Con's wife done to make these people love her so? Laurel thought about Brinna's words. It would seem that, despite living an ordinary life, visiting neighbors on market day, knitting a little coat and bonnet for a new baby, the lady Laurel had found a way to endear herself to the villagers.

Was there a lesson here? Had she ever really cared about the needs of her friends, or had she squandered all her energy on the pursuit of her career? Did she have anyone in her life willing to abandon everything to search for her? Would her friends openly weep if she were to return after a mysterious absence?

There was no time to ponder such things. Con and Donovan led her through the throngs to a table set on a raised wooden dais, so that it could be seen by all in the room. They climbed the steps and Con held her chair, then took his place at the head of the table, with Laurel to his right and Donovan to his left.

He signaled for Fergus and Dulcie to join them. Looking pleased, they left their table and climbed the steps before taking their places beside Laurel. The warrior Duncan was likewise summoned, and he and a tall, thin woman approached. While the woman bowed slightly, Duncan introduced her to Laurel as his betrothed, Mary. Before Laurel could offer a word of greeting, Mary reached out and caught both her hands, lifting them to her lips.

"Praise heaven that you've returned to us safely, m'lady. I felt as if I'd lost my own dear sister. And now you're back, and we have reason to smile again."

"Thank you, Mary." Overcome, Laurel had to swallow the lump that threatened to choke her.

Beside her, Fergus studied her with a keen eye. "You look pale, my lady. Are you not yet recovered?"

"Perhaps just a bit overwhelmed." She lifted a goblet to her mouth and drank, hoping the ale would settle her nerves.

With Con on her left and his half brother on her right, Laurel was able to observe them in close proximity for the first time. While servants moved slowly about the room, offering trays of plump partridge, thick slices of mutton, and bright red salmon, freshly caught in the nearby river, the two men spoke in solemn, hushed tones.

Fergus looked past her to his brother. "The barbarian died without another word."

Con nodded. "I expected as much. If he knew more, he'd have spoken of it rather than lose his life."

"I wasn't quite finished with him, but Duncan had had enough, and ended his life before I could ask more." Fergus studied his half brother. "Will you lead an army to find the invaders?"

Con stared out over the crowd. "I haven't the heart to ask these men to leave their families once more, when they've only now returned."

Fergus frowned. "Could it be that you're not willing to leave your own family, now that what was lost has been returned to you?"

Laurel turned to glance at Con's face, but instead of taking offense at the taunt, he merely smiled and touched a hand to Laurel's cheek. "Would you be willing to leave such as this, brother?"

Fergus, close beside her, heard his wife's hiss of annoyance and turned to her before saying to his brother, "Then perhaps you'd allow me to lead an army against the barbarians while you . . . grow soft in your pleasures."

Con's eyes narrowed, the only sign of annoyance. "We will speak no more of war this night. Have you forgotten that this is a time of celebration?"

"I forget nothing." Fergus glanced over his shoulder at a serving girl offering a basket of bread still warm from the oven, and scones drizzled with honey.

Filling his own plate and that of his wife, Fergus turned away from Laurel and bent to Dulcie. The two spoke in low tones, and though Laurel couldn't hear the words, she had the sense that their voices bore traces of anger.

Throughout the meal, tankards were filled again and again. The more the crowd drank, the louder grew their laughter. And the bolder became the villagers, as one after another of the men got to his feet to sing the praises of the lady Laurel, and to drink to her health.

At one point, Con signaled for Brinna to approach.

At his whispered command, she touched Donovan on the shoulder. "I'll take you to your chambers now."

The boy turned to his father. "Do I have to leave?"

"Aye. A young warrior needs his sleep."

"But I'll miss the rest of the speeches."

Con laughed. "When you've heard one, lad, you've heard enough. Go now."

The boy obediently nodded, before bending to kiss his mother's cheek. "Good night, Mother. I'll come to your chambers on the morrow."

Laurel watched as he followed the serving girl from the hall, and wondered at the curious warmth around her heart. Though he wasn't really hers, she felt a glow just looking at him.

"We've raised a fine son." Con's voice rang with pride.

Again, that sudden warmth, though she knew she had no right to this man's praise.

After some urging by Dulcie, Fergus stumbled to his feet. At once a hush fell over the crowd.

Fergus turned to his brother and the woman beside him. His words were halting at first, and it was clear that he felt awkward speaking to the crowd. "Let us drink to the laird, who was inconsolable at the loss of his beloved wife."

The crowd was on its feet, shouting and draining their tankards, while servants scurried about, refilling them.

"And let us drink to the lady Laurel, who has returned to her rightful place beside her husband, and has restored the laird's happiness."

Again there was much shouting and drinking.

Con leaned around Laurel to clasp his brother's hand. "I thank you, Fergus. It warms my heart to know that you share my happiness."

Fergus looked glum. "'Twas Dulcie's suggestion. For me, the happiness is clouded by the knowledge that the invaders go free, while we make merry in this place."

"There is time enough to make war, my brother." Con closed a hand over his brother's clenched fist. "We will speak again on the morrow. But for tonight . . ." He stood, and the crowd fell silent. Catching Laurel's hand, he drew her up to stand beside him. "I am thankful to the gods who have restored my heart to me. My wife and I are thankful for your love and loyalty. Now we retire to our chambers."

There was much laughter and knowing looks.

Con held up his hands for silence. "As for the rest of you, let the feasting continue through the night."

The crowd gave a roar of approval. Amid much clapping and stomping of feet, he led Laurel down the steps and through the great hall until, when the massive doors closed behind them, the sound of the crowd became little more than a low rumble.

Together they climbed the stairs to their chambers. As they stepped through the doorway and closed the door, Laurel found herself nearly trembling with the raw emotions assaulting her.

Most troubling to her was the knowledge that she wished, more than anything in this world, that she could give in and enjoy the pleasures this man was planning.

This man, who was another woman's husband.

It was a thought that greatly troubled her even while the man himself was more tempting than anyone she'd ever known in this world.

Or in the world she'd left far behind.

Six

A fire burned in the hearth. It was the only light in the room, sending flickering shadows dancing across the walls and ceiling. The fragrance of evergreen and wood smoke perfumed the air.

Con took Laurel's hand and led her through their chambers and past a closed door into a room beyond, where a figure lay amid a tangle of animal hides.

Staring down at the sleeping lad, Con squeezed her hand. "Each time I behold what you and I made together, my love, my heart is filled to overflowing. Is he not perfect?"

Too overcome to speak, Laurel merely nodded. How many times had she had just such a vision in her mind? A vision of standing, hand in hand with a man and staring at the face of their sleeping child. How often had she wondered what it would feel like to be a mother? To have a special someone who would love her unconditionally? The sight of Donovan, hair tousled, face angelic, stirred her heart as nothing else ever had.

"Poor Donovan suffered the loss of you as much as I did. But I was too lost in my own grief to give him the comfort he deserved."

Laurel touched a finger to Con's lips to silence him. "Don't punish yourself so harshly, Conal. The boy loves you so much that the only thing he wants is to be like you in every way."

He surprised her by taking her hands in his and lifting them to his mouth. "That isn't possible, for he has been shaped as much by you as by me, love. And because of you, he shall be a far better man than I. Kinder. Wiser. Stronger."

Laurel was moved to tears. How was it that this man's words, and the mere brush of his lips on her flesh, could have this effect?

Seeing the depth of her emotions, he led her out of the lad's chambers and closed the door before drawing her toward the warmth of the fire.

In their sleeping chamber, which could be seen through the open doorway, the soft animal hides had been turned down on the pallet, revealing snowy white linens.

On a side table stood a decanter of pale wine and two crystal goblets.

Con filled their glasses and crossed the room to hand one to Laurel. Though she was already feeling the effects of the ale from the feast, she accepted the goblet from his hand and absorbed the heat of his touch as his fingers brushed hers.

"The villagers drank to you, my love. Now I drink to us."

"To us." She echoed his words and sipped, before setting aside the goblet and straightening her shoulders. "About us, Conal, there are things I have to tell you."

"Aye, my love. And things I must tell you, as well." He followed her lead and set his goblet beside hers. "But all the words can wait. My feelings for you cannot."

As he reached for her she placed her hand on his chest. "You need to hear me."

"And I shall. But first, I have to kiss you, or my poor heart will surely stop beating." He dragged her close and covered her mouth with his, pinning her hand between them.

She could feel the pounding of his heart. Could taste the urgency as he deepened the kiss. Could sense the hunger in him as he plundered her mouth, giving her no chance to speak, or even to think.

This kiss was different from all the rest. Before, his kisses had been tempered with tenderness, gentleness. But now there was something deeper, darker. A depth of passion and need. Driving, desperate need.

Her head was spinning. The ale? Or the potency of his kisses? She wanted to be sensible. Needed to be. For she owed it to him to tell him the truth about herself, now, before all was lost.

But she was quickly losing control of the situation.

"You can't imagine the things I was thinking as I searched the forest for you, love." He held her a little away, staring deeply into her eyes so that she could understand.

The pain she could see there left her stunned and reeling, touching a chord deep inside her soul.

"Oh, my love." He drew her close and began pressing soft, moist kisses across her cheek, to her ear, where he nibbled and whispered, "Dear heaven, in my mind's eye I could see you at the hands of those barbarians. Enduring pain, humiliation, death."

"Stop, Conal. You mustn't torture yourself with . . ."

He ran light, feathery kisses down her throat and across her shoulder. "You've no idea the images that played through my mind. They caused me greater anguish than any wound I've ever endured in battle. I would rather die at the hands of my enemies than have to bear the loss of you again."

She struggled to catch her breath. Against her will her fingers curled into the plaid at his chest, drawing him closer. She had a desperate need to cling to him and never let go. She knew better than to give in to these feelings. This would surely lead to madness. But here she was, playing with fire. And welcoming the heat. His passion fueled her own, until she was drowning in needs.

She moaned as he changed the angle of the kiss and took it deeper. Her blood heated and pulsed as his hands, those strong, clever hands, moved over her, tempting and arousing. She felt a rush of pure adrenaline as his head dipped lower, to the soft swell of her breast. Despite the barrier of her wool gown, she could feel the heat of his lips as he began to nibble, to suckle.

She knew she'd allowed him to cross a line, but there was no fight left in her. She was weary of trying to hold back. Tired of fighting him, and her own desperate desire. The truth was, she wanted what he wanted. It seemed the most natural thing in the world to give in to the pleasure, and go with her feelings.

At her gasp of pleasure he lifted his head and kissed her long and slow and deep. Against her mouth he muttered, "The wound to my heart was far worse than any injury from an enemy's sword or dirk. I know in my heart that if I hadn't soon found you, my own life would have ended. I hadn't the will to go on without you, Laurel."

"We have to talk. There are things you need to know about me." She sucked in a breath and brought her hands to his chest, hoping for one last chance to tell him everything, before she lost control.

But he was beyond listening. Beyond reason. Beyond anything except the passion that had become a beast inside him, fighting to be free.

"The time for words is past, my love." With his mouth on hers he backed her against the wall and kissed her until they were both gasping for air.

She was hot. The flesh at the small of her back, where his hand was resting, was on fire. Even her blood had turned to molten lava, flowing hotly through her veins. She longed to be rid of the heavy clothes that only added to the heat.

As if reading her mind, he released her only long enough to take hold of her gown with both hands and tear it in two before allowing the remnants to fall to the floor. The sound of the fabric ripping could barely be heard above the pounding of their two hearts.

"Oh, Laurel. My beautiful, perfect Laurel. I'll have the village women make you a score of gowns to replace this one. But I must have you now."

With a moan she cupped his head and offered her mouth in a kiss that spoke of hunger and need and a desperate desire to forget everything except this man, this moment. She'd never known a man who could ignite such passion with but a touch.

There were dozens of arguments flitting through her mind. She was an imposter who had no right to this. And what about his right? The right to know the truth about her, and where she came from. The right to make an informed decision about the woman in his arms. Would he hate her in the morning, if she let this opportunity pass?

That thought stopped her for an instant. But as he deepened his kiss, even that last thought was swept from her mind. For now, for this moment, nothing mattered except this man, this kiss, and this hard, driving need that had taken her over the edge of reason.

He brushed soft, butterfly kisses across her shoulder, then lower, to the swell of her breast. This time, without the gown as a barrier, his mouth closed around one erect nipple.

Her knees buckled, and she would have slipped bonelessly to the floor if his hands hadn't been holding her. Hands that moved over her with all the skill of a long-lost lover who knew every part of her as intimately as he knew himself.

"You're so beautiful, Laurel. My wife. My life. And you're mine. All mine."

Stunned, she clutched at him as he found her, hot and moist, and drove her to the first stunning peak.

"I love watching you. In the firelight you look like a

goddess. My goddess of love." His mouth moved over her body, making her tremble with need.

She was desperate to touch him as he was touching her. She reached a hand to tug aside the plaid. It slid to the floor to join her gown.

"Conal." She struggled to speak over a throat gone dry at the sight of him. His body, lean and muscled, took her breath away. But it was his eyes that held her. Eyes dark and dangerous that seemed to see into her very heart, stripping her soul as bare as he'd stripped her body.

The darkness, the danger in those eyes excited her as much as any touch.

Trembling, she offered her lips and he took them with a fierceness that startled them both. And then they were lost in a swirling tide of pleasure.

The world beyond this room no longer mattered. The invaders, bent on destruction, and the traitor who had invited their evil, would be dealt with another time. The revelers in the great hall, consuming copious amounts of food and ale and sending up an occasional cheer, were forgotten. The world Laurel had left, and the strange one she'd entered, faded as they came together in a firestorm of passion.

No man had ever touched her like this. With lips and tongue and fingertips. One moment so gently she felt like weeping. The next, in a frenzy that had her pulse racing, her breath backing up in her throat. Taking her higher. Faster. Further. Until she moved in his arms, steeped in pleasure, eager to give as much as take.

With each touch of those clever hands, with each kiss, they were driven even further into the tide of madness.

Though the sleeping pallet was mere steps away, it seemed an impossible distance. He caught her hands and drew her to the floor, with only their clothes and the animal skins to cushion them.

Laurel could feel the tension humming through him. A tension that matched her own.

Driven by a need for release, she lay beside him and wrapped her arms around him, holding him to her.

"Take me, Conal. End this unbearable need." When she lifted her face to his, he allowed his gaze to move slowly over her.

"Aye, love. 'Tis the same for me. A need too great." His eyes were deep and unfathomable as they stared into hers. "Look at me, Laurel."

Her eyes were fixed on him as she gave herself up to him completely.

"I want to watch you as I love you. I want you to watch me, and know this. I love you always. Not just until death, but for all time."

When he entered her she kept her eyes steady on his, though her vision was blurred by tears. "And I . . ."

Her mouth opened. Her lips formed the words, but there was no time to speak as she wrapped herself around him, needing to move with him, climb with him.

Their breathing grew labored as they moved beyond words, beyond thought, beyond her world or his.

On the hearth an ember exploded into millions of tiny light fragments, mirroring the explosion of two hearts and souls as they seemed to reach the sky and shatter into millions of tiny star fragments, before drifting slowly back to earth.

It was the most incredible journey of their lives.

"Forgive me. I was too desperate." Con kissed away the tears that trickled from the corner of her eye. "I couldn't take the time with you that you deserved."

"That isn't why I'm weeping, Conal." She reached up to run a finger over the frown line between his brows. "I was just so touched by your declaration of love. You see, I don't deserve it."

"Love is not something we deserve. It simply is. I have loved you since I was no more than Donovan's age. I will continue to love you until these Highlands disappear from the earth. Do you not see? My love for you is never ending, Laurel." He smiled. "My father would surely agree. The first time he met you, he told me that the lass who had stolen my heart was a very old soul."

Laurel sat up, framing his face with her hands, staring deeply into his eyes. "Did he really say that?"

"Aye." He grinned. "Why do you find that surprising?"

"Because my grandmother used to say that to me. She often told me that I was an old soul. I was never quite certain what she meant by it."

"Nor I." Con drew her down, wrapping her close in his arms. "But I like to think it means that our souls have been united since the beginning of time." He stared into her eyes. "You're aptly named, my love. With the light that dances in those eyes, you could be our very own mountain laurel, freshly picked from the Highland hills. I love you, my mountain laurel. Now and forever, my darling."

She drew in a ragged breath, wondering what would happen to all his declarations of love when he learned the truth about her.

But not now. Not tonight. What they had just shared was too special, too earth-shattering, to spoil the moment. She was still so stunned by their lovemaking that she wasn't willing to risk this glow to the harsh light of reality.

Instead, she snuggled closer, wanting, needing, to draw out these special feelings for a while longer.

When she sighed, he drew her into the circle of his arms and pressed his mouth to a tangle of damp hair at her temple. "This is where you belong, my love. Here. Safe. With your heart beating in time to mine."

"Oh, Conal." She buried her face against his chest, breathing him in. "If only it could always be."

"Trust me, my love." He moved a little away, and tipped up her face for his kiss. Against her mouth he whispered, "As long as we have our love, nothing can ever separate us again."

And then, with tender touches and gentle kisses, he dried her tears and led her on a slow, easy journey back to that place known only to lovers.

Seven

"My love." Con's sleep-roughened voice, so close to her ear, had Laurel struggling to pull herself up from the deep, deep warmth of perfect contentment.

"What is it?"

"I must leave you. Duncan has alerted me that the barbarians are massing on our border."

"Another attack?" She sat up, shoving hair from her eyes, to see Con tucking a knife into his boot before taking up his sword. "Wait, Conal. There was no time last night . . ." A lie, she knew. There'd been all the time in the world, for they'd spent the entire night in each other's arms. But she had been reluctant to spoil their lovemaking with the things he needed to hear. He'd been so tender, so in tune with her every need. For this one special night she'd felt like a pampered, protected goddess.

Now she felt a sense of urgency. She would simply have to tell him her fears, and pray they didn't fall on deaf ears. "I need to warn you."

"As you do each time I go to battle." He chuckled. "I'll be watchful, my love."

"No." She caught his arm. "It's more than a simple warning. I believe my presence here has a deeper meaning."

"After the night we shared, I'd be a fool to argue with that." She saw the teasing light in his eyes and realized that her words were lost on him.

"Conal, you must listen to me. I believe that I was sent here to save you from those who would destroy you."

"Sent here? By the very ones who had captured you?"

"I don't know who sent me, or how I happened to be here now. Call it Fate. But I know things that you don't know. I want to keep you safe."

"Are you saying you would ride at my side into battle against the barbarians just to keep me from harm?"

"I would, if I were a warrior." It was the truth, she realized with sudden clarity. Though she had no right to his love, this man had become so important to her, she would gladly ride into battle to save him from harm. "That isn't what I meant. The invaders aren't the only ones bent upon your destruction." She saw a blur of movement in the doorway, where Duncan could hardly mask his impatience to be off.

She began speaking faster. "Think about it, Conal. The prisoner hinted that there was a traitor who had betrayed you to the barbarians. Someone within your fortress wants you dead." She took in a deep breath, determined to plunge ahead, no matter what the consequences. "I believe the traitor is your half brother."

He recoiled as though she'd slapped her. Then, taking a breath to compose himself, he touched a hand to her cheek. "I know the two of you have been at odds before, over Donovan, and the fact that you would keep our son a wee babe forever, while Fergus is determined to shape him into a warrior. But think about it, love. Fergus pushes him to become a warrior only because he wants the best for the lad. Know this, Laurel. Though Fergus and I had separate mothers, my brother shares my blood. I would trust him, not only with my life, but with the lives of those I hold most dear." His voice lowered, for her ears alone. "You need to sleep now, love. I gave you no time to rest at all last night, for want of my own pleasure. When we've vanquished the invaders, I'll return and show you, with much more patience, just how much I love you."

"Please listen, Conal."

From the doorway came an impatient voice. "Ye must go, m'laird."

"Aye, Duncan. You'll alert the others?"

"I will."

Conal tore himself from Laurel's arms and strode out behind Duncan, closing the door firmly behind him.

Laurel listened to the sound of their booted feet retreating along the passageway. Too agitated to sleep, she raced to the window and watched as the Highlanders milled about the stables until their leader strode into their midst. Within minutes they'd mounted their horses and were riding out in single file, gradually disappearing into the swirls of morning mist that shrouded the lochs and fells.

She paced the floor, arms crossed, mind awhirl. Hadn't she always considered herself a smart woman? She'd learned every trick in the book to persuade educated men, who thought they knew everything they could about every issue, to listen and accept her point of view. Yet she'd failed miserably to make the most important man in her life hear what she had to say.

The most important man in her life.

That thought caught her by surprise. When had this happened? How had she gone from New York sophisticate to medieval woman locked in the throes of love and domesticity? And why?

The why was easy enough. Conal MacLennan. Con the Mighty. He was everything a man should be, no matter the era. Strong. Brave. Gentle. Compassionate. A born leader, and yet humble enough to care about everyone under his responsibility. He had only to smile at her and she went all weak and feminine. But this wasn't some simple, wild vacation fling. This was serious. War and its bloody aftermath. Life and death.

She'd been yanked out of her comfortable life and dropped into the fifteenth century for a reason. It seemed reasonable to believe that she had something to teach these people who had become so important in her life. And teach them she would, even if they didn't want to learn.

To do that, she must begin by being honest about herself. To that end she discarded Laurel's night shift and dressed in her own clothes—the lacy bra and bikini underwear, the white, man-tailored shirt and designer slacks, before slipping her feet into the sexy sandals that still bore the stain of Con's blood.

She walked to the door and peered around. Assured that no one was about, she started along the passageway until she found the stairway to the tower.

She would return to the scene of the crime, in the hope that she would find enough incriminating evidence to prove, once and for all to Conal, and to anyone else who would listen, that her suspicions were correct.

Laurel climbed the stairs and paused with her hand on the tower door. It stood slightly ajar. Though a faint flickering light shone from within, she couldn't tell if it came from a candle or the dawn light. Believing the room to be empty, she was about to enter when she heard the sound of whispered voices from inside.

She froze in her tracks and strained to hear.

There appeared to be two people speaking. One a man, the other a woman, and both vibrating with passion.

The woman spoke first. "You're sure of this?"

"I know what I saw. She was dead before we tossed her body in the hole. But even if she were to revive, she could not have clawed her way out of the dirt that covered her in that grave. 'Twas far too deep."

"Then this woman is an imposter."

"Or the spirit of Lady Laurel, come back from the dead to avenge her death."

There was a moment of silence, as though they were contemplating the possibility of such a thing.

"If that be so, why did she not accuse us at once?"

"Perhaps she wishes to taunt us first. Or to wait for us to take a misstep."

"Or perhaps her mind was permanently damaged by that blow to the head."

"There is that. Either way, an imposter or a spirit, she must be stopped."

"How?"

"The same way we stopped her before."

"Knowing what she does now, she would never be persuaded to climb to the tower again."

"We will give her no choice."

"But how . . . ?"

"Leave it to me." The woman's voice was a hiss of scorn. "I know the one thing she cannot resist. Now go. And see that you do as instructed as soon as you are far enough from the fortress to be seen."

Hearing footsteps draw near, Laurel looked around for a place to hide. Just then the door was thrown open and she found herself pinned between the heavy, wooden door and the cold, hard wall.

With her heart slamming against her ribs, she heard a servant call out a greeting. "Would ye wish to break yer fast this morrow, m'lady? M'lord?"

As they descended the stairs Laurel heard their voices, though she couldn't see their faces.

"I'll take a meal in my chambers."

"I mustn't tarry. I must join the laird on his hunt for the barbarians."

"Aye, m'lady. M'lord."

As they disappeared from sight, Laurel wondered if her poor heart would ever stop racing. Filling her lungs deeply with air, she stepped cautiously into the tower room, leaving the door open behind her in order to make a quick exit if necessary.

The only furnishings in the room were a rough wooden table and chair. A taper burned in a sconce along the wall, its flickering light doing little to dispel the gloom. The stone walls gave off a chill, as did the narrow windows overlooking the Highlands below. With no panes to buffer it, the wind whistled into the tower with a mournful sound.

Despite the chill, there was a stench here. Death, Laurel thought with a shudder. She studied the stone sill, and the dark stain that had spilled down onto the floor.

Blood. She was certain of it.

Just standing in this room, Laurel felt her stomach lurch. With her hands pressed to her middle, she crossed the room and paused at a window. A dark cloud crossed the sun, blocking its warmth. At once the hairs at the back of her neck prickled, sending a series of shivers along her spine.

Had she been here before? Had she met a horrible fate in the tower? Was this why she was having such a violent reaction to this place? Or was this natural, considering the bleak setting and the bone-chilling cold?

She'd been a fool to come inside. Now that the partners in crime had left the scene, she must do the same. And never come back.

As if to mock her decision, the door slammed shut with a resounding crash. She was so startled she let out a cry and went rigid with shock.

When she was able to compose herself, she took a deep breath and moved to the door. The heavy latch had slipped into place, and though she tried, she couldn't budge it.

Had one of the two conspirators returned, only to find

her here? It would have been an easy matter to slam the door and throw the wooden brace into place, locking her in.

The thought that she'd made it so easy for them to take her prisoner had her clenching her teeth in anguish. *Fool,* she berated herself. *Stupid fool.*

To dispel her fear, she stiffened her spine. "You won't get away with this."

She leaned her weight against the latch and felt it lift. Though her hands were trembling, she managed to turn the knob and inch the heavy door open.

It had been the wind after all.

Free of the tower room she raced down the stairs and didn't stop until she reached the laird's chambers.

Once inside, she felt almost giddy with relief.

"My lady." At the sound of Brinna's voice, she jumped, and turned to find the servant placing a tray containing meat and bread and a goblet of wine on a table.

Beyond the open door, she saw Donovan in his chambers, tossing a length of plaid over his shoulder, much the way his father had earlier that morning.

Brinna studied her mistress clad in the hated clothes of the barbarians, and was quick to note the pallor upon Laurel's cheeks.

She lifted a brow in distress. "What has happened, my lady?"

"Nothing. I . . ." Laurel picked up the goblet and drank while she stalled for time. What must she look like to this simple village lass, wearing garb from another century?

As she set down the goblet, she realized that she need not explain herself. She was the laird's woman. The mistress of the castle. "Donovan and I will take our meal on the balcony." She picked up the tray and walked through the sitting chamber and out onto the balcony, with the lad trailing.

Brinna stood in the doorway, looking thoroughly confused. "Will you need anything more, my lady?"

"Nothing, Brinna. Thank you."

Laurel waited until the door closed behind the servant before greeting the boy. "Did Brinna tell you that the barbarians have returned?"

"Aye, Mother." He nibbled some bread and meat. "She said that Father and my uncle are even now battling the invaders in the Highlands. You should have awakened me. You know it is my fondest wish to be with them."

Laurel took a deep breath. "And so you shall."

Donovan's eyes went wide. "You will let me go to war?"

She nodded. "And I intend to go with you."

The boy was clearly shocked by her suggestion. "What are you saying? Father would never permit you to face the dangers on the field of battle."

"There are things I know that I must tell your father."

"You can tell him when he returns from battle."

Laurel shook her head. "I fear he will never return unless I tell him what I know to be true."

The thought had struck on her way back to these chambers. The last words spoken by the woman had sounded most ominous. The conspirators wanted Conal dead, as well as his wife. What better way than for one of his own trusted men to kill him and make it appear as though he'd been killed by the barbarians?

"Then you will tell me, and I, in turn, will carry your words to Father."

Laurel smiled. He was so like Conal. He had a clever mind and a firm resolve. But she was equally firm. She would not be dissuaded from her plan of action this time.

Lifting a sword and knife from above the fireplace, she handed the sword to Donovan, while tucking the knife into the pocket of her slacks.

The boy stared at the sword in his hand. "This belonged to my father when he was a lad. And to his father before him."

"Now it is yours. I know you'll handle it with honor."

She drew in a breath. "Hurry to the stables and prepare two horses, Donovan. We ride together to your father."

She watched as he danced away. Then she turned and began readying things she might need on the battlefield. She filled a sheep's bladder with ale for disinfectant. She carefully folded clean linen for dressings.

Again she thought about the medical miracles available in her own world, and the amazing skills of twenty-first-century surgeons.

Time was too precious to waste on wishful thinking. Gathering her meager supplies together, she tied them into a bundle and dashed from the room, eager to join Donovan.

If indeed Conal was being led into a trap, she needed to do all in her power to arrive in time to warn him.

Eight

As Laurel raced down the stairs and out the door toward the stables, she was glad to be rid of that clumsy gown and in her own clothes. Though she'd felt elegant, almost regal, wearing Laurel's gowns, there was something to be said for the freedom of modern slacks and a shirt.

As she drew near, she saw two horses grazing near the doors to the stable. What was Donovan thinking? They should have been saddled and ready to ride by now.

Perhaps he was accustomed to the services of a groom, who would no doubt be riding with the warriors.

She set down her bundle and hurried inside, ready to lend a hand.

"Donovan? What are you up to?"

There was no answer.

Laurel looked around. Then, spying a stall door standing open, she stepped inside. Her heart stopped. Lying in the dirt was the lad's sword.

He'd been so proud to carry it. So eager to join the

warriors in battle. There was no way he'd have willingly tossed it carelessly to the ground.

Willingly.

The word sent a splinter of ice along her spine.

Had someone accosted the laird's son? But why?

The two in the tower room had been scheming against her and the laird. She'd never given a thought to the safety of the boy.

With a cry she turned and retraced her steps to the fortress. Once inside, she took the stairs two at a time until she was standing once more in the laird's suite of rooms.

"Donovan." She crossed to the boy's sleeping chambers.

The room stood empty.

As she stormed across the room she saw a scroll. A knife had been thrust into the center of the scroll, pinning it to the lad's sleeping pallet.

She grasped the knife and freed the scroll. The words made her blood freeze in her veins.

We have your son in the tower. Come alone or he dies.

The traitors had given her no time to seek out Conal's help. No time to think of a plan to save the boy. Instead, they were using the invasion by the barbarians to distract Conal while they worked their evil.

That innocent's life was in her hands. Unless she did as they bade, she had no doubt of Donovan's fate.

As she started along the passageway that led to the tower stairs, she could feel her skin begin to crawl with the knowledge that she must once again enter that hated tower room. Everything about that room made her violently ill. Now she understood why.

After all her grand thoughts of teaching these ancient people the knowledge acquired through the ages, it all came down to the most basic of all facts.

This day she must die as she had once before, in this very place. This was her fate.

For there was no doubt that she would willingly exchange her life for the lad's.

"Donovan." Laurel flung open the tower door and cried out his name at the shocking sight that greeted her.

The lad was seated in a chair, wrists and ankles bound. Blood oozed from a cut over his eye. His eye was swollen half shut, the tender flesh already turning a sickening shade of black and blue.

It would seem the lad had put up quite a fight. Yet the woman standing behind him bore not a single mark. She'd used an accomplice, no doubt, to overpower Donovan.

As Laurel started toward the boy, Dulcie pressed the blade of her knife to his throat.

"Stay away, or I'll slit him like a lamb to be slaughtered."

"He's your nephew, Dulcie. You told me you love him like your own. How can you bear to see him harmed?"

"This is your doing." The younger woman's words were spoken between clenched teeth. "Had you not returned, the lad would have been allowed to continue to live in his ignorance. But you've made that impossible."

Laurel fought to keep her tone reasonable. "You don't have to do this, Dulcie. Just allow Donovan to leave this place, and you can do with me what you will."

"Oh, I have every intention of killing you." The young woman's eyes narrowed with fury. "But now the lad must die also. He knows too much to be allowed to live. It's all your fault. If only you'd stayed dead."

Donovan's head came up sharply. "Mother, what does she mean by this?"

Laurel saw the way the knife remained firmly pressed against his throat. She needed to distract the woman from her intentions while she figured a way to free him. "Ask Dulcie."

The lad swallowed and felt the scrape of her blade on his flesh. "You thought my mother dead?"

"I've been assured of her death by the one who killed her." She glared at Laurel. "How did you escape your grave?"

Laurel took a tentative step toward her. "Perhaps I'm a spirit, come back for vengeance. Have you thought of that, Dulcie?"

The young woman instinctively stepped back before firming her resolve and moving close behind the lad again. "Spirit or no, I'll kill him if you come closer."

"What good will that do you? Can you honestly believe that his father will calmly accept the death of his son without seeking retribution?"

"His father will die this day before he can return to the fortress."

Dulcie's words cut like the knife in her hand.

Laurel saw the look of anguish in Donovan's eyes and wondered if the same expression was mirrored in her own. "How can you be sure the barbarians will win?"

The young woman laughed. "I see that you are not as quick-witted as you claim."

At Laurel's puzzled look the woman's smile grew. "War is indeed a way to end a laird's life without question. But suppose there is no war? The wise man invents one, to cover his deed."

"I feared as much. There is no invasion, is there?" Seeing the slight nod, Laurel caught her breath. "Conal will soon tire of the empty chase and order his men back to the fortress."

Dulcie gave a smug smile. "Sometimes, in order to gain power, a man must first gain the trust of the one in power." Her smile faded. Her tone sharpened. "And in order for a woman to gain the power, she must charm a man into doing her bidding."

"This was all your idea?" Laurel studied the young

272 RUTH RYAN LANGAN

woman with new interest. At their first meeting, Dulcie, pale and somewhat vapid, had struck her as surly, but not threatening. Now she was revealing herself to be both shrewd and cunning. And thoroughly evil.

"I am cursed with a man who would be content with nothing more than a hovel, as long as it was filled with his woman and pack of bairns." She spat the word as though it were vile.

"Is that why you and Fergus remain childless?"

Dulcie merely smiled. "There are ways to prevent a babe. There are certain women in my village who know which herbs to take for such things."

"And so you've withheld a child from your husband, in order to force him to do your will?"

The young woman threw back her head and laughed. "Again you prove your ignorance."

Before Laurel could comment, Dulcie shot her a look of triumph. "I am with child. And now, my man will do whatever pleases me, if . . ." she added in silky tones, ". . . he wishes to see his bairn thrive."

Laurel felt a wave of sickness. The evil in this room was a living, palpable thing. She no longer knew whether it was the tower or the woman standing before her. Both had the power to strip her of whatever strength she had left. But for Donovan's sake, she needed to fight back.

Dazed, disoriented, she thought about the knife in her pocket. What good would it do her if it cost the boy his life? She had to find a way to distract this evil woman.

Dulcie lifted the blade from Donovan's throat and used it to point to the window across the room. "You know what you must do. Go."

When Laurel hesitated, she slid the knife across the boy's flesh in one swift motion. He cried in pain and Laurel watched in shock as a thin line of blood began oozing from the wound.

"The next will be fatal if you disobey me again. Go to the window ledge."

At Dulcie's command Laurel forced herself to move, despite the fact that her rubbery legs were threatening to fail her.

She needed to get closer to Donovan and Dulcie, not farther away. But to disobey the woman's command would cause the boy to die anyway.

With each step her mind was awhirl with ideas.

If only she could think of a way to get Dulcie to leave Donovan's side. It was their only chance.

She had but one option. She was prepared to fight this woman to the death, if necessary, in order to spare the lad's life.

Con reined in his mount. "How many did you see, Duncan?"

"A score or more, m'laird."

"Where could they have gone?"

"Hiding in the brush, I'd wager." Duncan urged his horse along the trail, using his sword to move aside the low-hanging branches of the trees that hugged the ground.

Fergus, riding ahead with several warriors, splashed through a stream, sending a spray of water into the air. On the other shore, he paused, and looked toward the laird before shaking his head.

The morning sun had burned off the last wisps of fog that had been hanging over the loch, leaving the sky a clear, cloudless blue.

Duncan looked up, shielding the sun from his eyes. "A fine day for fighting."

"Or loving." Frustrated, Con thought about the night he'd spent in Laurel's arms. He'd wanted to spend the morning with her, kissing her awake, and then perhaps stealing yet another hour in their bed before having to face the day.

And here he was, doing the very thing he'd been doing

on the day she'd disappeared, lost to him for what had seemed an eternity.

How long had she been gone? He'd lost track of the time. Days had turned into nights, each one an endless round of torment, wondering if he would ever be able to hold his beloved in his arms again.

When his man-at-arms finished searching the trail ahead, Con waved him over. "Duncan. I would confer with you."

"Aye, m'laird?"

"There's been no sign of the barbarians. 'Tis time to return to the fortress."

"A while longer, m'laird. I sense them somewhere nearby."

Con had always trusted Duncan's instincts. The man was a fine warrior, as well as a devoted friend.

"Fergus." He cupped his hands to his mouth and shouted.

His half brother turned, then wheeled his mount and galloped up to where Conal and Duncan were mounted. "Aye, Con? What is your wish?"

"Any sign of the invaders?"

"Nay." Fergus shook his head. "Unless they were on foot, for there are no fresh horse droppings."

Con nodded. "I agree. Duncan wants us to continue the search. What say you?"

Fergus shrugged. "If you so order it, I suppose I could take some of the men and go on."

Duncan smiled his encouragement. "Aye. No sense in wasting the day."

" 'Tis settled then." Con clapped a hand on his brother's shoulder before turning to Duncan. "Will you ride with them?"

Duncan decided instantly. "I ride with ye, m'laird."

"Always watching out for me, are you?" With a smile, Con turned his horse toward home.

Duncan remained, watching until the others disappeared into the forest before wheeling his mount.

Ahead of him on the trail, Con was deep in thought when he abruptly slid from the saddle and knelt to study a trail of fresh prints in the dirt.

Deer, he thought in disgust. Not horses.

At that very moment an arrow sang out, just missing him, and landed in the trunk of a tree overhead. Had he been astride his mount, the arrow would surely have caused a mortal wound.

He ducked behind his horse and looked around. The trail was empty. He felt a moment of triumph. The one who'd fired would be caught in a trap, for somewhere behind him, Duncan was bringing up the rear.

Pulling himself into the saddle, he quickly backtracked, but found no invaders.

He came across Duncan kneeling in the dirt.

Alarmed, he was on his feet within seconds, hurrying to his friend's side. "Did they get you, too? Are you hurt?"

"Aye." Clutching his arm, Duncan got slowly to his feet.

Though the forest trail was shaded, a glint of sunlight found its way through the canopy of leaves and reflected off something shiny in the warrior's hand.

Caught unawares, Con didn't react quickly enough as he brought up his arm to block the thrust of the knife. The blade found its mark, lodging deep in his chest. Pain ripped through him, dropping him to his knees.

As Duncan stood over him, watching the blood spill from his wound, Con brought his fist into the warrior's groin.

With a sharp hiss of pain, Duncan fell to one knee. At once Con was on him. The warrior wheezed out a breath, then struggled to his feet, with Con's arm wrapped around his neck. Duncan realized that, though his friend was mortally wounded, he was in for the fight of his life.

"Why?" Con's knife was already in his hand, lifted to his old friend's throat.

" 'Twas all part of the plan."

"What plan?"

"To distract you, while your wife and son die."

"Nay!"

Con wasn't even aware of his blade slicing through flesh and bone. He had no recollection of the limp body dropping to the ground as he turned and weakly pulled himself onto the back of his horse. He saw nothing but a haze of shadows through the mist of fury mixed with terror that glazed his eyes as he urged his mount toward the distant fortress.

The pain of his wound was forgotten. His only thought was that he had to be in time to save those he loved, or his life would be forever meaningless.

Nine

Once at the fortress, Con slid weakly from the saddle and stumbled inside, his feet too numb to feel the stairs that led to his chambers. Finding it empty, he looked about in desperation, when the flutter of a scroll caught his eye.

Picking it up, he read the words before crumpling it in his fist. With a vicious oath he drew his sword and raced up the steps to the tower, praying that he wasn't too late.

Hearing the approaching footsteps, Dulcie looked up in anticipation. "I was beginning to think . . ." When she saw Con in the doorway, her eyes widened in stunned surprise. "You! You're alive."

"Aye. And the murdering bastard who thought to use his position of trust now lies dead in my place."

Though the woman paled, she kept her wits about her, continuing to hold the knife to the lad's throat.

Con saw the blood that oozed from his son's wound, staining the front of the lad's plaid. He lifted his sword menacingly. "Release Donovan at once."

"You will stay away, m'laird, or my blade will sever the lad's head from his shoulders before your sword can stop me."

Con could feel his strength waning, and knew that he had to act quickly, or all would be lost. The wound was draining him so that even a puny female like Dulcie would soon be able to best him in battle.

Leaning heavily on his sword, he struggled to keep from swaying. "Why, Dulcie? What is it you want?"

She smiled now. "I see my laird is as compliant as his wife, while I hold the lad's life in my hands. You will do whatever I tell you, rather than see your son killed before your eyes."

Through gritted teeth Con demanded, "I ask you again, woman. What is it you want?"

"What I have always wanted. Power."

"And you think to have it by killing me and mine? What of the villagers? Do you think they will stand behind the woman who robbed them of their laird?"

"Your death will not be laid at my hand. 'Twill be blamed on the barbarians."

"And these?" He indicated Laurel and Donovan. "Will their deaths be laid at the feet of the barbarians, also?"

"It will appear that a lone invader was able to slip into the fortress. Perhaps I will have a few others join these two in death to make it look like a proper invasion. Brinna, I think." She was speaking to herself now, as though unaware of the others in the tower room. "And Cook. She never forgot that I was once the daughter of a slut, before coming to live in the laird's fine fortress."

"You're mad."

"Am I? Then think of this. Once the proper time for grieving has passed, the villagers will choose a new laird."

"The one you had chosen to replace me now lies dead in the forest."

"If you expect me to go limp with remorse over the death

of Duncan, you are sadly mistaken, m'laird. I was only using him to do my bidding."

"Duncan was my friend. How did you get him to do your bidding?"

When she said nothing, he turned to Laurel for an answer. "Can you explain it to me?"

Laurel stared across the room at the evil woman. "She knows how to give a man his most cherished possession."

He arched a brow. "And what would that be?"

"A child."

He turned to Dulcie in astonishment. "You are with child? It is Duncan's?"

She merely smiled, the smug little cat smile of a woman with many secrets.

His eyes frosted over. "Have you forgotten that you're still wed to my brother? Does Fergus know?"

Laurel stepped up beside him and drew a handkerchief from her pocket, pressing it to stem the flow of blood from his chest. "Don't you see, Conal? She and your brother are in this together."

He closed a hand over hers. "Nay, my love. I know in my heart that Fergus has no knowledge of this evil deed."

She gave a sigh of impatience. "There's no time to argue the point, Conal. You're wounded."

" 'Tis nothing."

She studied her handkerchief, already soaked with his blood. His skin had turned an ominous shade of gray.

Her voice lowered with feeling. "You said that once before. But this time, I can see that the wound is grave."

He drew in a breath and turned to Dulcie. "When your husband learns of your deed, he will see you punished, even if it be by his own sword."

Again that smug smile as she whispered, "Like Duncan, Fergus will do my bidding."

"How can you be so sure?"

"It is as you said. I am still wed to your brother. He is

the logical choice to replace you. Without anyone to say otherwise, he will believe the bairn his. He has long yearned for a child. He would never do anything to harm its mother."

Laurel saw a shadow in the doorway and knew she had to act quickly to distract Dulcie.

She took a step toward her. "You know how the laird and I love Donovan. Release him and we'll do whatever you ask."

"Do you think me a fool? Do not come closer." Dulcie kept the blade of her knife against Donovan's throat.

In defiance, Laurel took yet another step, keeping the young woman's attention focused on her and away from the door. "You're enjoying this sense of power, aren't you?"

"Aye. I knew the lad would be your weakness. You and the laird will do as you're told, as long as this precious life hangs in the balance."

"Wouldn't you do the same?" She had to keep this madwoman talking. Had to figure out a way to wrestle that knife from her hands.

"Only a fool lets someone, anyone, have power over her. I'll not put anyone else ahead of my own life."

"Not even the child you carry?"

"The child will live within me only as long as it serves my purpose." Dulcie gave a dry laugh. "I told you that there are women in my village who know what herbs to take to conceive a child. There are plants that can take life, as well. And I know all of them. Now then." Her tone shifted. There was a note of finality in her voice. "We will do what we came here to do."

Laurel kept her gaze fixed on Dulcie. "You mean you'll do what you did the last time I disappeared? When you had me thrown from the tower window?"

Dulcie gave a quick laugh. "Aye. Only this time, when I've finished with these two, I shall go below stairs and drive the laird's sword through your heart myself, to assure that you'll never again return."

Caught up in her sense of power, she pointed dramatically with the knife. "Climb to the balcony rail. Now! 'Tis time for you to leave us."

Con used that instant of distraction to reach out and kick his son's chair out of Dulcie's reach. At the same moment, Fergus, who had been watching and listening from the open doorway, charged across the room with his sword lifted.

Laurel, believing that Fergus meant to kill Con, pulled the knife from her pocket and leapt into the fray, determined to protect the wounded laird, even if it meant losing her own life.

Seeing what she intended, Con snatched the knife from her hand just as Fergus brought his sword through Dulcie's heart.

Stunned, Dulcie could only stare at him in horrified silence as she dropped to her knees.

Fergus stood over her. "I knew you didn't love me when you agreed to our betrothal. I knew in my heart that had I not been kin to the laird, you'd have never looked at me." His hand curled into a fist as he watched the blood spread in ever-widening circles down the bodice of her gown and onto the floor. "But I was lonely. All my life I've been alone. And seeing the love between my brother and his wife, I foolishly believed that if I loved you without asking anything in return, it would be enough." He lowered his head in shame and disgust. "Now I know that you're incapable of loving, because you can't see beyond your own selfish ambition."

"Fool," she cried. "You have killed not only me, but your bairn, as well."

"No more lies, woman. I stood just outside the tower door and heard everything. The child isn't mine. Nor would you have ever permitted it to live."

With her last breath, Dulcie spat at him. "I would have made a better laird than you or your . . ." Whatever else she'd been about to say was lost as she gave up her life.

Fergus felt for a pulse at her throat. Finding none, he turned away, unable to even look at her.

Together Con and Laurel untied Donovan, and with tears of joy and relief, gathered him into their embrace.

Still weeping, Laurel crossed to Fergus, catching his hand in both of hers. "Forgive me, Fergus, for doubting you."

"Knowing what I do about Dulcie, you had every right to believe the worst of me."

"Mother!"

At Donovan's cry, Laurel turned to see Con drop to the floor, his hand clutching his chest. Blood spilled in an ever-widening river from between his fingers.

"Oh, my darling." Laurel used his plaid to mop at the blood, but there was no stopping the flow.

She stared in horror at the blood that spilled from his wound. So much blood.

Fergus dropped to his knees beside his brother. "What can I do?"

"Promise me that you will love Donovan as your own."

"I swear. He will grow to be a Highlander you will be proud of."

"I can ask nothing more."

The two men clasped hands. As Fergus stepped away and drew Donovan with him, Laurel caught Con's hands in hers. "There are things I must tell you, Conal. I've tried so many times, but now they can't wait."

"Aye, love." Pain glazed his eyes. His skin had lost all its color.

"My name is Laurel Douglas. But I'm not your Laurel. I come from another world. The twenty-first century. Something happened. I don't know what, but somehow I found myself here with you. I thought I was sent here to teach you all the things we'd learned in the past hundreds of years. I thought I could change the course of history. I didn't mean to . . ." She paused, struggling to find the words. "I had no right to your love. And now, if you should die, it's all been for nothing. Oh, don't you see? None of this makes any sense if you die."

Despite his pain, he managed a weak smile. "I care not where you came from, love. You're my Laurel. My own true love."

"But I . . ."

Though it cost him, he touched a hand to her cheek. "It matters not where you were, or how long we were separated, we belong together. As for all that you would teach me, think of this: Perhaps you were really sent here to learn."

"To learn what?" She was fighting tears now. She could feel them, tightening her chest, struggling to break free of the hard, tight lump in her throat. She bravely swallowed them back.

"Perhaps over the centuries you'd forgotten what it is to be truly loved. Perhaps you came back, not to teach, but to learn."

Her eyes went wide as she digested the truth of his words.

"But if that's so, and if you truly love me, you can't die. You can't leave me, now that I've found your love."

"I have no choice. My wound is mortal. But know this." He stared into her eyes, willing her his strength. "Love such as ours never ends, even in death. It lives on for all time."

She could no longer hold back the tears. They fell freely, spilling down her cheeks, running in rivers down the front of her shirt.

"I can't bear to lose you, now that I've only just found you, Conal."

"I'll never leave you alone, my love. Will you trust me in that?"

She wiped her tears and clasped his hands. "But you're dying. How can you be with me if you . . . ?" She swallowed back the word she couldn't speak, and managed to whisper, "I'll try to believe, Conal."

"You must believe it. I will be always with you, my love. Until the end of time. And beyond."

She felt his hands go slack in hers. And though his eyes were still open, the light had gone out of them.

Shattered, Laurel continued to kneel beside him, her hands holding his in a death grip, as her tears mingled with his blood.

As if from a great distance she felt a touch on her shoulder, and looked up to see Fergus, his arm firmly around Donovan's shoulders.

"The lad and I will fetch the women of the village to prepare the laird for burial, my lady." He added softly, "They will stay with you, for you cannot be alone now."

"Thank you, Fergus." Laurel caught Donovan's hand, squeezed.

He lifted her hand to his lips, before trailing his uncle from the room.

When they were gone, she pressed a kiss to Conal's lips. Already they were cold and unresponsive.

Drained beyond belief, she stretched out beside him and gave in to a feeling of profound exhaustion and grief.

Ten

Laurel awoke from a deep sleep and looked around, hoping against hope to discover that everything she'd experienced was just a dream. Instead, she felt her heart sink as she realized she was in the fortress chambers, on the sleeping pallet she'd shared with Conal.

Conal. The pain of loss was like a knife to her heart.

In the other room, Donovan and his uncle were talking in low tones.

Bits and pieces of the previous day began flitting through Laurel's mind, as if in a nightmare. The burial of Con the Mighty, with clan members from all over the Highlands arriving to pay their respects. The women offering her food, ale, quiet comfort. The whispers about Dulcie and the shame she brought upon her husband, whom she married only because he was kin to the laird.

Laurel could recall speaking softly to Fergus, determined to let him know that, despite her earlier misgivings, she trusted him completely. She'd told him repeatedly how much his brother loved him. He, in turn, assured her over and over that he wished to honor his brother's memory by helping teach Donovan to be a brave and honorable Highlander.

When the villagers declared Fergus to be their new laird, he announced to the clan that he would remain so only until Donovan was old enough to claim the title. And he asked that Laurel continue to be regarded as mistress of the fortress. Though she was honored and touched by his declaration, she had refused, saying that one day he would meet a woman worthy of him to fulfill that duty, as would her son when he reached manhood.

Lying very still, Laurel thought again about the things Con had told her before he died. What a fool she'd been, thinking she'd been sent here to teach these poor, ignorant people all the fine things her world had discovered through the ages. She'd been the student, learning about the most basic of all lessons—life and death, honor, integrity, and most of all, love. Real, abiding love, not the stuff of movies.

"You're awake, Mother." Donovan hurried over and knelt beside her as she sat up, tossing aside the covers.

She was surprised to see that she was still wearing her clothes from the previous day. Why had she clung so tightly to her twenty-first-century uniform? As long as she was here, why didn't she simply give in and wear the garb of the other women?

"How long have I been asleep?"

"Not long." Fergus walked up to stand behind his nephew. "You insisted upon remaining with the others while they mourned the laird. It was only when we insisted that you lie down that you gave in to exhaustion." He gave her a gentle smile. "You should sleep awhile, my lady."

"Maybe later." She got to her feet and offered her hand to Fergus. "Thank you for your love and loyalty, and for all that you've done for Donovan."

"I give you my solemn vow, as I gave to my brother on

his deathbed, that I will do all I can to serve you and the lad. And I will do all in my power to see that Donovan becomes a Highland laird worthy of the love of his clan, for I love the lad like my own."

"I know you do. And that greatly eases my mind." She drew Donovan into her arms and kissed him. "Your father died knowing you would live a life that brings him honor."

"I will, Mother. I will make you and Father proud."

"I'm already proud of you. I couldn't be more proud." She started toward the door, then paused and turned. "I need to go to Conal's grave. Alone."

"I understand, my lady." Fergus drew an arm around the lad's shoulders.

Laurel studied the two of them and felt a sense of relief that Donovan had such a fine man to see him through the grief and loneliness that was bound to follow.

She walked along the passageway until she'd left the fortress. Conal's grave was but a few short steps away.

As she knelt beside the fresh mound of earth, it occurred to her that one day a new castle would be built over this very spot. It seemed a fitting tribute to the man who had taught her about true love.

She thought of his words, on the night they'd made love.

As long as we have our love, nothing can ever separate us again.

And then came the realization that, though he'd told her often how much he loved her, she'd never said the words to him. At first, she simply hadn't realized how much he meant to her. And by the time she knew just how deeply she loved him, there hadn't been time.

"Conal." She wasn't aware at first that she was speaking the words aloud. She was simply compelled to say all the things that were in her heart. "I don't know when it happened, or how. But I do know that I lost my heart to you. I tried not to. I didn't feel worthy. But your love was so pure, so honest, and so all-consuming, there was no way I could deny it. I simply fell in love with you. Completely. Your life and your death have affected me so deeply, I'm not sure I'll ever recover. I love you, Conal. I will spend a lifetime missing you so . . ."

The words died on her lips as a wild rush of wind sent her hair flying about her face. A dark shadow seemed to blot out the sun. Darkness overtook the land, and Laurel shot to her feet, trembling in fear.

The darkness frightened her until she saw a bright light moving toward her.

Seeing it, she felt a strange sense of peace, along with a hint of anticipation. As though the light was a symbol of life. Of hope. Of all that she'd been longing for.

As the light drew near, she blinked against its brightness. At first she'd thought it was a torch, but this light didn't flicker like a flame.

An electric torch, she realized. A high-powered flashlight.

She looked around, dazed and more than a little confused, only to realize that the ancient fortress was no longer towering in the background. In fact, it was nowhere to be seen.

She was back in the five-star hotel, which had been built over Conal's gravesite. She was once again standing in front of the tapestry.

The voices of their tour and guide had faded away. The only sound to break the stillness was the tread of footsteps on the highly polished wood floor.

A man approached, surrounded by a halo of light. When she lifted a hand to shield her eyes from it, he lowered the flashlight away from her face.

"Sorry." The voice was deep and cultured, with a hint of Scottish burr. "We've had a power failure, but only in this wing, apparently. An electrician is already working on it. Looks like you got separated from your tour group. They were ushered to the dining hall in another wing of the castle. Lucky for you, I thought I'd make certain no one was stranded in the darkness."

Couldn't he see that she'd been crying? Wasn't he wondering about the bloodstains on her clothes?

Laurel glanced down at herself and realized that she looked exactly as she had when all of this adventure had begun. Her slacks and shirt as neat and tidy as if she'd only now put them on.

But not quite.

He pointed the flashlight toward her sandal. "Is that blood? Have you injured yourself?"

"It happened . . ." She wondered how she could possibly explain to him all that had occurred, when she couldn't even explain it to herself. "It happened some time ago."

"Are you certain? I assure you, if you've been harmed in any way, I'll make it up to you. As the current owner of MacLennan Castle, it's my duty to see to even the most minor of inconveniences."

She peered at him in the dim light. "You're the laird?"

There was a hint of laughter in his voice. "That's what I would have been called in earlier times. Now I'm just plain Conor MacLennan, the eighth Earl of Heath, and Lord of the MacLennan Clan. Just a fancy way of saying I'm the innkeeper. And you are . . . ?"

"Laurel Douglas."

"Laurel." He lifted the flashlight to her face. "That's a special name in our clan. But I'm not surprised. With the light that dances in those eyes, you could be our very own mountain laurel, freshly picked from the Highland hills. We wear the laurel as our heraldic badge." He pointed the light to his lapel pin in the shape of a laurel leaf.

His words, so like those spoken by another, had her head spinning. To settle herself, she reached out and touched a hand to the wall.

And then she thought of Conal's words as he lay dying:
I will be always with you, my love. Until the end of time. And beyond.

Oh, Conal. You kept your word.

"I beg pardon. Did you say something?"

Laurel studied the way he was dressed, in a navy blazer and gray pants, the collar of his white shirt open at the throat. "Just thinking aloud. I'd have expected the lord of the castle to wear a kilt."

"I do, for formal occasions." He paused. "Since you've missed dinner with your tour, why not join me for a bite of supper in my suite?"

"You actually live here?"

"My family has called this place home for hundreds of years." He offered his arm, and though her mind was reeling from all she'd been through, it seemed the most natural thing in the world to place her hand on his arm and move along by his side.

Within minutes they'd passed through the portrait gallery and had moved on to the private section of the castle, which was off-limits to the public.

They rounded a corner and blinked against the light of the hall sconces.

"Good. It seems the electrician has restored power all through the castle."

Laurel glanced over at the man beside her. "Do you make it a habit to invite guests to your suite for dinner?"

"As a matter of fact, you're the first." He smiled down at her, and in the clear light she saw Conal's eyes, Conal's smile. Her heart did a series of somersaults in her chest, and she wondered that she could still breathe.

"It's the strangest thing." Conor paused outside the doors to his suite of rooms and tipped up her face, staring deeply into her eyes. "But I feel as though I've been waiting for you all my life."

Laurel wondered at the lightness around her heart.

She would never know if all the things she'd experienced in the fortress were real, or if they'd been the result of some sort of extreme fear when the power went out, leaving her alone in the dark without the comfort of her tour group. But this much she knew. Because of her introduction to Conal MacLennan, and the adventure they'd shared, she was a different woman from the one she'd been before arriving here. Whether real or a figment of her imagination, Con the Mighty had taught her to believe in love.

Laurel returned Conor's smile. "I was just thinking the same thing."

"Well then." Instead of moving aside, he remained just so, watching as the light in her eyes deepened.

The smile he gave her was absolutely dazzling. "I can't wait to give you a proper Highland welcome."

On the Fringe

MARY KAY MCCOMAS

This story is dedicated to my sister,
Karen Aris,
who gave it to me.

One

"Mauu-uum!" Susan bellowed up the narrow stairwell, her voice like a dental drill on the back of Bonnie's neck. "Mom! Aunt Jan's here."

Great. Could this day get any better?

She stood, brushed dust off the denim that covered her knees and, stretching her back, looked up to the rafters, praying for patience . . . clearly the one thing sweet old Pim hadn't stuffed in her attic. Her grandmother was an accumulator. *Was, is now, and ever shall be*, she supposed.

"Bonnie?" Her sister's voice was firm and demanding, usually critical, sometimes irate . . . but always a comfort in its familiarity. "Come down. We need to talk," she said, though her attention was riveted on her niece. "Does your mother know you're answering the door in this getup, young lady? Do you even own a bra?"

Susan, Bonnie's fifteen-year-old daughter, had two older brothers, a father, fraternal grandparents, and cousins— Janice was not the only family she had and so she tended not to . . . value her as much as Bonnie did.

"I own a few, if it's really your business, and my *mother* bought me this getup, old—"

"Susan." Her sister and daughter could have been old and new versions of the same person standing together at the bottom of the attic steps looking up at her: both long and lean, short dark hair framing their faces—one artfully gray-streaked, the other neon pink–tipped—eyes wide and blue, the same do-something-about-her expression on their faces. "Would you bring me two bottles of water from the fridge? Please," she added when the stormy expression didn't immediately dissipate.

Astutely noting that her afternoon off might well be in peril, Susan turned on her heel, cast one last resentful glance at her aunt, and stomped off in her low-rider stretch jeans and short knit cami.

"You're just asking for trouble with that girl."

"I'm picking my battles." Bonnie sat on a dusty step halfway down and gave a weary sigh. "She's okay. She's just . . . being a kid."

"She's sassy, rude, and you can see her nipples through that . . . top, I guess you'd have to call it since it wouldn't cover her bottom any better."

"That's all true, but she's not a runaway crack whore; she's hardly bitched at all about helping me out here at Pim's this morning, and frankly, I'd rather die than inflict on her the insecurities that I had about my body at her age."

"What was the matter with your body?" She frowned, trying to recall as her gaze skimmed over Bonnie's thirty-pounds-too-heavy, five-foot-eight-inch frame; the spider-web laced through her thick, shiny, auburn waves of hair; the dust on the dark lashes around her gray-green eyes. She looked to be exactly what she was, an almost-forty-year-old mother of three, a third-grade teacher's assistant, and a newly lapsed Republican.

"Nothing. That's the point. There was nothing wrong with my body back then. I was a little taller than everyone else for a while, including most of the boys, and I had breasts . . . not even large breasts, just normal, really, a respectable C cup . . . but I thought I stood out like a giant pink cow in a flock of white sheep. I was always trying to hide and blend in and cover myself up. I was twenty-five before I knew how beautiful I was in high school and thirty-eight, with two boys in college, before I realized how great I looked at thirty."

"And that's my fault?"

"No. Did I say it was your fault?"

"No, but you sound angry. Like you were the only teenager in the world who ever felt weird and ugly. You weren't. While you were busy being tall and voluptuous, oh poor you, I was dealing with Dad's hawk nose *and* I was smart, so I *was* essentially invisible to everyone but the teachers and the geekiest nerds until some moron in a football jersey came to me looking for a miracle one short week before he's due to flunk out of geometry and then, of course, it's *my* fault he doesn't get to play in a tie-breaker game where college scouts *might* have picked him up so he could play and party for another four years before he had to come back to Leesburg to sell cars at his father's dealership where, thirty years later, they can actually—did you know?—refuse to let you test drive the most beautiful moss-green Lexus that you want your husband to buy you for your anniversary and then have to wait three months for after special-ordering it from a different dealership and . . ." She glanced away like she'd lost her next thought and let her body sag against the doorjamb. "I always padded my bras . . . so that in the event that someone actually did see me, they wouldn't try to run a flag up my leg."

She appeared so sad and sounded so dejected that when she finally looked up Bonnie burst into snorting laughter. It was the first heartfelt laugh she'd had in weeks.

"Oh sure." Janice tried to look outraged, then shrugged and gave a grudging chuckle.

As far as Bonnie knew, there was nothing in her sister's life that wasn't bigger or better, sadder or worse, more or less than what she had—and that wasn't always as annoying as it sounded.

"Actually, it's Susan's hair that concerns me most," Bonnie said. It was a relief to finally admit it out loud. "It's like one of those mood rings we used to have when we were kids, remember? In the four weeks since her dad left it's gone from Cool Angry Blue to Royally Mad Magenta to Truly Pissed Pink. When she goes for Furious Flame Red I'm afraid her head'll explode."

Neither sister laughed. They both knew the frustrated, explosive feeling she was talking about and it wasn't funny.

"Then you have to do something." Janice made it sound so easy.

"Like what?"

"Beg Joe to move back in."

"No."

"Just until the two of you can work things out. See a marriage therapist or something. But stay together."

"He chose to leave, Jan. I didn't kick him out. And he's welcome to come back if he wants to, but I'm certainly not going to *beg* him for anything."

"Is this a menopausal thing? They say menopausal women have renewed urges for autonomy."

"Autonomy?" She chuckled in disbelief. "No. I'm not menopausal."

"And you're sure there isn't another woman?"

Joe Sanderson with another woman. This would have made everything less complicated for Janice—a lying, cheating, no-good womanizer like her first husband was something she had experience with and knew how to handle. But a smart, charming, handsome, hard-working, and faithful man who wasn't feeling content in his life—and therefore with his wife—was a puzzle to her. And the fact that her sister felt pretty much the same way about the good, honest man made it a real conundrum.

"I'm sure. There is no other woman."

There wasn't even a good fight to clear the air . . . much less one to stir up any dust . . .

Bonnie could still hear the wind tapping rain against the window that Sunday morning four months earlier—clearly not when their problems began but when they started to surface, like dead bodies from the bottom of a dark lagoon.

It was cold and dreary and too early to get up. She cuddled into Joe's warmth beside her in bed as if he were a pot-bellied stove in winter. He was always so warm. Even his toes were a comfort as they automatically reached for hers, rubbed, and then held them between his feet to heat them like slices of bread in a toaster. She knew he wasn't fully awake when he rolled more completely toward her, lifting his leg so she could slide one of hers between his, or when he drew the covers more tightly around her shoulders as his arms came about her, because they'd cuddled like this hundreds and hundreds of times before and he rarely remembered the next day.

She knew, too, that he would hold her like that, safe and protected, forever . . . if she didn't screw up and give him *the signal*—or what he always seemed to *think* was a signal.

In truth it was just a reflex she'd tried to harness for years. It was that pleasured moan when skin meets skin or cold meets warmth or lonely meets companion; that uncontainable hum from the back of the throat at the sudden, sharp awareness of the senses; that instinctive noise; that . . . *signal* that inevitably turned a perfectly glorious Sunday morning cuddle into full-blown sex—which, admittedly, could go either way, depending on her mood.

As it happened, her mood was favorable that morning . . . well, not at first, but Joe was nothing if not persuasive. His lips and hands knew all the right places to go and which buttons to push. *He can't remember to hang the toilet paper with the loose end on top or to readjust the driver's seat after he drives my car or wait for the commercials to talk to me during* Grey's Anatomy, *but Joe Sanderson can make love to his wife in his sleep,* she thought, heavy-lidded and drowsy.

In fact, the more she thought about it and the more predictable his moves became, the more she began to suspect that he was . . . making love to her in his sleep. As his mouth kissed and nibbled its way down her neck, her mind fought the euphoria in her sex-drugged brain to listen to his breathing. Panting . . . he could be dreaming of sex. And if he was dreaming, well, how did she know if he knew he was making love to her? *I could be anyone!*

He pushed at her nightgown and his warm, wet mouth covered the tip of her breast. She sobbed in a breath of excitement as she started to wonder if she ought to speak—ask him if he knew who he was having sex with, ask him to say her name. But they always advised against waking sleepwalkers, not because of that old heart attack hooey, but because they wake up confused and disoriented and sometimes swinging their fists. This might be true of sleeping . . . sex participants as well, and she was in a precarious position here.

Moments after he entered her, Joe's skin grew warmer and moist against the palms of her hands as he increased his efforts for an orgasm. She stroked him and kissed him and wondered how he could have been so angry with her just last night when he discovered—at the hardware store while buying a small replacement part for her broken garbage disposal—that she'd maxed out the Visa card again, and still want to make love with her this morning. *That is, if he's aware it's me . . .* For all she knew a hole in the mattress or a knothole in a tree would have been just as convenient for his dreams of . . . oh say, Nicole Kidman.

But Joe didn't hold grudges. He was a blow-up-and-it's-over kind of guy. She was the grudge holder. *That's true,* she admitted to herself with a large sigh. But she wasn't irresponsible with the money. *We have children, children want stuff and stuff costs money.* Yes, she was a little overindulgent with them but she didn't mean to be and if she was spoiling them and ruining their character—not that he ever actually accused her of it—it was a little late to change things now. *To suddenly cut the children off for no particular—*

"What the hell are you doing?" Bonnie's eyes snapped open to see Joe staring down at her, his strong, angular face flushed with exertion, his breath coming in short, desperate gasps. He looked ready to explode. "Baby, you're killing me!"

"Oh! You're awake." Did she say that out loud?

In the dim light he looked surprised, then incredulous—so she must have—and then almost amused before he closed his sleepy hazel eyes, gave a soft chuckle, and lowered his forehead to hers. "This does feel familiar, sweetheart . . ." He took two more gulps of air. ". . . but not so much that I can do it in my sleep."

"No, of course not. That was a stupid thing to say. I don't know why I said—"

"You're not into it, are you?"

"No. I am into it. I am. It's great. Wonderful. I just . . . I was . . . I got . . . sidetracked."

"Sidetracked." His expression as he studied her was curious. After a moment, he sighed and rolled off her, asking, "Sidetracked where? To what? Problems at work? Here?"

"Nowhere. I was here. With you." This wasn't a conversation she wanted to have this early in the morning, under these particular circumstances, so she turned her back to him, bunched up her pillow, and tried to settle in again. "I was cold. I wanted to cuddle."

"Okay. Good. Then why'd you give me the signal for sex?"

She pulled the covers up close to her face and mumbled into the pillow. "I didn't."

"What?"

"Nothing," she said through her breathing space in the sheets. "I'm sorry, honey. Go back to sleep."

"I'm awake now and don't be sorry. Talk to me. What did you say just then?"

Oh, Christ! Well, fine. Maybe twenty years was long enough not to mention that an instinctive hum was not a fucking signal!

So to speak.

"I said . . ." She flipped the bedding back and half-turned toward him. "I didn't."

"You didn't what?"

"I didn't give you a signal. I gave a loud sigh, a purr. I was cold, you were warm, it felt good, I hummed. It's an instinctive noise. I do it when I eat ice cream. I do it when I take a bubble bath and when I hug Susan or the boys and after my first sip of a really cold beer. It doesn't mean I want to have sex. It's just something that happens when something feels good or tastes good or . . . or *is* good, *like* sex. But it doesn't mean I *want* it."

She watched as his eyes scanned the ceiling, waited while he came to the inevitable conclusion.

"Are you telling me that all these years I've been thinking you wanted sex with me and you didn't?"

"No. I love making love with you. You know I do. And when I'm not in the mood I tell you I'm tired or mad or whatever. Don't I tell you?" He nodded. "All I'm saying is that most of the time when I make that noise, that nice moan, I'm just . . . making that noise. I can't help it."

"Why haven't you ever said anything?"

She shrugged. "At first because I thought it was you wanting sex and that was fine with me—great in fact—but then after a few years I discovered I could get just the cuddle I wanted without all the bother of sex if I didn't make that noise. And by then it was too late to tell—"

"The bother of sex?"

"You know what I mean."

"I think I'm beginning to."

"Stop it. We have a great sex life and you know it or you wouldn't have stopped just now. You could tell I wasn't really into it and you stopped. How many times has *that* happened?"

"How do I know you weren't just too sleepy to do a better job of pretending this time?"

Proof of orgasm. Even having children wasn't corroborating evidence.

"Have I ever lied to you?"

"I don't know."

"No. I haven't. I make tiny omissions . . . for your own good, but I have never lied straight to your face." She finished rolling over to face him more directly. "Do you believe me?"

"Maybe."

"Then I am telling you straight to your face that I've only had to fake an orgasm maybe . . . eight times the whole time we've been married. You're that good," she added as a sugar coating.

His sweet tooth was still asleep. He came up on his elbow, more curious than wounded. "Which eight times?"

"Oh." She groaned. "Give me a break. I don't remember. I— Yes, I do. Both times you went out fishing with Greg Morris and came back sunburned and drunk and, unfortunately, amorous. You were done before my head hit the pillow, so I had to pretend I was done too so you'd roll over, pass out, and leave me alone."

His keen green eyes narrowed as he tried to remember. "And the other six times?"

"I don't know. And . . . and that's not the point anyway. Actually, I've forgotten the point. What is it?"

"That what I always thought I knew about you might not be true. Maybe I don't know you as well as I thought I did."

"Oh, yeah. Well . . ." What could she say? She was a bride a month after she graduated from RFK High School in May. He was the ripe old age of nineteen when they married. How well could two people know each other after living side by side for twenty years? Did other couples discuss every little opinion or thought that passed through their minds? And how often were they allowed to change their minds? How could something not bother her too much the first dozen times it happened early in her marriage but drive her *completely insane* the last six dozen times in the last eight years? At what point in a marriage did it become okay for one to assume they knew the other so well that they could presume to know how the other would respond or react? And, come to think of it, she wasn't the only one who didn't always speak her mind. "Well, what about my mushroom soup meatloaf that you ate and hated for years before you said anything?"

"You can't compare meatloaf to sex."

"Yes, I can. It's the same thing. I go to all the trouble of making what I think is a perfectly good dinner for you and you eat it and you say it's fine and years go by before you mention to Susan that you used to *luuuv* your mother's meatloaf and that she used the recipe off the oatmeal box."

"Mushrooms have no taste."

"Why didn't you just say so? Why say it's fine and choke it down if you hate it?"

"Because you hate to cook and you went to all the trouble of cooking the meatloaf for me, so I ate it."

She sighed, loud and short-tempered. "Did you ever think that if I'm going to the trouble of cooking at all that I'd rather go to the trouble of making something you like than the trouble of making something you can barely tolerate? At least I usually enjoyed the sex I didn't ask for."

They studied one another in the weak morning light until Joe finally leaned over and dropped a kiss between her eyebrows, fell back onto his pillow, and closed his eyes. But he didn't go back to sleep. She could hear the rumble of the gears grinding in his brain, even over the constant stream of questions in her head. What did this mean? Was their marriage in trouble? Were his feelings hurt? Was it better to get these things out in the open or, if they didn't make you nuts, just let them go? Why'd she have to finally explain about the hum? And what were they going to use for a signal now?

Two

That was just the beginning. In the weeks that followed, more minor irritations and misunderstandings came to light, and after those a few more. Nothing worth fighting about, nothing that changed the fundamental love they had for one another, but certainly enough to make them question, even more, how well they really knew each other . . . or if over the years they'd grown apart, become different people and if deep fondness and friendship—and kids and bills and habit—rather than true love, held them together.

"Maybe a few weeks apart," Joe suggested after a vigorous bickering about who put what clutter in the basement and whose priceless possessions needed to be disposed of first.

"You're *leaving* me?" Stunned, she stopped stacking boxes and turned to face him. "I want to keep seventeen boxes of *Vogue* magazines that I've been collecting since I was sixteen years old and you're *leaving* me?"

"No. Of course not. It's just something I've been thinking about lately."

"*Leaving* me?" She glanced at the ceiling-high pile of boxes. "Look, I can probably whittle these down to . . . say, thirteen boxes, less maybe. And I don't really care if you want to keep all the old fishing and camping stuff. None of the new stuff is broken or has any holes in it, but if you want to keep the old stuff, too, that's okay. None of this junk is worth breaking up our marriage for."

"Someday I'm going to wish I got all that in writing." He chuckled and stepped forward to wrap his arms around her. "And you're right. None of this is worth breaking up our marriage. Nothing is. I just think that . . ." He grasped her shoulders and held her at arm's length. "God, Bonnie, do you realize how long we've known each other? We met at Chicky Davis's birthday party when you were this . . . God, this luscious, funny, smart, completely *un*self-absorbed junior and I was a . . . just the opposite senior and . . . and aside from our daughter and my mother you're the only woman I've ever loved. We fell in love young, we got married young, had kids young. We both gave up dreams to be together and I wouldn't have it any other way but . . ."

"But what?" She braced herself.

"But maybe we need to step back a little, take a look at who we are . . . now. Who we are alone, who we are together. We're not teenagers anymore; we've changed. A lot. Hell, we have a son who's older than we were when we got married. Maybe it's time to get reacquainted with ourselves . . . and then with each other again."

She once heard or read somewhere that if the word *divorce* was never brought up during a fight or in a discussion with your spouse then it could never be an option in your marriage—and was acutely aware that Joe hadn't gone anywhere near the word . . . yet.

And he was right about them changing over the years. Sometimes, she didn't know where he stopped and she began. Other times, she felt a distinct division between him and a self she kept quiet and hidden away like an undesirable relative. As if that part of her was someone she didn't think he'd understand, someone she wasn't sure he'd even like . . . and yet it was still *her*, acting out from time to time, pushing to the foreground when she least expected it, surprising everyone—including herself.

Like now. Time alone was suddenly very appealing.

"I don't know how you plan to spend time apart without leaving me." She hoisted a box of magazines to the floor so they'd each have one to sit on. "But I'll at least listen."

His proposal was simple. They'd take two months—a negotiable time if either of them found it too difficult—and he'd rent a small, furnished apartment just minutes from the house.

"In case you need me to open a jar or kill a spider." He grinned and she simpered back. He was joking, of course. He'd seen her deliver three babies, watched her napalm gopher holes with gas and matches in the front yard, and he had even cleaned up the mess after she killed a snake to death by hysterically chopping it into two dozen pieces with a garden hoe. She wasn't a helpless female. "Or if one of us starts to go blind without sex."

Now *that* might actually happen.

Everything else in their plan was to remain the same. The same joint bank account, same jobs, and the same car pool schedule for Susan.

She'd still be at home, but he'd be gone. And that's why it wasn't working . . .

Susan returned and handed both frosty, cold bottles of water to Bonnie with the silent, profoundly put-upon service only a teen can deliver.

"Thanks, honey." Bonnie passed a bottle to her sister. "You've been a great help this morning. So if the floors are done and the rugs are back where they belong and all the

crystal is washed, you can go ahead and leave if you want."
She was used to speaking to the girl's back these days and
pretended it didn't bother her. She heard rather than saw
her start down the front stairs and lifted her voice. "First
check on Pim for me, will you?" Then in a low mutter, she
added, "And when you see your dad tell him I'm wide open
to the concept of joint custody."

Bonnie took a long drag off her water bottle. Janice
watched her thoughtfully for a few seconds before she
broke the seal and drank from her own.

"Don't give me that look." Bonnie twisted the cap back
in place. "You know, I thought he'd be back in a day or two
with all this time apart to 'find ourselves' business out of
his system. You said every couple could use a few days
apart once in while, that it wouldn't hurt us, that the kids
would understand if we explained it to them. Now it's been
four weeks, the kids hate me because they think I drove
him off, and you're suggesting there might be another
woman. If I'd known he could hold out this long *I'd* have
been the one to move out. How come I'm still here with the
kid and the big house to clean? Obviously, he's the one who
thought the plan through, not me. Plus, now they're changing the aides around at school so I'm not sure which grade
or teacher I'll get when school starts next month, and
Pim's accident, and now she's home from rehab and . . ."
She sighed and stood to go back up the steep attic stairs,
but she didn't. "Pim still doesn't know about Joe. I don't
know how to tell her."

Pim wasn't just their grandmother, she was the only
mother Bonnie could remember clearly, their parents having died in a train accident when she was five and Janice
was almost seven. A young, independent eighty-eight, Pim
wouldn't allow even her great-grandchildren to call her by
anything other than the silly nickname she had picked up
in her own childhood, back when postcards cost a penny,
Marlboro cigarettes were twenty cents *a pack*, and the

country had a total of 131 golf courses and just thirty AM radio stations.

A freak fall in her garden and a broken hip shortly after Joe left kept Pim stiff and housebound these days, and the lack of everything normal in her life was taking its toll on her mind: She was as loopy and unpredictable as a wire spring.

"Don't try. It'll just confuse her more. Besides, he may come home before she realizes he's gone and you might not have to tell her anything." Janice's uncharacteristic optimism should have been Bonnie's first clue that her day was taking a strange new twist, but it was so nice to hear she barely paid attention to it.

"I hope so. And I hope he comes back with enough answers for both of us, because with all that's been going on here I haven't had any time to get reacquainted with myself, much less ask myself questions ... which sounds ridiculous when I say it out loud, doesn't it?"

Janice smiled and nodded. "So what are you doing up here?" She peered into the dimly lit space above the stairs and grimaced. "Looking for a good hiding place?"

"That's not a bad idea, but I'm actually looking for Pim's *magic carpet*." Janice arched a single brow. "I know, but she's so insistent about having it with her that I think there must be some sort of rug up here that reminds her of a magic carpet. Maybe a mat or a throw or something from her childhood that'll help her rest easier if we put it on the floor in her room.

"She's been so restless since we brought her home. You've seen how agitated she gets, late at night. The other night, when I covered for the nurse's night off, I caught Pim trying to get out of bed, saying she had to get to the rug before the dead of night or the magic would be gone. I had to promise her I'd look for it."

"When exactly is dead of night, I've always wondered?"

Bonnie shrugged.

"And pretending to look, then reporting it gone . . . ?"

"Has occurred to me . . . about a hundred times." She grinned. "But I figured a quick look wouldn't kill me and if I find something that helps her rest, so much the better. I hate seeing her so weak and feeble. It breaks my heart."

Something in that statement caused Janice to look away as if she suddenly remembered some bad news. Bonnie knew the look well.

"I don't want to hear it, Jan." She started up the steps. Janice followed.

"But this is good news . . . potentially."

"Right." She glanced back at her sister's attire—one of her best summer linen pant suits, pale blue, crisp, and tidy with low-heeled sandals that matched—which meant the news was really, *really* bad if she was chancing the dust and dirt in Pim's attic. It was a cramped space at the top of an American foursquare, filled with junk and treasures that may not have been cleaned since the roof went on nearly a hundred years earlier. "As long as you're up here, come over and help me move this rug out of the way. I think there's something behind it, but it's wedged in tight between the floor and that rafter there."

"That's not *the* carpet, is it?" Her face was a wince of disgust as she surveyed the sloppy cylinder of dusty gray and dark blue matting.

"No. I know this one, don't you? She used it outside for her garden parties, remember?" Janice shook her head. "Doesn't matter. Come help me."

Janice held out her hands to display the professional Realtor look she had going, then waved her hands at her eyes and nose—which had convenient tendencies to plug, puff up, turn red, and run in the presence of dust, dogs, and fresh-cut grass—then shrugged helplessly. "Want me to try to catch Susan?"

"Oh, come on." Bonnie climbed over several old beer boxes, a tatted footstool, a copper birdcage, and around the steamer trunk she'd been going through when Janice arrived. "You're not going to get out of here clean anyway and it'll only take a sec. Hold your breath."

"All right, but then you have to listen to me."

"I'll have to listen to you anyway, won't I? Take that end."

All Janice had to do was push a little at the top of the rolled-up floor covering while Bonnie pulled from the bottom . . . well, shove hard when she jerked vigorously . . . okay, ram it with her shoulder as she wrenched with all her might before it fell like a tree in a forest. Dust billowed and they both turned their faces away until the cloud settled.

"Oh, for—"

"Wow. Look at this, Jan."

Janice turned to see Bonnie straddle-walking the rug they'd just brought down, making her way to a smaller carpet, rolled up and leaning against the wall. Clearly the other carpet had shielded this one from the light and years of grimy neglect because even the outer, downside of this smaller carpet was bright with color.

It came out of its hiding space easily, not even as wide as Bonnie was tall.

"I bet this is it," she told Janice, excited, feeling like something was *finally* going right in her life. "Look at the colors. And it's not huge so it won't be hard to get it down, and it won't take up too much space in Pim's room."

"You don't think it's magic, do you?" There was a tone in her voice that assured Bonnie she would be locked up if she gave the wrong answer.

"Of course not, but if Pim thinks it is and if it helps her rest, that's magic enough for me." She settled the carpet lengthwise on the old dusty rug and climbed over both. She guessed she could manage to get it down the steps on her own and wouldn't risk Janice's health any further. Letting the lid to the steamer trunk fall back in place, she secured the straps and said, "I guess I can handle some *potentially* good news now."

"I'm having an end-of-the-summer dinner party tomorrow night and I want you to come."

"Boy, that *is* potentially good news." Watching her sister curiously, she transferred the smaller carpet over to the top of the steamer trunk. Janice's parties were always . . . comfortably elegant and catered, big or small. Still watching her sister suspiciously, Bonnie walked across the attic to her and, without looking away for more than a second, bent and picked up the far end of the big dirty rug and began walking toward the wall, lifting the rug higher and higher until she could push it back where it had been. Janice was looking very guilty; the eye contact was getting to her. "But that isn't all your news, is it?"

"I invited Joe, too."

Was that all?

"That's fine. I keep telling you we don't hate each other. We're not even fighting. Neither one of us will make a scene in front of all your guests. I promise."

"There are no other guests."

"Jan—"

"The two of you need to deal with this, whatever it is. I don't get it, but I think it's gone on long enough. We'll sit down and hash it out together."

"Just stay out of it, will you?" She sat on the edge of the dusty old trunk, the carpet behind her. It felt warm against the small of her back. Nice. "Joe and I will work things out, alone. I don't need you to do any *hashing* with my marriage, thank you very much."

"Well, you need something. This much time apart isn't healthy. You need to talk. You need counseling. You need something. Maybe you just need to go over to that place he's living at and kick his ass around the room a couple times. That'll get his attention."

Bonnie ran a hand over the fine, colorful weave of the carpet, vaguely wondering if it might not be more of a mat than a rug, instinctively recognizing the craftsmanship and its antiquity as something special and rare.

"Maybe I need my own magic carpet," she said absently, enjoying the soft underbelly of the carpet against the palm of her hand, eager to see if the show side was just as silky. She looked back at her sister, folded her arms across her chest, and tried to concentrate on the moment. "Maybe I should have stayed home the night of Chicky Davis's birthday party. I sometimes wish I'd never gotten married, you know, and I wonder a lot about how my life would have turned out. Not that I'd ever—"

She watched as Janice's face slowly elongated, her mouth and eyes stretching to form perfect Os of shock, amazement, and fear.

"Jan?" As she spoke, a shadow crossed her face, something passed between them and the bald lightbulb hanging from the rafters. Something in the room was moving . . . *Bats*! came to mind.

But before she could move or cover her hair and her face, darkness enveloped her. It came from above and behind her and fell like a curtain in front of her, leaving daylight on the sides. She stood to escape toward the light, felt a gentle nudge from behind, and fell up against it. At that moment it tipped, like it was going to fall on Janice. Bonnie's body followed and she screamed . . . She felt herself falling.

Three

Bonnie braced herself to land flat on her face, bringing her arms in to protect herself, trying to turn to one side, hoping to get her knees up to her chest so . . . What, she could bounce like a ball?

As illogical as that thought was, so was the fact that she hadn't landed yet. In fact, she wasn't falling anymore, she was . . . floating. She relaxed her arms a little and opened one eye to be sure.

Yep. Floating—like on an air mattress in a swimming pool.

"Jan?"

"Bonnie?"

"Jan?" She straightened her legs and stayed chest down for a minute, then slowly propped herself up on her elbows and looked around.

It was Pim's rug, soft and bright in some Oriental pattern that was truly lovely or could have been, she thought, if she wasn't floating on it eight feet off the ground.

"Bonnie?"

Carefully, as the carpet was prone to waffle a bit when she moved, she inched her way over to the edge, took a firm grip on the fringe, and eased her head over the side. She couldn't remember the last time she'd been so happy to see her sister.

"Jan?"

"Bonnie, my God, what are you doing?"

"Floating?"

"Well, stop it. Get down from there."

No need to tell her twice. She moved the rest of her body over, preparing to ease herself over the edge and land on the trunk below. She'd worry about corralling the carpet later. But just as she was about to shift her weight over the side, the rug curled in on itself, flipping Bonnie onto her back so she was staring straight into the rafters.

"I think it likes me."

"Not funny."

"Not really meant to be, but it won't let me off." And yes, she knew how that sounded, but she didn't know how else to explain it. She sensed a power or energy from it and remembered the warmth she'd felt earlier. "Maybe you'd better go talk to Pim."

"Pim?"

Bonnie rolled over and crawled over to the edge again. Janice looked up, impatient, her hands on her hips. She was frazzled and covered with dust, her eyes and nose turning red, hair mussed, her only sister hovering above her on a carpet. And somehow, she still looked like the boss of everything.

"Pim's the only one who knows anything about this thing."

"She's also broken and feeble."

"Not feeble. She knows about this. She's been trying to get to it. She can tell you how it works."

"Like a secret word or something?"

"Yeah. Like . . . bibbidi-bobbidi-boo!" They both held their breath expectantly.

"Sim sala bim!" Janice pointed her arms out in front of her and wiggled her fingers at the rug.

Nothing.

"Go ask Pim."

"I'll call Joe."

"Joe?"

"And Roger, too. They should both see this. Joe can come to your rescue and you can hug and kiss and make up and then I think we should call both the *National Enquirer* and *Star* magazines to start a bidding war for picture rights to this. No one is going to believe it. I wonder if Susan's gone yet. She can go next door and get the neighbors— We should get as many nonfamily witnesses as possible, I think."

"I think you need to get a grip down there and go talk to Pim. It's her carpet. She may not want the whole world to know about it. It was hidden, remember."

For several seconds Janice looked like she wanted to argue, but all she said was "Well, all right, but take this." She whipped her cell phone from her pocket and tossed it up onto the rug. "At least call Roger. He'll get such a kick out of this."

And off she went, her heels clattering on the steep steps as Bonnie sighed and let her forehead rest on the rug. *Someone should get a kick out this,* she thought, trying to put it all together in her mind.

A magic carpet. Her sister was right, no one was going to believe it. She didn't believe it and she was stuck on it. Stuck on a flying carpet . . . no, it hadn't actually flown yet.

Maybe all it did was float.

She lifted her head and looked around for Janice's cell phone. It had slipped down the carpet into the valley her body made and was resting against her thigh. Clutching it in her hand, she heaved her body over to the center of the rug and drew her legs up under her to slowly sit up. She hated feeling helpless and started looking around for escape ideas.

If she stood up, she could easily reach the rafters and maybe get *off* the rug, but that wasn't the same as getting herself *down*. She bucked a little to see if she could get the carpet to scoot forward to one of the columns holding the roof up, so she could stand and perhaps push it to the floor, but all it did was readjust itself to keep her from falling off.

She perceived that as well . . . that the carpet was taking care of her, keeping her safe. It wouldn't let her off and it wouldn't let her fall. To test this, she got to her feet. It wobbled like a table with one slightly shorter leg, then it was steady and sure. She walked from one end to the other, measured it in her mind as approximately five feet by nine feet, and was again struck by the color and vibrant pattern. She jumped on one corner, knowing it could give way and she might fall, but also knowing that it wouldn't. It held like concrete.

"Okay. I admit it. You're a really cool carpet," she said out loud and then laughed because she didn't know what else to do.

She couldn't resist a hop to the center to stand like a surfer, bending her knees and swaying as she rode the imaginary crest of a . . . tsunami. After that, it was high-stepping, and the rug gave gently like one of those inflated moonwalk things they have for kids at picnics and fairs. Finally a high jump, then two, and then she raised her legs and landed softly on her bum, but she didn't bounce like she would have on a trampoline, not like she hoped she would as she invented and discarded one escape plan after another in her head.

She still had Janice's cell in her hand. As she stared at it she realized she was trying to remember the number that all her phones had on speed dial—Joe's number.

She dropped the phone in her lap, covered her face with both hands, and growled with her teeth clenched. She didn't want to be the first to give in, the first to break, the first to admit that she couldn't handle her life without him—not that her life ordinarily involved situations like this, but still . . . He was the one who had left, he had to be the one to come back.

"He just has to be," she murmured as though in prayer.

Stretching her stiff neck from side to side, she tried to quell her impatience with Janice for taking so long. She was sure Pim was doing her best to remember—she always did. Her best, that is. A thousand images of Pim coming to aid and rescue her over the years rushed to her mind . . . and then it went blank as something else, completely unrelated, tried to surface.

It came slowly as she studied the dark border around the edge of the carpet. At first it looked like part of the design, it was so well-blended in the weave of the rug, but on closer examination she could see that what looked like boxes all around was actually a series of lines and dashes placed high, low, and in between: vertical, horizontal, and diagonal. Some repeated, but there was no pattern to the order.

"These are your instructions, aren't they?" She spoke more to herself than the carpet. Really. "This is some sort of language, but it doesn't look Asian like the rest of you or even Middle Eastern. Not as fancy as hieroglyphics. Not runes either." She'd come to the end of her knowledge of what foreign and ancient languages looked like, but she'd bet her life she was right about it being some sort of message. "Jan's the brainiac, she might know."

She sighed in frustration. "God, I wish you were in English."

And then it was.

"Oh. Thanks."

She knew she should be frightened, hysterical even, at

least disbelieving, but the plain fact was, she wasn't. She didn't foresee any imminent danger: It wasn't trying to hurt anyone and there wasn't a single reason not to trust her own eyes.

She looked at the words *alter* and *change*, *end* and *make*, trying to figure out where to start. After several minutes she had it.

> *For one day one second will alter the years.*
> *Change sorrow to laughter and joy to tears.*
> *Wishes alone can't make it right.*
> *And dead of night will end the flight.*

"Dead of night." Definitely Pim's magic carpet. She knew about it, must have known about it for years. But what did it mean? Did Pim want a ride on it . . . or was she already *on* a ride . . . one that would end at dead of night?

"So when the hell is dead of night?" She repeated Janice's question from before and, still speaking to the rug as if it had ears, she added, "She's in no shape to travel right now, so can we renegotiate this dead of night thing? Does it matter which night it is? Or can it be just any dead of night?"

Oddly enough, she got no answer.

Feeling a little desperate now, knowing that if she didn't figure the carpet out it could affect Pim in some way, she started over, reading the directions again.

They didn't make sense.

"What did I do? What did I do?" she chanted as she tried to remember what she'd been doing, what she had said, what she'd been touching or thinking when the rug came to life. It had to be her or the rug would have scooped up Janice instead, right? "What did I do?"

She recalled Janice's stupid dinner party and asking Janice not to meddle with her marriage, rubbing the carpet, and wishing it was real and saying . . .

"I said, 'I sometimes wish I'd never gotten married'." She waited for the carpet to acknowledge her revelation. "That's a horrible thing to say, I know. But I do sometimes. I wish I'd never gotten married."

Tremors vibrated beneath her. "Uh-oh."

A ripple started at each corner of the rug and worked its way along the fringe toward the opposite end, causing the carpet to turn slightly to the right. As the rippling picked up speed so, too, did the circling, until the rug had turned a full rotation and was starting on a second, a little swifter this time.

"Jan?" Something was very wrong and she was getting dizzy. She wanted off, but not by being thrown by a high-speed, centrifugal force. "Janice! Abracadabra! Okay, I take it back— Actually, I didn't mean it anyway. I love Joe. I've always loved Joe. I'm glad we got married. Stop. Shit. Shazam! *Jaan-ice!*"

Faster and faster . . . the carpet was in full spin. And so was she. Her stomach roiled with nausea and her eyes couldn't focus on anything; she wanted to close them but it just didn't seem like a good idea. She needed to stay aware, watch for opportunities to save herself, maintain what little control she had left.

"Jan! Help me! Anyone! *Jaan-ice!*" Her scream rang in her ears as she drew her legs to her chest and buried her face in the small space between them. Her heart throbbed in her throat and she fervently wished she'd spent more of her life in church.

A whirring noise grew louder as the whirling accelerated, so she didn't hear Janice holler, "What? I'm here. I'm coming," from the bottom of the attic steps or see her arrive at the top and mutter, "Holy shit."

Four

The caller ID displayed her sister's name as Bonnie scurried across the polished hardwood floors of her upscale condo in her stockinged feet, very late for work.

Great. Can this day get any better?

She flipped open her phone and put it to her ear as she lowered herself to the floor to look under the couch. "Jan. Jan. I love you. You're my favorite sister. But I don't have time to talk right now."

Her hand slid across the Chinese silk the sofa was covered in and she remembered why she loved it.

"You sound out of breath. What are you doing?" Janice asked.

"I'm looking for a file that I brought home last night to review for a very . . ." She scrambled over the plush area rug to the wing chair she paid too much for at a White House auction—even with photo verification of it in Lady Bird Johnson's bedroom—and looked under the cushion. ". . . very important investment meeting this morning. Shit!"

"What?"

"I snagged my panty hose." She looked behind pillows, on top of shelves, in drawers, and along ledges as she made her way back to her bedroom to change. "I also got up thirty minutes late and my hair dryer blew up . . . After five years, out of the blue, it picks today to die. Think it's an omen?"

"Of what? The coming of the Antichrist?"

"Maybe. I've heard that the man I'm meeting with this morning can be a little . . . not devilish, but . . . prickly."

"Maybe it means the man you're meeting with this morning is . . . *the* man."

"Don't be ridiculous. Hang on." She tossed the cell phone on the bed, smoothed down her slim, navy, same-size-she-wore-in-college skirt, and adjusted her white silk blouse—no synthetic fibers for her . . . She picked up the phone again. "Have you told me why you're calling yet? I can't remember. And I'm in a hurry so it better not be about some man you think I have to meet. I meet plenty of . . . Oh, thank God!" She whipped the Watson folder off the shelf in her bedroom closet, as confounded as she was relieved, and focused next on shoes. On the bed disheveled sheets began to undulate slowly and with purpose as her overnight guest came awake. "Ah . . . I meet plenty of men on my own. I do. I'm thirty-nine, almost forty years old, and I have a great job that I love, a great car, a great condo. I've traveled all over the world and I can't think of one single thing a man can give me that I can't get on my own."

Tony, a thirty-two-year-old magazine ad for healthy Italian living, cocked his manly brow at her in a lustful challenge. Clearly he thought he knew at least one man who could give her something special. Silently, she laughed at him with mild affection and opened the drawer in the bedside table to enjoy the expression of deflated fascination on his face as he peered in.

"Me either," Jan said. "Not one single thing. Which is

why I haven't set you up with anyone for almost two years. No one I know needs that kind of a hammering."

Hammering? She glanced at Tony and touched the side of his face, and when he looked away from the drawer she smiled at him. Pressing the cell phone against her thigh, she kissed him softly on the lips and whispered, "None of that stuff in there is as good as you are." His dark umber eyes twinkled knowingly and she turned to leave the room . . . so much for hammered.

"So why are you calling me?"

"Just to hear your voice?"

"Jan. I have my jacket, my purse, and my briefcase. I'm walking toward the door. Speak."

"I know you were just out here Sunday, but I was wondering if you could come again this weekend."

"Is it Pim? Is she still loopy and confused?"

"Oh yeah. And she's still harping on that carpet or whatever in the attic. She says you have it and that your life is in danger. I told her I'd call and check on you and she got very agitated. She told me to tell you that 'dead of night will end the flight.' That's what she said. And you have to set things right again before that."

"Before dead of night . . . which is when exactly?"

"How should I know? You're the one with a nightlife." Bonnie rolled her eyes, but didn't correct her. If Jan knew how many early mornings and late nights were business-rather than pleasure-related she'd be . . . Well, Bonnie didn't like to burst anyone's balloon.

"I was going to call and let her talk to you herself—"

"Thank you, so much, for rethinking that one." She pushed the button for the elevator to the parking garage. "I just don't have time this morning. But I'll drive over early Saturday and spend the night with her. Tell her I'll bring everything I need to make her one of those chocolate souf-flés she likes."

"She's not supposed to eat a lot of chocolate."

"She's eighty-eight years old, Jan. She can eat whatever she wants."

"I'm just saying . . ."

The elevator doors slid open. Bonnie would lose reception when she stepped inside, so she stood on the threshold and held the doors open with one hand. "Sure you are, and I'm just saying there will be plenty of soufflé for all of us to have some. How's that?"

"That's better."

"I thought so. I've got to go. Tell Pim I love her. I love you. See you Saturday." She stepped back into the elevator, flipped the phone closed, and started looking for her keys as the elevator doors shut.

Ninety-six minutes later, the rapid tapping of her low-heeled shoes announced her arrival at the business offices on the fourth floor of Superior Atlantic Bank—one of the largest independent banks on the East Coast.

Her spine always stretched and straightened with pride when she walked through the waiting area and down the hall to her office because . . . well, she didn't like to brag but she knew she belonged there, she deserved to be there, she was good at the work she did there. It was her bank. She came to Superior Atlantic right out of college with an MBA and a few courses in economics, political science, and commercial law—and with a burning compulsion to excel. Which she did, from the bottom up—from a brief stint as a teller to loan officer to operations. And when the opportunity arose to move upstairs and have her own office—with a view of the nation's Capitol building—as a trust officer, she grabbed it. That was eleven years ago.

Her secretary, Angela, knew her step and raised her head from the task on her desk like a doe sensing danger. Sensing but not fearing. She and Bonnie were a team, had been for almost eight years, and they knew each other well.

"Please," she whispered to Angela when she was close enough to be heard. "Don't tell me the Watsons arrived early." Looking around for her clients, she marched straight past the outer desk through the open door to her office. "You won't believe the morning I'm having. The only thing I've escaped so far is a bomb in my underwear drawer."

"Actually, Mr. Watson just called to say they were running about twenty minutes late."

"Bless him. That's my first lucky break today." She set the briefcase on the shiny cherrywood desk and stashed her purse in the right-hand bottom drawer. With a weary sigh she fell back in the big, soft, red leather chair and stared at the large, brightly colored carpet she had framed over the alpine green sofa in the seating arrangement across the room. She usually found it refreshing, energizing. Today it made her nervous. "I locked my keys inside my condo . . ." She decided to omit the part about having to call the doorman to let her in because Tony was in the shower and couldn't hear her screaming and beating on the front door. "And when I finally got to my car, one of the tires was flat. I had to take a cab to work."

She swiveled in her chair and extended one of her legs.

Angela dutifully obliged and leaned over the desk to take a look.

"I was wearing my new Ferragamos this morning to impress Mrs. Watson, but then I changed to these at the last minute. I thought she might be more impressed if I didn't fall off my shoes and break my neck today. I'm serious." Angela's skeptical smile made her feel foolish, like she was making up absurdities. "But she'll be even more impressed if I don't sound like a raving lunatic when she gets here, won't she?"

Angela nodded, but her expression was sympathetic. "But after the Watsons leave we'll bite the heads off live chickens and burn smelly candles. We'll make all your bad luck go away."

"Okay." Bonnie slowly sat up, turned her chair to the desk, and took the Watson file from her briefcase, along with a folder full of preferred investment interests. "But you have to do the explaining if we get something nasty on the carpet."

"Deal." Angela's good-natured smile was a comfort. "Do you need coffee now or do you want to wait for the Watsons?"

"I'll wait, thanks, but I think I might take this opportunity to use the ladies' room, freshen up a bit, so I don't feel so frazzled."

"Don't be long. Your twenty minutes are almost gone."

"Check. I'll be back in two seconds."

She felt better now that she was in the bank where she belonged. In fact, she'd often thought that the atmosphere of the bank was a huge part of what she loved about her job. The dustlessness, for instance, was always the first thing she noticed in every bank she visited, how dust-free they were . . . and not just the teller stations and desks, but the picture frames and plants as well. And the quiet— even when people were talking it was quiet. Even when they weren't speaking in the hushed tones that might be respectful, or might be secretive, or might just be laryngitis, it was quiet.

Taking a deep breath as she crossed the large elevator bay toward the ladies' room, she murmured a polite good-morning to a man about her age waiting for an elevator and inhaled again. Angela said she couldn't smell it. Actually, most people she mentioned it to thought she was nuts, but what she loved best about banks was the smell of the money. She gave herself a reassuring nod as she passed by the mirror in the restroom—like now there were two of them who wished for the scent of money in an aerosol can.

She was almost finished when she heard the door to the hall open and close. Half hoping it was Trudy Campbell, who'd recently returned from an island cruise with her husband of twenty-five years, Bonnie opened the stall door with a tell-me-everything grin on her face . . . and froze.

The man who'd been waiting for the elevator a few minutes ago was now in the ladies' room. He was tall, built rugged and lean, and that's about all she noticed because he was also holding a gun, aimed straight at her chest. The sight of him was so unexpected, so outrageous, so terrifying that for some reason that had nothing to do with her high-level cognitive processes, she stepped back into the stall, then closed and locked the door.

"Oh, come on," he said, with no small amount of scorn and disbelief in his voice. "What's that? You can't see me now so I don't exist?" She could tell by the sound of his voice that he was walking in front of her door. "That a bank policy or something? Pretending not to see people?"

A disgruntled customer. Clearly angry, but he didn't sound flat-out crazy.

"Or are you thinking I can't shoot you through the metal door?"

Not so much can't shoot as *won't* shoot through the metal door, she calculated, because he couldn't see where she was standing exactly so he'd have to shoot more than once to make sure he hit her—and it would only take one shot to alert security to her situation.

Her heart was beating so fast she was afraid it would burst.

She pressed her lips and held her fingers together as she leaned from side to side to see what she could through the small spaces on either side of the door. Suddenly, loud and furious, the toilet flushed when she triggered the motion detector. She released a startled, high-pitched gasp, and he . . . chuckled.

"Nervous?" There was a taunting amusement in his voice that he'd regret when she testified against him in court. "You don't need to be. I don't want to hurt you."

That's when she realized he *could* tell where she was by

simply looking under the stall at her feet. Feeling frazzled and vulnerable, she hiked her skirt up to micromini level, reached up to hold on to the top of the left-hand side of the stall, then awkwardly planted both feet on the toilet seat. She needed to stay low so he couldn't see her over the door.

How on earth had he gotten a gun past security? Man, that was maddening! They'd spent several million dollars on security and this wacko just breezed in with a gun, waltzing around like . . . Well, crooks could be very clever sometimes.

She felt tapping on the fingers of her left hand and looked up into his face over the left wall of the cubicle. Instinctively, she pulled her hand away as if he'd burned it and immediately lost her balance on the slippery lid. Desperate, she grabbed the wall with both hands, this time to keep from falling, and he grabbed one of her wrists to make sure she wouldn't.

She quickly kicked off her shoes, righted herself, and yanked her arm out of his grasp.

"You're going to break your neck if you stay there." He rested the hand with the gun in it on the top of the wall—not exactly threatening her with it but casually reminding her that she didn't have one. "Get down now and come out."

Though the tone of his voice wasn't harsh or menacing it left no room to doubt what he expected of her—full compliance. And in the fleeting seconds she took to decide if she would give it to him, she memorized the angles of his face, the small scar in his left eyebrow, the way his dark brown hair curled close to his forehead. His hazel green eyes were so keen and so aware they seemed capable of seeing through anything . . . including her.

Bonnie jumped the seventeen inches to the floor—always a better bearing than falling—and slipped her shoes back on. He did the same in the stall next to her and exited while she straightened her blouse and rearranged her skirt. She was appalled that she had nothing to defend herself with: no purse, no cell phone, no semiautomatic of her own.

He didn't smile, but he nodded his head in approval when she left the stall. She edged forward and made a vague motion toward the sink. He waved his gun briefly. "Sure. Fine. But hurry." He stepped up beside her at the sink. "Just so you know, I'm only taking one hostage today, and I've picked you. So anyone else who gets in my way from now on gets shot, and that includes anyone who tries to come in here while you're stalling with the soap there."

Immediately, all her friends on the fourth floor came to mind and Angela's name came up neon red with fireworks and a marching band. The Watsons were bound to have arrived by now and Angela would be looking for her.

"S-so where are you planning to go next? From here, I mean."

"You do speak." She nodded and took note of the gently worn jeans and brown tweed sports jacket he was wearing—nice-looking on him but misconstrued by so many these days to be proper business attire. "I'm not sure where to go. I didn't come in here planning to rob the place. I wanted . . . I don't have a real plan yet."

What? What kind of burglar was he to have no plan? This wasn't some drive-through branch bank in the suburbs that passed out lollipops and coupons for a two-pound bag of grits with every transaction. This was Superior Atlantic, and everything about it—from the safe to the lamps to the locks on the front door—was state of the art. He was going to need a plan, a good plan.

"Well, this is a busy bathroom so . . . so maybe we can . . . um . . . Oh! The small conference room. All the windows have blinds and there's a lock on the door. We-we'll be safe there until you iron out your plan."

He studied her face. "Are you setting me up for a trap so you can escape?"

"No. Not yet. I . . . I need time to iron out my plans, too."

One corner of his mouth curved up—like what she said was only half-funny. "Are you always this truthful?"

"I try to be, but no, not always."

"Fair enough." He took her by the arm and slipped the gun in the pocket of the jacket. "You look like a smart woman. Do I have to remind you not to do anything stupid? Don't try to be a hero because I'm not going to shoot you—I'll shoot your friends. Got it?"

"Yes."

Five

There was no one in sight when they left the lavatory. They stopped briefly at a large support column, surveyed the territory, hurried forward. Her knees wobbled, she was so afraid of making a mistake. His hand was very warm around her arm, his grasp firm but not painful. She was aware of his height and the strength of his body as he walked beside her, close and dangerous.

She wanted to scream—for several reasons—when she caught sight of the pinched-face and snide Valerie Barson from Mortgages coming toward them. Bonnie shuddered and shook her head, tried to feel shame for the overwhelming urge she felt to call out to her.

"What is it?" His voice was deep and low in her ear. "You okay? You're not getting sick on me, are you?"

She turned to him slightly. "Please. Just please don't shoot the woman in the purple dress coming toward us or I'll go to hell for it."

His expression was only slightly more curious than it

was confused. And the self-inflated mortgage broker was oblivious to his stare when she passed.

"Bonnie."

"Valerie," she responded, though any other day she'd have said "Val" to annoy her—and just like that the encounter was over and behind them.

The Val/Valerie signal was weak and ambiguous, she knew that, and she didn't expect Valerie to pick up on it, but she had to try. She had to stay aware and alert to any opportunity that presented itself.

"Not a good friend of yours, I take it." She shook her head in confirmation. "And you were thinking of doing something to get her shot." She shook her head again in denial and disbelief. "I like the way you think, Bonnie."

She turned her head in surprise, remembered how he'd gotten her name—thanks a lot, Val—and decided that the more information she gathered about him . . . well, the more information she'd have.

"What's your name?"

"Cal."

"No last name, Cal?"

He turned his head and glanced over her shoulder when he heard a door close behind them. His grasp on her arm kept her from doing the same. She couldn't see if someone was going into an office or coming out, if they were walking toward or away from them. "No last name. Keep moving."

"This is your first bank robbery, isn't it?"

"What makes you say that?"

"Well, no offense, but you're not very good at it." She met his eyes when he turned his head to look at her. They were a striking combination of deep green and golden brown—not too far apart—actually, really beautiful eyes for a thief. "There's no real money above the first floor. No cash. Just forms, applications, a few checks, a lot of—" She stopped short and felt the small end of his gun in her ribs. Two young tellers came out of Human Resources chatting and happy. They smiled at both Bonnie and Cal as they hurried by.

"Careful," he said, low and light and somehow making that innocent word sound threatening.

Bare minutes elapsed before someone else emerged from another office and stepped into their path. Another and then another. They would smile or speak if they knew her—it was almost like leaving bread crumbs for the police—and then suddenly, she remembered why she didn't come this way very often.

"Bonnie."

"Oh gosh, hello, Kevin," she said, in much the same way Seinfeld greeted Newman. He was tall and so thin there was an inch of dead space inside his collar, with large brown eyes and a perpetually botched short, dark haircut. She was embarrassed to admit that they had had a very brief thing, nonsexual, thank God, several years ago, briefly, fueled by pity, for a short time. Big mistake. *And* he was married. Automatically, she stepped away to keep him out of her personal space and felt the robber at her back. She knew she should be too scared to stand so close to him, but frankly, Kevin was scarier.

"It's good to see you, Bonnie. How've you been? What brings you down to our end of the hall?" She could picture saliva dripping from his wolfish fangs as he contemplated an early lunch—her.

"I'm fine. I'm showing my friend here, my good friend Cal around the bank."

"Right. Good. Hi." He stuck out his hand to the robber. "Kevin McNally. Good to meet you."

Bonnie held her breath, unsure of what her captor would do. But then she had to wonder how, if he was holding her right arm with his left hand, he would hold the gun and shake hands with his right. And yet somehow, when he brought his right hand forward and locked his long-fingered, work-worn hand around Kevin's soft, paper-pushing paw, it was empty.

Her mind instantly pulled up several spectacular scenarios of making a dash for the stairwell, or for an office with a phone in it while his hand was empty, but every plan came up with the same snag—too many people in the hallway.

"How's it going?" Cal said, shaking Kevin's hand like it was any old day on the calendar.

"I didn't catch the last name."

"He didn't pitch it." Bonnie stepped back into the exchange, to give the robber an easy out. She was aware that criminals needed plenty of choices and options. It was when they felt cornered or pinned down that the real trouble started "You don't have to tell him, Cal, but if you do be prepared to get buried in loan flyers and credit card applications."

She glanced up at Cal and caught him staring at her, bewildered and more than a little intrigued. A long second passed between them before he gave an indolent shrug and said, "I'm already on the mailing list."

"That's right. I forgot." Trying to suppress any unnecessary gestures that might attract attention, she slipped her hands behind her back. "And more than the people who are our potential customers, we love the people who already are . . . more . . . than that." Denim brushed against her fingers and for a quarter of a second they robotically palpated the leg underneath . . . at least she hoped it was a leg! She instantly made two fists and brought them to her sides. "Okay. That's all. We have to go now. Bye, Kevin."

"It's great seeing you, Bon. Don't be such a stranger."

Cal was all but running to keep up with her. "Hey. Hey. Slow down. I won't let him bite you."

"Is that because you're planning to bite me yourself? Because if you are you might as well shoot me now and get it over with, because I know what rape is about, buster."

"Rape?"

"It's about power and humiliation and . . . and little, bitty penises and I'm not going to give you the kind of reaction you want. Even if I feel it, I won't show it to you. And . . . and that gun doesn't really scare me either, you know. There are only five or six bullets in it and once they're gone, they're gone, and you're dead meat. I'll testify—"

"Be quiet." The pressure of his grasp and the stern set of his jaw sealed her lips. Looking up, she saw that his eyes were murky green and hard as stone. "I don't plan on hurting anyone unless I have to, okay? And I don't rape. I don't know what kind of bug crawled up your—"

"I put my hands behind me and felt your leg by accident."

"So?"

"You moved." His features softened with bewilderment. He looked totally unaware of the incident—and she felt like a fool. So she lied. "And I . . . well, I didn't want anyone to see that you were holding my arm. People don't walk around holding arms much anymore, and I hurried us away so no one would see and we could get to the small conference room quicker and . . . it's there, behind you."

He turned, looked both ways down the hall, and led her forward.

"Don't go getting weird on me now, okay?"

"No. No, I won't. That was . . . a misunderstanding. I'm better now. Much better."

"Good."

"Oh, you know what, though? Wait. Wait."

"No."

"I have a better idea."

"Tell me inside." He opened the door, turned on the light, pulled her into the room, and let go of her arm for the first time since they left the ladies' room. It looked like one continuous move as he locked the door and twisted the knob to close the blinds, which were inside the window that was set inside the door. Then he hurried across the room to do the same to the the window that overlooked the street.

This was her moment and she was taking it. Two steps to the door and half a second to wrap her hand around the doorknob, just another spark of time to get the door open and she'd be gone.

"So who do you think will be faster, Bonnie? You getting through that doorway or me putting a bullet through your head?" he asked casually. He came up slowly behind her and gently steered her away from temptation.

And that was it. She was locked in a room with a robber and his gun. Her legs suddenly went weak and she sat down.

The small conference room was . . . small, and that's why people didn't use it often. There was space enough for the standard ten-foot table and the chairs if they were tucked neatly under the table, but put a body in a chair and there was no way to get around it. So Bonnie sat on the end where she had legroom. There was a cordless phone in the center of the table, no bathroom, no sink, no snack bar or soda machine.

"Are you okay? You look pale."

She nodded. "I'm fine. I'm just not used to guns and thieves and missing important meetings and lying to people I hate."

"You're missing an important meeting?" he asked, and again she nodded as she ran a hand through her chin-length auburn hair—with really fabulous highlights at the moment. "What do you do? Do you think they're looking for you already?"

"Oh yeah." She was proud of the fact that people would miss her right away. A stupid thought at a time like this, she knew, but who wanted to be one of those invisible people who disappear and no one misses them. People with no friends and no family and no one who cares. One of those lonely people she was so afraid of becoming. "I'm a private banker." She glanced at her watch. "And I'm about twenty-two minutes late for a meeting with a couple who made most of their money in car parts and wine. Interesting combination, don't you think?"

"So you don't work at this bank?"

"No, I do. I just don't work with the general population anymore. I used to, but now people with certain amounts of money can hire me—through the bank, of course—to help them manage their finances, with everything from investment counseling to tax planning to legacy and philanthropic strategies to cash management. What about you? What do you do . . . when you're not robbing banks, I mean."

"Construction." He finished looking through the blinds in all directions on the street side of the room and did an awkward step-sidestep combo in the eighteen inches of space between the conference table and the wall, to check out the hallway. "People with certain amounts of money, you said. What's a certain amount?"

"Usually it's at least $250,000 annually . . . although I do have two clients who started out with half that much." She tapped her nails on the table, pinky to index finger. "One of them is my sister and her husband, even though I firmly believe that you should never do business with family . . . or mix family with money for that matter, so I'm actually doing both, but fortunately it's working out fine." She put her elbow on the table and hid her mouth behind her fist. "Sorry about that."

"What?" His eyes were focused on the hall.

"I babble when I'm anxious."

He glanced at her briefly and went back to his surveillance. Then, after a few minutes, he said, "My mother used to talk all the time. Constantly. Even when she wasn't nervous."

"And it drove you crazy, right?"

"Sometimes. Mostly it was like having a bell on a cat; it helped us to hear her coming so we could vanish."

"Us?"

"I have a brother and a sister."

"Do they know what you're up to this morning?"

"Hell, I don't know what I'm up to this morning." He left his post at the door and step-sidestepped his way back to the window. "Got any suggestions?"

"On how to rob my bank? I don't think so. But if you'd like to change your mind, you should do it pretty soon, before the police get here. The two of us can walk out the door together, part at the elevators, and go on about our lives. No one has to know about the past thirty minutes."

He shook his head. "Someone's going to know I was here this morning. Someone in this place is going to pay attention to me."

She held her arms out wide. "What about me? You've got my full attention."

"Can you get me a loan for half a mil?" His tone was testy. "Personal or business, fixed rate or not, I'm not picky. I'll pay it back any way you want—if it's fair. I just need the money."

"For . . ."

"Land. Enough to build two hundred new houses on one-and-a-half-acre lots between The Plains and Markham."

"For half a million?" She knew the area. It wasn't far from Pim's house and he was going to need more than half a million.

"Well, we already have $500,000 and the landowner says he'll hold a note for that much more off the top."

"I see. And your collateral?"

"Our business, our share of the land, my home, whatever you want."

"Not your brother's home?"

He shook his head once and lowered a blind with the nose of his gun. "He's got kids."

She couldn't say for sure that she'd ever fantasized

about being kidnapped or held hostage but she'd bet the villain was never as decent a man as Cal seemed to be. "I do think I can get you a loan, Mr. . . . um . . ." She smiled at his profile as he peered down at the street. "You still haven't told me your last name, Cal."

"I also haven't told you the reason your . . . colleagues turned me down. And not just me but my brother, too, because he's my partner." She waited attentively—after all, talking money was her life. "I have a record."

"Under the circumstances, I don't know why I'm so surprised, but I am. You don't seem like a criminal to me."

"I'm not. Not anymore. The last time I was in jail was eleven years ago, for something I did four years before that. I was young. I was a punk. I paid my dues. Since then I've been busting my hump with my brother to keep our business together. And now that we're at a place where we can finally take some risks and spread our wings a bit, we can't because of my record."

Felony arrests were covered by a bank policy, she knew, but at the moment she couldn't say it was a good one, nor would she say it was fair. He had paid his debt to society; he had turned his life around and made something good for himself, but he was still being penalized.

And, no, the irony of discussing his sustained rehabilitation with his kidnap victim was not lost on her.

"Well, we're not the only bank in town, you know," she said optimistically. "I can't believe those words came out of my mouth, but it's true. Did you try anywhere else?"

It was time to move to the other side of the room again, so he nodded when he went by and said, "Three. Three other places. Same answer, same reason. What kills me is that if I weren't around, my brother could do it on his own, easy."

She felt miserable for him. "I'm sorry, Cal. I really am. It doesn't seem fair to me either."

"Don't. You don't have to say things like that just because you're scared. I told you I wouldn't hurt you."

"I didn't. I meant it. I am sorry everything turned out badly for you. And I'm sorry that what you're doing now isn't going to help matters," she said, matter-of-factly. "But as much as I'd like to change things for you, I can't." She frowned. "Which makes me wonder why you picked me? Why not someone from Loans and Acquisitions?"

"What was the better idea you had before we came in here?" He smoothly changed the subject.

"Oh. It wasn't important. I just remembered that Gil Hopkins's office is empty for a while. He's out having a couple hernias fixed. He's a pretty big man and hernias can be dangerous if they're not taken care of surgically." He was looking at her with tolerance, like he might his chatty mother. "He's in Accounting? There's a computer in his office and a water machine and it's just across the hall from a bathroom and there's no street window, but it's not as big as this. Do you get claustrophobic?"

"Seven years in prison and you get used to small places."

"Seven years?" For some reason she'd been thinking a year for forging checks or hacking computers or jaywalking, maybe. "Can I . . . ?"

"What?"

"Never mind. It's none of my business."

"What was I locked up for?"

"Yes, but don't tell me. I'm just being nosy."

"I got three years for taking a beat-up piece of shit truck when I was eighteen." He wagged his head. "And I deserved that one, I guess. I thought I was real big stuff in high school . . . Someone your mother would have told you to steer clear of, I bet." His smile was small and rueful. "If they hadn't gotten me for the truck, they'd have caught me doing something else. Eventually. I was long overdue. But the second time, and this is seven years later when I'm about . . . twenty-five, I guess, I was almost completely innocent."

"Almost completely?" She caught herself enjoying his story and tried to stop. It was bad enough that she liked looking at him so much.

"I resisted arrest. But you would, too, under the circumstances."

"What circumstances?"

He glanced out the window in the door and crossed over to the street side, saying, "It was winter, right? So it was cold out but not *freezing* cold, you know what I mean?"

"I think so. When you can go without a hat but not without a coat."

"Right." He turned to look at her and she was struck by how peculiar it was to imagine him, with his open expression and easy manner, in jail, and it was flat-out weird to have to keep reminding herself that he was robbing the bank . . . and that she should be terrified. "That's exactly what I did, too. I took off my hat, one of those knit caps, and stuffed it in the pocket of my coat. Everyone was wearing those big, green army coats back then, remember?" She shrugged, not really. "Anyway, I went to a buddy's house to play poker one night, just an innocent nickel-and-dime game, and about twenty minutes into the game I get hot, take off my coat, and toss it on the guy's couch. There were six of us and this seventh guy who came late; we made room for him and then he bailed before anyone cashed out. Some friend of somebody's friend.

"So the game's over. It's about 2:30 in the morning. I grab my coat off the couch and head home. I'm not in my car ten minutes before I get flashing lights and pull over because I know about the busted taillight I haven't fixed yet. I figured I'd give the same spiel I gave the other two times I got stopped, about the damage being new and having an appointment to get it fixed next week."

"Haven't you ever heard that honesty is the best policy?"

He gave her a quizzical look that amused her. "Don't give me that, you'd have lied, too. Admit it."

"I admit it." She tried not to grin. "But you're holding a gun on me so does that count?"

Cal's lips curled up at the corners and his eyes sparkled with glee for a whole minute before he remembered the rule about not having fun with the captives.

"They didn't believe me anyway. And when they called my plates and license in and found out I was a con they were all over me like a bad rash. I told them they could search the car, I had nothing to hide. I got out and put my hands on my head so they could frisk me. I'm an innocent man, right?" A derisive laugh slipped out. "I thought my head would explode when they pulled a baggie full of pills out of my pocket."

Bonnie gasped, covered her eyes with her hands, and muttered, "It's not your coat." She slipped her hands down to cover her mouth and waited for him to continue.

"Also the bulk in my pocket that I thought was my cap—the cap I didn't even check on after I stuffed it in my pocket because it was warm enough to go without it—was a gun. And it wasn't just a concealed weapon, it was also a parole violation." He let her groan and fall back in her chair in defeat. "You ever watch those cop shows and wonder how stupid the crook must be to try and outrun a cop car . . . and then a whole fleet of cop cars? Well, fear makes people stupid . . . and reckless. It made me *real* stupid and reckless. I head-butted one cop and rammed the other in the gut with my shoulder. They both went down, and I started running through the neighborhood, in the dark, with handcuffs on. Real smart."

"And, of course, no one believed it wasn't your coat."

"Would you?"

Reluctantly, she shook her head. And okay, she was being pretty stupid and reckless herself because she believed him. She believed him and she liked him; liked the way his clear hazel eyes looked straight into her soul when he spoke and the solid, uncomplicated tone of his voice. She liked that his hands were rough and well-used but the nails were clipped neat and clean. There had to be some way to help him.

She watched as he crossed the room again. "Look, if we leave here now I swear I'll do everything I can to help you get the money you need." He was looking out on the hall-way, taking a peek in both directions. "I know a few venture capitalists, maybe we can work something out there . . . or maybe a private investor . . . there are loans and grants from the government that hardly anyone uses. We'll look every-where and we won't stop until you have all the money you need."

He turned, leaned back into the corner behind the door, and looked at her. His eyes were soft and warm and scalpel sharp all at the same time. She felt a familiar, airy, boosting sensation below her diaphragm and immediately reminded herself that *she* was the captain of her own ship.

"Where were you a couple hours ago?"

"I know," she said with sympathy. "And two hours ago I'd have had to turn you down for your felony arrests, too. The bank has rules. But I didn't know you two hours ago and I wasn't willing to use my own personal time to help you find the money you need."

"Because now you know all about me."

"Of course not, but I know more about you than when we first met, and I know I want to help you."

For a long minute he stared at her, so long she finally squirmed in her chair. Eventually, he pushed away from the wall, saying, "Thanks, Bonnie, I appreciate the offer, but it's a little too late. The cops are here."

Six

"No! Don't answer it," she said, when the telephone rang. She sprang from her chair and clamped her hand over his on the receiver. "Let me answer. I'll tell them we came in here for a quiet, private meeting. I'll tell them someone overreacted, that I'm here because I want to be."

He shook his head and the phone kept ringing.

"Please, Cal, once they know this is a hostage situation for sure there's only one way this can go—badly; our options will be gone and we won't be able to turn back."

"I understand. Now move your hand."

"Um." She scratched around inside for a minuscule amount of courage and used it all to say, "No. Now you're making a mistake. Take another minute and think it through. Think about your life. About your brother's life, and your sister's. What about . . . do you have a wife?"

"Divorced."

"Kids?"

He shook his head, his gaze on hers. "What about you? I bet some rich guy gobbled you . . . no ring?"

It was her turn to shake her head and she couldn't remember the last time she permitted herself to feel self-conscious about never having been married. She withdrew her hands slowly and hid them out of sight, saying, "I was busy doing other things."

"I'd like to know what, but first . . ."

A startled cry spilled out of her when she realized she'd been duped into freeing his hands. Her desperate lunge to secure them again ended in a sudden, frozen halt when a loudspeaker screeched outside the door.

"Joseph Sanderson, this is the police. Please pick up the phone so we can talk. Joe Sanderson. We know who you are, now all we want is to know what you need."

He was a kidnapper and a thief and she couldn't believe how hurt she felt that he'd lied to her about his name.

"Joe? Joe is your real name? Great. Fine. I suppose I get to call you Joe now?"

"You can if you want. My mother does, and a few people I grew up with, but I've been Cal to everyone else since I left home. Poor Joe had a reputation to live down, remember? My middle name is Calvin. Can you beat that for a stupid name?"

"Come on, Joe, pick up. Tell us what we can do for you."

Cal held out both hands helplessly. "They're asking so nice, I gotta pick up now."

"No. I can still do it. I can defuse the whole thing right now. Please, Cal."

An expression of wonder and . . . something close to fondness softened his features as he looked at her. He put his fist under her chin and gently swept the pad of his thumb across the rounded tip of her chin and said, "You asked—"

They both jumped when the phone rang again. He snatched it up impatiently and pressed the speaker end against his side.

"You asked why I picked you . . . I must have talked to a

dozen people in this bank today. You were the only one who looked me in the eye, smiled at me, and wished me a good morning. If I hadn't seen you I'd have gotten on the elevator and gone home empty-handed again. I'd have gone home to watch my brother pretend he doesn't know it's me that's holding him back. But I did see you and . . . Damn it!" he said when the bullhorn in the hall started up again. He lifted the receiver to his mouth. "Can you wait a damn minute? I'm busy here. And it's not like I'm going anywhere." The phone went back to his waist. "Where was I?"

"But you did see me."

He smiled and Bonnie's knees went weak. "That's right. I did. And I thought to myself, 'Now there's a woman. Friendly, honest, smart. A woman who would never give up, she'd never take anything on the chin and accept it. She'd fight.' "

"You got all that from a smile, a look, and a polite good-morning?"

"Was I wrong?" She shook her head—her rather inflated head—slowly. "But none of that is why I picked you. The reason I picked you to take as my hostage is . . . you were available."

The gasp and the outrage and the humor and chagrin all arrived in the same breath moments before he burst into good-natured laughter. Swallowing chuckles, she whacked his left arm and then added her hand to his as he held the phone to his waist.

"That's funny, Cal, but this *isn't*. You're in serious trouble, so get a serious attitude before you talk to them."

"Yes, ma'am." He scowled "Did I mention bossy? You looked bossy, too."

She was about to make a retort when he put a finger to his lips and put the receiver to his ear.

"Sorry to keep you waiting. My hostage was giving me some flack . . . No, she's fine, she's just real mouthy." His grin was teasing and so was her indignant eye roll. He held out the phone. "Tell them you're okay." She called out that she was and he took over again. "Here's the deal, Ted, I haven't decided what I'm going to do yet so back away from the door and stop calling every five minutes. I don't want to go off half-cocked so don't force me to. When I know what I want to do, you'll know. Oh, and no more of that bullhorn, it makes my fingers twitchy." He hung up. "How was that?"

"I think it was good. But don't give them any reason to think I've been hurt or that you're being abusive or they'll storm us. Help me push the table up against the door. And turn out that light. You really are horrible at this."

"You, on the other hand, are acting suspiciously adept at it." He set one chair atop another and another, using them all to barricade the door. "Which leads me to wonder, why are you helping me?" He looked around and realized he'd stacked all the chairs and she had nowhere to sit but the floor.

"Thank you, but leave the chair. We should sit on the table anyway, for extra weight. Get under it if they try to break in."

The looks they exchanged said it wasn't a matter of *if* they tried to break in, but when—and if they both knew, why say it aloud?

"That's another good suggestion. Have you thought of writing a book? *How Not to Bungle a Burglary*, and its follow-up, *How to Be a Happy Hostage*."

Ignoring him, she sat on the tabletop next to him and started swinging her legs. She couldn't help it—she hadn't had a legitimate excuse to sit on top of a table since she was twelve.

"I'm helping you because I think you got a raw deal—not that any of this is going to make any difference. You know that, right? You can't win this."

"When you write your book be sure to stress the importance of faith and staying upbeat." Bonnie turned her sternest look on him. He winked at her and she . . . gave up.

"Actually, I'm helping you because this is all my fault. When I walked by you, out near the elevators, you got sucked up into the vortex of my morning from hell." He gave a soft, dismissive chuckle. "I'm serious. I woke up thirty minutes late today, my hair dryer blew up, I snagged my pantyhose, locked all my keys inside my condo, had a flat tire, took a taxi to work, was kidnapped, and held hostage." She lifted her left arm. "And it's not quite noon yet." She turned her head to find him staring at her. "What?"

"Do you think that'll hold up in court? Your Honor, I was just standing at the elevator, minding my own business—which, by the way, is grossly limited because of my two felony arrests—when this very pretty woman came along and I got sucked into her bad morning."

"Works for me." She especially liked the very pretty part.

"That's the story I'll use then. I like it."

Bonnie nodded. "I'm going with Stockholm Syndrome." He tipped his head and gave her a you-always-get-all-the-best-excuses face. "Well, why else would I be helping you?"

Cal sobered slowly and thoughtfully. "Don't tell anyone, not even your best friend, that you did anything to help me in here. Not the slightest little thing. Okay?" She nodded. "And don't make me out to be a monster either, all right? My niece and nephews might see the news."

"You're not a monster. I'd never call you one."

He tipped his head in gratitude and slid off the table to check the window overlooking the street.

He was in great shape for a man his age . . . for a man almost any age, she decided, her gaze wandering from broad shoulders to trim waist, down long, lean legs. It was a fit, working man's body.

Though he hadn't said it aloud yet, they both knew that taking her hostage had been a gigantic mistake made in a rash moment of anger, fear, and frustration and now he was in over his head. If he could, she knew he'd surrender immediately, apologize to her, a vice president of the bank, and the cops, and go home. As it was, he was simply putting off going back to jail for as long as he possibly could. And she wanted to wait with him.

Knowledge and instinct were what she was all about . . . since doing her job was basically her whole life. She'd be the first to admit, but not to her clients, that the managing, projecting, planning, investing, and building of other people's money was commonly an educated crapshoot—that she was pretty good at, by the way . . . And she wasn't the first to say *that*.

But at the moment, what she knew in her head and felt in her gut was all wrong, backward, all tangled up.

She was in danger, his hostage, a stranger to him, but she felt like his friend and his partner—and okay, lover had crossed her mind once or twice, briefly, perhaps under different conditions. He'd had a gun in his hand the whole time she'd known him but he was no more a criminal than she was, she'd swear to it.

She looked across the room at him. He was holding his gun in both hands, staring at it as if it were a toy or like he could clearly see that it was way too small to defend him against the cannons he knew were coming.

The cops hadn't given up and were calling every few minutes or so. It was her turn to pick up and hang up for a while.

"You know what?" She spoke softly into the silence that had stretched out between them for close to an hour. He looked up immediately, happy for the reprieve from his thoughts.

"What?" He pushed off the wall and walked halfway across the room to match her position: feet on the floor, butt on the table, arms propping up the torso.

"I was just thinking . . . I have a sister who's eighteen months older than I am."

He gave her a little smile and humored her. "What's her name?"

"Jan. Janice. She's Jan Everly now, but she used to be Jan Simms. Janice Simms? I'm Bonnie Simms." A slow pucker started between his brows, but all he did was nod to encourage her to get to the point. "We . . . well, she mostly, went to school with a boy named Joe Sanderson. In Leesburg. What a coincidence, huh?" His pucker was now a Stage 4 frown. "Interesting, isn't it?"

"It's weird, is what it is. And I remember your sister. She's the one who tutored Billy O'Neal for some test that he failed so he couldn't play football on scout night and missed out on a college athletic scholarship."

"Oh, give me a break. Billy O'Neal is a moron and that's why he failed the test and couldn't get into college."

"And you . . ." He pointed an accusing finger at her, which she found unnerving. "You. God. Chicky Davis waited all night for you to show up at his birthday party and you left him hanging."

"I was hanging, too, over a toilet bowl. I had the flu."

"That . . ." He bonked her on the end of her nose with his finger. ". . . is a lie."

"No."

"Yes. I saw you. Peeking through the bushes on the other side of the garage at Chicky's house that night. Just for a second, but it was you—but I didn't know that until Monday. I even thought about exposing you . . . people hiding in bushes at parties are called entertainment, usually."

"Why didn't you?"

He shook his head once. "I don't know."

"I'll never forget it. It was the first time a senior asked me out, *and* it was Chicky Davis, *and* it was his birthday—a special occasion—that he could have invited a million other girls to . . . The pressure was immeasurable. It's no wonder I was nauseous . . . I threw up in those bushes, you know." She hesitated, waited several beats. "So, is that all you remember about us?"

"About your sister, yeah. Nerdy chicks weren't exactly my type."

"She's exceptionally bright."

"Okay." He looked away briefly, then came back to search her older face with younger eyes. "Your hair was more red back then, a lighter, brighter red. I'm amazed I didn't recognize you, because you look pretty much the same—different haircut, softer curves but . . . you still have the greatest legs to ever walk out of Robert F. Kennedy High School."

Her brows popped upward. "I was your type?"

He gave a short laugh and spoke bluntly. "No. Not even close. But there was a time when I would have made an exception. I wished I was more *your* type."

"Mine?" Like, totally awesome. So rad, man. Really bitchin . . . Her inner teen was flippin' out.

And he saw it. He smiled, pleased, and an amazing thing happened when he looked away in a surprisingly bashful fashion. She felt herself teetering on the brink of deep like . . . very deep like.

He cleared his throat. "The Monday after Chicky's party, I asked around until someone pointed you out. I was curious. I wanted to see what kind of nobody junior would stand up a popular senior, an all-district quarterback . . . someone with Chicky's clout."

"I bet you were surprised." She didn't mean to sound self-deprecating.

"I was," he said, still staring at his boots. "I felt . . . stunned, for weeks. I couldn't believe that I didn't see you first. You were all legs and . . ." He brought his hands up in front of his chest. They paused there for a fraction of a fraction of a second and went straight to his head. "And you had all that red hair." He leaned close and looked at her. "What happened to your freckles?"

She shrugged. "My hair got darker and my freckles faded. Even trade." He hummed and lowered his gaze to their hands, so close on the table between them. "So why didn't you ever ask me out?"

He scoffed. "Well, for one thing, you stood up Chicky—"

She laughed. "I had the flu!"

"You were tested and proven undependable. You were unpredictable. You were a social disaster waiting to happen to the next guy who asked you out."

"Maybe I didn't like football players, what about that? Maybe I didn't like Chicky."

He gave her a look. "Everybody liked Chicky." When he saw she couldn't argue with that, he went on. "So what do you remember about me? Anything?"

"Yes, but wait just a second. What's the other thing?" He frowned. "You said, for one thing, I stood up Chicky. What's the other thing?"

"Oh. You weren't my type. You were clean and bright and beautiful and innocent and the girls I dated . . . weren't, for the most part. We liked to have all kinds of fun, if you know what I mean."

"I think I do. Yes. I remember some of those girls." He pretended to hang his head low. "And I knew who you were when I was a sophomore. You spent a lot of time with Max . . . um . . ."

"His name was Fred Maxton."

"Yes. He made a friend of mine pull his gym shorts over his head and wear them around his neck for almost a month."

He nodded like he was remembering, unhappily. "I grew up next door to Max. He was a year older, but we were pretty good friends—not that I approved of the things he did sometimes. And it's not a good excuse for the things he did, but when he was a sophomore, he was a big, stocky guy and he got tipped, headfirst, into the cafeteria trash cans. Regularly. Kids are cruel to each other. And it goes around and around and around."

"Can I ask a personal question?"

"Sure."

"Earlier you said you didn't have children. Is that by choice or . . . ?"

"No. Definitely not by choice. I like kids. My brother's kids are great. Having a few of my own would be . . . totally amazing. Great. But now . . ."

She didn't want to think about now, at the moment.

"Did you come from a broken home?"

He shook his head. "I remember you used to live with your grandmother, right? Or was that someone else?"

"Pim is her name. My parents were killed in a train accident when I was five."

"She's still alive?"

"Oh yes." She laughed softly and affectionately and started to tell him about Pim and the exciting life she led until she had to settle down again to raise the offspring of her only daughter. He listened while she told him of the faraway and exotic places Pim had been to, the magical and powerful people she'd met, and the many lessons and stories she learned to pass on to her and her sister. Everyone knows that being reprimanded or warned or alerted was always taken better and remembered longer if a fairy or a sultan or an evil dragon was involved . . . at least until middle school.

About halfway through the memories, she realized what they were doing—playing catchup. They were hurriedly cramming as much personal history into what little time they had to feel connected to one another; trying to live a lifetime together in a day.

Automatically, she answered and hung up the phone when it rang.

"You're going to need to say something soon. Cops don't play well in the dark." He gave her a curious look and she smiled. "Okay. They don't play well in any light."

"Joe. You need to say something soon, man." The man with the megaphone sounded frustrated. *"Don't keep us in the dark. Tell us how we can help you. Tell us what you want."*

"See?" They chuckled a little because the cop had used so many of her words. "And I have an idea of what to say . . ."

Seven

"Did you get that, Ted? I want a development loan for half a million dollars to be repaid to the bank at the going rate. I've already filled out all the paperwork. It's in one of those offices down the hall."

"Loans and Acquisitions," Bonnie whispered helpfully, as she had been throughout the entire "demands" process.

"Loans and Acquisitions," Cal repeated. "That's where they are, all the forms I filled out. I do not want to steal the money, I just need to borrow it. Got that?" All Bonnie could hear of the negotiator was a buzzing noise from the phone at Cal's ear. She watched Cal's face for his reactions to what was being said. It was particularly expressive, his face . . . or she was particularly excellent at reading it. "I tried it that way, Ted, but they can't put my past behind me."

"Finish up. They're talking to keep you distracted."

He looked straight into her eyes and nodded; she reached out and took a light hold of the table edge for balance, and waited for the flutter in her chest to subside.

"That's number one. Number two: I want total amnesty

for everything I've done in this bank today. My hostage has agreed not to press charges if she walks out of here unharmed, so all you have to do is speak to the bank and the district attorney. And I want it in writing, both of them. I want loan papers and amnesty papers so I can read them." He listened. "How long?" Bonnie held up four fingers and looked askant at him. He grimaced and shrugged. "Four hours. You have four hours, Ted. Is there anything you don't understand?" His shoulders slumped in a frustrated fashion and he closed his eyes for several long seconds. "No. I meant is there anything about my demands that you don't understand?" He covered the mouthpiece with his hand. "I think I'm Ted's maiden voyage. He keeps talking to somebody else."

"Like you do?"

He gave a silent laugh and turned back to the negotiator. "I don't know. I'll check and see if she wants to talk to you." He covered the mouthpiece again and raised his brows at her in question; the choice was hers. When she looked hesitant, he tried to help. "They might not be as jumpy and anxious if they know you're okay."

She stepped closer and took it from him. The handpiece was warm from his palm and the moist scent of his breath lingered lightly as she pressed it to her face.

"Hello?"

"Ms. Simms, are you all right?"

"Yes. I'm fine, but . . . I'd appreciate it if you would meet Mr. Sanderson's requests as soon as possible so we can all go on about our lives."

"Is he armed, Ms. Simms?"

"Yes, of course. And also, could you tell my secretary, Angela, to contact my family and tell them I'm okay? And to be sure to apologize, profusely, to the Watsons. And to set up another appointment for the earliest possible day next week?"

"Is there a bomb in there, ma'am? Any kind of incendiary device?"

"Did you hear what I said?"

"Yes, ma'am. This conversation is being recorded, ma'am. Any bombs?"

"One moment, please." She covered the lower half of the phone with the palm of her hand and met Cal's eyes with hers. "He wants to know if we have a bomb."

"Me," he said firmly. "Not we. Don't forget that."

"A bomb could hold them at bay awhile longer."

"It also might cause them to storm us sooner and harder with no thought to the hostage. You know, sacrificing the life of one to save the lives of many? Better say no."

She did, but Ted was a suspicious soul.

"Is he forcing you to lie, ma'am?" Ted was eager for her to say something horrible about Cal, something incriminating or dangerous. What she wanted to do was extol his virtues . . . and not just the expression in his eyes or the grace of his big, calloused hands. She liked the way he protected his brother and concerned himself with her comfort and safety. She appreciated the kindness he'd shown her and his decision not to terrorize her by swinging the gun in her face all the time. She wanted to pummel the people who rejected his loan application, refusing him the second chance that everyone deserved. Angry and stressed, Bonnie's hands trembled with frustration. "Ma'am, are you being coerced?"

"No! He wouldn't do that! I have to go now." She held the phone out to Cal who took it and then followed her with his eyes until she came to rest against a wall on the street end of the room.

With the shades drawn, the lights out, and the sun settling slowly on the other side of the building, it was getting dark and hard to see details—like cheeks flushed with emotion and a quivering chin. Then again, sometimes you don't need any light to see.

"Four hours, Ted. Don't disappoint me," he said, keeping it short and to the point. He put the phone in the charger, then turned around to watch Bonnie with no little concern on his face. "Bonnie? Are you okay? Want me to add having Ted filleted to my list of demands?"

Her soft, nearly silent chuckle gave her body a slight shake and she turned around, her eyes brimming with unshed tears she was embarrassed for him to see. She held up one hand to stop him when he started to approach her, and swiped at a stray tear with the other.

"I'm okay. Honest. I'm having a minor meltdown. Not a big thing. Venting a little stress is all. I'm a girl. It happens."

He kept coming and inside she groaned her dismay. What if she did something stupid and humiliating like . . . cry on his shoulder? What if she went temporarily insane and kissed him? It was intensely tempting. What if she totally lost it and allowed herself to care about him . . . care too much about him . . . maybe love him even? What if she . . .

So what if she did?

"I'm sorry, Bonnie. Really sorry," he said, tipping his head to see her face. "This was such a bad idea. I'm sorry I dragged you into it."

"You were angry and frustrated. That's a lethal combination."

"Doesn't mean I get to take it out on you." He took off his sport coat and tossed it onto the air-conditioning unit under the window. He peered through the blinds—up, down, all around—then opened them to let in the low glow from the streetlights, car lights and storefronts four stories below. "We need to stay down now, but at least we'll have a little light. I think they've turned off the electricity. The good news is that once it gets too dark to see it should cool off a little."

"Always looking on the bright side," she said, teasing him. Stepping out of her shoes, she started to loosen the button at her throat. "Hot air rises, right?"

"Right," he said, watching her slide down the wall to sit on the floor. "You want my jacket?"

"Thanks, but it's not that much cooler down here." She smiled cordially at him and he was about to explain that she could *sit* on his coat until he caught a glimpse of the glint in her eyes and realized she was teasing him.

"Smart-ass."

"I am going to need a hand getting up, though. Straight skirts aren't built for anything but looking good."

"Well, I gotta tell ya," he said, lowering himself to his knees and sitting back beside her. "Yours is looking very good."

"Oh, I bet you say that to all your hostages." She was unbuttoning the cuffs of her white silk blouse and rolling up the sleeves.

"As a matter of fact, I do. But I don't mean it unless I'm saying it to you."

She blushed. She did. He was playing with her and she was flattered . . . and she was also an idiot. There was no future for her with this man—no off-white wedding, no kids, no rocking chairs on the wide front porch at sunset.

Yet, she more than liked most everything about him. His humor and concern for her. His looks, of course, but also the strength it had taken to turn his life around after being in jail. And to throw it all away on a dream? What was that? Heroic? Reckless? Insane?

"I'm very proud of that, you know."

"What's that?" he asked, shifting slightly closer to her, as if the wall was too lumpy where he sat before.

"My weight and being able to fit into the same size clothes I wore twenty years ago."

He smiled like she'd just told him an interesting body fact—like her foot was the same length as her forearm.

"My weight is one of the many things I am inordinately proud of—one of the many vain and frivolous and self-satisfying things I fill my time with because, aside from my job, there is nothing in my life that is real or true or praise-worthy."

He was looking confused and a little wary now. "Everybody feels like that sometimes. I bet if you—"

"No. Not me. There are no service clubs in my life or charitable organizations, no music, no art, no white-water rafting, no neurotic obsession with a hobby. All I do is work." She sighed deeply and leaned her head back against the wall. "I used to be a firm believer that having a husband and children was no way to define yourself. But it has recently occurred to me that if 'wife and mother' isn't a definition then neither is 'banker.' Isn't that right? Or 'president' or 'dishwasher' or 'Indian chief.' Really, in the end, it's not what I do with my life, it's what I do every day that matters."

After several long seconds of silence crawled by, she opened the eye closest to Cal and had to smile at the thoughtful mystification on his face. She had to like a man who at least *tried* to understand the deepest, darkest inner workings of a woman's mind.

"Right?" she asked just to get his reaction.

"Well . . . maybe . . . And maybe your blood sugar's low from not eating all day. Want me to see if they'll slide a cheeseburger under the door?"

She opened both eyes then and laughed. "No. Thanks." She hesitated. "Actually, all that was a prelude to me telling you that I . . . admire you. I mean, this whole thing was a fiasco, of course, and you'll probably end up in jail—"

"That's so admirable."

"*But* your heart was in the right place. Your intent was good. You didn't do it solely for yourself: You did it mostly for your brother, so he wouldn't be punished for something you did . . . and already paid for. You haven't hurt anyone. You've been kind and sweet."

"You think I'm sweet?"

"I can't even remember the last time I did something brave or self-sacrificing."

"I'm sweet?"

"Everything in my life revolves around me."

"Sweet?"

"I don't know when I became so selfish . . . so empty. Pim taught me better." She turned her head and looked at him. He was already looking at her. "I don't normally need this kind of . . . hammer to fall on my head to get me to recognize that I've strayed too far off the path. It's insane, I know, to thank you for taking me hostage, but I'm afraid I'm going to have to because—"

As slow and smooth as a cake rises, as natural as water flows downstream, Cal leaned forward and pressed his lips against hers. They were soft and warm and jerked her pulses through the roof. He pulled away briefly, but she could still feel his breath on her lips, across her cheek, the heat of him inside her personal space. When he kissed her again his mouth was open and his tongue probed. She obliged, and the blood in her veins caught fire.

She could smell fresh sawdust and wind on him, and the large, calloused hands she so admired were unexpectedly tender as they stroked her cheek and slipped over her throat to the back of her neck, to support her head while he took the kiss deeper.

She lifted one jelly-muscled arm to his shoulder to cling—pooling on the floor beside him being out of the question. Her arm couldn't stretch the breadth of his shoulders; the muscles in his arms and back were like stone—and she couldn't recall feeling safer or more protected . . . or more vulnerable. Ever.

She *loved* it.

"I knew it," he said breathlessly, his lips on her cheek and temple, then her throat. "I knew the first time I saw you, that day at school, I knew kissing you would be outstanding." He kissed her other cheek and then the space between her eyebrows, like he couldn't stop himself, like he couldn't get enough. "I knew about your lips, too. So soft." He caressed hers with his and then looked at her. "I even knew you'd taste special . . . like that one drop of pure sweetness you get from a honeysuckle. Remember? Did you do that as a kid, suck on honeysuckle?"

She nodded vaguely, palming his face and stroking the side of her right thumb across the stubble on his left cheek. "I did. I also did it last summer in Pim's garden."

His smile was wide and bright and quite possibly the sexiest thing she'd seen in fifteen years. "You . . . in the honeysuckle . . . in the summertime. Pretty picture."

She shook her head and gave a soft laugh before averting her eyes. "My mental picture of you is pretty . . . clichéd, I'm afraid." She peeked up through her lashes at him. His smirk and his laughing eyes were worth her discomfiture. "Tool belt, no shirt, jeans tight enough not to get caught in machinery . . . a black metal lunchbox."

"What's in my lunchbox?" he needed to know.

This was fun. She scooted back against the wall and wiggled around to get more comfortable on the floor.

"Need a cushion?" he asked.

"Yeah. But a couch would be better. Oh! Wait!" Too quick to stop him, he reached behind her, took hold of her waist on both sides and hauled her up onto his lap—sidesaddle because of her skirt. She immediately attempted to get off. "Cal, don't be crazy. I'll break your legs. At the very least, I'll put them to sleep. You can't be comfortable. The floor is hard enough without adding the weight of a second person to—"

Without word or warning he leaned forward, wrapped his arms around her stiff, awkward body, pulled her close to his chest, and then slowly lowered them back against the wall.

"Isn't this killing your back?"

"Shhh. Relax. You might well be the last woman I hold in my arms for a while."

"Oh. I'm so sorry . . ."

In the near dark his finger found her lips. "That was a statement, not a complaint."

"Oh." She felt her body relax on his, like butter relaxes on hot toast. "I see . . ."

"Good. I want you to see. Now tell me what's in my black metal lunchbox."

She laughed softly, then smiled as she picked up the steady, unhesitating rhythm of his heart with her ear against his chest. She realized then that it wasn't what they talked about now as much as the intimacy of talking in the dark, the touching, the trust and closeness that mattered most. "Two sandwiches, two peach fruit cups, a spoon, a paper napkin, and a thermos of chocolate milk."

She bounced on his chest a little when he chuckled. "What kind of sandwiches?"

"One is peanut butter and marshmallow." He groaned. "No, it's really good. You'll love it. And the other one is this tofu-tuna stuff my sister makes that'll have you crying it's so—"

The clatter of metal on wood came first and immediately after the noise was so loud it took several seconds to determine that the chairs stacked at the door had fallen.

The signal.

They were coming in.

Eight

Cal pitched her into the darkness but she instinctively knew he'd sent her somewhere toward the table so she could crawl under it for protection.

"Cal?" She put her head down to let her eyes adjust— and to pick up the reins of what nerves she had left—then crawled cautiously away from the pale light from the street toward the dark shadow of the table. A loud, ramming boom reverberated in the room, and she screamed when they hit the door again. In the near darkness there was no way to tell how much space the table had given them. "Cal!"

"Right behind you."

But he wasn't. It was true that losing one sense—like sight—made the other senses—like hearing—stronger and more sensitive. And Cal was across the room to her left; he hadn't moved yet.

She tried to picture what was there, what he might be after. A third resounding crash and she heard the table shriek in protest as it moved. Still, the noise and the force and the tremor through the room were nothing compared to the pressure and the power of each quaking beat of her heart.

Finally, she made contact with the table and put her back to it. She knew the other long wall was directly in front of her, the door was on her right and to her left was Cal, the street window, the air-conditioning unit below it, Cal's jacket . . . and his gun in the pocket thereof.

"Cal, what are you doing? Leave it there. Get away from it."

"Christ. Go back under the table, Bonnie. Please. I'll be there in a second."

"What are you doing?" Their voices rose and fell with every assault against the door, and with every blow the table moved a little more and the door opened a breath wider.

For an analytical, numbers kind of girl, she was acutely aware that what felt like slow motion was in fact flashing by in milliseconds, and that wisdom, practicality, and education were meaningless when fear prevailed and instinct took over.

Her instinct just then was strong and piercing. She needed to be with Cal. Good thing, too, as she found she'd been following the sound of his voice from the start.

However, she didn't have the time to probe that instinct or the meaning of the relief that passed through her body like a frigid chill when she caught the subtle movement of solid in shadow. Her heart embraced this tiny piece of peace, protecting it from a world of fear and noise and danger.

"Cal?"

"Oh God, Bonnie!" She watched the black form, low in the shadows below the shine from the streets, lean forward, waving his arms through the space in front of him. "Baby, go back under the table. You'll be safe there."

"Come with me." She reached out and touched him; he immediately had a solid grip on her and pulled her to her feet . . . into the light and into his arms. "Be safe with me."

"Man, I wish things could have been different for us."

"It still can be. There can still be an us. There might be a little jail time but, well, we'll have the longest engagement ever." He chuckled and she leaned back so she could see the shadows of his face; her hands moved to his waist. "This reminds me, though . . ."

The crash came again and they trembled as one.

Much better.

"This reminds me that when we get out of here I may . . . assault Ted. He's a lousy negotiator. Both our demands were perfectly reasonable."

"Mine, Bonnie. My demands, remember that."

"Should we be sitting on the table? More weight?"

She felt his chest rise and fall with a resigned sigh, felt his arms tighten around her shoulders. She tightened hers around his waist—just in time for another room-rocking wallop.

"No. We won't get that much more time," he said. "And we don't want to piss them off by resisting."

"Then come back and . . ." She faltered when she moved her arm a little and felt something hard and unbodypart-like beneath her forearm. ". . . and get under the table with me. Please, Cal."

She felt his fingers skim lightly over her face, coming to rest on the closed seam of her mouth as her fingers detected the open seam of the pocket in the jacket he'd put back on.

"I can't," he whispered, his face so close she could feel his breath on her lips—though she could barely make out any part of him or the pocket that she was slipping her hand into. "I need to stand and take responsibility for what I've done here, not cower under the table with my hostage. And I need to know you're safe. Please. It's almost over. I promise. Now go!"

He gave her a light, halfhearted shove and she staggered backward into the dark. But she wasn't as disoriented as she might have been. The next blow didn't just reveal the location of the door, it also let in a small wedge of the bright light from the hallway. It was both helpful and terrifying as it shed a momentary light on the gun in her hand.

The gun she'd pulled from Cal's pocket. The suspiciously lightweight gun. The gun that wasn't the cold, smooth, metallic texture of tempered steel, but the tepid, rough, brittle touch of plastic made in China.

"What the hell is this?"

"How'd you get that? Bonnie. Give it back."

"A toy? A squirt gun? You kidnapped me with a squirt gun?"

"Bonnie . . ."

The police rammed the door again and let in enough light to show Cal searching the air for her with his arms outstretched. Their eyes met briefly before the darkness engulfed them again. He looked angry and determined. She immediately went to the floor and crawled six feet away.

"I told you I didn't want to hurt anyone," he said, like she didn't know that if she spoke he'd have a bead on her location. "And no one will sell me a gun because of my record, you know. A plastic gun from the gift shop across the street was the best I could do."

"There is no gift shop across the street." She shouted over the racket at the door, which probably masked her location, but she moved three feet to her left anyway. "And I bet that squirt gun belongs to one of your nephews. This was your plan all along." She moved to the right this time, and when the next crash on the door came she was hidden in dark shadow. "No wonder you didn't have any trouble getting it through security."

"The gift shop is in the lobby of the hotel across the street. Between the bar—where I went after getting hammered by your bank—and the men's room—where I went after getting hammered on my own. It was in the window, and that's when I got the idea. I just wanted to scare them.

I wanted them to feel real fear, fear for their futures, let them see how it feels but . . ."

"But what?"

"Give it back, Bonnie."

"But what?"

"I didn't want to go back to prison," he hollered in frustration. Then more calmly added, "I don't ever want to go back to prison. So I walked back to the elevators and while I was waiting I decided that going back to my brother without the loan again was just another kind of prison I didn't want to be locked up in."

"Then I came by."

"And you were everything I said before," he said, sounding a little uneasy. "In fact, you'd already disappeared into the bathroom before I came up with a way to get my brother what he needed most."

"By kidnapping me with a plastic gun. A plastic gun . . . to kidnap me with." She knew it didn't make sense but thought if she said it often enough it would . . . eventually. "But that's just stupid. It's crazy. It's . . ."

It's suicide came to mind mere seconds before his hand latched onto her left arm.

"No, Cal. No. Suicide by cop is not what your brother needs." Struggling to get free of him and to keep him away from what looked like a very real gun at the same time, she knew their fracas wouldn't last long—he was bigger and stronger than she was.

However only a few were more clever than she was . . .

"Your brother loves you. And your sister loves you. And what about my long engagement?" She brought her knee up between his legs and tagged him with a warning. It made him release her immediately, step back, and bend a little to protect himself—long enough for her to tuck the squirt gun in her bra because her waistband would be the first place he looked for it when he discovered her hands were empty. "I can't let you do it, Cal. I care about you. Very much."

And the police were taking their own sweet time . . .

She wrangled with him to keep her hand just out of his reach, but he easily overtook her, coiled his arm around her waist with her back against him in quest of the toy, and ultimately put his hand flat on her chest—her second best hiding place.

Next time she kneed a man she would have no mercy.

"Help!" She was hoping to distract him until she could get free. "Help me! The gun is plas—"

He silenced her with his hand.

"Shhh." His breath was warm on the side of her neck—and all he did was hold her, seeming to be in no hurry to retrieve his deadly weapon.

Two easy jerks of her head and he freed her mouth immediately. She felt him at her back—shielding her, supporting her, enjoying her weight and form against him. He sighed and she guessed he was in another world for a few seconds, a happier world, a world where he'd made different choices, had a different life. She wanted to be there with him.

What they did have was one perfect moment—as warm as a lifelong friendship, as thrilling as sex, as intimate as any kiss—and they relished it.

Suddenly the table screamed one last time and the door gave way. Light flooded into the darkness of the small conference room like a Hollywood spotlight. Then everything happened at once.

In milliseconds she felt Cal's fingers skim across her breast; the cops were shouting and screaming like they were going to war; Cal's other arm was like something mechanical as it drew her to his left and then pushed her backward, behind him, as far as he could. Hard to throw backward. She did a short spin off the end of his right hand and without hesitation shot straight to his left and the stupid plastic gun it held.

She heard him say, "Please, Bonnie, get away from me,"

like she was accustomed to obeying his orders. Then he refused to give her the toy . . . so she had to scratch his arm, deeply, and dig her nails into the back of his hand.

"Son of a bitch!" Either the surprise or the pain loosened his grip enough for her to twist the weapon free. She held it in the air as high as she could and turned away from him toward the officers tripping over chairs as they streamed into the room.

"It's over," she hollered back at them, holding the toy out to them for the taking. "No one's been hurt. I have the weapon." Two rapid claps of violent thunder wobbled the room. "It's a toy. A plastic squirt gun. See?"

She frowned at the hot, searing pain in the middle of her abdomen and . . . high on her right shoulder. Not a good time to be sick, she knew, as the room teetered around her. Maybe it's just aftershock . . .

"Oh God, Bonnie!" Cal put his arms around her, so warm and strong, pulling her back and down to the floor so he could cradle all but her legs on his lap. "Why did you do that? Why?"

The lights came back on with a glaring vengeance. She had a flash of a thought that the light had taken all the romance from the room, made it look small and . . . functional, but that was when she noticed the blood on Cal's hands.

"Cal."

"I wasn't going to do it, I swear," he was saying, trying to sound at least as angry as he was fearful for her and failing pitifully. "I had everything under control. I was going to surrender."

"Are you . . . ? Oh. Oh! It's me! Cal, I think I've been shot!"

"I know, sweetheart, just be still. You'll be fine. There's an ambulance coming."

There was a policeman standing behind Cal, but Cal kept jerking away from him.

"Cal," she said, turning slightly in his direction and hissing when a stabbing pain ripped through her stomach. She was getting sleepy. "Cal, listen, I'm . . . I'm really sorry everything turned out badly."

"Shhh."

"I'm sorry I hid at Chicky's party."

"Me, too." He leaned forward and quickly buzzed her lips with his, then barely breathed the word, "Honeysuckle."

She grinned and closed her eyes to slow the spin of the room, let her senses float to every part of her body that touched his and soaked in the bliss of being near him.

Time may or may not have passed, but the next thing she heard was someone asking for directions to the patient.

"Cal, Cal," she said, unable to hide the panic in her voice. "Stay with me."

"Shhh. The ambulance is here. You'll be fine."

"I'll never be fine again. They'll take you away."

"Shhh. I'll be fine. I promise."

She let her forehead rest on the stubble of his chin and for a moment they shared a minim of peace. Then she whispered, "I wish life could have been better for us."

Even with her eyes closed, she felt the spinning begin— not a swirling spinning like inside her head, but spinning-spinning like . . . a Frisbee . . . or . . . a magic carpet . . .

Cautiously, she opened her eyes, but either the room or the rug was spinning so fast it made her eyes ache trying to see anything. She closed them again. The next attempt was better as she limited her field of vision to the end of her arm and . . . there was the beautiful, brightly colored rug she had framed and hung on her office wall. Only she didn't have an office and . . . and it was Pim's rug. And Cal . . . no, Joe was going to prison and . . . no, Cal was.

Suddenly, she cried out in panic and uncurled like a party favor—flat on her back. Her fingers scurried over her torso like crazed spiders, looking for bullet wounds and blood. She found none and for a moment was torn between enormous relief and wretchedness.

She rested her hands on her soft, loose-muscled abdomen, felt the pull of her tummy-tuck jeans, and came close to weeping with joy. She loved her flab! She did. She didn't want any more of it but loved what she had. It was a reminder that her original life was so much better than it could have been, that there was some . . . divine, celestial reason that things turned out the way they did instead of how they might have transpired.

Looking up into the rafters, she thought the rotations might be slowing down, but closed her eyes again to keep from getting sick. She couldn't really recommend carpet travel . . . except to those who had lost their way or needed to see what was truly important in their lives . . . It was nauseating and disturbing on several levels.

When the rotating slowed and the whir started to fade, she thought she heard her name being called. Seconds later, she was positive.

Nine

"Jan? Is that you?" She sat up, using her hands on the carpet to support her. She opened her eyes. The carpet wasn't going any faster than a merry-go-round now and shapes were . . . taking shape.

"Bonnie? Can you hear me?"

"Yes. Yes." She put a hand over her heart. "You sound so good! I've missed you so much."

"But you didn't go anywhere, honey." She watched the carpet stop and hover high for several seconds—like it had its motor running. "You've been spinning up there for the last four or five minutes. I was afraid to leave you, in case I was hallucinating. And you had my cell so . . . Oh! Here it comes. I think it's landing. This is so bizarre."

And you don't know the half of it, sister, Bonnie thought.

As if it had a crack pilot at the helm, the rug settled gracefully over the steamer trunk and positioned Bonnie like she was sitting on a high bench. She felt the heat of it against her palm and the nicest kind of thrill passed through her body as the gentle guardian—or whatever—in the rug bid her farewell.

"Thank you," she murmured softly, spreading her fingers wide and pressing down significantly. "I won't forget."

Bonnie hopped down off the trunk and crushed Jan in her arms like an avocado heading for guacamole. "You are the *best* sister. You're the only constant in my life," she told Jan. "No matter what version of my life I'm living in, you're there with me."

"Of course I am. So what happened? You were awfully quiet up there. Thank God you're all right. You are all right, right?" Jan was nervous and excited all at once and talking very quickly.

Startled, they both squealed as the carpet moved suddenly, lifting swiftly and hanging in the air, then rolling up like a shade in a window. It came down again softly, draped itself gracefully across the steamer trunk. Then it lay still, and Bonnie sensed it was inert, like the dollhouse or the birdcage in the corner. Jan kept a wary eye on it as she said, "What happened to you?"

"So much," she said, walking backward, pulling her sister excitedly toward the attic steps. "You're not going to believe it . . . and I can't tell you right now . . ."

"Ah, come on!"

"*And* I need you to stay with Pim for a bit, can you do that?"

"I do have clients, you know. I'm a professional real estate broker."

But more than a savvy businesswoman, Bonnie knew her sister was a bone-deep romantic.

"That's fine. It's not a big deal, I guess. I was going to tell Joe about all this, but it can wait until after the nurse comes. Oh, here's your cell phone."

"Joe?"

"Yes. My husband?"

"But I thought you were going to wait for him to come back to you, for your self-esteem."

"More like my pride. And I don't think there's any room for pride when you've seen how fragile life is." She turned off the overhead light and started down the attic steps. "When you've seen how one decision can alter your whole destiny."

"You saw something up there? What'd you see? A premonition? A past life?"

"No." Bonnie held the door open at the bottom and waited for her sister to come through. She closed it and shook the handle to make sure it was tight, then turned to Jan. "I saw my life as it might have been. I lived it."

"In five minutes?"

"I think that must be part of the magic, because it felt like one very long day in a very different lifetime."

"Different how?"

Bonnie sighed in frustration and palmed her sister's cheeks. "Please. Stay with Pim. I'll be back as soon as I can and then I'll tell you all about it. I promise."

"You'd better. I also want to know what happens when you see Joe."

Bonnie grinned, then skipped down the main staircase while Jan remained on the second floor, leaning over the railing.

"I'll be back soon. Put on a pot of coffee."

"Hi," she said when he opened the door. She was as anxious and jumpy as she had been on their first date—and even more in love. Just the sight of his face was a balm to her soul and the sound of his voice was like heaven.

"Hey." His surprised expression dissolved into a hesitant happiness. "Is everything okay? The kids?"

"Yes. Fine. Everybody's fine. Can I come in?"

"Sure." There was still a small ripple of concern on his

brow as he watched her pass by. He twisted a bit to close the door. When he turned back, she hurled herself at him— and the ripple was gone. He wrapped his arms around her and buried his face in the curve of her neck. They clung to one another for a long moment.

"Come home now," she murmured close to his ear, her eyes closed, her senses absorbing his every nuance like she hadn't absorbed them all before. The strength of his arms, the scent of warm shampoo and fabric softener around his neck, the sound of the hum—*that hum*—from deep inside him when he was overwhelmed with happiness.

She started slipping down his body and opened her eyes in time to meet his hazel gaze.

"I'm not going home until you hear why I left." When her feet touched the floor, he released her. "I don't want to be at home if you're not there. And you haven't been there, Bonnie."

"I know. I wasn't." She hesitated. "But I didn't know I wasn't . . . and that's just the first of a lot of strange things I'm about to say, so I need you to trust me."

"I always have. Do you want to sit?"

"Not just yet. I'm nervous."

"Okay." The corners of his mouth twitched, but he didn't laugh. He leaned back against the wall just inside the door. "I'll stand, too."

She nodded and was taken aback at how much better that made her feel.

"All right, now I know how this is going to sound but . . . I've been on the other side of the fence."

"What fence?"

"The one where the grass is always greener on the other side . . . that fence. Only the grass isn't greener, Joe, not even close. And anyone who says it is will only find out that it's . . . you know, the green stuff the football players like?"

"Money?" His tone was dubious.

"No. Ah . . . Astroturf. The grass on the other side of the fence is Astroturf. It just looks real, but . . . well, maybe it is real and not Astroturf, because it seems like a life but it's a life where we've made all the wrong choices . . . or just different choices, maybe, but we, you and I, we've made our best choices in this life. We're so lucky, Joe." She banded her arms around his torso and hugged tight. "We have so many of the things you can't buy with money."

"So then . . ." He rubbed her back slowly. ". . . we can afford a couple of black plastic squirt guns?"

Her heart stopped and a flush of fear washed over her. Which life was she in? *Her* life or her if-only life? Was this Joe or was it Cal in her arms . . . and if it was Cal, where was her Joe?

"Joe?" she raised her head to look up at him.

"Yes."

"Cal?"

"Not really."

"Then what . . . how do . . ." She caught herself, unsure if her mind could handle any more magic today.

He scooped her up close to his chest again and dropped a kiss on the top of her head.

"I'll try to explain what I know so far." She heard him swallow and knew he was thinking it through to get it all straight. "When I—*Cal* in the other life, got out of jail ten years after you died . . ."

"I died?"

He nodded. "One of the first things he did was to drive over to Pim's house. Not our Pim, the Pim in his world."

"Right."

"He wanted to explain what had happened and apologize to her and your sister. He told her everything, even about the plastic gun. He was still devastated. He just couldn't forgive himself for what happened. He started to cry and . . . Pim took mercy on him."

"She took him up to the attic."

"Yes. And explained about the carpet on the way up."

"Explain it to me."

"I'll tell you what I know. Wanna sit yet?"

"Is this story going to get weirder?"

He smiled encouragement and pulled her down beside him on the couch.

"First she had him . . . Cal, dig the carpet out of its hiding place in the attic, haul it down the steps, and roll it out in the big part of the hallway by her bedroom door. She said it would take him anywhere in his life he wanted to go if he wished it. He could stay there for only one day to fix wrongs or to relive something that made him happy, but if he didn't make *a second wish* to bring him back, before dead of night, he'd be stuck there forever.

"*There*, apparently, is a parallel world, his life because he made certain choices. And yours, if you'd chosen differently. The carpet takes you to what might have been."

"But I didn't know there was a 'this life' in that one, not like I know about that one in this one . . . did that sound like English to you?"

He laughed. "Yes. And actually I wondered about that, too, when Pim was explaining it—after all, Cal was falling for you and you did sacrifice yourself for him . . . not that I'm the least bit jealous."

"You're not really, are you, because I didn't know—"

"No, honey, I'm not. Bad joke. Anyway, Pim says it's part of the magic in the carpet: You don't remember traveling to a different life, but you remember everything when you get back to yours."

"That makes sense. So I can see how much fuller my life is and how the choices I made, like marrying you, made me a better person, less self-centered, more caring, not as rich, but perfectly comfortable, with time to cuddle with the man who loves me, who I adore and never want to be apart from again?"

"I believe so." He chuckled and leaned forward leisurely

to give her a slow, warm, wet kiss that made her want to cry for some reason. "Want to hear the rest of this now or go straight to bed?"

"I better hear the rest now—I might not be in any kind of shape to hear it later."

"Okay. Um . . . Oh. The memory-loss business . . . You also forget about the second wish to get back. Apparently, that's the chance you take, the danger of the magic; it has to come from you spontaneously."

"For the same reasons, don't you think?" she asked quietly, her mind drifting back. "And because if it were too easy . . . no one would . . ."

"What?"

"Pim. The other Pim, she tried to warn me. She knew I had the rug—and I did—framed over the couch in my office, and that I was in danger and had to make things right before dead of night."

He shook his head. "I keep hearing that. When the hell is 'dead of night'?"

She shrugged and they both chuckled, glad simply to be talking, alone, in a quiet place, together, at the same time.

Joe let loose a full-sized sigh and took another step toward bedding his wife. "Cal considered going back to the day he met you but he figured that would only turn out the same. He thought of going back to before his felony arrest, but then he never would have met you . . . and he wanted very much to meet you so . . . he went back to the night of Chicky's birthday party."

She gasped. "But that's the night *we* . . ."

"And when I saw you hiding in the bushes I had the same choices Cal had—ignore you and assume that you'd find your own way home or flush you out and make sure."

"Ha. Flush me out. That's a good one."

"*But* Cal hadn't made the worst choice of his life yet—which was not meeting you—so he was still Joe, me, at the time. There was no parallel life for him yet. And it was *me* who went around behind the garage and started to pretend I was going to whiz in the bushes and . . ."

". . . heard you scrambling to get out of the way."

". . . heard me scrambling to get out of your way."

They said it together and laughed.

"I wonder why the kids don't ask how we met more often."

"I love how we met," she said, a dreamy look on her face. "You very patiently listened to me tell you who I was and how nervous I was and that I only agreed to go out with Chicky because I didn't know how to tell him no and I felt kind of nauseated and he wasn't really my type and I might actually die if I had to join the party. And you told me to wait there and came back two minutes later with two cans of Coke and you gave me one. You said that you told Chicky that you heard I had the flu and not to tell anyone any different. And then you walked me home, in the moonlight, with your hands in your pockets. And I was in love before we reached the front gate."

"For me it was when you came thrashing out of the bushes all flustered and pissy and indignant. Like you had every right to be sitting in those bushes without getting peed on. *Then* you got embarrassed, which was almost as much fun."

"*Pht.*" She sobered. "So meeting me kept you from becoming Cal."

They searched one another's face and it didn't seem to matter that they'd seen it millions of times before. Every day there was something new—a new laugh line, a single gray eyebrow hair, the fluctuation of fat in their cheeks, worry and wonder.

Joe drew his hand up between them and traced the edges of her lips with his finger while saying, "When dead of night came I was sound asleep in my bed in my mother's house."

"He didn't make a second wish."

He shook his head and released a long breath. "He did in a way. While he was at Pim's he wrote the whole story in a letter, everything he could remember. He attached it to the carpet and when he was ready to go he made both wishes at once—to go back to the night of Chicky's party and for the rug to return immediately to Pim without him."

"The Pim in his world."

"But with you dead and him basically pre-Cal that parallel didn't exist for either of you anymore so the rug went back to the nearest Pim it could find."

"Ours."

He nodded. "And, of course, she read the letter when she found the carpet in her upstairs hallway. I've known this story for years—Cal's story. Pim and I have talked about it and she said we should let it happen naturally, that we knew you wouldn't be hurt . . . in this life so . . . so when you started acting, what's the word . . . ? Sidetracked? Sort of far away and unfocused . . . I thought you might need some space to think and . . . to do whatever you had to do to get you here this afternoon."

Her smile was as slow to her lips as the twinkle was to his eyes—but everything else was picking up speed. Her pulse was off the charts.

"And so, my Bonnie wife," he said, grabbing her shirt at the throat to hold her head steady for a slow kiss. "Whether or not the grass is greener depends on which side of the fence you're looking over, doesn't it?"

"I guess it does." They locked their lips together, disengaging only once to pull his T-shirt over his head. Then she forced him back on the couch cushions—though it didn't take much forcing.

"I'm thinking we should keep this place until Susan goes off to college," he said, out of the blue, ducking her lips to see the buttons on her shirt. He zigged when she zagged, but she weaved when he bent, and she landed a solid kiss on his mouth. In seconds, he was helpless.

"Why?"

"Wa— Why what?"

"Why would you want to keep this place?" She kissed him again, deeply, and he mumbled his answer.

"Privacy."

Giving him a moment to catch his breath, she looked around and nodded. "It could use some paint, but . . . What can we do here that we can't do at home . . . when Susan's babysitting."

He grinned at her, taking her hand firmly in his. "Come on, I'll show ya."

Ten

It was after dark so the porch light was on and the door was locked. Bonnie knocked firmly on the etched glass windowpanes set in the door to get Jan's attention.

She came down the hall from the kitchen with her arms crossed at her chest and an annoyed expression on her face. She stopped in the hall to flip her hair in the narrow mirror, then moseyed up to the door to stare at her sister. But she didn't open it.

"I'm sorry. I know I'm kind of late."

"Kind of?"

"Definitely. I'm definitely late and I'm sorry."

"Did you bring anything to eat?"

"No. No, but I put frozen brownies in the freezer yesterday. Two seconds to thaw."

She continued to survey her for several more seconds before she asked, "Anything of interest happen while you were away for these many, many long hours?"

"Well, Joe and I had sex."

"What?"

"Sex! Joe and I had sex *this afternoon!"* she screamed while her sister climbed all over the door trying to get it open.

"What is the matter with you? Get in here. All the neighbors can hear you."

"Got the door open, didn't it?" Bonnie buzzed her sister's cheek. "Didn't the nurse show up?"

"Yes, but you said you were coming back so I waited."

"I'm glad you did."

"What about Joe?"

"I bet he's glad, too. Shall we call him and ask?"

"For God's sake. Are you high?"

"No, I'm just . . . real happy about my life again. It's not midnight yet, is it?"

Bonnie started walking up the wide front steps and Janice followed.

"Maybe 11:15 or so."

"Good, because I've been thinking . . . dead of night must be the darkest, quietest, loneliest time of night. Midnight is the middle of *Letterman* so you know people are up and watching. Two or three in the morning is when most bars close. So between three A.M. and five A.M. is the deadest part of the night."

"That's about what I calculated, but with the discrepancy between the hours worked for men and women of 7.9 versus 7.1 and people with degrees working 3.1 hours versus high school grads working 7.1—"

"Okay, I got it," Bonnie said. "Tough problem, but we both came to the same general deduction. Right?"

"Yes." They arrived at the top of the stairs. "So?"

"So, I'm going to need you to help me haul the magic carpet from the attic into Pim's room." She saw the pained grimace on her sister's face and slung an arm across her shoulders as she led her toward the attic door. "Man, that rug was spinning so fast earlier I bet there isn't one iota of dust on it." Janice didn't look impressed. "Just think of all the favors I'm going to owe you after this."

That perked her up. She lifted a single brow to let her sister know that she wouldn't forget and that payback was hell—but she didn't really scare Bonnie.

"Tell me what happened," Jan said softly and seriously, having reached the limit of her patience.

With great relish, Bonnie told her everything from the thrill of Cal's kiss to being the proud owner of more than one pair of Ferragamo pumps.

"So you were always meant to be with Joe. God, that's so romantic."

"Our paths were meant to cross, that's for sure. But whether we die and go to prison or become high school sweethearts who get married and have kids and live relatively happily ever after all depends on the decisions we make in the time it takes our hearts to beat." She reached past her sister and opened the door to the attic. "I'll never take what I have for granted again." She paused. "If I do, you smack me, okay?"

"With pleasure."

"You didn't come up here after I left, did you?"

"You mean deliberately? Without force or impending disaster? No."

"I don't remember turning out the light, but I must have," she said, pulling the cord that turned it on again.

And there it was, the amazing, spectacular carpet—its field and medallion, the brackets and borders crisp and bold and subtle at once; every warp and weft woven together with great skill and beauty . . . and magic.

"Are you sure Pim's up to, you know, riding her magic carpet?" Janice asked as they approached it.

"I don't know, but I want to give it a try. If she's got something important to do I want to give her the chance. We owe her at least that."

"What about me? Should I take a spin on this thing? Literally."

"Do you want to?" Bonnie let out a labored *ugh* when

she lifted the center and one end of the special rug, shuf-
fling backward to face the steps and the door.

"Not really."

"Maybe when Pim . . . doesn't need it anymore or when
you have a question with no good answer."

"Are you going to ride it again?"

"No." Bonnie said, quick and firm. "Never again."

"Hmm. And Joe?"

"I love Joe . . . even when his name is Cal. And he
doesn't want to ride it again either."

"What?"

"Joe is moving home as we speak, then he's going to
pick up Susan and a pizza and we're going to live happily
ever after. Lift your end higher over the railing there.
That's it. Good."

"Well, that's the best damn news ever," Jan said, groan-
ing laboriously. "I can't believe we're doing this ourselves
when we both have big, strong husbands to call."

"We're doing it because we can, and because the fewer
people who know about the rug, the better, right?"

"Not even Roger? I'm horrible at keeping . . ." Her sister had made the turn out the door at the bottom of the
steps, but the last eighteen inches of the rug were jammed.
Janice rammed it through like a pro. ". . . secrets from
Roger. Even when I want to."

"Then it's okay to tell Roger, but I have to warn you
he'll probably think you're insane."

Janice laughed from the caboose. "That wouldn't be
something new, you know."

They set the rolled-up rug against the baseboard in the
hall a few feet from Pim's bedroom, then tiptoed to the
door. Bonnie tapped lightly and the middle-aged night
nurse answered.

"Hi, Lucy, how are you?" Bonnie asked, smiling too big.

"I'm good. Can I get something for you? Pim is asleep
finally."

"No. We don't need anything. But it's getting late and Jan and I were thinking of going home. We thought you might like to take a break first." She waved an arm. "Bathroom, food, drinks . . . Run around outside to stir up your blood a little."

"I have taken care of my patients for many years at night," Lucy said, more than a little huffy. "And I have never fallen asleep or needed to have my blood stirred."

Janice stepped forward. She was the people handler in the family. "What my sister meant to say was that we'd like you to go downstairs until we call you to return because we want some private time with our Pim."

Lucy made a *tsk* noise, grabbed her sweater off the rocking chair she preferred, and hurried out of the room.

"If that woman quits, you'll be doing the nightshift until *you* can replace her," Bonnie muttered, bending over the rug and picking it up again.

"Well, you had her running around outside to stay awake. The truth is so much simpler." She picked up her end, always aware of her manicure, which was less than a week old.

"I'll remember that."

They waddled and pushed and jerked the rug, then stood still as statues, hoping that what they were feeling wasn't happening. Bonnie made a half-turn to see Janice's face go pale.

"It's for Pim, Jan," Bonnie said, feeling she had an affinity for the spirit of the carpet—all she could feel from it was gentleness and an eager desire to be near Pim. "Don't be afraid. The carpet's getting warm for her, not for us. Come on."

They put their burden carefully on the floor . . . just in case . . . and closed the door. And neither one of them hesitated long before approaching the old woman's bed.

She was tiny and thin-skinned. Bonnie had seen plenty of pictures of her with the raven-black locks of her youth, but in real life she'd never seen anything but the continually neat waves and curls permanently pressed into her silver-white hair.

"Look at her," Jan said in a whisper. "Always the lady: She's got blush and lipstick on. Isn't she something?"

She nodded. "She's one of a kind, our Pim."

"But she isn't dead yet so why are we whispering?" Pim asked, opening only one eye . . . which was enough. Her eyes were the bluest of blues, laser-quick, and shrewd.

"Oh! You scared me half to death, Pim!" Jan was more surprised than annoyed.

"Pim, you old possum." Bonnie laughed. She had kids and kids played possum. "You better behave now because we found your magic carpet."

"Oooooh." Pim's eyes and mouth became perfect circles. "My sweet, darling girls, you have saved me." She clapped her hands, once, dramatically, then threw back the bedsheets like she planned to leap out of bed in her long, white, cotton nightgown. Both women automatically held their hands out, fingers up, to stop her. "Oh, don't be silly. I'm not going anywhere . . . I'm slow as a county worker." She looked straight at Bonnie. "I wasn't sure if I was making sense when we talked last night. I'm not used to taking so many different prescriptions. Makes me fuzzy."

"Makes you a little more than that, Pim. I thought you were hallucinating."

"You were completely *crazy* is what you were," Jan said.

The old lady's laugh was elegant and infectious—a sound Bonnie would always cherish and remember.

"So how do you want to do this, Pim? Do you want to try getting up? Or do you want it in bed with you?"

"It is a lovely piece of art, but that still doesn't win it a place in one's bed. Carpets belong on the floor. So if you, my sweet girls, would be so kind as to unroll it there in the space in front of my dresser, I believe I can handle the rest of this operation on my own."

While Pim straightened out her nightie, smoothed out the hair on the back of her head, and got her new walker ready for the ride, Bonnie and Janice wordlessly opened up the rug in front of the chest of drawers—but that didn't mean they weren't commenting. Head jerks, shoulder rolls, and severely contorted facial expressions were as easy to read in siblings as their DNA.

"Ah, what operation is that, Pim?" Bonnie suspected that she already knew, but with her grandmother's mental acuity lately . . .

Pim's blue eyes rose and took aim, drilled through Janice first and then Bonnie before she looked satisfied and spoke softly. "I think one of you already knows the operation I refer to."

"I do," Bonnie admitted freely—to be healthy, clear-minded, and fracture free. "And I think maybe I should or . . . or Jan should or the nurse or someone should be here with you—just in case something goes wrong."

"The nurse?" Pim clearly saw her as a security breach.

"Okay. Me or Jan . . . or Joe."

She lifted her head with a jolt and for the first time in . . . ever, looked guilty—though she gave no explanation or excuse or apology and went back to her business.

"Nothing will go wrong, dear." She cheek-walked to the edge of the bed and lowered her legs into the square of space between the bed and the walker. Matter-of-factly she asked, "And did you, Bonnie girl, make your second wish before dead of night?"

"Yes, ma'am." The idea of how close she'd come—because of her ignorance of the carpet's power—to staying on the other side, to being dead right now, nauseated her. "I did. Luckily. The whole thing was an accident . . . and so was the second wish."

"I apologize, dear, for sending you to fetch it. I forgot how sensitive it can be. I should have waited for Joe."

Bonnie opened her mouth to speak, but Janice's voice came out: "Joe's been really busy this last month, Pim. Bonnie's hardly seen him."

"Too busy to come by and see me even once?"

"He did come . . . twice . . . that I know of, maybe more, but you were sleeping."

Bonnie frowned at her sister, appreciating her willingness to lie for her husband, but fixed on the fact that her timing was a little off. Now that she and Joe were together again, she didn't care who knew they were apart.

Pim nodded silently, looking at both of them expectantly. They looked back quizzically, clearly wanting to be helpful.

"Go!" she said, when their hovering finally started to get on her nerves.

"But are you sure—"

"Yes. Go."

Pim was standing independently with her walker as they backed out of the door together, Bonnie's hand on the doorknob.

She heard the latch click.

Janice said, "Do you think she'll be all right?"

From behind them in the hallway Pim answered, "Will who be all right?"

Both sisters screamed and fell back against the door . . . which blocked their exit.

Their hearts hammered under their hands as they took in Pim's usual healthy color and the lack of a walker. Her favorite cross-trainers were on her feet and a tall glass of milk was clasped in her hand.

"It's too early for Christmas and Halloween, so you're not hiding gifts or putting rubber snakes in my bed . . . though you're a little old for that now, aren't you? So why aren't you at home this time of night?"

"We . . . we . . ." Jan was still trying to catch her breath as Pim opened the bedroom door.

"We, ah, were driving by and saw the light on."

"We just wanted to kiss you good-night."

Pim smiled her delight. "My sweet girls. Well, come in and let me get settled in bed. You can tuck me in like you used to, when you were up and thought I was still asleep."

"You were awake?" Jan asked.

"Yes, indeed. I could have spent hours watching you play with my cosmetics, sweet Jannie." She drank half her milk, slipped out of her sneakers, and climbed into bed with her long, white cotton nightgown tucked in around her. Bonnie went to the far side of the bed while Jan stayed near and together they pulled the sheets tight, stuffing the ends between the mattresses. "Oh, nice and cozy. Thank you, girls."

Jan leaned in front of Bonnie. "Thank you, Pim, for everything. I don't say that often enough." She kissed the lady's cheek and then her forehead. "I love you."

"Oh, sweetheart, I love you as well. You've made my life an intrepid adventure."

They smiled warmly and Janice walked lightly across the room to the door.

Bonnie tucked one of Pim's silver curls behind her ear and smiled into the warm blue waters of her eyes. "Goodnight, my Pim. Sleep well." She kissed the hollow of her cheek. "Light on, down, or off?"

"Lights off in a moment but . . . but don't forget, my girl, that *wishes alone can't make it right.*" Bonnie froze in place. She realized then that she'd been half-hoping this Pim didn't know about the carpet or what had transpired in the last few hours. "My darling, wishes are not enough to make your life what you want it to be. Even with a little magic, wishes aren't enough to make you happy. Courage and faith and love and humor. Friendship. You need hard work and tenacity and a helping hand sometimes. You need good judgment, a sense of fairness, and—"

"A Pim to love you."